OPERATION WHITE COAT

DOUG BISHOP

ROSEWOOD PUBLISHING LLC

DEDICATION

To my father, Don Bishop, An alum of Operation White Coat. Whose courage, selflessness, and unwavering faith exemplify the highest ideals of service.

This is for you.

PROLOGUE

Into the Stainless-Steel Bubble

May 25, 1963

I didn't know what to expect when they first told us about Operation White Coat. All they said was that we'd be part of something bigger—the future of warfare, the next evolution of the soldier. The words sounded grand and essential, and I was stupid enough to believe them. They promised us power, control, and purpose. They didn't tell us the price we'd pay for it.

We weren't soldiers to them. We were experiments.

Everything felt clinical and too clean the first time they took us inside the lab. The walls were white, the floors sterile, and the air smelled like disinfectant and steel. We were told to wear surgical scrubs and follow a group of men in white lab coats. They moved like machines—efficient and emotionless. They didn't see us as people. We were data points, test subjects, and the foundation of a twisted dream.

And at the heart of that dream was the stainless-steel bubble affectionately called the 8 Ball.

Welcome to the Machine

Under the shadow of a 30-foot steel sphere, ten test subjects sat motionless in isolated cubicles arranged in precision within the cavernous hangar. The air was tense, and only the faint hum of machinery reverberated off the cold, sterile walls. This wasn't a place of hope but of control—designed to push human limits in the face of the unimaginable.

Each subject wore a sealed mask, their breaths audible in the stillness. Above, the sphere contained a volatile, invisible force—a biological agent poised for release. It hovered like an unseen predator, waiting to strike.

Behind the thick glass, scientists monitored the scene, fingers poised over switches. A hiss broke the silence as gas spiraled down, infiltrating the masks. It was a silent invasion, testing resilience and survival.

This experiment at Fort Detrick wasn't for humanity's benefit. As the gas filled the chamber, the subjects unknowingly faced a moment that would redefine—or end—their existence.

Into the Bubble

The scientists explained the procedure using chilling detachment. "Enter the hanger and proceed to your cubicle. There, you'll breathe a calibrated gas. This gas will introduce a controlled infection," they said, the word "infection" stripped of gravity as if it were routine. "It will begin the enhancement."

Operation White Coat wasn't a place for questions, only orders. We sat in silence, awaiting the gas. One by one, soldiers donned masks, faces hidden behind feigned courage. When Parker emerged, he was twitching, his pupils blown wide, his body convulsing as if rewriting itself. He collapsed before reaching the recovery room, dragged away without a word. That's when I knew—this was no enhancement.

The Chamber loomed in the hanger, a perfect steel sphere, ominous and mesmerizing. My name was called. Hands shaking, I entered the cubicle and was strapped into the cold chair. The gas flowed. I breathed.

The Infection

At first, breathing in cold air felt sharp and dry, like the sting of winter on bare skin. I exhaled slowly, trying to stay calm, but something strange immediately happened.

The gas wasn't just cold—it was alive. I could feel it spreading through my lungs, crawling into my bloodstream like tiny, invisible fingers. My body reacted violently—I coughed and gagged, but the mask stayed tight. There was no escape.

Then the pain hit.

It started in my chest—a deep, burning ache that spread outward, coiling through my limbs like fire. My vision blurred, and I felt my muscles tense and twisting under my skin. It felt like my body was trying to tear itself apart from the inside.

I remember clutching the arms of the chair, my knuckles white with strain. The room spun, and my heart pounded in my ears. But they kept yelling for me to breathe— "Breathe! Breathe! Breathe!"

The gas was in control now. And it was changing me.

Rewriting the Code

They said the infection was "calibrated"—designed to break us down and rebuild us. The gas wasn't just a toxin—it was a biological program, a living algorithm that rewrote every cell in our bodies.

I could feel it working—my bones ached, my muscles trembled, and my mind raced with thoughts that weren't mine. Memories that didn't belong to me flickered in my head—snippets of people, places, faces I didn't recognize.

It was as if the gas was implanting something—altering my body and mind.

Time lost meaning. I don't know how long I was in that bubble—seconds, minutes, hours. But I knew I wasn't the same when the process finally ended.

The scientist unstrapped the mask, and I stood up from the chair. I stumbled out, gasping for air. My limbs felt foreign, heavier, and more precise as if I were wearing a suit of armor made from my skin.

The scientist waiting outside looked at me with a cold, satisfied expression. "You'll adapt," he said as if I were nothing more than a successful prototype.

Aftermath: The Price of Perfection

In the days that followed, my changes became undeniable. My reflexes sharpened, and my senses heightened. I could predict movements before they happened and react faster than my thoughts could process. Sleep became a distant need, as though my body had transcended exhaustion. Yet, these enhancements came at a cost.

The dreams were relentless—vivid, violent, and filled with faces and places I couldn't recognize. Strangers' voices called to me in the dark, echoing memories I didn't own. Then came the soft whispers, like fleeting thoughts, not mine. Over time, they grew louder and more insistent, pushing into my mind. The infection wasn't merely physical; it reshaped me, transforming my essence.

He sat amidst the remnants of his children's playtime, toys scattered like fragments of a distant joy. Small cars, toppled blocks, and a plush animal lay forgotten on the floor. His gaze drifted absently over the chaos, his thoughts consumed by memories of his wife—her smile, warmth, and how she made their house a home. But that warmth was gone, leaving an unbearable void.

The grief became a storm. His body trembled uncontrollably, his breath shallow and erratic. Tears burned down his cheeks, unbidden and unrelenting. The weight of his anguish pressed down on him, an unbearable heaviness. In desperation, his eyes found the Colt 1911 on the coffee table. Its cold, metallic presence seemed to offer finality, a way to escape the pain.

He held the gun, its weight solid in his hand. His memories surged—a disjointed flood of laughter, love, and loss. As his finger hovered over the trigger, a memory flickered—a voice, a face, a reason to stay. His hand trembled violently, the Colt impossibly heavy.

With a deep, shuddering breath, he slowly inserted the gun into his mouth, his chest heaving as if he had just climbed a mountain. His heart pounded in his ears, but the storm inside him had quieted, if only a little. The Colt remained in his hand, the grip even stronger than before.

He closed his eyes for the last time.

CHAPTER 1

A Whisper of Secrets

Present Day

The lights of Washington, D.C., twinkled outside Rhett Kardon's apartment, a facade of calm that only deepened the storm within him. He sat hunched on his couch, elbows resting on his knees, his fingers locked tightly together. Despite years of CIA training that had instilled in him the discipline to control his emotions and thoughts, tonight was different. Something was slipping through the cracks.

The apartment itself mirrored his state of mind. Shadows lingered in every corner, the dim lighting from scattered lamps casting uneven patterns on the walls. It wasn't neglect—it was deliberate. Harsh light felt invasive, and Rhett had no desire to invite clarity into a space he'd built for solitude. The few bulbs that worked illuminated the clutter at the center of the room: papers, case files, and notes—a chaotic but functional system that reflected the constant churn of his mind.

It wasn't a home in the traditional sense. It was more of a command center, a base of operations for a man who lived and breathed his work. There were no photographs, artwork, or personal touches. The couch was serviceable but worn, and the coffee table was battered from years of use. A lone chair sat at his dining table, symbolic of his self-imposed isolation. The desk near the window, covered in stacks of files and an ever-present laptop, was the heart of the space.

This was Rhett's world: quiet, detached, and utterly devoted to his mission. Relationships were distractions he couldn't afford. The cases, the files, and the pursuit of answers were the only constants. The few who had ventured into his life were long gone, pushed away by his inability to give anything beyond his focus to his work.

But tonight, the quiet was different. The shadows seemed heavier, the air thicker. His thoughts wouldn't settle. Memories he had buried long ago began to rise, unbidden and relentless.

Men in dark suits walking through his family's house. Hushed conversations that ended abruptly when he entered the room. The cold, detached figure of his father, Dr. James Kardon, viewed the world through a lens of logic and calculation.

As a child, Rhett had thought his father's peculiarities were just part of being a scientist. The mental exercises, the chess games, the endless puzzles—he'd believed they were his father's way of bonding. However, as he grew older, the interactions became more clinical, like experiments in which he was the subject.

"Strategy is everything, Rhett," his father would say, moving chess pieces with mechanical precision. "Control the game, or the game will control you."

There was no warmth in those moments, only an unyielding demand for perfection.

Rhett pressed his palms against his temples to force the memories away. They weren't helpful. They weren't relevant. Yet they clawed their way back, refusing to be ignored.

"Ping."

The sound jolted him out of his thoughts. He turned toward his desk, where his secure terminal glowed faintly. It was a line reserved for classified work, impossible to trace. The timestamp read 3:00 AM. Who would contact him at this hour?

He crossed the room, his bare feet silent against the floorboards. Sitting down, he leaned forward as the screen came to life. The message had no sender ID, and the subject line read:

"Operation White Coat."

Rhett's brow furrowed. It was a name he hadn't heard in years, not since his father's funeral. At the time, it had seemed like a passing reference—just one of many classified operations his father had been involved in during the Cold War. But now, seeing it again, unease settled in his chest. He clicked the message.

From: Unknown

Subject: Operation White Coat

"Your father lied to you, Rhett. Operation White Coat was never shut down."

The words hit like a hammer. His father lied. The operation wasn't dead. And someone out there knew who Rhett was—and what his father had done.

Rhett reread the message, his pulse quickening. It was vague, but the implications were enormous. What had his father hidden from him? More importantly, why now?

His instincts screamed at him to treat this as a threat. The message could be bait, a trap to lure him into dangerous territory. He had seen this tactic before—false breadcrumbs leading operatives into the lion's den. But this was personal. It's too personal to ignore.

He typed out a response:

"Who are you? What do you know?"

He hit send and waited. Nothing.

The silence pressed against him, thick and suffocating. Rhett pushed back from the desk and began pacing, his mind racing through possibilities. Whoever sent the message had gone to great lengths to ensure they couldn't be traced. They knew how to stay hidden—just as his father had for most of his life.

Rhett's thoughts drifted to his father's funeral. It had been a closed casket, sterile, impersonal affair, attended by a handful of government officials who spoke coldly about Dr. Kardon's "contributions." Even then, Rhett had felt like an outsider, left to piece together fragments of a man who had been more of an enigma than a parent.

The message on the screen refused to leave his mind. What if Operation White Coat wasn't just a relic of the past? What if it was alive—and active?

He stopped pacing and stared out the window. The city below moved on, oblivious to the storm brewing inside him. But Rhett couldn't ignore the feeling that his life was about to change forever.

Turning back to the terminal, he refreshed the screen. Still no reply.

Rhett exhaled slowly and shut the laptop. He leaned back in his chair, staring at the ceiling as the weight of the message settled over him. If his father had lied about Operation White Coat, there was no telling how deep the deception ran.

One thing was sure: Rhett wouldn't stop until he uncovered the truth. No matter the cost.

CHAPTER 2

Operation White Coat

Rhett sat at his desk, fingers still hovering over the keyboard, the message about Operation White Coat lingering on the screen like an open wound. The harsh glow of the monitor was the only light in the room, casting long, jagged shadows across the walls. His breath felt shallow, his mind swirling with fragments of memory that didn't quite fit together. What the hell had his father been hiding? The words on the screen seemed to pulse with every beat of his heart:

"Your father lied to you, Rhett. Operation White Coat was never shut down."

His chest tightened at the thought. The man who had raised him—the same man who had taught him how to ride a bike and stood stiffly at his high school graduation—had built his life on lies. He didn't want to believe it, but the message gnawed at him, a tiny sliver of doubt lodged in his mind, threatening to unravel everything he thought he knew.

There was only one person Rhett could think of who might be on the other end of this communication, and that would have the answers he so desperately needed—an informant who thrived in the murky waters of government secrets. Rhett had crossed paths with him years ago during a covert mission in Eastern Europe when both had been neck-deep in a web of espionage and back-alley deals. The guy had been jittery and skittish as a rabbit, constantly looking over his shoulder, but he had an encyclopedic knowledge of the black-ops world.

If anyone knew about Operation White Coat, it would be him.

Rhett took a deep breath, his fingers finally moving across the keyboard. He typed a brief message to the informant through a secure, encrypted channel.

"Saint Petersburg?"

While waiting for a response, Rhett considered the mission, which started at the Hermitage Museum.

The response came quicker than Rhett thought it would.

"Hermitage."

The informant responded like a precise exchange between two computer technicians: one initiates with a "Ping," and the other immediately replies with a "Pong," confirming the connection.

"Need to meet. Urgent. Place?"

For a moment, the room was silent. Rhett leaned back, staring at the screen, half expecting no reply. Then, suddenly, a response blinked into view:

"Tomorrow night. At Casey's Bar in Georgetown. 8 PM."

The message was terse, but it was enough. Rhett closed the encrypted terminal and leaned back in his chair, his mind buzzing. What the hell was Operation White Coat about? He couldn't stop thinking about the cryptic message. His father—the man who had always been so guarded, so distant—had led a Cold War-era Operation involving genetic experimentation.

He had grown up idolizing his father despite the man's aloofness. Rhett had assumed the distance between them was just part of who his father was—a man absorbed by work, always involved in some classified operation that couldn't be discussed. Rhett had followed in his father's footsteps, becoming a covert operative himself, thinking that maybe he could finally understand the man. But now, as he stared at the flickering computer screen, he realized he had been chasing a ghost.

His mind raced back to his childhood, sifting through fragmented memories of moments that suddenly felt too rehearsed, too calculated: the impromptu physical training sessions his father would insist on, the strange psychological tests disguised as "games," and the medical checkups that were always conducted at odd hours with doctors who never introduced themselves.

What did his father do to him? And if Operation White Coat was still active, why had someone reached out now?

Rhett knew he wouldn't sleep that night. The hunt had already begun.

The Bar in Georgetown

The streets of Georgetown buzzed with life, a medley of laughter, conversation, and the hum of car engines. Street vendors called out their wares, mingling with the crisp autumn air, heavy with the scent of roasted chestnuts and damp leaves. For Rhett Kardon, none of it mattered. He moved through the crowd with purpose, his head low, collar turned against the chill, eyes scanning the throng for signs of danger. Years of training had made vigilance second nature.

Slipping into a shadowy alley, Rhett quickened toward a nondescript bar tucked into the city's forgotten corners. Its flickering neon sign cast an intermittent red glow on the cracked pavement. The bar's anonymity made it a haven for secrets—and the people desperate to share them.

Inside, the air reeked of stale beer and cigarette smoke. Dim lighting obscured faces, creating an atmosphere where anonymity thrived. The jukebox hummed a melancholy blues tune, the perfect backdrop to the room's gritty ambiance. Rhett moved to the back, where his contact waited in a shadowed booth.

The informant was a wreck—hunched over, sweat beading on his pale forehead, eyes darting toward the door every few seconds. His fingers drummed anxiously on the scarred table as Rhett slid into the seat across from him. Silence hung between them, heavy and deliberate. Rhett's steady gaze applied unspoken pressure, forcing the man to speak first.

"I don't have much time," the informant muttered, his voice shaky. "They're watching me."

"Then stop wasting it," Rhett said flatly. "Talk."

The man leaned in, his paranoia palpable. "They've got something planned. Big. And soon."

"What do you know about Operation White Coat?" Rhett asked, his tone sharp.

The informant froze, his wide eyes darting to the door. "Jesus, Kardon. You don't want this. It'll wreck you."

"I'm not here for warnings," Rhett said firmly. "Tell me."

The man's voice dropped to a whisper. "Your father didn't just work on White Coat. He led it."

The revelation hit like a punch. Was Rhett's father—cold, methodical, yet never sinister—the architect of an operation steeped in darkness? The informant pressed on, describing genetic experiments designed to create enhanced operatives—faster, stronger, smarter, and superhuman.

"And you," he added, his voice barely audible, "were the first success."

The words sent Rhett's world spiraling. Childhood memories of tests, checkups, and his father's detached gaze snapped into focus. He wasn't a son—he was a prototype.

Before Rhett could react, the informant bolted, leaving Rhett alone with the suffocating weight of the truth. As he stepped back into the cold night, one thing became clear: he would uncover the whole story, no matter the cost.

The Next Steps: Digging Deeper

As night settled over Washington, D.C., Rhett Kardon paced his dimly lit apartment, his thoughts in turmoil. Outside, the city lights flickered indifferently, but inside, Rhett was unraveling. Hours earlier, he had learned two devastating truths: his father, Dr. James Kardon, had spearheaded the infamous Operation White Coat, and Rhett himself had been one of its test subjects. His carefully constructed reality now felt like an elaborate illusion.

Memories he had buried clawed to the surface, demanding a second look. Childhood moments—routine medical checkups, probing questions, and his father's relentless scrutiny—now took on sinister undertones. What Rhett once dismissed as quirks of a brilliant but distant man now revealed themselves as calculated manipulation. His father had not been a parent; he had been a handler, methodically shaping Rhett into something unknown.

Rhett remembered the countless evenings he spent sitting across from his father, solving puzzles and answering abstract questions while being watched with the cold detachment of a scientist. Success brought no praise, and failure no comfort. Every interaction was a test, another step in an experiment. The weight of betrayal pressed on Rhett's chest. His father had shaped him not out of love but as part of a grander, dehumanizing design.

The informant's jittery warnings replayed in his mind: Operation White Coat wasn't dormant. It was still active, hidden in the shadows, shaping others like him. The thought of other lives twisted by the operation stoked his determination.

He stared out the window, the hum of the city distant and irrelevant. The path to the truth wouldn't be safe; the secrets he sought to uncover were fiercely guarded. But Rhett couldn't turn back. This was personal—it was about reclaiming his identity.

Turning to his desk, Rhett jotted down names from half-remembered conversations and glimpses of his father's notes. One name stood out: Carter, a reclusive former intelligence officer with a talent for unearthing secrets. Though Rhett hadn't spoken to him in years, Carter owed him a favor.

Contacting Carter wouldn't be easy or safe. Rhett drafted an encrypted message, careful to obscure his intentions. Each keystroke felt like crossing a threshold into dangerous territory. As he worked, a chilling thought gnawed at him: if Operation White Coat had shaped him, could he trust his memories, instincts, or identity?

The hours dragged on until, at dawn, Rhett dialed Carter's number. A gruff voice answered, "Kardon. Took you long enough."

"I need your help," Rhett said, his voice firm. Carter chuckled darkly. "What is it this time?"

"Operation White Coat," Rhett replied. "I need everything you can find."

Carter paused. "You're playing with fire. Are you sure about this?"

Rhett's jaw tightened. "I don't have a choice."

"Alright," Carter said. "But once you start, there's no going back."

"I'm ready," Rhett said, though his conviction wavered.

The call ended, and Rhett stared at his notes. The journey ahead would be treacherous, but this wasn't just about the past. It was about reclaiming the life his father had stolen.

Flashback: The Father's Study

Rhett Kardon parked on the desolate road leading to his father's house past midnight. The headlights illuminated a once-stately mansion now succumbing to decay. Ivy choked the stone walls, shattered windows glinted like hollow eyes in the moonlight, and the overgrown driveway bore the weight of years forgotten. Like its former owner, the house was a shell of its former self.

Rhett gripped the steering wheel, memories clawing at him. The house symbolized order and control, and its pristine facade reflected Dr. James Kardon's meticulous nature. Yet to Rhett, it was a prison—a fortress where his father's authority cast a cold shadow. Now, it stood as a crumbling monument to the secrets he had come to confront.

Cutting the engine, he stepped into the chilly night. The air was thick with the scent of damp earth and decay as he made his way up the overgrown path. Each step echoed with the weight of unanswered questions. The tarnished doorknob, cold under his hand, was a sharp reminder of the boy who had once hesitated there, seeking his father's approval.

With a deep breath, he pushed the door open. The house greeted him with silence, cloaked in dust and abandonment. Sheets covered the furniture, their ghostly forms shimmering in the moonlight streaming through broken windows. The floor creaked beneath him, amplifying the eerie stillness. The emptiness felt alive, every shadow a fragment of the past.

Rhett moved toward the study, the room that had always been forbidden. As a child, he had often lingered outside its closed door, straining to hear muffled conversations and the typewriter's rhythm. Now, it was his gateway to answers.

The study door hung ajar, and Rhett stepped inside. The room, frozen in time, was lined with bookshelves holding volumes on genetics, military strategy, and obscure sciences. The mahogany desk, once his father's symbol of authority, was cluttered with yellowing folders and handwritten notes. One folder caught Rhett's eye, its cryptic label promising revelations.

Flipping through the pages, his pulse quickened as a phrase leaped out: Operation White Coat. One entry made his stomach drop: "Test subject shows promising results. Cognitive and physical responses exceed expectations. Observation continues."

The truth hit him like a blow. He didn't need to guess who the test subject was. His father had raised him not as a son but as an experiment.

Anger surged through Rhett as he slammed the folder shut. His eyes landed on a photograph buried beneath papers: himself as a boy, his father's hand resting on his shoulder, a rare smile on his face. Was it love or pride in a creation?

Shaking off the thought, Rhett turned back to the desk. There was more to uncover. Whatever darkness lay ahead, he was ready to face it.

CHAPTER 3

Memories Resurface

The streets of Georgetown were eerily quiet as Rhett Kardon returned to his apartment, his mind tangled with memories and the weight of the informant's revelations. The usual hum of late-night traffic was replaced by an oppressive stillness, the shadowed, winding side streets of Washington, D.C., feeling darker and more foreboding than usual. Each step brought him closer to home, but the journey felt endless, his thoughts colliding like waves in a storm.

The informant's words replayed relentlessly in his mind, each syllable cutting more profound than the last. Dr. James Kardon, his father, was not the man Rhett thought he knew. Once, he had been a distant but brilliant figure in Rhett's life—a scientist whose focus bordered on obsession. But now, the truth painted a different picture: his father wasn't just involved in Operation White Coat; he had been at its heart. And worse, Rhett himself had been a part of it. He wasn't merely James Kardon's son—he was an experiment, shaped and studied under the guise of paternal care.

When Rhett finally parked his car in front of his apartment building, he didn't move for a long moment. His fingers gripped the steering wheel tightly, his knuckles white against the dim glow of the dashboard. Memories of his childhood surged to the surface, moments once innocent now stained with sinister intent. His father hadn't been raising him—he had been molding him, documenting every step of Rhett's life with the detachment of a scientist observing a test subject.

The informant's account had been rushed, delivered with the nervous energy of someone running out of time. His eyes had darted around the dimly lit bar, and his voice had trembled with fear. Every detail he offered came with a sense of urgency, a warning Rhett couldn't shake. Yet, a part of him resisted the truth. Could his entire childhood have been a lie? Was this revelation a carefully crafted manipulation, or was it the unvarnished reality he had avoided for so long?

Pushing the car door open, Rhett stepped into the chill of the night. The cold air bit at his skin, grounding him as he crossed the deserted street to his building. The dim streetlights stretched his shadow long against the pavement, a distorted reflection of the turmoil within. His movements were automatic, his body on autopilot while his mind churned over the pieces of his past, now fitting into a darker puzzle.

Inside his apartment, the familiar space felt alien. The walls seemed to close in, the weight of the evening pressing against him. He dropped his keys onto the cluttered desk and ran a hand through his hair, trying to steady himself. The room, once a sanctuary from the world, now felt like a prison, filled with echoes of memories he couldn't escape.

His childhood replayed in his mind, unrelenting. The medical tests—routine and invasive—now took on a new meaning. Back then, Rhett had trusted his father's assurances that these exams were necessary. He had accepted the cold, sterile rooms, the probing questions, the detached doctors with their clipboards and unreadable expressions. As a boy, he had chalked it up to his father's meticulous nature. But now, those memories were tainted. He could see them for what they indeed were: experiments.

And the visitors—always the visitors. Men in dark suits who arrived unannounced, their presence heavy with unspoken authority. They had lingered in his childhood home, their conversations with his father hushed and secretive. Rhett had always felt uneasy around them, their stares too sharp, their words too measured. His father dismissed them as colleagues or advisors when he'd asked, brushing off Rhett's curiosity. Now he understood. These weren't just associates—they were handlers, agents of a program that had turned Rhett's life into a controlled study.

Pacing the length of his apartment, Rhett felt anger rising with every step. His fists clenched at his sides, his jaw tight. His childhood—the years he had thought were his own—had been stolen, replaced by a framework designed to push him beyond his limits. His father's approval had always felt conditional, tied not to who Rhett was but to what he could achieve. And now he knew why. Rhett wasn't a son to his father; he was an operation.

He slumped onto the couch, his head in his hands as betrayal crushed him. His father's pride in his physical and mental feats had been data points, not moments of connection. Every milestone had been measured, cataloged, and analyzed as part of a grander, more twisted ambition. Rhett's stomach churned at the thought.

But it wasn't just about his father. The informant had been apparent: Operation White Coat wasn't over. It had simply gone underground, its influence lingering in the shadows. Rhett wasn't alone. There were others like him, lives twisted and manipulated by a program that valued results over humanity. How many more children had been sacrificed? How many others were living with the same scars?

Rhett leaned back, staring at the ceiling. He couldn't walk away from this. He had spent years unearthing secrets as a CIA operative, navigating the dark alleys of classified operations. But this was different. This was personal. He needed answers—not just for himself, but for everyone who had been a part of Operation White Coat.

Reaching for his phone, Rhett scrolled through his contacts, hesitating over familiar names. Old allies, contacts from his past—people who might help him find the truth. But trust was dangerous. A single misstep could expose him to the people he was trying to uncover.

Setting the phone down, Rhett exhaled deeply. Fear gnawed at him, but he pushed it aside. This wasn't just about uncovering a conspiracy but about reclaiming his identity. His life had been shaped by forces he hadn't understood. Now, he was determined to confront them.

He poured himself a glass of water, staring at the city lights. His reflection in the window looked back at him—a man caught between who he thought he was and who he might indeed be. The path ahead was murky, but he couldn't turn back.

This wasn't just a search for answers. It was a fight for his humanity. And Rhett Kardon was ready to face whatever lay ahead.

Memory 1: The "Checkups"

At eight years old, Rhett Kardon lived in a world filled with unspoken mysteries. His father, Dr. James Kardon, was a figure of authority and intellect, distant yet commanding admiration. While Rhett's mother provided warmth and stability, her absence on a business trip that week left the house feeling empty and cold. His father's detachment became more pronounced without her presence, casting a shadow over Rhett's otherwise ordinary childhood.

One morning, Rhett woke to find his father standing in his bedroom doorway. The pale morning light filtered through the blinds, creating wall patterns. Still groggy, Rhett clutched his blanket and blinked at his father, who calmly informed him they were going for a "routine checkup." The phrase was familiar to Rhett, a normal part of life with his father. Yet these visits weren't like his friends' cheerful, playful medical checkups.

The clinics his father frequented were cold, sterile places hidden in plain sight—industrial buildings devoid of warmth or personality. Rhett had long since stopped wondering why. It was simply the way things were. These visits were always quiet and shrouded in secrecy. There were no friendly nurses, no waiting room posters, and no other patients—just white walls, empty spaces, and detached doctors whose gazes seemed to pierce right through him.

That morning, as Rhett and his father drove out of the city, familiar streets gave way to an industrial landscape of warehouses and factories. Rhett fidgeted in the passenger seat as they approached a narrow, unmarked building. Its gray concrete walls and small windows felt uninviting, almost forbidding. Inside, the reception area was equally lifeless—gray walls, sparse furniture, and a silent figure barely acknowledging their arrival. Rhett clung to his father's hand, seeking comfort, but his father's silence deepened his apprehension.

They walked down a long, sterile corridor, their footsteps echoing off the tile floor. At the end, they entered a stark examination room. A metal table under harsh fluorescent lights dominated the space. Rhett obediently climbed onto the cold surface, his tiny legs swinging nervously. His father stood in the corner, arms crossed, watching him with an unreadable expression.

A tall man in a white lab coat entered the room, his sharp features framed by glasses that reflected the fluorescent glow. "Hello, Rhett," he said with clinical detachment. "We're going to ask you a few questions today." Rhett nodded, glancing at his father for reassurance, receiving only a tiny, emotionless nod in return.

The questions started innocuously—about school, friends, and his feelings. But they quickly grew stranger, probing his thoughts, problem-solving abilities, and reactions to stress. Then came the tests: puzzles, shapes, and tasks assigned with precise instructions and timed meticulously. Rhett approached them like games, eager to do well, but the somber atmosphere drained all joy.

When it was over, the doctor turned to his father. "The results are promising," he said, his voice devoid of warmth. "He's showing significant adaptability." Rhett didn't understand the words but felt their weight, sensing he was more operational than a person.

On the drive home, Rhett stared out the window, unease settling deep in his chest. He couldn't articulate why, but something about the day felt wrong. Years later, he would realize these weren't checkups. They were experiments, and he had been his father's subject.

Memory 2: The Chessboard

A vivid and cold memory rose unbidden in Rhett's mind, like a shadow emerging from deep waters. He was a teenager seated across from his father at the kitchen table, a chessboard spread between them. His father's face was as impassive as always, his gaze fixed on the board with a detached intensity. Chess was their ritual, a silent battleground where his father tested him relentlessly.

The chessboard, worn and scratched, was one of the few constants in their transient lives. To Rhett, it was more than a game—it was a fragile bridge to connect with his father, Dr. James Kardon. But for his father, it was a tool to mold Rhett's mind into something precise and valuable, like the chess pieces themselves.

His father's every move was calculated and deliberate, as though rehearsed countless times. The silence during their matches was heavy, filled with unspoken critiques and expectations. Occasionally, his father would break it with words that echoed through Rhett's memory: "It's all about strategy, Rhett. You either control the game, or the game controls you." The phrase grated on Rhett, its meaning burrowing deeper into him with each repetition. It wasn't wisdom; it was a command devoid of affection.

One game, in particular, lingered in Rhett's memory. That night, frustration simmered as his father captured piece after piece. Desperate to win, Rhett played aggressively, pushing forward with reckless determination. His father, unfazed, waited for Rhett to falter. His father broke the silence when Rhett's queen fell to a decisive counterattack. "Impatience is a flaw," he said clinically. "Strategy requires patience. You don't seize control; you wait for it."

The lesson stung, not for its accuracy but for its emptiness. Rhett didn't want strategy—he wanted connection. But to his father, life was a chessboard, a series of calculated moves where mastery mattered more than relationships.

As the years passed, Rhett began to resent the games, realizing they weren't about teaching him to think but shaping him into a reflection of his father's ambitions. The breaking point came when he was seventeen. Playing with rebellion in his heart, Rhett attempted to outmaneuver his father. But his father dismantled his strategy effortlessly, ending the game with another cutting remark: "Control isn't taken; it's earned."

The words haunted Rhett, cementing the realization that he would never be seen as a son—only as an operation. Those games had been manipulation tools, shaping him into an extension of his father's vision.

Years later, Rhett sat alone, the memory as vivid as ever. The chessboard symbolized his father's control, a reminder of the autonomy and identity stolen from him. But as anger bubbled up, it gave way to resolve.

Rhett vowed to dismantle that chessboard—not with strategy, but with freedom. He would rebuild his life on his terms, no longer a pawn in his father's game.

Back to the Present

Rhett stopped pacing, his mind whirling with fragmented memories and revelations that came faster than he could process. He ran a hand through his hair,
breathing heavily as each recollection resurfaced, forcing him to confront a reality
he had never known existed. The memories were slipping together like puzzle
pieces, creating a picture he had been blind to his entire life. How had he missed
it? How had he allowed himself to go on, believing that his childhood, however
distant his father had seemed, had been expected?

He stood there momentarily, stunned, his fists clenched at his sides as realization sank in. His entire childhood had been an experiment, carefully orchestrated
and controlled. Every interaction with his father, every "checkup," every cold
glance, every calculated word—they had all been meticulously planned as part
of something greater, something his young mind had been unable to grasp. The
weight of it pressed down on him, a slow, suffocating realization that made him
feel small and helpless, like a pawn in a game he hadn't even known he was playing.

Unable to stand any longer, he sank onto the couch, his head heavy with
thoughts that refused to settle. His gaze drifted around his apartment, landing on
nothing in particular. His mind was too focused on the internal chaos to register
the room's familiarity. Everything felt different now. The memories flooding back
painted his life in a new, disturbing light, and the anger simmering within him
threatened to boil over.

Was this why his father had always seemed so detached and utterly unemo-
tional? Had he never seen Rhett as a son, as someone to nurture and care for, but
instead as an operation—a subject in an experiment? The thought made him sick,
made his stomach clench in anger and sorrow. His father, the man he had spent
years trying to understand, had never truly cared for him as a father should. He
had been more interested in the results of his experiment, in observing Rhett's
reactions, in seeing how his "subject" would develop.

The anger flared in Rhett's chest, and heat surged through him with a force
that shook him. It was a primal anger from years of betrayal, from realizing that
someone else's agenda had shaped his life. He clenched his fists tightly, nails
digging into his palms as he struggled to keep himself from losing control. Part
of him wanted to scream, punch the wall, and let out the frustration that had

been building ever since the memories had started to resurface. But he held back, forcing himself to breathe, to keep his focus. He knew this anger was only a piece of his uncovered truth.

His father had lied to him. His entire life had been manipulated, controlled, and conditioned by a man who saw him as nothing more than a tool, a carefully crafted operation to fulfill a hidden purpose. And now, with the knowledge of his father's betrayal heavy on his shoulders, Rhett knew there was no turning back. The truth had changed everything.

The Sleepless Night

Rhett stared at the ceiling, unable to sleep. The memories played on a loop in his mind—the tests, the conversations, the men in black suits. Everything felt so clear now, so obvious. His father trained, shaped, and molded him into something beyond human. And Rhett hadn't even known it.

But now that he did, he couldn't ignore it.

There was a knot of anger and grief in his chest that wouldn't go away. He wanted to confront his father and demand answers, but Dr. James Kardon was gone—buried with his secrets. But if Rhett knew one thing for sure, it was this: Operation White Coat wasn't over.

The message had been clear—someone out there knew.

CHAPTER 4

An Old Friend

The truth Rhett had uncovered pressed on him like an unforgiving weight. Every revelation about his father twisted the fabric of his childhood into something unrecognizable. Dr. James Kardon had never been a distant, preoccupied man immersed in government work. No, he had been far more calculated, far more sinister. His father had seen Rhett not as a son but as a subject—a living experiment. The memories Rhett once clung to for understanding were now warped, poisoned by the revelation of a secret so dark it was whispered only in the deepest corridors of intelligence.

The betrayal churned within him, a storm of anger and confusion threatening to consume him. Sitting alone with this knowledge felt unbearable. The questions roared in his mind, the scattered pieces of his life too fragmented to understand. Rhett knew he couldn't face this alone. He needed guidance, someone who understood the world he had stumbled into. And there was only one person he trusted for that: Garrett Westfield.

Garrett had been more than a friend. During their years as Navy Seals, he was Rhett's closest confidant. Together, they navigated chaos, survived impossible missions, and learned to rely on each other when nothing else made sense. Garrett thrived in uncertainty, able to see clearly through the fog of war. If anyone could help Rhett make sense of his father's web of lies, it was him.

Without hesitation, Rhett picked up his phone and scrolled through his contacts. His thumb hovered over Garrett's name as doubt flickered in his mind. How could he explain something so immense? How could he describe the discovery that his entire life had been a carefully constructed illusion? But he couldn't let doubt paralyze him. He pressed the call button and listened as the line rang.

After a few seconds, Garrett's familiar, gruff voice came through. "This better be good, man. I was about to enjoy my first decent beer in days."

Rhett exhaled, a tension easing slightly in his chest. "Garrett, it's been a while."

The line fell silent momentarily as if Garrett sensed the call's gravity. "Yeah," he said, his tone shifting. "What's going on, Rhett?"

"It's complicated," Rhett admitted, his voice shaky. "I need to see you. There's something I need to tell you in person."

"Where and when?" Garrett's response was immediate.

"Tomorrow, 9:00 p.m. The old bar by the docks."

"Got it," Garrett said, no hesitation in his voice.

Relief surged through Rhett as he hung up. The bar by the docks had always been their refuge, a place to decompress after long missions. It was only fitting they would meet there now as Rhett faced the unraveling of his life.

Meeting Garrett

The bar was a dive tucked away on the city's outskirts, a place where no one asked questions and no one looked too long at anyone else. The kind of place Rhett and Garrett had always found comforting—safe, in the way dangerous places are when you know how to survive them.

Rhett stepped inside, scanning the dimly lit room. It smelled of beer, old wood, and cigarette smoke. His eyes found Garrett immediately, sitting at the bar nursing a bottle of beer. He looked the same as the last time Rhett had seen him—broad-shouldered, with the scruffy beard of a man who lived by his own rules.

Garrett glanced up and gave Rhett a lopsided grin, his sharp blue eyes flickering with recognition. "Well, look what the cat dragged in." He raised his bottle in a mock salute. "Still alive, I see."

Rhett smirked, though it didn't reach his eyes. "Barely."

Garrett motioned to the empty stool beside him. "Figured you'd show up eventually. Whiskey? Or are you pretending to quit drinking again?"

Rhett shook his head and signaled the bartender. "Whiskey. Double. Neat."

As the bartender poured the amber liquid, Garrett studied Rhett, his easy grin fading slightly. "So, what's eating you, brother? You don't look like a man who just came in for a drink."

Rhett took a long sip of his whiskey, the burn sliding down his throat, grounding him. He stared at the glass for a moment before speaking. "I need to ask you something... and I need you to be straight with me. No bullshit."

Garrett raised an eyebrow, leaning back on his stool. "When have I ever given you bullshit?"

Rhett gave a short, humorless laugh. "Fair point."

He set his glass down and turned toward Garrett, lowering his voice. "Have you ever heard of something called Operation White Coat?"

Garrett's expression didn't change, but Rhett noticed the subtle shift in his posture—the slight stiffening of his shoulders, the way his hand gripped the beer bottle a little tighter.

"Where the hell did you hear that name?" Garrett asked, his voice low.

Rhett didn't answer immediately. He knew Garrett well enough to recognize that reaction—the reaction of a man who knew exactly what kind of danger they were discussing.

"I need to know what it is," Rhett said quietly. "And how it connects to my father."

Garrett exhaled slowly, rubbing the back of his neck. "Jesus, Rhett..." He took a swig of beer, his gaze flicking toward the door as if someone might be listening. "That's a dangerous road you're walking down. You sure you want to keep going?"

"I don't have a choice, Garrett," Rhett said, his jaw tightening. "I got a message—anonymous. Someone knows about White Coat, and they know my father was involved."

Garrett set his beer down with a thud. "You're telling me Dr. James Kardon was mixed up in that mess?"

Rhett gave a grim nod. "More than mixed up. He ran it."

Garrett swore under his breath, dragging a hand down his face. "And now someone's stirring up old ghosts."

"What do you know?" Rhett pressed.

Garrett hesitated, his eyes narrowing. "I know it was some deep black-ops Operation—Cold War stuff—the kind of thing they bury so far down that no one ever finds it. I heard whispers about it when I was in the teams. A lot of money disappeared into that hole."

He leaned closer, his voice dropping to a near whisper. "But listen to me, Rhett. The people connected to things like that. They don't just disappear. They stick around, waiting for the right moment. You dig into this; you'll find yourself on a lot of radars—the kind you can't outrun."

The Rabbit Hole

Rhett Kardon stared into his whiskey glass, the amber liquid catching the bar's dim light. The last sip burned as it slid down his throat, doing little to dull the betrayal coiling in his gut. His thoughts churned relentlessly, each one circling back to the same question: What did my father do to me? Garrett, his oldest friend and the only person he trusted to share what he'd uncovered. Rhett's voice was low but unwavering as he spoke.

"I have to find out the truth, Garrett. I need to know what my father was involved in."

Garrett's face remained calm, though his steady gaze betrayed a flicker of unease. They had faced unimaginable dangers together as Navy SEALs, but this was different. This wasn't a mission against a clear enemy but a dive into dangerous, personal shadows. After a long pause, Garrett leaned back and sighed.

"What makes you think there's anything left to find?" he asked. "I heard that operation went all the way to the top. And I mean the top. Maybe it's better to let sleeping dogs lie."

Rhett shook his head slightly, the motion firm, resolute. "Not this time. I can't move on—not without knowing the truth. This is personal now."

Garrett studied him, the flicker of concern in his eyes growing. He'd seen what happened to people who chased secrets that didn't want to be found. The deeper you dug, the darker it got. He knew the danger Rhett was inviting, but he also knew his friend well enough to understand there was no stopping him. Once Rhett had decided to pursue something, no force on Earth could hold him back.

With a resigned sigh, Garrett ran a hand through his hair, his frustration evident. "Alright, listen," he said, leaning forward. "If you're going to do this, you've got to be careful. This isn't like tracking terrorists in the desert. If they're still around, these people don't leave loose ends, and they never quit."

Rhett's eyes hardened, his voice steady as he replied, "Neither do I."

Garrett's lips curved into a faint, humorless smile. "That's what worries me."

The silence between them grew heavy. Garrett could see the weight of determination in Rhett's expression but knew the risks. This wasn't just a hunt for information but a journey into a place where truths were deadly and survival wasn't guaranteed.

Finally, Garrett broke the silence, his tone serious. "If you're going down this road, you can't do it blind. You will need resources—contacts who know how to operate off the grid. Official channels won't help you here."

Rhett nodded, absorbing his friend's words. He was fully aware of the danger but couldn't care. "I've got a few leads. There's someone who might know where to start. But I'll need backup. Someone I can trust."

Garrett frowned, his reluctance plain. "You know I'm with you. I don't like this, but I know I can't stop you. Just tell me what you need."

The relief Rhett felt was immediate. Garrett's support had always been a constant, and now, more than ever, he needed it. "There's a man named Simon Reiss," Rhett said. "An old intelligence contact my father mentioned years ago. He's in the private sector now—consulting on 'risk management.' If anyone knows where my father's files are, it's him."

Garrett's expression tightened. "Reiss... I know the name. He's not the kind of guy you approach lightly. If you plan to deal with him, you better be ready to pay. And not just with money. He'll want something valuable."

Rhett grimaced. "I figured as much. But it's worth it if he can get me closer to the truth."

Garrett nodded slowly, though his concern didn't fade. "Reiss is in the business of secrets. He'll play every angle to get what he wants. If you go to him, you'll need leverage—something he can't get anywhere else."

"What kind of leverage?" Rhett asked, already calculating his next steps.

"Information," Garrett replied. "A favor he can cash in later. Or access to something he's locked out of. Reiss doesn't deal fairly, and he doesn't give anything away for free. You need to make it worth his while."

The reality of Garrett's warning sank in. Rhett wasn't just stepping into the unknown—he was walking into a game of manipulation, where alliances shifted like quicksand, and trust was a liability. But his resolve didn't waver. He had to do this, no matter the cost.

"Do you have anything on him?" Rhett asked. "Something I could use?"

Garrett thought for a moment, his brow furrowed. "Not much. But I've heard he's been trying to gain access to certain intelligence networks—ones he's been locked out of since he left the game. If you can offer him a way in, he might listen."

Rhett nodded, already forming a plan. "Thanks, Garrett. I knew you'd understand. I need someone watching my back."

"You've got it," Garrett said firmly. "But promise me something—don't let this obsession take you down. You go too far, and you might lose more than you're trying to find."

Rhett looked away, his jaw tightening. "If I don't do this, I'll lose myself anyway."

Garrett's face softened, his loyalty outweighing his hesitation. "Then let's get going, my brother."

For the next few hours, they planned meticulously. Garrett laid out contacts, routes, and contingencies, treating this like one of their old missions. But this time, there was no clear objective, no official orders—just Rhett's unrelenting need for answers.

As the bar emptied, the weight of their task loomed heavy, but so did Rhett's determination. He was stepping into a world of shadows and deceit but wouldn't back down. Too much of his life had been shaped by secrets, and now it was time to take control.

When they finally left, Garrett clapped a hand on Rhett's shoulder. "You're not in this alone. Keep your head clear, and don't let your emotions call the shots."

Rhett managed a faint smile. "Thanks, Garrett. I don't know what I'd do without you."

Garrett smirked, though his voice carried a warning. "Probably get yourself killed. Just remember—once you open this door, there's no closing it."

Rhett nodded. He knew the risks. He knew the pain that awaited him. But he also learned one thing: he couldn't keep living in the dark. With Garrett by his side and his resolve unshaken, Rhett was ready to face the truth, no matter where it led.

CHAPTER 5

The First Clue

T he next few days passed in a blur of sleepless nights and obsessive research. Lying in bed, staring at the white textured ceiling with a slowly rotating ceiling fan pushing cool air onto Rhett's clammy and sweating body, lying with the sheets in tatters. Rhett Kardon's mind was locked in a relentless loop. Every memory of his father, every cryptic moment from his childhood, every conversation about Operation White Coat now felt like a puzzle demanding to be solved. What exactly had his father done to him? And, more importantly, why?

The meeting with Garrett had grounded him but lacked the clarity he needed. Answers were still out there—hidden, buried in the past. Rhett knew he couldn't rely on anyone else to find them. This was his fight now.

A Package with No Return Address

R hett sat at his desk, the dim overhead light casting shadows that seemed to stretch and shift across the cluttered surface. Folders and documents lay scattered around, evidence of his restless search for answers. His laptop was open before him, and various secure sites and encrypted databases were blinking on the screen. He was digging into CIA archives, black-market information brokers, and old government documents—anything that could illuminate the truth he was desperately hunting. Yet, no matter how many avenues he explored, he kept hitting dead ends. Files were redacted beyond recognition, links were broken, and databases were restricted, denying him the needed access. Frustration gnawed at him, a tension building in his chest as each road led to a brick wall.

Just as he was about to slam his laptop shut in exasperation, a sudden knock at the door broke the silence. Rhett tensed, his instincts taking over. Years of training kicked in, and his hand moved without thought to the Springfield hidden under his desk. He kept his movements silent as he stood and crossed the room, every muscle on high alert. Approaching the door, he peered through the peephole, scanning for any movement outside.

Nothing. The hallway was empty.

Rhett's pulse quickened. He tightened his grip on the Springfield, then cautiously pulled the door open, bracing himself for whatever might be waiting. But there was no one. The only thing on the floor was a small, nondescript package, plain and unmarked. There was no label, address, or sign of where it had come from—just a simple cardboard box sealed with heavy-duty tape.

He stared down at it, his mind racing through possibilities. It was risky; the package could be anything. For all he knew, it might contain a tracking device, a listening bug, or even an explosive. But there was something about it, something deliberate. It didn't feel like a random threat or a careless gesture. This felt targeted and personal.

Taking a slow breath, Rhett bent down and picked up the box, noting its surprising weight. He shut the door behind him, locking it securely, and carried the package to his desk. Placing it down, he stepped back, his eyes narrowing as he studied it. His mind worked through a mental checklist—possible threats, triggers, traps. But his instincts told him to proceed. Whoever had left this hadn't meant to harm him, not yet, at least.

Moving carefully, he retrieved a small tactical knife from his drawer. He used the blade to slice through the tape, and his movements were precise and controlled. As he opened the box, a faint scent of dust and age wafted out, filling the air with a smell reminiscent of old libraries and forgotten memories. Inside, wrapped in brown paper, was a stack of documents, yellowed with age. The ink had faded over time, but the text was still readable, and there was a sense of purpose in how each paper had been carefully bundled and protected.

Rhett unwrapped the paper slowly, a sense of foreboding washing over him as he revealed its contents. What he saw made his blood run cold. Familiar names, government seals, and classified stamps stared back at him. Some documents had his father's signature alongside operation titles he recognized from his fragmented memories. Each page was a piece of the puzzle, confirming the existence of experiments he had only begun to suspect—experiments with names he had seen before, whispered in dark hallways and locked in restricted files.

The First Clue: Operation White Coat Documents

The documents were blueprints from Operation White Coat. Written in his father's precise handwriting, they contained diagrams, genetic markers, and psychological evaluations. Each sheet felt like a piece of a much larger, darker puzzle.

Rhett's heart pounded as he flipped through the files, eyes scanning the neatly printed lines. This wasn't just research. It was meticulous documentation—everything from physical data to behavioral observations—and in the middle of it all was his name:

Rhett Kardon is circled in red and underlined twice.

He stared at the sheet in disbelief. They had been monitoring him since childhood, cataloging every stage of his development: reflex tests, cognitive assessments, and emotional evaluations. Nothing had been left unmeasured.

"Jesus," Rhett muttered under his breath. His hands trembled slightly as he continued flipping through the documents. It wasn't just monitoring—it was control. His father had carefully guided every aspect of his life, treating him like an experiment.

There were handwritten notes in the margins, scrawled in his father's distinctive handwriting:

The subject exhibits above-average reflexes under stress.

Emotional conditioning: incomplete. Further testing is required.

The entries span years—childhood, adolescence, and even early adulthood. His entire life had been a controlled environment. Every achievement, every failure, was part of a larger plan.

Rhett felt the walls closing in around him. His father hadn't just experimented on him—he had built him.

The Psychological Profile

One document made Rhett's blood turn to ice. It was a psychological profile his father wrote when Rhett was only fourteen. The tone was clinical and detached as if the writer were observing a lab rat rather than his son. The words were cold, calculated, and utterly devoid of parental warmth or care. Rhett scanned the page, barely able to process the language that dissected his adolescent mind as if it were a specimen under a microscope.

The subject demonstrates signs of advanced strategic thinking but resists emotional manipulation. The phrase made Rhett's stomach tighten. Emotional manipulation—his father had studied his responses to it like a behavioral experiment. He'd documented Rhett's ability to resist as though it were a shortcoming or obstacle needing correction. As Rhett read on, his father's intent became even more apparent. Increased exposure to stressors is recommended to promote detachment and resilience.

The words hit Rhett like a physical blow. He realized that his father had intentionally subjected him to stress, strategically manipulating his environment to see how he would respond. His father used psychological theory not to understand him as a person but to control and shape him as a subject. It was a chilling application of conditioning, designed to break down normal emotional responses and replace them with strategic detachment—a kind of psychological armor against the vulnerabilities of human connection.

Rhett closed his eyes, and flashes of his teenage years flooded back to him. The calculated distance his father had kept, the constant tests of endurance and critical thinking, and the relentless focus on pushing his mental and physical limits made sense now. Every moment he had thought was a typical interaction was, in fact, part of a calculated process. His father hadn't just been preparing him for life; he'd been conditioning him, stripping away his natural responses to forge a new personality.

He could feel the weight of psychological theories his father had employed, perhaps theories rooted in behaviorism, classical and operant conditioning. Every experience and every challenge his father had set up was designed to re-inforce desired traits and eliminate those considered weaknesses. Emotional responses, empathy, vulnerability—all had been identified as obstacles to be minimized, carefully trained out of him to produce someone capable of cold precision and complete emotional control.

Rhett's mind spun with anger and disbelief. This wasn't parenting. This was engineering. His father had applied the principles of behavioral psychology with clinical precision, creating a calculated environment in which Rhett's emotional independence was actively suppressed in favor of controlled detachment. Each test and every confrontation had been another reinforcement of his father's agenda: resilience through isolation and strength through emotional distance. His father had even anticipated that Rhett might seek closeness or empathy, and he had designed scenarios to teach him the futility of those needs.

In suppressing emotional responses and nurturing cognitive control, his father had also tapped into cognitive behavioral theories that emphasized rationality over emotional awareness. By teaching Rhett to value strategic outcomes above all else, he had encouraged what psychologists might call a "highly adaptive but emotionally avoidant" personality. Rhett's cold precision, difficulty forming close relationships, and tendency to remain distant from those around him weren't traits from life's natural challenges. They were intentionally crafted responses, instilled in him by someone who had seen his mind as something malleable to be shaped, honed, and perfected.

He opened his eyes and threw the paper onto the desk, his chest heaving. His father hadn't just raised him; he had molded him, using theories of resilience and conditioning to suppress any form of emotional vulnerability. Rhett wasn't just shaped by life; he was shaped by one man's clinical vision of perfection—a machine of self-control, of cognitive precision, devoid of emotional weakness.

Staring down at the discarded profile, Rhett felt his sense of self crumbling. His whole life had been a lie. The man who should have been his greatest ally and protector had reduced him to a subject in an experiment.

The Puzzle Deepens

Rhett leaned back in his chair, running a hand through his hair. His mind was spinning, struggling to process the enormity of what he had just uncovered.

Why had his father done this? What was the ultimate goal of Operation White Coat? And why was Rhett's development so important?

He flipped through more pages, desperate for answers. Some documents mentioned other subjects, such as failed experiments and people who didn't survive the process. Rhett shuddered at the thought.

But his name was the only one marked as a success.

The last page in the stack was a letter from his father, written in neat cursive handwriting. It was dated just a few weeks before his father's death.

Rhett—if you're reading this, you've found the truth. I never wanted things to turn out this way, but you were always destined for more. You're the future. What I did... I did it for you. I only hope one day you'll understand.

Rhett stared at the letter, his hands trembling. It wasn't an apology. This was a load of shit. It was nothing more than a lame justification.

In his father's narcissistic view, he believed in what he was doing. He had thought that turning his son into a superhuman was somehow a gift.

But all Rhett felt was a betrayal.

Confronting the Past

Rhett stood up, pacing the room. He had spent his entire life trying to be the man his father wanted him to be—disciplined, detached, and focused. But now he realized that every choice he had made, every step he had taken, had been guided by his father's invisible hand.

His anger boiled inside him, fierce and uncontrollable. He wanted answers, so he tried to tear down every wall around him, find the people who had been part of this twisted operation, and make them pay.

But more than anything, he wanted to understand.

He stopped pacing and stared at the documents spread across his desk. Somewhere in those pages, beneath the technical jargon and data, was the truth—the real reason his father had turned him into a prototype.

And Rhett was going to find it.

The Decision

R hett sat at his desk; he knew he couldn't return to the CIA without this information. Someone inside the agency wanted Operation White Coat to stay buried. If they found out what he knew, they'd stop him, silence him, or worse.

He sat down at the desk again, staring at the documents. He was alone in this. But that was nothing new. Rhett had spent his whole life alone, even when surrounded by people.

Now, it was time to turn that isolation into an advantage.

He carefully rewrapped the documents in the brown paper, hiding them in a secret locked drawer beneath his desk. He couldn't trust anyone—not yet.

But he knew where to start. There were names in those documents—scientists, agents, people connected to the operation. One of them had to have answers.

The discovery of the documents gave Rhett his first real lead—but it also deepened the mystery and anger. His father's betrayal is not just a possibility but a fact. As Rhett prepared to dive deeper into the secrets of Operation White Coat, he knew the road ahead was filled with danger. But he was ready. He had nothing left to lose—and everything to uncover.

Rhett exhaled slowly, his mind sharpening with purpose. He had a mission now. And nothing—not the CIA, not the ghosts of his father's past, not even the people trying to bury Operation White Coat—was going to stop him from finding the truth.

CHAPTER 6

The Informant's Fate

T he faint hum of the city outside did little to calm Rhett Kardon's racing mind. The discovery of the documents had been more than just a revelation—it was a confirmation that everything the informant had told him was true. His father had experimented on him. Rhett's entire life, from childhood to adulthood, had been a meticulously orchestrated lie.

But the trail was still cold. The files provided some answers, but not enough. He needed more. There were too many missing pieces and too many questions without answers. The only person who might have filled in those blanks was the informant.

Rhett grabbed his jacket from the back of his chair, his movements sharp and deliberate. He needed to talk to the informant again—now.

To the Informant's Apartment

The drive across Washington, D.C., was quick and tense, the city lights flashing by as Rhett's mind churned through every possibility. He had to know more. If the informant had survived this long while carrying the weight of such dangerous knowledge, he had to know something more significant.

He pulled up to the informant's apartment building, a nondescript brick structure tucked away in an old part of town—the kind of place that hid secrets well. Rhett scanned the street from his car, ensuring he wasn't followed. The night air felt heavier than usual, and an unsettling sense of foreboding settled over him.

Rhett exited the car, every muscle in his body tense as he approached the building. His instincts were humming, but something didn't feel right. The building was too quiet, too still.

He took the stairs two at a time, his heart thudding with adrenaline and dread. The informant lived on the third floor, in a corner apartment with a view of the alley—perfect for someone who liked to see trouble coming before it arrived.

When Rhett reached the door, he immediately noticed the lock had been tampered with.

A chill ran down his spine. He was too late.

The Scene Inside

Rhett drew his Springfield and slowly pushed the door open, the hinges groaning in protest. The apartment was dark, and the air was stale, smelling of cigarette smoke and rotting food.

He flipped the light switch. Nothing.

The dim glow from the flickering streetlights outside offered just enough illumination for Rhett to see the state of the room. The place had been ransacked. Furniture was overturned, drawers pulled open and emptied, and papers scattered across the floor. It wasn't a robbery. It was a message.

Rhett's stomach twisted. They'd found him.

He moved through the apartment, stepping carefully to avoid making noise. His instincts told him someone might still be watching. He scanned the room, his sharp gaze flickering over every detail.

And then he saw him.

The informant lay slumped against the wall, his body twisted into a disturbingly unnatural position. Rhett's eyes adjusted slowly to the dim, flickering light, but the grotesque details began to take shape. Brain matter was smeared across the wall behind him, an ugly stain marking the spot where his last moment had been etched into the decrepit room. Dried blood had pooled down the remnants of his face, streaking over the worn and dirty fabric of his clothes, collecting in dark patches that spread across his torso, then dripping to the floor, seeping ominously into the cracks between the floorboards.

His hand, frozen in a final gesture of casual habit, held a half-smoked cigarette, now cold, the ashes long scattered on the ground below. The sight was jarring, a mix of violence and eerie calm. This was someone who had tried to stay composed, even at the edge of death.

The silence of the room pressed in on Rhett. Dust hung thick in the stale air, disturbed only by his shallow breaths. He took a cautious step forward, every sound amplified in the stillness, and felt a faint chill as though the room remembered the last moments of the man's life. This wasn't just a death—it was a message.

A Closer Look

Rhett stood, scanning the room for anything the killers might have missed. He knew how these operations worked—clean and efficient. But no one ever cleaned up perfectly. There were always traces, tiny pieces left behind.

He knelt beside the informant's desk, sifting through the scattered papers. Most were junk—old newspapers, coffee-stained files, grocery lists. Nothing important. But then he found something.

Tucked beneath a stack of newspapers was a small notebook. The leather cover was worn, and the pages were filled with the informant's cramped handwriting. Rhett flipped through it quickly, skimming the notes: dates, locations, code words—pieces of a puzzle.

One name kept appearing over and over: Operation White Coat.

And beneath it, circled in red ink, was another word: "Montenegro."

The Montenegro Lead

R hett stared at the name, trying to place it. Montenegro. It wasn't familiar, but it had to mean something. The informant wouldn't have highlighted it otherwise.

He took out his phone and snapped a picture of the notebook page. Montenegro might be the next piece of the puzzle. Whoever—or whatever—it was, it had something to do with his father's work.

Rhett slipped the notebook into his jacket pocket, his mind already racing. He needed to move quickly. Whoever had killed the informant might still be close by—and if they found Rhett here, he'd be next.

A Close Call

J ust as Rhett stood to leave, he heard the soft creak of a floorboard in the hallway.

His body reacted on instinct. He moved to the side of the doorway, pressing his back against the wall, his Springfield raised and ready.

The door creaked open slightly, and a shadow moved inside.

Rhett acted fast. He grabbed the intruder by the arm, twisting hard and forcing them against the wall. The Springfield was at the person's temple before they had time to react.

"Who the hell are you?" Rhett growled, his voice low and dangerous.

The figure—a man in his thirties with dark hair and a scar running down his cheek—didn't flinch. His expression was calm, too calm.

"You're too late, Kardon," the man said quietly. "The game's already over."

Rhett's grip tightened. "What game? Who sent you?"

The man gave a thin, humorless smile. "It doesn't matter. They're coming for you next. You should've stayed out of this."

Before Rhett could press further, the man's hand twitched toward his pocket—a cyanide capsule.

Rhett acted fast, slamming the man's head against the wall hard enough to knock him out. He wouldn't let this guy die—not before he got answers.

Interrogation

Rhett dragged the unconscious man through the narrow doorway, his shoulders heaving as he dropped the man onto the cracked, grimy floor of the dilapidated apartment. Dust stirred as the man's limp body hit the ground, settling again on the walls and floor as if eager to cloak the scene in silence. Rhett quickly scanned the room, his eyes landing on a length of electrical cord discarded near an overturned chair. He snatched it up without hesitation, deftly binding the man's hands together, ensuring he wouldn't get away anytime soon. This man held information—something crucial, something Rhett needed if he was going to survive. Tonight, he would get answers.

The man began to stir, a low groan slipping from his lips as he gradually regained consciousness. His eyelids fluttered, and his eyes opened, quickly registering his predicament. His gaze landed on Rhett, looming over him, cold and unmoved. The man's bravado flickered slightly, but he kept his face impassive, slipping into the calculated calm of someone accustomed to fear.

"Start talking," Rhett commanded, his voice a deadly whisper. The tone was enough to make most people crumble, but the man responded with a faint, derisive smile, mocking even as he looked up from his bound state on the floor.

"You really think you're going to get answers?" he taunted, lifting his chin as if daring Rhett to try harder.

Rhett's expression didn't change. He crouched down, his face inches from the man's, his eyes sharp and unrelenting. The shadows in the dimly lit apartment accentuated his features, casting him in a sinister light. "I've got time. You don't," he said, his voice low and cold, each word laced with a dangerous promise.

The man's defiance faltered, just for a moment. Rhett could see it in his eyes—the slight shift, the flicker of doubt breaking through the forced arrogance. But the silence in the room was suddenly interrupted by a phone buzzing. Rhett's eyes darted to the sound. He reached into the man's pocket, quickly retrieving the phone.

A message glowed on the screen, stark and chilling: Target identified. Execute extraction.

Rhett's heart pounded as he read it, his blood turning to ice. This wasn't just some small-time thug he was dealing with. This man was connected to something bigger that was now closing in fast. They weren't just watching him; they were coming for him.

The man's expression had shifted, a slight smirk pulling at the corners of his mouth, seeing the reaction flicker in Rhett's eyes. "Too late," he whispered, a smug satisfaction replacing his earlier defiance. "They're coming, and there's nothing you can do to stop it."

Rhett's grip tightened on the phone, his mind racing. But he wouldn't let this man have the upper hand, not now. He leaned in close, his voice low but filled with a deadly calm that betrayed the storm brewing beneath. "You think they'll get here in time to save you? Think again."

With that, Rhett grabbed a chair, dragging it across the floor with a grating scrape and placing it in front of the bound man. He sat down slowly, his gaze never wavering, locking onto his captive with a steely focus. "Last chance. Who sent you, and why are they coming for me?"

The man's confidence seemed to waver for a moment, his eyes darting toward the door as if hoping for salvation to arrive any second. But he realized then that he was truly alone, at the mercy of a man with no spare. His mouth opened, the hint of words forming on his lips, but Rhett didn't need to hear them to understand the truth. This wasn't just an interrogation anymore; this was survival, a deadly game where every second counted.

The clock was ticking, and Rhett knew he'd do whatever it took to make it alive.

The Next Move

Rhett didn't waste another second. He grabbed the notebook from his Jacket pocket and the man's phone, shoving them both into his pocket.

He stood over the bound man, his expression hard. "If you leave here alive, tell your bosses I'm not done."

The man's grin returned, though it was weaker now. "You're in over your head, Kardon."

Rhett didn't bother with a response. Threats meant nothing to him. With swift, brutal force, he slammed the butt of his gun into the man's skull, the impact crunching like the skin of a ripe tomato bursting open. The blow tore a jagged gash across his brow, and thick, dark blood began oozing down, pooling over his face in a slow, relentless stream. He slipped out of the apartment, moving quickly and quietly down the stairs. The hunters were closing in. But Rhett wasn't running.

He was just getting started.

CHAPTER 7

Hidden Truths

The weight of the informant's death hung over Rhett Kardon like a shadow. The man's lifeless eyes, the staged crime scene, and the veiled threat from the captured operative burned into Rhett's mind. He was in the middle of something far more significant than he had imagined—something deadly. The danger increased with every step he took deeper into his father's legacy, but Rhett knew one thing: the truth was buried inside those old documents. And Montenegro—whoever or whatever it was—held the next puzzle piece.

Back at the Apartment: Assembling the Pieces

When Rhett returned to his apartment, he locked the door behind him and paused, scanning the room for any signs of intrusion. He couldn't afford to be careless. The CIA, whoever had killed the informant, and other unseen forces were all converging on him. He felt it in his gut.

Every shadow could hold an enemy. Every open connection is a trap.

He moved toward his desk, dumped the notebook's contents, and Montenegro lead onto the surface. He had to work fast—there wasn't much time before they came for him, too.

The familiar hum of his laptop filled the silence. Rhett spread out the pages of the documents on the desk, using the notebook's scribbled notes as a guide to connect the dots. Operation White Coat's scope was more significant than he'd realized. Each new detail painted a picture more disturbing than the last.

The Scope of the Operation

The documents showed that Operation White Coat was about more than just creating enhanced soldiers. It was an evolution of warfare. The program aimed to create a new breed of operators—capable of functioning beyond human limitations, with enhanced physical, mental, and cognitive abilities.

It wasn't just reflexes and strength they were enhancing—they were tampering with genetics, conditioning minds, and suppressing emotions. The goal was to build soldiers without fear, remorse, or hesitation. Operatives who could blend in perfectly, kill without question, and operate under unimaginable conditions. Machines wrapped in human skin.

Rhett was the first success.

The documents detailed his childhood conditioning: psychological evaluations, stress testing, and reflex training. His father's cold detachment made sense now. Dr. James Kardon hadn't seen Rhett as a son—he had been a prototype. And those "medical checkups" Rhett endured as a kid? They were tests designed to monitor his development and ensure the enhancements held.

His father had documented every success, every failure, and every adjustment along the way.

The Ethical Nightmare

What Rhett found next made his blood run cold. There were others.

Pages and pages of files referenced additional subjects—other children, other prototypes. Some were listed as "incomplete" or "terminated," meaning they hadn't survived the experiments. Rhett flipped through the profiles, his horror mounting as he realized how far the program had gone to perfect its design.

These weren't ordinary soldiers being groomed—they were weapons created from the cradle, children stripped of agency, individuality, and emotion. Lives were sacrificed in the name of progress.

Rhett's stomach churned. He hadn't been the only one. And worse, the program hadn't ended with him. It had continued—quietly, in the shadows.

One report caught his eye, hitting closer to home than anything he'd seen.

Subject: Rhett Kardon

Date: January 23, 2003.

Assessment: Full reflex optimization achieved. Emotional suppression: partial success. Further conditioning is required.

Recommendation: Increase exposure to life-or-death scenarios. The subject demonstrates loyalty but is resistant to complete detachment.

His father's words echoed in his mind:

"It's all about strategy, Rhett. You control the game, or the game controls you."

Even his emotional distance had been deliberate. Dr. James Kardon had not just been building a soldier and a son without weaknesses.

The Montenegro Connection

Rhett forced himself to push the personal horror aside—he didn't have time to dwell on it now. He flipped back to the notebook, focusing on the name circled in red: Montenegro. The same name had been cross-referenced multiple times in the old documents, usually tied to clandestine meetings in South America.

Montenegro had been involved with the operation from the beginning. The documents hinted that he was a key scientist who helped Dr. James Kardon develop the protocols and enhancements that shaped the program. If anyone had answers about why Operation White Coat was still active, it would be Montenegro.

Rhett found coordinates scribbled in the notebook's margins. Argentina. A specific location—remote, hidden deep in the countryside.

Rhett stared at the coordinates, his heart pounding. If Montenegro was still alive, he was the key to everything.

But there was no time to waste. The people hunting Rhett would be on him soon. If he wanted to find Montenegro, he had to disappear—now.

The Final Warning

Rhett leaned back in his chair, letting the enormity of the situation settle over him. He couldn't trust anyone—not even the CIA. His gut told him that someone inside the agency was involved—maybe even the same people who had silenced the informant.

He thought of Garrett's warning:

"You dig into this, and you're putting a target on your back."

The target was already there. But Rhett wasn't backing down.

His encrypted phone buzzed on the desk, cutting through the silence. He picked it up and checked the screen: a message from an anonymous number.

Walk away, Kardon. Or you'll end up like the informant.

Rhett's jaw clenched. They were watching him.

He shut off the phone, dropped it into a glass of water, and watched as bubbles rose to the surface. He wasn't going to be threatened. If they thought they could scare him off, they were dead wrong.

He'd spent his life fighting in the shadows—he wasn't about to stop now.

Packing and Preparing for the Hunt

Rhett stood and moved with precision, grabbing his go-bag from the closet. He didn't know how long he'd be gone, but he knew one thing: he wasn't coming back until he had answers.

He inventoried his bag:
- •Fake IDs and multiple passports
- •Cash in USD and EUR, $20,000 in each currency
- •Encrypted satellite phone
- •Burner phone
- •SOG combat knife
- •Signal jammer
- •200 rounds of 10mm ammo
- •2 Springfield Armory XDm handguns
- •4 magazines for his XDm
- •2 Silencers for his Springfield

He then grabbed the notebook containing Montenegro's name and coordinates. The old Rhett Kardon might have waited for permission and followed the rules. But not anymore. The old Rhett was gone.

This was personal now.

His father's lies. The informant's death. The shadowy forces are closing in. It all led to the same place—Argentina.

CHAPTER 8

Danger Close

R hett had just slung his jacket over his shoulders, his mind already
on his next move, when a prickle of awareness crept up his spine.
His instincts flared—a warning honed over years of dangerous encounters.
Something wasn't right. He paused, his hand hovering near the Springfield
concealed under his arm, as he strained to listen. At first, there was nothing
but the muffled hum of the city beyond his window. But then, faint and
almost imperceptible, came a sound from the hallway—a soft creak, the
barely-there weight shift on an old floorboard. Someone was outside his door.

He knew right away: these weren't amateurs. Professionals. They were
moving with precision, with purpose, but not quietly enough for someone
like him. Rhett had been trained for situations like this—moments where
a single sound could mean the difference between life and death. His heart
quickened, but his mind remained cold and calculating.

He considered his options. The first was to fight, to stand his ground
and face them head-on. But that was precisely what they expected. They'd
be waiting, positioned, and prepared for him to engage. This wasn't just
a random ambush; they'd designed a trap, banking on him choosing the
apparent route. He needed to outthink them, sidestep their strategy, and turn
their plan against them.

With swift, silent precision, Rhett grabbed his go-bag, already packed for contingencies like this. The weight was familiar, reminding him how often he'd had to leave in a hurry. Without a second thought, he turned to the window. The fire escape outside was narrow and weathered, the metal coated in a thin sheen of rust. Fourth floor—high enough to make a jump risky but low enough for the fire escape to be an option.

He moved calmly, slinging the bag over his shoulder and reaching for the window frame. With deft hands, he pried it open, each movement careful and controlled, avoiding even the most minor sound. He knew that the slightest slip would alert them, giving away his change of plan.

Just as he swung one leg out onto the fire escape, he heard the doorknob turn with a soft click. Whoever was out there had decided to make their move. Rhett didn't look back. His mind was entirely in the moment, every nerve on edge, calculating his next step. He slipped out onto the fire escape, his body low to keep his profile small. He exhaled, the rush of adrenaline sharpening his senses as he began to descend, the metal of the fire escape groaning softly beneath his weight.

Once he reached the third floor, he paused, crouching low and pressing himself against the side of the building, listening intently for any sign of pursuit. Above, he heard the door to his apartment open, followed by the faint sounds of footsteps and low murmurs. They'd find his empty apartment and realize he'd slipped through their fingers. But by then, he'd be long gone, blending into the city like a shadow in the night.

Escaping the Net

Rhett moved down the metal staircase swiftly but quietly, every step a calculated movement. Above him, the door to his apartment swung open, and he heard the soft shuffle of boots. The men were inside now, and it wouldn't take long for them to realize Rhett had slipped away.

"Clear!" one of the men whispered above. "He's not here."

"Check the fire escape," another voice ordered.

Rhett didn't wait to hear the rest. He dropped to the third-floor landing and then the second, his movements fluid. Years of Navy SEAL training had conditioned his body to move without hesitation, to blend into the darkness like a shadow.

As he reached the ground, he spotted two figures at the alley's mouth—lookouts. Armed, alert. They were part of the team hunting him.

Rhett flattened himself against the wall, waiting for the right moment. He could feel the weight of his Springfield under his arm, but shooting them would draw attention. He needed to move without being seen.

The lookouts paced the alley in practiced rhythm, their eyes scanning the street. Rhett waited, counting their steps, timing their movements.

He slipped behind them like a ghost on the third pass, keeping low and out of sight. The adrenaline coursed through him and heightened his senses. He knew this game well—it was survival, pure and simple.

He reached the street without a sound, blending into the night. The hunt was on—but Rhett was already one step ahead.

A Desperate Call to Garrett

Once clear of the alley, Rhett kept his pace brisk but calm, weaving through the quiet streets until he spotted the glow of an all-night diner ten blocks away. The neon sign buzzed in sharp pink and blue, casting a surreal glow onto the sidewalk below. It wasn't much, but it was safe enough, a place where he could catch his breath and figure out his next move.

He slipped inside, the bell over the door giving a faint jingle as he entered. The diner was nearly empty, just a tired waitress behind the counter and a couple of bleary-eyed patrons nursing mugs of coffee. Rhett quickly slid into a booth at the back, where he could keep an eye on the entrance but remain mostly out of sight. The garish lights buzzed overhead, harsh and cold, but he welcomed it—anything that kept him awake and alert.

Settling into the booth, Rhett pulled a burner phone from his pocket. His fingers were steady, but he felt the weight of every second slipping by. He dialed Garrett's number, his mind racing through what he'd say, the urgency of the situation pressing down on him.

The line rang twice before Garrett picked up. "Tell me you're not dead," Garrett said, his voice taut with concern.

"Not yet, but not from a lack of them trying," Rhett replied, glancing out the window and scanning the street for any hint of movement. "But it's close. They just hit my apartment. They're moving fast, Garrett. I barely made it out."

There was a moment of silence on the other end, then Garrett took a long breath. "Jesus. You need to get out of D.C., man. They'll have every exit covered by morning."

"I know," Rhett said, his voice low and resolute. "I've got a lead—Argentina. There's someone down there who knows more about Operation White Coat, someone who can give me answers. But I can't get out clean on my own. I need your help."

Garrett didn't even pause. "I'll handle it. Meet me at the old freight yard in an hour. I'll have a ride waiting. It won't be comfortable, but it'll get you out of here."

Relief washed over Rhett, but he kept his tone even. "Thanks, brother."

"Don't thank me yet," Garrett replied. "This is only the beginning."

Rhett ended the call, slipping the phone back into his pocket. He glanced around the diner one last time, the diner's hum and the distant clatter of dishes grounding him. This was his only chance, his one way out. With a deep breath, he rose from the booth, already mapping out his path to the freight yard, every step calculated.

As he entered the night, the city felt darker and more sinister, with shadows stretching long under the dim streetlights. But Rhett had a destination and a plan, which gave him the focus he needed to see this through.

The Freight Yard

The freight yard on the outskirts of D.C. was the perfect meeting spot—abandoned, sprawling, littered with rusting metal and crumbling concrete; it offered countless places to hide or quickly escape. The silence here was thick, almost tangible, broken only by the occasional creak of an old metal beam or the rustle of distant animals disturbed by his presence. Rhett arrived early, moving with practiced caution, keeping to the shadows as he surveyed the area. Every muscle in his body was tense, his senses on high alert. His Springfield pistol was in his hand, the familiar weight reassuring as he prepared for whatever might unfold in this deserted place.

A few minutes later, the soft crunch of gravel broke the quiet. Rhett's eyes darted to the end of the yard, where an old beat-up pickup truck crept forward, its headlights off to keep a low profile. The vehicle was barely more than a silhouette in the dim light, its paint chipped and body-worn. As it pulled up beside Rhett, the window rolled down, revealing Garrett's face, rough and hardened by years of experience in the field. His expression was tense, the urgency unmistakable in his eyes.

"Get in," Garrett said, his voice low and edged with impatience. Rhett didn't hesitate. He slipped into the passenger seat, settling in just as Garrett floored the gas pedal, the truck lurching forward and tearing down the old gravel road, sending clouds of dust billowing up behind them.

The silence stretched as Garrett navigated the winding path out of the yard, his hands gripping the wheel tightly. Finally, he shot Rhett a sideways glance, a half-grin flickering across his face, though his eyes held a sharper edge. "You've sure stirred up a hornet's nest, huh?"

Rhett let out a short, humorless chuckle. "Wouldn't be the first time."

The truck rattled as Garrett pushed it harder, each bump and pothole jolting them in their seats. The landscape around them blurred, but Garrett focused on the road ahead. After a moment, he said, "You're flying out of Baltimore—a cargo plane. Leaves in three hours."

Rhett's eyebrows shot up, impressed. "How in the hell did you pull this off so fast?"

Garrett shrugged, his gaze never leaving the road. "You're not the only one with connections, brother," he replied, a trace of amusement in his tone. But there was a tension behind his words, a sense of stakes higher than either of them wanted to acknowledge out loud.

The miles passed in silence as Garrett steered them through the dark backroads, keeping off the main highways, avoiding the eyes that were undoubtedly watching for any sign of Rhett. This wasn't just an escape—an exodus, a desperate run to Rhett's only chance. As they approached the city's edge, the lights of Baltimore glimmered faintly on the horizon.

The Flight to Argentina

The cargo plane was cold and uncomfortable, the metal floor complex against his back and the rattling walls amplifying every shiver that wracked Rhett's body, but he didn't care; he wasn't focused on the biting cold or the stale smell of diesel and dust in the air. If it got him out of the country undetected, he was willing to endure whatever discomfort the plane threw his way.

He sat alone in the dim, cavernous hold, surrounded by stacks of crates and metal containers that cast eerie shadows with every shake of turbulence. The darkness felt oppressive, thick enough to suffocate, but it suited him; it gave him the cover he needed to focus. His mind raced as he stared blankly at a dented steel crate across from him, barely noticing the occasional jolt that made the crates around him groan under the strain.

One name played on repeat in his mind, as if his brain couldn't let it go: Montenegro. The man was more than just a lead; he was the keystone to everything Rhett had been searching for. Montenegro held the secrets Rhett needed—the truth about the enigmatic Operation White Coat, the twisted reasoning behind his father's dark experiments, and, maybe most importantly, the people's identities still pulling the strings, hidden away in the shadows.

But Rhett knew this wasn't going to be a simple extraction. Argentina was more than just a destination on a map. It was a powder keg, a battlefield waiting to erupt. Whoever was desperate to keep Montenegro's lips sealed wouldn't just stand idly by. They'd throw everything they had to make sure Rhett never got close. He almost felt their presence, like a swarm of faceless enemies waiting just beyond the clouds.

As the plane shuddered through the night sky, Rhett pulled his backpack closer, unzipping it to reveal his weapons and ammunition, laid out with precision. He ran his fingers over the cold metal, mentally reviewing his plan again. There was no room for error. He would have to be quick to stay steps ahead of the hunters who would surely guide him, and, above all, he would have to get to Montenegro before they did.

Every second in the air was closer to the fight that awaited him.

The First Steps in Buenos Aires

The plane touched down in Buenos Aires just before dawn, tires screeching against the runway, jolting Rhett from his anxious thoughts. The moment he stepped off the aircraft, the humid air enveloped him, thick and almost suffocating—a stark contrast to the cold, biting air he'd endured on the cargo plane. Buenos Aires greeted him with a blend of unfamiliar scents and distant city sounds as the morning light began to creep over the horizon, casting the sprawling metropolis in a soft, golden glow.

Moving quickly, he adjusted his cap low over his eyes, blending in with the few early risers already stirring in the streets. A stream of workers, street vendors, and city-dwellers began to trickle out, yawning and bleary-eyed, the pulse of the city awakening with each passing minute. Rhett moved through them like a shadow, slipping into alleys and backstreets, ensuring he left no trail for any potential eyes tracking his arrival.

His first stop was a small, nondescript building in a quiet neighborhood on the city's outskirts. The place was unremarkable—a narrow, forgotten apartment in a faded high-rise, the place people walked past without a second glance. Garrett had arranged it all with typical precision, a safe house meant to be as invisible as its tenant. The apartment was modest, just a cot in the corner, a table strewn with basic supplies, and a single, flickering lightbulb casting a dim glow over the peeling walls. It was far from comfortable, but it was safe, and that was all Rhett needed.

As he closed the door behind him, Rhett took a deep breath, letting the silence settle around him. His heart was hounding from the tension of his journey, but now, with a few moments of respite, he forced himself to calm down and focus. He placed his bag on the table, methodically laying out his weapons, ammunition, and a single map marked with the intel Garrett had provided.

But his thoughts kept drifting to one thing—Montenegro. The name felt like fire, searing through his mind, a beacon that refused to dim. Montenegro was somewhere out there, hidden in the vast stretches of the Argentine countryside. The intel was sparse, but Rhett knew this man held the answers to everything—answers that he had been chasing for too long to back down now.

He stared at the map, eyes tracing the towns, rivers, and mountains scattered across it. Finding Montenegro in this rugged terrain would be like finding a needle in a haystack, but Rhett's resolve was unshakable. This man was the last link to the truth about Operation White Coat, his father's secrets, and the shadows that had torn his life apart. No matter how daunting the search appeared, he wouldn't let this opportunity slip through his fingers.

After a few moments of quiet contemplation, Rhett packed up his gear, secured his weapons, and marked his watch, calculating the time he had before the city fully awoke and prying eyes started to watch. He had one chance, one slim opportunity, to find Montenegro before his pursuers caught up to him.

Danger Close

As Rhett stood at the window of the safe house, the early morning light casting long shadows across the narrow street below, he felt a familiar tension settle in his chest. The city was waking up, oblivious to the silent war unfolding within its confines. Vendors began setting up their stalls, children hurried to school, and the hum of daily life grew steadily louder. But for Rhett, each passerby was a potential threat; each sound was a possible signal of impending danger.

The recent memory of the informant's abrupt silence gnawed at him. Someone had gotten to them first, someone who was now undoubtedly closing in on Rhett's trail. The weight of unseen eyes pressed upon him, a constant reminder that the hunt was far from over—it was just beginning.

He turned away from the window, the dim interior offering little comfort. The safe house, with its peeling wallpaper and sparse furnishings, was a temporary refuge, not a sanctuary. He couldn't afford to stay hidden for long; every moment of inaction was a moment the enemy gained ground.

Rhett's gaze fell upon his gear, meticulously laid out on the rickety table: a map marked with potential leads, two handguns with full magazines, a knife, and a burner phone with a single contact—Garrett. He checked his weapons, ensuring they were ready for immediate use. The cold metal felt reassuring in his hands, a tangible means of fighting back against the faceless adversaries pursuing him.

He knew that confrontation was inevitable. Whoever was hunting him would eventually catch up, and when they did, Rhett intended to be prepared. His training had taught him the importance of readiness, anticipating the enemy's moves, and countering them precisely. But until that moment, he had to stay ahead, keep moving, and continue his search for Montenegro.

The path forward was fraught with uncertainty and peril, but retreat was not an option. Rhett steadied himself, determination hardening his resolve. The only way forward was through the danger that lay ahead. He would navigate the treacherous landscape, confront his pursuers, and uncover the truths hidden from him for so long.

With a final glance around the room, Rhett gathered his belongings, secured his weapons, and slipped the burner phone into his pocket. He took a deep breath, calming the storm of thoughts swirling in his mind. Then, without hesitation, he stepped out of the safe house and into the bustling streets of Buenos Aires, ready to face whatever awaited him.

CHAPTER 9

The Trail to Argentina

The humid air of Buenos Aires clung to Rhett Kardon like a thick, oppressive blanket, weighing down every breath and adding to the tension already coiling within him. He stood in the shadow of an old, crumbling apartment building, its faded paint and rusted balconies a reminder that he was far from the polished streets of Washington, D.C., and even farther from the safety of home. The escape from D.C. had been a close call—too close, a hair's breadth from disaster. Every move and turn felt like he was one step ahead of a ghost, an invisible hand pulling him back into the clutches of those who wanted him silenced.

Now, thousands of miles away, with only the dim, early morning city sounds as his company, Rhett knew that the miles he'd put between him and the United States offered little security. The danger hadn't vanished with the distance; it had only latched onto him, following him across continents like a dark shadow. He could almost feel it lurking, an unseen presence lingering just out of sight, waiting for the opportune moment to strike. Operation White Coat—the very thing that had upended his life, his family, his trust in everything he thought he knew—still held him captive in its web, its architects relentless in their pursuit.

And then there was Montenegro. The name had become his only guiding star, a single beacon in the fog of deception and violence surrounding him. This man was his only lead, the last thread connecting him to the truth about Operation

White Coat and the sinister forces that drove it. Montenegro was out there, a ghostly figure hiding in the vast stretches of Argentina's countryside, keeping secrets Rhett needed to survive. This man knew the insidious details that Rhett had only begun to unravel—the experiments, the betrayals, the influential people who wanted Rhett gone.

Rhett pulled himself from his thoughts, scanning the street once more. He had no time to waste. His adversaries were coming, and he had no illusions that they would show mercy. Every instinct told him that finding Montenegro was his only hope, his only chance to get the answers he sought—and maybe, just maybe, a way out of the deadly game he'd been forced into. But for now, all he could do was keep moving, stay sharp, and be ready for the moment danger closed in.

The City of Ghosts

The city streets began to stir with the sounds of morning life, a symphony of early risers moving through Buenos Aires like clockwork. Shopkeepers unlocked their doors with the clank of metal gates, vendors rolled out carts stacked with fresh produce, and the steady rumble of buses filled the narrow avenues as commuters prepared for another day. The air was still thick with the night's humidity, though a faint breeze carried the promise of the day's heat. Rhett leaned casually against a graffitied wall, his form blending into the urban canvas as he observed his surroundings, assessing each face and movement with silent intensity.

He checked his watch, feeling the weight of the seconds slipping by. His window to find Montenegro was shrinking with every passing minute. The last lead had warned him of the urgency and danger: Montenegro wouldn't stay in one place long, and Rhett's pursuers were closing in. There was no time to linger and no margin for error.

The informant's last message played in his mind, a dark omen: "Trust no one." Rhett was no stranger to deception in his line of work, but he knew the warning wasn't meant lightly. This was a web of lies and betrayals; any move could mean his end. He would have to stay one step ahead, deciphering friend from foe without a single misstep.

With one last glance down the street, he saw a small café. Rhett pulled the collar of his jacket up and moved into the flow of pedestrians. The crowd provided the cover he needed, an ever-shifting wall of anonymity that allowed him to move unseen. But even as he walked, every sense remained alert, watching, listening, waiting for the faintest hint of danger.

A Ghost Named Montenegro

Raúl Montenegro had been a key engineer of Operation White Coat during the shadowy years of the Cold War. As a lead scientist, he spearheaded the genetic engineering protocols that forever altered Rhett's life. Montenegro's work wasn't just innovation; it embodied a dangerous ideology—the belief that humanity could be refined and reshaped through genetic manipulation. The experiment left deep scars, not just on Rhett but, if rumors were true, on countless others.

When Operation White Coat was "officially" shut down, Montenegro didn't fade into obscurity or academia like others. He vanished, erased from records as if he'd never existed. There are no final reports, no archived files—just silence. Whether he orchestrated his disappearance or had influential figures do it for him, his trail has gone cold until now.

According to Garrett's contact, Montenegro had resurfaced in Argentina, far from where anyone would expect. In the countryside near Bariloche, locals spoke of a reclusive foreign doctor. Rumors whispered of advanced medical equipment and strange knowledge, hinting at a past steeped in secrets. If true, Montenegro hadn't abandoned his work—he had relocated it away from prying eyes.

For Rhett, Montenegro was the last link to the truth behind Operation White Coat and his father's role. If anyone could illuminate the scope of the experiments and who still pulled the strings, it was him.

Reaching Montenegro, however, would be no easy task. The rugged terrain of Argentina's countryside, with its dense forests and towering mountains, offered plenty of hiding places. A natural recluse, Montenegro would be vigilant for strangers, making it nearly impossible to get close.

But Rhett wasn't deterred. Montenegro wasn't just a lead—he was the keystone to uncovering the truth. Rhett's resolve hardened. He would find Montenegro, no matter the cost.

Elena Morales: A Risky Ally

R hett leaned back in his chair, exhaustion pressing down as he rubbed his temples. Days of relentless pursuit had led him nowhere, the trail to Montenegro growing colder by the hour. The harsh truth settled in—he couldn't do this alone. To find Montenegro in Argentina's sprawling wilderness and tangled underworld, he needed help. —someone who understood the terrain and the dangers lurking beneath it.

That someone was Elena Morales.

Elena wasn't just a journalist; she was ex-military and a powerhouse. Known for her fearless pursuit of hidden truths, she had earned a reputation for exposing secrets others feared to uncover. Her work had often brought her dangerously close to covert Cold War programs, including rumors of missing scientists and clandestine experiments. Elena had a knack for navigating perilous paths, unearthing connections in Argentina's shadowy corners. Her tenacity matched Rhett's own, making her a potential ally he couldn't ignore.

Rhett had stumbled across her name in his retrieved documents—a surprising but promising lead. Elena had ties to the Argentine underground and risked her life chasing threads connected to Operation White Coat. She was resourceful, sharp, and driven by an insatiable need for truth. But she wasn't safe.

Elena's methods were unconventional, often skirting the edge of ethics. She wasn't the kind to forge alliances out of loyalty. If helping Rhett served her agenda, she'd do it. If not, she'd walk away—or worse. Relying on someone so unpredictable set Rhett on edge, but he was out of options.

With a resigned sigh, he dialed her number and picked up his burner phone. This wasn't the plan he wanted, but it was the one he had. He hoped that if Elena could lead him closer to Montenegro, the risk would be worth it.

The First Meeting with Elena

Rhett found Elena in a tucked-away café in San Telmo, a quiet corner of Buenos Aires with cobblestone streets and colonial charm. The scent of coffee lingered in the crisp morning air as ivy draped over the café's facade, concealing it from the casual eye. Inside, the dimly lit space buzzed with subdued conversations, a haven for private meetings like the one he'd arranged.

Elena sat at the back, partially shadowed, as she sipped coffee. She exuded quiet confidence—a dark leather jacket, sharp green eyes framed by long black hair, an athletic physique, and an air of constant vigilance. Although she seemed to blend into the setting, her presence was magnetic, commanding attention without asking.

As Rhett approached, her gaze locked onto him, recognition flashing in her eyes. "Rhett Kardon," she said smoothly, her voice low. "I wondered when you'd show up."

Sliding into the chair across from her, Rhett kept his expression neutral. "You know who I am."

Her lips curved into a slight, calculated smile. "Your name comes up in places people don't want it to."

Rhett didn't flinch. "I need to find Montenegro."

The mention of the name erased her smile. She glanced around, ensuring they weren't overheard. "That's a dangerous name to throw around," she said quietly. "Especially here."

"I'm not looking for warnings," Rhett replied firmly. "I need answers."

Elena studied him for a long moment, her eyes sharp with curiosity and caution. "Why Montenegro?" she asked.

Rhett hesitated. "Unfinished business."

Elena tilted her head, weighing his words. Finally, she nodded. "I can help, but it won't be easy—or safe. Montenegro has powerful enemies. If you go looking, they'll notice."

"Easy isn't my style," Rhett said with a faint smile.

Elena smirked, a flicker of understanding passing between them. "Good. Let's start with a fixer who might know his location. But be ready—this will test you."

Rhett leaned forward, resolved to harden. "Let's go."

Into the Countryside

The following day, Rhett and Elena set off in a battered SUV, its engine sputtering before roaring to life. Leaving Buenos Aires behind, the urban sprawl gave way to Argentina's vast countryside. Concrete and steel faded into rolling hills, fields of wild grass swayed in the wind, and dense forests loomed over the winding road. The landscape felt infinite and unyielding as if it could swallow them whole.

Elena drove with practiced ease, her hands steady on the wheel. Her dark hair was pulled back, and her sharp gaze stayed fixed on the road ahead. The silence between them stretched until she finally broke it, her tone light but probing. "So, what's your plan with Montenegro?" she asked, her voice loud enough to rise above the engine's hum.

Rhett stared at the horizon, his jaw tight. "He worked with my father," he said after a pause, bitterness threading through his voice. "I need to know what they were doing."

Elena glanced at him, her expression skeptical. "And you think he'll just hand over the truth?" she asked, one eyebrow arching. "Men like Montenegro don't give up their secrets easily."

Rhett's grip on the armrest tightened. "He doesn't have a choice," he said, though he knew convincing Montenegro would be far from simple. The man had vanished for years, leaving only shadows behind. But Rhett couldn't afford doubt now—he had come too far.

The air between them remained tense, and their unspoken wariness was palpable. They were allies out of necessity, and neither fully trusted the other. Rhett sensed Elena's guarded glances, as she likely felt his reservations. They were two sides of the same coin: calculating and prepared for betrayal.

The road stretched endlessly ahead, leading them deeper into the unknown.

A Dangerous Roadblock

As they approached the narrow mountain pass, the road twisting between sheer cliffs, Rhett felt a familiar unease settle over him. His senses sharpened, and he scanned the terrain. Something was wrong. "Slow down," he said, his voice low but commanding.

Elena glanced at him but obeyed, easing off the gas. Ahead, a black SUV sat parked at an angle, blocking the road completely. Sleek, unmarked, and menacing, it screamed trouble.

Rhett's hand instinctively moved to his Springfield, his fingers grazing the cool steel. His voice dropped to a warning. "It's an ambush."

The words barely left his mouth before gunfire erupted, shattering the windshield in a spray of glass. "Out! Now!" Rhett shouted, shoving his door open and rolling into the ditch. Pain shot through his shoulder as he hit the ground, but he ignored it, already scanning for cover.

Elena moved fast, diving into the ditch beside him as bullets tore through the air above them. The attackers were disciplined and precise, moving with military coordination. This wasn't random—it was a hit, methodically planned.

Peeking over the edge of the ditch, Rhett counted four gunmen clad in tactical gear, rifles trained with deadly focus. He steadied his aim, squeezing the trigger. One attacker dropped, then another.

"We're pinned," Elena muttered, her breath ragged. "They're flanking us."

Rhett's eyes darted to the treeline across the road—dense, dark, and their best shot. He looked at Elena. "On my signal, run for the trees."

Elena's eyes narrowed. "You better not get me killed, Kardon."

He allowed a brief grin. "Trust me."

Firing suppressing shots, Rhett shouted, "Go! Go! Go!" They sprinted toward the treeline as bullets ripped the ground around them. Diving behind trees, they found cover, but their attackers were closing in.

Rhett reloaded, glancing at Elena. "Stay close," he said, his voice steady.

She smirked, gripping her weapon. "Easy isn't my style."

Together, they braced for the next wave, ready to fight through the shadows.

The Escape

At Rhett's signal, he and Elena leaped from the ditch, guns blazing as they charged forward. Their sudden offensive caught the attackers off guard, and their hesitation in responding bought precious seconds. Bullets ripped through the air, forcing their enemies to scatter, and their carefully planned ambush fell into disarray.

Rhett and Elena sprinted across the exposed ground, the forest looming ahead. Gunfire erupted behind them, bullets snapping through branches and sending leaves cascading as they dove into the cover of the trees. Elena's lungs burned, her heart pounding, but adrenaline kept her moving. The attackers' shouts and footsteps echoed close behind, but the dense forest offered a reprieve. The thick underbrush and towering trunks provided camouflage, making the terrain a natural ally.

"This way," Elena whispered, gesturing to a barely visible trail beneath the tangled brush. It twisted and turned, obscured from view, a path only someone familiar with the woods would know.

Rhett nodded quickly, following her as they navigated the narrow trail, ducking branches and sidestepping dense foliage. Their movements were synchronized, and their breathing was harsh but muted. The sounds of pursuit gradually faded, swallowed by the layers of trees and the heavy stillness of the forest.

Only when the attackers' shouts and gunfire became distant echoes did they slow. Rhett leaned against a tree, his chest heaving as he scanned the surroundings. Beside him, Elena crouched low, her sharp eyes fixed on the path they'd taken.

For a moment, silence enveloped them, broken only by their ragged breaths and the faint rustle of leaves. Rhett allowed a measure of tension to ease but remained alert. The attackers were still out there.

"They'll keep looking," Elena murmured, her voice steady but low. "But they don't know these woods like we do."

Rhett straightened, resolve etched on his face. "Then we use that to our advantage." He adjusted his grip on his weapon. "Let's keep moving."

With a brief nod, Elena led the way. Together, they vanished more profoundly into the forest, shadows swallowing them whole.

A Moment of Respite

When they stopped to catch their breath, Rhett leaned against a tree, his chest heaving as he struggled to steady his racing heart. The forest around them was eerily quiet, its stillness heavy, as though the trees themselves were listening. Elena slid down beside him, her face pale and smeared with dirt, but her eyes remained sharp, glinting with determination.

She wiped her brow, letting out a strained chuckle. "You weren't kidding about the danger," she said, her voice tinged with exhaustion.

Rhett managed a wry smile, shaking his head. "I don't do easy," he replied with a hint of grim humor.

Elena exhaled a weary laugh, though tension undercut her words. "We need to move," she said, her voice firm. "If the same people from Montenegro sent those guys, they won't stop until we're dead."

Rhett's nod was brief but telling. Her words confirmed his suspicions. These weren't just mercenaries—they were part of something far more dangerous, a shadowy force desperate to keep Montenegro's secrets buried. Their relentless pursuit only strengthened Rhett's belief: they were on the right trail.

He inhaled deeply, his mind already plotting escape routes and contingencies. Every ambush, every close call pointed to one undeniable truth—Montenegro was real. And whatever the man was hiding was explosive enough to warrant bloodshed.

Rhett let the weight of the realization settle. This wasn't just about answers for himself. Montenegro's secrets could upend powerful lives, unraveling legacies built on lies. The mission had evolved into something bigger—a reckoning.

Glancing at Elena, who watched him expectantly, he gave a firm nod. "Let's keep moving," he said, pushing off the tree.

Without hesitation, they pressed deeper into the forest, their steps cautious but resolute, knowing each one carried them closer to the truth—and more profoundly into peril.

Chapter 10

The Beautiful Distraction

The sun dipped lower, painting the rugged Argentine countryside in a warm amber hue as Rhett Kardon and Elena Morales pressed forward, navigating the unforgiving terrain. Their original route had been lost after the ambush—a precision strike that left no doubt about its intent. Forced to deviate into a web of dirt roads and overgrown paths, they plunged deeper into a wilderness that seemed determined to swallow them whole.

Rhett noticed an old, rundown vacation house with an SUV parked nearby. He and Elena quietly crept over to the vehicle. When Elena opened the door, she spotted the keys clipped to the sun visor. Wasting no time, she started the engine, and the two drove off down the dirt road.

The SUV jolted over uneven ground, its tires crunching against loose rocks while the thick underbrush scraped noisily along its sides. The rugged terrain mirrored Rhett's unease, its unpredictability amplifying the sensation of being hunted.

Rhett couldn't shake the feeling that the ambush wasn't random. Its timing, its precision—it all hinted at a shadowy network intent on protecting its secrets. Whoever was pulling the strings behind Operation White Coat had eyes everywhere, an omnipresent force that shadowed his every move. And as each mile brought them closer to the truth, Rhett could feel their invisible grip tightening.

The fading light filtered through the trees, creating an interplay of flickering shadows that danced across the forest floor. The woods felt alive, their gnarled branches reaching out like skeletal hands, whispering secrets of those who had passed through and never returned.

Elena drove silently, her knuckles tight on the wheel, her gaze fixed ahead with unwavering focus. Yet Rhett noticed the subtle signs of tension in her jaw clenching and the rhythmic tapping of her fingers against the steering wheel—a steady metronome of suppressed anxiety.

"You alright?" Rhett broke the silence, his voice cutting softly through the low rumble of the engine.

Elena quickly glanced at him, her lips quirking in a faint smile. "I've had worse days. You?"

Rhett's chuckle was dry, almost humorless. "Still breathing. I'll take it."

The sun sank below the horizon, leaving behind a cloak of shadows that seeped into the woods. Darkness crept in like a predator, wrapping the landscape in foreboding quiet. The headlights illuminated a narrow path ahead, but Rhett thought of the unseen dangers lurking just beyond their reach.

Elena's voice broke the stillness again, softer this time. "You're not what I expected, Kardon."

Rhett raised an eyebrow, intrigued by her tone. "What did you expect?"

She hesitated, then shrugged. "Someone colder. Less... human."

The corner of Rhett's mouth lifted in a faint smile. "Like my father."

Her silence spoke volumes. Dr. James Kardon's name carried weight—a reputation carved from ambition and calculated ruthlessness. It was a shadow Rhett had spent his life trying to escape.

Offering her a wry smile, Rhett said, "Let's just say I'm full of surprises."

Elena's expression softened, her lips curving slightly as she repeated, "Full of surprises."

For a fleeting moment, the shared purpose that bound them seemed to transcend the suspicion and secrecy that had defined their partnership. But as the SUV's headlights cut through the deepening night, they both braced for what lay ahead. The road to Montenegro—and the secrets he held—would demand more than either of them could anticipate.

The Safe Haven

They reached the village just after dusk, the SUV grinding to a halt amidst a cloud of dust that settled slowly over the cracked road. The place was more of a forgotten relic than a functioning community, its handful of weathered buildings clustered together as if for mutual support against the encroaching wilderness. Peeling paint flaked from walls battered by relentless sun and time, and dim yellow lights flickered weakly in a few scattered windows.

Rhett and Elena stepped out of the vehicle, the crunch of gravel beneath their boots drawing the attention of the few locals lingering outside the cantina. Their quiet conversations died as wary eyes turned toward the strangers. Outsiders were an anomaly here, and Rhett felt the weight of their scrutiny—a silent interrogation disguised as indifference.

Elena turned her head toward the cantina, her voice low. "This place is off the map," she murmured. "We'll be safe here for a night. They won't think of looking for us in a place like this."

Rhett's eyes swept the surrounding shadows. "Safe" was relative in his world. A place like this might hide them for a while, but he knew better than to let his guard down.

Inside, the cantina was dimly lit, its flickering bulbs casting a warm amber glow over scarred wooden tables and walls worn with age. The air was thick with the mingling scents of stale beer, tobacco, and the faint mustiness of forgotten places. Behind the bar, a grizzled man glanced up, his sharp eyes betraying a practiced wariness. He said nothing as Elena ordered two beers, his silence louder than words.

Elena handed Rhett a bottle, her fingers brushing his briefly before she raised her drink. A faint smirk tugged at her lips. "To staying alive."

Rhett clinked his bottle against hers. "To finding Montenegro," he replied, the steel in his voice undercutting the levity of her toast.

They drank quietly, the low murmur of the locals' conversations forming a backdrop almost comforting in its ordinariness. But Rhett's instincts wouldn't let him relax. He studied the room, cataloging the exits, memorizing the placement of every patron and the rhythm of their movements. The danger was never far away.

"You ever think about walking away?" Elena's voice broke the silence, soft but deliberate.

Rhett hesitated the weight of her question settling heavily on him. "I've thought about it," he admitted. "But I'm in too deep. There's no turning back now."

Elena nodded slowly, her gaze introspective. "Some things pull you in. You can't just let go."

The unspoken understanding between them deepened, binding them in their shared purpose. The smell of rain drifted through the open door, carrying the sounds of villagers readying themselves for a stormy night. They allowed themselves the illusion of peace for a fleeting moment, though both knew the calm would be short-lived.

Secrets in the Cantina

The weight of unspoken truths hung between them as they nursed their beers, the dim light painting shifting shadows across their faces. Rhett's mind raced, the reality of Montenegro's elusiveness gnawing at him. Somewhere out there, in the vast wilderness of the Argentine countryside, Montenegro held the key to unraveling Operation White Coat.

"You know," Elena began, her voice heavy with unspoken worry, "they'll send more men."

Rhett nodded, his gaze steady. "They already are. They won't stop."

She exhaled sharply, setting her bottle down with a faint thud. "This isn't just some Cold War relic, is it?" she asked, unease creeping into her tone. "It's still active. Whatever your father started, it's still happening."

Rhett's jaw tightened. He had carried this burden alone for so long, but now, with Elena at his side, the time had come to share the truth.

"Yeah," he said quietly. "And it's worse than we thought."

In measured tones, he told her everything: the experiments, the genetic enhancements, the twisted vision that sought to create soldiers who weren't just stronger but entirely controllable. He spoke of children taken from families, raised in sterile labs, tools of war. And finally, he revealed the most brutal truth: that he was the program's first success.

Elena's expression shifted from disbelief to horror. "You're telling me... you're one of them?"

Rhett let out a bitter laugh. "Whether I like it or not. I've spent my life trying to outrun it, but here I am, right back in the middle."

She leaned back, her gaze searching his face as if trying to reconcile the man before her with the nightmare he described. "And Montenegro?" she asked, her voice edged with anger. "He was part of this?"

"He designed it," Rhett replied, his tone heavy with regret. "He and my father thought they were building a legacy. If he's still alive, he knows how to stop it."

Her fingers tightened around her bottle. "So, he's not just hiding. He's running from what he created."

Rhett nodded. "And the people chasing him? They need his knowledge to take the program further. It's not just active—it's evolving."

The gravity of his words settled between them like a storm cloud. Their mission had taken on new dimensions, and the stakes had never been higher.

"Then we don't stop until we find him," Elena said firmly, her resolve unshakable.

Rhett raised his bottle. "To end it."

Their bottles clinked, a solemn declaration of purpose. Together, they braced for the fight ahead, knowing there was no turning back.

A Fragile Sanctuary

The respite didn't last long. Just before midnight, Rhett's genetically enhanced instincts snapped at him. His senses were sharp, every nerve attuned to the faint crunch of tires on the gravel outside. His hand instinctively found the cold steel of his Springfield beneath his Jacket.

"They're here," he whispered, his voice tense.

Elena stirred, instantly alert. Her eyes met his with an unspoken question. Rhett gestured for the backdoor. They crept to the SUV and slowly pulled away from the cantina.

CHAPTER 11

A Dangerous Liaison

The storm had left its mark on the Argentine wilderness. Drops of rain clung to leaves and branches, illuminated by the SUV's headlights as it pushed deeper into the forest. The air was thick with the scent of damp earth and petrichor, heavy and oppressive, amplifying the quiet tension in the vehicle.

Rhett Kardon's hands gripped the wheel, his knuckles white, steering through the uneven, muddy terrain. The SUV lurched over rocks and splashed through puddles; each jolts a reminder of their narrow escape. His focus remained sharp, his eyes darting between the road ahead and the rearview mirror. Somewhere out there, their pursuers regrouped, planning their next move.

Elena Morales sat beside him, her body tense, eyes flicking toward the back window every few moments. She felt the danger as acutely as Rhett did. The ambush they had narrowly evaded wasn't just a warning but a declaration. Their enemies were relentless, and they grew bolder with every mile closer to Montenegro.

The headlights illuminated the forest ahead in brief, shifting bursts of light. The trees loomed like sentinels, branches reaching across the narrow road, dripping water from the recent downpour. Beyond the illumination of the beams, darkness swallowed everything. The forest felt alive, as if it were watching them, complicit in the danger surrounding them.

Elena broke the silence, her voice steady despite the edge of weariness. "They're getting closer, aren't they?"

Rhett nodded without taking his eyes off the road. "They've spent years burying Montenegro's secrets. We're too close for them to stop now."

She glanced at him, her expression unreadable. "And us?"

"They'll come after us until there's nothing left to chase," Rhett said bluntly. "But we've got one advantage—they don't know this terrain like we do."

Elena gave a wry smile. "Good thing I'm not ready to turn back."

Their eyes met momentarily, a silent exchange of determination and trust. Whatever lay ahead, they were in it together. Rhett pressed harder on the accelerator, the SUV surging forward as the forest seemed to close tighter around them.

A Fragile Sanctuary

The rain began to pick up again as the SUV crept into a clearing. Rhett killed the engine, plunging them into silence save for the gentle water drum on the roof. He scanned the area, his sharp eyes cutting through the darkness. They were miles from any road or settlement, deep within the wilderness. If their pursuers had any advantage left, it wouldn't be geography.

Elena shifted in her seat, wiping condensation from the window to peer outside. The forest seemed to press against the clearing, its edges blurred by the downpour. "We can't stay here long," she murmured. "They're probably tracking us."

Rhett nodded, checking his weapon as he spoke. "We'll rest here for a bit, then keep moving north. There's a river ahead."

Elena leaned back, exhaling a long, steady breath. Her fingers tapped idly against the edge of the seat, betraying the tension she was trying to suppress. "Do you ever get tired of this?"

Rhett glanced at her, his expression unreadable. "Tired of what?"

"Running. Fighting. Being the guy who's always two steps ahead or two seconds from dead."

He considered her question, leaning back in his seat, his gaze drifting to the rain-streaked windshield. "Every damn day," he admitted, his voice quieter than usual. "But I don't get to stop. Not until this is done."

Elena turned to face him fully, her eyes soft but piercing. "What happens when it is? If you find Montenegro, if you get your answers—what then?"

Rhett didn't answer right away. He didn't know. The chase had consumed him for so long that he hadn't allowed himself to think about what came after. "I'll figure it out when I get there," he said. Now, I only care about stopping whatever my father started."

Elena nodded, sensing the weight of the conversation was pulling him inward. She let the silence stretch between them, a shared pause that allowed the tension to dissipate slightly. Outside, the rain began to ease, its rhythmic pattern softening to a gentle drizzle.

The Ambush

The quiet was broken by a sharp, distant sound—footsteps crunching on wet earth. Rhett froze, his senses sharpening as his hand instinctively reached for his weapon. He motioned for Elena to stay quiet, his other hand raised in a signal to wait.

The footsteps grew louder, more deliberate. There were voices now, low and indistinct but unmistakable. Rhett peered through the rain-slicked window, spotting faint beams of flashlights cutting through the trees. He counted at least four figures, moving with military precision, their movements too coordinated to be casual hunters.

"They're here," he whispered, his voice barely audible.

Elena's eyes widened, and she reached for her weapon, her fingers tightening around the grip. "What do we do?"

Rhett's mind raced. "We move. Now."

Without another word, they slipped out of the SUV and moved low and quiet through the wet grass. The rain muffled their movements, making the ground slick and treacherous. Rhett led the way toward the dense tree line; his senses tuned to every sound around them.

The attackers moved closer, their flashlights sweeping the clearing where the abandoned SUV lay. Rhett could hear their voices more clearly now—orders were being exchanged, and their search intensified. He motioned for Elena to stay low as he circled behind a large tree, positioning himself for a better vantage point.

The first attacker stepped into the clearing, his flashlight casting a harsh glow across the SUV. He raised his weapon, signaling to the others as he approached. Rhett moved swiftly, raising his Springfield and firing a silenced shot. The man dropped instantly, his body crumpling to the ground without a sound.

Elena moved as well, circling the clearing to flank another attacker. She spotted him through the trees, his back turned as he scanned the shadows ahead. Bracing herself, she raised her weapon and fired, the shot striking true. The man staggered before collapsing, his flashlight rolling away in the mud.

The forest erupted in chaos. The remaining attackers shouted to each other, their flashlights darting wildly as they scrambled to locate the source of the gunfire. Rhett and Elena used the confusion to their advantage, moving swiftly and silently, picking off their enemies individually.

The rain intensified, turning the ground into a slippery, muddy battleground. Rhett slid behind a fallen log, firing at an attacker who had taken cover behind a tree. The man fell with a sharp cry, his weapon clattering to the ground. Rhett didn't wait to see if he was finished; he moved again, always staying one step ahead.

Elena found herself face-to-face with one of the attackers, his flashlight blinding her as he raised his weapon. Without thinking, she lunged forward, slamming the butt of her rifle into his face. He stumbled backward, blood streaming from his nose, and she fired twice, the shots echoing through the forest as he fell.

Aftermath

When the final attacker fell, silence descended over the forest once more. The rain had eased to a drizzle, its gentle rhythm masking the distant sounds of the wilderness. Rhett and Elena regrouped near the tree line, their breaths heavy, their bodies slick with rain and mud.

"You, okay?" Rhett asked, his eyes scanning her for injuries.

Elena nodded, wiping rain from her face. "Yeah. You?"

"Still breathing," he said, a faint smirk tugging at the corner of his mouth.

They stood there momentarily, catching their breath, the adrenaline still coursing through their veins. The forest around them was a mess of broken branches, muddy footprints, and the lifeless bodies of their attackers. But they had survived—again.

"We need to keep moving," Rhett said, his tone serious. "This was just the first wave. They'll send more when these guys don't report back."

Elena nodded, her expression hardening with resolve. "Let's go."

Together, they disappeared into the forest, their figures swallowed by the shadows. The wilderness pressed in around them, silent and watchful, as they pushed forward into the unknown. Montenegro was still out there, waiting, and the secrets they sought were closer than ever. But so was the danger, and they both knew there was no turning back now.

CHAPTER 12

A Shared Past

The forest consumed them utterly, its towering trees and dense undergrowth closing around Rhett Kardon and Elena Morales as they ventured deeper into the wilderness. The air hung thick with moisture, the suffocating humidity turning every breath into labor. Each step they took was muffled by a soft carpet of decaying leaves and the damp, loamy earth, their progress marked only by the subtle rustle of disturbed foliage. The memory of the recent ambush still lingered like a shadow over them, the adrenaline humming faintly in their veins—a constant reminder of how perilously close they had come to death. Though they had escaped by the narrowest margins, Rhett knew the reprieve was temporary. Every second they spent out in the open allowed their enemies to close in, tightening the invisible noose around them.

The stakes were painfully clear: this wasn't just about completing their mission. Losing meant far more than failure. It meant forfeiting their lives and risking everything they had fought for.

They moved in silence, their breaths controlled, their footfalls careful to avoid the snap of a twig or the rustle of a bush. Yet the tension between them was palpable, a taut string vibrating with something unspoken. It wasn't just fear that weighed on them—fear of the relentless pursuers or the deadly trap that surely awaited them more profoundly in the forest. No, the tension was rooted in something more profound, a bond forged through shared peril and necessity. Rhett and Elena were bound not only by their shared mission but also by a connection that had grown unbidden, a thread of camaraderie that had steadily deepened with every brush with death.

Rhett glanced at Elena, watching her as she navigated the uneven terrain with a quiet intensity that belied her petite frame. Her sharp green eyes missed nothing, scanning every shadow, every swaying branch, and every whisper of movement with unerring precision. She wasn't who he had expected when this mission began—a journalist with a penchant for digging up dangerous truths. But she had repeatedly proven herself, standing her ground when others would have faltered. Her resilience had earned his admiration, though he hadn't admitted it aloud. Yet, there was something else, too—something more personal. How she carried herself and met his gaze with trust and determination had begun to chip away at the walls he had spent years fortifying around himself.

Elena must have sensed his gaze because she turned her head, her eyes meeting his for a fleeting moment. It was a silent exchange, heavy with unspoken words. Her faint smile—a momentary, private gesture—wasn't one of confidence but acknowledgment. They were in this together, and the stakes were higher than either could face alone.

The silence around them was deceptive, broken only by the occasional rustle of leaves or the distant trill of unseen birds. Yet Rhett's instincts were on edge, his senses finely attuned to the faintest suggestion of danger. He knew their enemies were relentless and unyielding, lurking somewhere in the shadows; relentless White Coat wasn't just a mission—it was a specter, a ruthless force driving them forward and threatening to crush them under its weight.

They pressed on, the unspoken tension between them as much a source of strength as a reminder of all they stood to lose. Every step deeper into the forest brought them closer to Montenegro, the elusive figure who held the key to unraveling the past. But with every step came the certainty that the forest seemed to conspire against them, the oppressive darkness closing in like a living thing.

The Weight of Trust

The uneven trail demanded their full attention, and each step required a calculated decision on where to place their feet. Rain dripped from the leaves above, the rhythmic pattern creating an almost hypnotic backdrop to their silent progress. Occasionally, a branch would snap underfoot, or the squelch of mud would momentarily break the stillness. But even those sounds were muted, swallowed by the oppressive silence of the forest.

Elena moved ahead, her movements deliberate and precise. She seemed to flow through the underbrush, disturbing as little as possible, her eyes darting between the shadows. Behind her, Rhett kept a steady pace, his every muscle taut, his grip on his Springfield tight. His gaze swept the forest, scanning for any sign of their pursuers. Every shadow, every rustling leaf was a potential threat, and his mind worked in overdrive, assessing and reevaluating their surroundings.

"We need to stop soon," Elena whispered, glancing back over her shoulder. Her voice was barely audible, but her tone carried an edge of quiet authority. "We're getting close to Montenegro's territory, but we need to rest if we're going to make it."

Rhett hesitated. He hated the thought of stopping, of allowing even a moment for their enemies to gain ground. But Elena was right; pushing forward in their current state was a gamble that could cost them everything. He nodded, his jaw tightening.

Elena pointed to a narrow clearing where the dense trees formed a natural canopy, shielding them from prying eyes. "We can take shelter there for a while," she suggested. "It's not much, but it'll allow us to regroup."

The clearing was tiny, with barely enough room for them to settle without exposing themselves to the open. They sat with their backs against the thick trunks of ancient trees, their eyes on the dark forest silence them grew heavy, filled with unspoken thoughts and unanswered questions.

Rhett broke the silence first. "Why are you here, Elena?" he asked, his tone low and probing. "You could've walked away from this a long time ago. Why didn't you?"

Elena hesitated, her eyes fixed on the darkness beyond the clearing. It seemed she might deflect the question momentarily, but then her shoulders relaxed slightly. She leaned back against the tree, her expression softening.

"It's personal," she said quietly.

Rhett arched an eyebrow. "How personal?" His voice held an edge of curiosity but was tempered with caution. He sensed there was more to Elena's story than she had let on, and he wanted to understand what drove her.

The Story of a Lost Brother

E lena let out a slow breath, her eyes distant as though staring into a painful memory. When she finally spoke, her voice was soft, barely more than a whisper.

"My brother, Mateo," she began. "He was... brilliant. A scientist—genetics, biochemistry, experimental biology. He was always pushing boundaries, always asking the questions no one else dared to ask. But a few years ago, he disappeared."

She paused, her throat tightening. Rhett oversaw her, his expression unreadable but his focus unwavering.

"At first, it was small things—missed calls, canceled meetings. Then, he stopped responding entirely. He was caught up in his work, but the rumors started. Whispers about Cold War-era operations resurfacing, about people vanishing. And his name kept coming up, always tied to Montenegro and his experiments."

Her voice faltered, and she closed her eyes briefly before continuing. "I started digging. I followed every lead, every scrap of information. But the deeper I went, the darker it got. People warned me to stop, but I couldn't. I couldn't just let him disappear without knowing why."

Rhett nodded slowly, pieces of Elena's story falling into place. He understood what it meant to be consumed by a search for answers and driven by a need for closure. He had been there himself.

"I think Montenegro knows what happened to Mateo," Elena said, her voice steady despite the emotion beneath it. "And I'm not leaving until I find out the truth."

A Shared Determination

R hett met her gaze, his expression softening. "We'll find him," he said quietly. "And we'll get the answers you're looking for."

Elena looked at him for a long moment, something unspoken passing between them. "Thank you," she said.

Their bond, forged in danger and tempered by trust, felt unshakable. Whatever lay ahead, they would face it together.

The Cabin in the Hills

B y mid-afternoon the next day, they found a small, weathered cabin tucked into the hills, nearly invisible beneath the dense foliage. The air around it felt charged, as though the forest was holding its breath.

"This is it," Elena whispered, her heart pounding.

Rhett approached cautiously, his weapon drawn. The cabin's door hung crookedly on its hinges, and the interior was cloaked in shadows. Papers littered a wooden table, and diagrams and notes hinted at Montenegro's work. In the corner, a monitor flickered faintly, casting an eerie glow.

"He's been here," Elena said, her voice filled with relief and dread.

Rhett didn't have time to respond before the door slammed shut behind them—a trap. The explosion came seconds later, the blast shaking the cabin and throwing them to the floor. Before they could recover, armed men stormed in.

The Escape

"**M**ove!" Rhett barked; his voice sharp with urgency as he shoved Elena toward a concealed trapdoor hidden beneath a weathered rug. She pushed it open without hesitation, and they dropped into the narrow tunnel below. Gunfire rattled through the air above them, each shot like a hammer blow in the confined space. Dirt and debris trickled as the chaos continued, but there was no time to look back.

The tunnel was pitch-black, the air thick and oppressive. Each step forward felt heavier than the last, desperation pressing down on them. Rhett held onto Elena's arm, guiding her through the suffocating darkness as the echoes of pursuit faded behind them. Every breath was a struggle, every heartbeat a reminder of how close they had come to an end.

After what felt like an eternity, they reached the exit and climbed out into the forest. The sudden flood of sunlight was disorienting, blinding them momentarily as they shielded their eyes. The crisp scent of pine and earth was a stark contrast to the stifling air of the tunnel, but the forest was no haven.

Rhett scanned the trees, his weapon drawn and his senses on high alert. The forest was eerily quiet except for the rustling of leaves in the wind. "We're not done yet," he said, his tone grim and resolute.

Elena, her face streaked with dirt and her chest heaving from exertion, met his gaze and nodded—determination burned in her eyes. Whatever lay ahead, they would face it together.

CHAPTER 13

Secrets in the Shadows

The forest canopy filtered the waning afternoon sunlight, scattering shifting patterns of gold across the muddy trail. With each step, Rhett Kardon and Elena Morales pushed forward, their boots sinking into the rain-soaked earth. Their clothes clung to their bodies, damp from the relentless morning downpour and stained with the grime of the jungle. The thick air carried the scents of wet foliage, decaying wood, and earth—a stark reminder of their isolation deep within the Argentine wilderness. Towering trees loomed above them, their intertwined branches creating a suffocating sense of enclosure. Every sound—a snapping twig, the distant call of a bird—set their nerves on edge, a constant reminder of the dangers lurking just beyond sight.

Rhett adjusted the strap of his pack, rolling his aching shoulders as they trudged onward. Despite the oppressive humidity, the chill of the damp afternoon air gnawed at him. His thoughts drifted back to the failed ambush at the cabin: the crack of gunfire, the acrid sting of smoke, the metallic taste of blood. They had barely escaped alive, but the lingering questions were like splinters in his mind.

Why now? Why had Montenegro's enemies become so desperate to silence him? And what was it about Operation White Coat that remained so deadly, even after all these years? Rhett kept his thoughts to himself, unwilling to add to Elena's burden. She already carried enough.

A few paces ahead, Elena clutched a battered map, her eyes scanning its smeared ink and torn edges. It was cobbled together from fragments they had risked everything to recover in Buenos Aires. Though the lines were faint, they had been clear enough to guide them. Yet, Rhett could sense her doubt in how she gripped the map too tightly, her shoulders stiff with tension. She doubted herself, doubted the map. Her uncertainty was like a pulse in the air, unspoken but palpable.

The stakes were higher than ever, and their time was running out. Montenegro wasn't just a target; he was the key. To Rhett, he was the last thread that might untangle his father's connection to the shadowy experiments of Operation White Coat. For Elena, he represented hope—answers about her brother Mateo, who had vanished into the same dark web of lies and secrets.

"Stop," Elena said suddenly, her voice sharp but quiet. She crouched, brushing aside a layer of moss to reveal a faint carving at the base of a tree. Rhett knelt beside her, his hand instinctively moving to the weapon. The symbol was unfamiliar, but its intent was unmistakable: a warning or an invitation.

Elena glanced at him, her dark eyes alight with resolve and fear. "We're close," she whispered.

"Close to what?" Rhett asked, his voice low. "Montenegro—or a trap?"

Elena's lips pressed into a thin line. "We'll find out soon enough."

The forest around them grew eerily still, the hum of insects fading into silence. Rhett rose, scanning the dense trees for any sign of movement. Every shadow felt heavier, every rustle more sinister. There was no turning back now. Montenegro waited somewhere in this vast, untamed wilderness—and with him, the answers they had sacrificed everything to find.

The Abandoned Facility

The trail wound through increasingly dense foliage, leading them to the remnants of an old government research facility hidden beneath creeping vines and moss. The crumbling walls were streaked with dark stains and shattered windows gaped like hollow eyes. Time had taken its toll, but the building's structure still hinted at the cold precision of its original purpose. Graffiti scrawled in faded colors suggested that others had passed through, but the silence around them was absolute. Whatever activity had occurred here was long gone—or so it seemed.

Rhett crouched low, his sharp gaze sweeping over the decaying structure. It looked like nothing more than an abandoned ruin to an untrained eye, but Rhett's instincts told him otherwise. Its isolation beneath the dense forest canopy, the remnants of reinforced barriers—this was no ordinary ruin. It was the perfect place for a man like Montenegro to operate in secrecy, far from the prying eyes of the outside world.

"This is it," Elena said, breaking the silence. She unfolded the map, her finger tracing a faded set of coordinates. "The documents said this was part of Operation White Coat—an off-the-books lab for experiments they couldn't conduct anywhere else."

Rhett nodded, his jaw tightening. Facilities like this didn't just fade into obscurity. They left behind dangerous legacies—unfinished experiments, volatile materials, and people willing to kill to keep them buried.

"We need to check for recent activity," Rhett said, rising to his feet. His voice was calm, but his hand rested on the grip of his weapon. He scanned the perimeter with heightened awareness, looking for any sign of disturbance—fresh footprints, hidden sensors, or the glint of a concealed tripwire. "If Montenegro's been here, there'll be something useful. Or a trap."

Elena nodded, slipping the map back into her pack. Her face was resolute, though her green eyes betrayed a flicker of unease. "We don't have much time," she said, glancing over her shoulder. "If someone's watching this place, they'll know we're here soon."

Together, they approached the building with deliberate caution. The closer they got, the more the forest seemed to press in around them, amplifying the sound of their footsteps against the silence. The main entrance loomed ahead, a rusted door barely hanging on its hinges. Rhett motioned for Elena to stop as he crouched to inspect the threshold. His fingers brushed the faint indentations around the frame—pressure sensors, just as he'd suspected.

"Someone's been here recently," Rhett muttered. He glanced back at Elena, his voice firm. "Be ready."

Exploring the Ruins

They slipped through the rusted doorway into the darkened interior, the air inside thick with the smell of decay and chemicals. Their footsteps echoed faintly on the cracked tile floor, unnaturally loud in the stifling silence. The walls were lined with rusted cabinets and faded posters, relics of a bygone era. Elena shone her flashlight down the corridor, revealing shards of glass and discarded lab equipment strewn haphazardly.

"This doesn't feel abandoned," she murmured, her voice low.

Rhett didn't respond. His focus was on the room at the end of the hall, where a faint glow beckoned. They moved toward it, their movements cautious and deliberate. The door at the end of the corridor was ajar, and Rhett pushed it open with the barrel of his Springfield, his senses on high alert.

The room was eerily pristine inside. A steel table stood in the center, surrounded by medical monitors and humming machines. Shelves of vials lined the walls, their contents glowing faintly in the dim light. Elena moved to the table, her breath catching as she scanned its surface. Papers lay scattered across it, filled with dense scientific notation and diagrams.

Rhett approached a nearby bulletin board cluttered with files. His eyes scanned the yellowed documents, their brittle edges curling with age. A name caught his attention, scrawled in neat handwriting on the corner of one file: Dr. James Kardon—his father.

His heart clenched as he opened the file, scanning the dense text. Dates, locations, and experiment codes leaped off the pages, each cutting more profoundly than the last. It wasn't just his father's involvement—it was the scope of the operation. The notes detailed human experimentation on an unimaginable scale, and the implications were staggering.

A Grim Discovery

Elena's hands shook as she flipped through the brittle, yellowed pages, her horror deepening with every word. The files detailed Montenegro's experiments in clinical, detached language. Subject after subject was listed as "deceased" or "discontinued," their identities were reduced to numbers and footnotes. But then, among the grim entries, a few were chillingly marked as "successful."

Her breath caught as she turned the page and froze. A photograph stared back at her: a young man, his face gaunt and pale, his eyes hollow with despair that seemed to pierce the page. Beneath it, scrawled in bold letters, was a name that hit her like a knife to the heart.

Mateo Morales.

Elena's legs gave out, the weight of the revelation too much to bear. Rhett lunged forward, catching her before she hit the ground. She clung to the file as if letting go of it would erase the last thread connecting her to her brother.

"No... no, no, no," she whispered, her voice breaking. Tears streamed down her face, her words trembling. "They said he disappeared—they never said... this."

Rhett knelt beside her, his pulse pounding in his ears. His eyes darted to the photo, then to Elena, and the pieces clicked into place like a horrifying puzzle. Mateo hadn't vanished. He had been taken—dragged into the same monstrous experiments Rhett had barely escaped.

His fists clenched, the rage inside him boiling over. "Montenegro didn't just stop," he said bitterly, his voice low and fierce. "He kept going—long after the operation was supposed to be shut down."

Elena's sobs quieted, but her hands still trembled as she gripped the file, her knuckles white. Her brother was alive once—but what had they done to him?

Rhett placed a steadying hand on her shoulder, his expression resolute. "We'll find out what happened to him," he vowed, his voice a promise carved in stone. "We're not stopping. Not until we know the truth—nor until we end this."

Elena looked at him, her tear-streaked face hardening with determination. "Then let's make them pay.

The Surveillance Room

They searched the rest of the facility, moving with renewed urgency. Rhett found what they were looking for at the far end of the hallway: a small surveillance room hidden behind a false wall. The equipment inside was old but still functional.

Rhett powered up the monitors and scanned the camera feeds. Most of the screens were filled with static, but one camera still worked—it pointed toward a hidden entrance at the back of the facility.

"Someone's been using this place," Rhett muttered. "And they didn't leave through the front door."

Elena leaned over his shoulder. "What's that?"

On the screen, a blurry figure moved through the shadows—a man wearing a hooded Jacket. He disappeared through a metal hatch on the floor, and the camera became static.

"That's Montenegro," Rhett said, recognizing the figure from old photographs. "He's still here, and he knows we are here too."

Into the Underground Lab

They found the hidden hatch on the floor and pried it open. A narrow staircase led down into the darkness, the air growing colder with every step. Rhett led the way, Springfield drawn, as they descended into what felt like another world.

The underground lab was vast, with rows of cryogenic chambers, medical equipment, and vials of strange substances. Most of the chambers were empty, but a few still held bodies, their occupants frozen in eerie silence.

Elena stared at the chambers, her expression unreadable. "What the hell is this place?"

Rhett's jaw tightened. "It's the next phase. They didn't stop with the original operation but moved it underground."

They moved deeper into the lab, the sterile smell of chemicals growing stronger with each step, until they reached a small office tucked away at the far end. The door creaked open, revealing a dimly lit space cluttered with papers and laboratory equipment.

Inside, a man sat slumped over a desk, his body motionless and lifeless. A small glass vial lay tipped over near his hand, its contents a faint trace of residue on the desk's surface. The acrid, bitter smell lingering in the air made the scene unmistakable.

Elena leaned in closer, her hand covering her nose and mouth. "Cyanide," she murmured, her voice tinged with recognition and unease.

Rhett inspected the scene grimly, noting the hastily scrawled note beside the man. The words were smudged but readable—short and desperate. Whatever secrets the man had carried, he had chosen this irreversible escape rather than let them be discovered.

"He knew they were closing in," Rhett said, his tone low. "This was his way out."

Elena nodded, her expression solemn. "Let's hope whatever he protected didn't die with him."

The Final Message

R hett checked for a pulse, but it was too late—Montenegro was dead.

"Damn it," Rhett muttered, slamming a fist against the wall. "We were too late."

Elena searched the desk, her hands shaking. Amid the clutter of papers and notes, she found a small, encrypted laptop.

"This might still have the answers," she said, opening the laptop and powering it on. A single video file—Montenegro's final message—was displayed on the screen.

They watched in silence as the screen flickered to life.

Montenegro's Confession

The grainy video flickered to life, casting a ghostly glow in the dim room. Montenegro's face appeared on the screen, haggard and pale, his sunken eyes shadowed by exhaustion. His voice was barely a rasp, each word strained as if it cost him everything to speak.

"If you're watching this," he began, his gaze piercing through the lens, "it means I didn't make it out. But you need to hear the truth. Operation White Coat... it was never about making soldiers."

He paused, his chest heaving with a violent, hacking cough that rattled like death itself. It seemed he might not continue for a moment, but then he swallowed hard and forced himself to go on.

"It was about control," he said, his voice trembling with bitter disdain. "Controlling the next stage of human evolution. Your father believed he could create a new kind of human—perfect, obedient, without flaws."

Rhett's fists clenched at his sides, his breath shallow as the weight of the words sank in. This wasn't the dark secret he had imagined—it was far worse.

Montenegro's eyes flickered with a mix of sorrow and fury. "The subjects... they weren't volunteers," he confessed, his voice breaking. "They were taken. They were stolen from their lives and their families. And they were meant to replace us. A new species, designed to serve without question."

The camera zoomed closer, capturing every line etched into Montenegro's face. He leaned forward, his voice dropping to a chilling whisper. "You have to stop it. If they restart the operation, it won't just be the soldiers they're making. It'll be everyone. No one will be free."

The screen abruptly went dark, the silence that followed deafening. Rhett stared at the blank monitor, his jaw tight, his mind reeling. Elena sat frozen beside him, her hands gripping the table's edge as if it were the only thing keeping her upright.

Rhett exhaled shakily, his voice a low growl. "This isn't just about revenge anymore. This is war."

A New Mission

Rhett shut the laptop, his mind racing. The stakes were even higher than he'd thought. Operation White Coat wasn't just a relic of the past but a blueprint for the future. And if their enemies succeeded, it would change humanity forever.

"We can't let this happen," Rhett said, his voice low but determined.

Elena nodded, her eyes fierce. "Then we finish what we started."

Rhett reached for his bag, checking his weapons. The hunt wasn't over—and the fight was beginning.

Together, they moved back toward the surface, leaving Montenegro's secrets behind, carrying the weight of a new mission.

CHAPTER 14

The Russian Connection

The forest behind them seemed to whisper warnings as Rhett Kardon and Elena Morales pushed through the narrow trails, their faces hardened with grim determination. They had uncovered more than they bargained for in Montenegro's underground lab. The truth about Operation White Coat was worse than anything Rhett had imagined. And now, as the pieces began to fall into place, it was clear that their enemies were more numerous—and more dangerous—than they had anticipated.

Montenegro's warning still echoed in Rhett's mind: The operation was never about soldiers—it was about control. It wasn't just a relic of Cold War paranoia but a blueprint for the future—a plan to engineer a new breed of humanity.

But Montenegro's trail didn't end in Argentina. The recovered documents hinted at another key player: Viktor Volkov, a former Soviet scientist. If they were going to stop the resurrection of Operation White Coat, they needed to find Volkov—and they needed to find him fast.

Their next destination was Copenhagen, Denmark.

Leaving Argentina Behind

As twilight descended, the crumbling village where they had stashed their SUV appeared. Its dilapidated buildings cast jagged silhouettes against the dimming sky. The air was damp and thick with the scent of earth and rot. Rhett's eyes scanned the treeline, his hand never far from the weapon holstered at his hip. Their enemies wouldn't stop hunting them just because Montenegro was dead. If anything, his death might intensify the pursuit, throwing more bodies and resources into the search.

The vehicle was parked where they had left it, hidden beneath a tangle of vines near the village's edge. Rhett approached cautiously, scanning the area for signs of disturbance. Satisfied, he quickly nodded to Elena, who moved to cover him as he unlocked the doors. She remained alert, her weapon ready, her sharp eyes darting between the darkened windows of the surrounding buildings.

Rhett climbed into the driver's seat, his gaze flicking to the fuel gauge. The needle hovered dangerously close to empty. "We've got enough to make it to Bariloche," he said grimly, starting the engine. "But that's it. No detours."

Elena settled into the passenger seat, her expression distant but focused. "Bariloche it is," she said. "From there, we get to the airport and out of Argentina by morning."

The vehicle rumbled to life, the sound jarring against the quiet of the village. As they drove onto the dirt track leading out of town, the last rays of sunlight disappeared, replaced by a deep indigo sky streaked with crimson. The road was rough, each bump jarring but necessary as they put more distance between themselves and the shadowy forces pursuing them.

Elena broke the silence as they approached the main road. "What's the plan in Copenhagen?" she asked, her voice calm but edged with tension.

Rhett's grip on the wheel tightened. "Find Volkov," he said. "If he's part of this, he's our best chance at dismantling it. If he's not..." He didn't finish the thought. He didn't need to.

Elena nodded, a grim smile touching her lips. "Then we end it," she said softly. "One way or another."

Her words hung between them, heavy with unspoken promises. The road stretched on, winding through the forest as the stars began to emerge overhead.

Neither of them spoke again. Their focus was forward—on the path that would take them to Denmark and, with luck, to the answers they so desperately needed.

Arrival in Copenhagen

The sharp chill of Copenhagen's air was a stark contrast to the humid jungles of Argentina, cutting through Rhett and Elena as they stepped off the tarmac at a private airfield. Their breath puffed visibly in the cold, and the wind gnawed at their exposed skin, seeping through layers of clothing. They moved quickly, loading their bags into a waiting car parked at the edge of the airstrip. Rhett scanned the perimeter as he climbed into the driver's seat, his instincts on high alert.

The city unfolded before them in muted tones; its cobblestone streets and historic facades shrouded in the soft glow of streetlights. The damp pavement glistened underfoot, reflecting the warm hues of the lamps and the occasional flicker of passing headlights. Copenhagen was beautiful, but Rhett barely noticed. His eyes were locked on the road ahead, his mind consumed with calculations and contingencies.

Elena sat beside him; her focus split between the map on her tablet and the shifting scenery outside. Her expression was unreadable, her mind running through the same mental exercises as Rhett's.

"Volkov's last known location was a safe house in Nyhavn," Rhett said, breaking the silence as they neared the historic district. "If he's smart, he's moved on. But we don't have time to assume that."

Elena nodded. "If he's still there, he won't stay for long."

Nyhavn's vibrant energy greeted them as they arrived—a sharp contrast to their somber mission. Tourists thronged the waterfront, their laughter and chatter blending with the clink of glasses and the soft creak of boats bobbing in the canal. It was a scene of life and celebration, but to Rhett and Elena, it was another layer of camouflage hiding the shadows they sought.

Rhett parked in a narrow alley just off the main strip, seamlessly blending with the other vehicles lining the street. They moved quickly, their steps purposeful, approaching a weathered building with peeling paint and crooked shutters. To most, it would look abandoned, a relic of a bygone era. But Rhett knew better. Safe houses were built to be overlooked.

"This is it," he murmured, his hand brushing against the holster at his side.

Nyhavn: A City of Secrets

They slipped inside the side door, their movements silent and precise. Guns drawn, they advanced through the dimly lit interior, their breaths shallow in the still air. The smell of dust and old cigarette smoke clung to the walls, mingling with a faint metallic tang that hinted at past violence.

The safe house was sparse, its furnishings functional but battered. Papers littered the floor, and a desk lamp flickered weakly in the corner. A rusted filing cabinet stood against the far wall, its drawers ajar. Rhett scanned the room, his sharp eyes catching the telltale signs of a quick departure—disturbed dust, an overturned chair, a single cigarette crushed into the floorboards.

"Volkov was here," Elena whispered, kneeling to examine the desk. Her fingers brushed against a faint smudge where something had been hastily moved. "Not long ago."

Rhett's gaze shifted to the wall above the desk, where a collage of photographs caught his attention. Each image was carefully pinned to the plaster, connected by a web of red string. Faces stared back at him—scientists, soldiers, officials—all tied to Operation White Coat. At the center, two figures loomed more significant than the others: Viktor Volkov and his father, to Rhett's shock.

Rhett's breath hitched as he stepped closer. His father's face was unmistakable, his expression stern as he stood beside Volkov in what appeared to be a high-tech laboratory. The realization hit him like a blow, the implications twisting in his gut.

"Your father," Elena said softly, joining him. Her voice was steady, but her eyes betrayed her concern. "He was part of this."

Rhett's fists clenched at his sides, the weight of his father's secrets pressing down on him like a crushing tide. "He didn't just work on it," Rhett said bitterly. "He built it."

Elena's hand rested briefly on his shoulder, a silent gesture of support. "We need to keep moving," she said. "If Volkov left a trail, we must find it before someone else does."

The Hunt Begins

The next several days were a blur of motion and desperation. Leads were chased, informants bribed, and surveillance systems hacked, all in pursuit of a man who seemed to exist everywhere and nowhere at once. Copenhagen became their battleground, its labyrinthine streets hiding their prey and the forces hunting alongside them.

Every step forward felt like a gamble, every uncovered clue a potential trap. The safe house was only the beginning—Volkov's web of connections stretched deeper than they had imagined, and as the days wore on, the realization grew: they weren't just chasing Volkov. They were being hunted themselves.

Ultimately, it wasn't brute force or careful planning that brought them to their quarry. It was luck—or perhaps desperation. A late-night message from one of their informants pointed them to a derelict industrial complex on the city's outskirts. There, hidden among the rust and decay, Volkov waited.

The Final Confrontation

The complex loomed before them, a sprawling maze of crumbling warehouses and abandoned machinery. The air was thick with the scent of rust and oil, and the faint creak of shifting metal echoed in the darkness. Rhett and Elena moved precisely, their steps muffled against the cracked concrete.

They found him in the heart of the largest warehouse, hunched over a cluttered workbench beneath a single hanging bulb. The light cast long shadows across his gaunt face, his wild gray hair framing sharp, calculating eyes. Viktor Volkov didn't look up as they approached, but his voice cut through the silence.

"You've come a long way to find me," he said, his tone carrying both amusement and resignation.

Rhett's gun remained steady as he stepped forward. "We need answers."

Volkov finally turned, a faint smile playing on his lips. "Answers?" he repeated. "You already know more than most. But very well—if it's the truth you want, let's begin."

The Truth Revealed

Over the next several hours, Volkov unraveled Operation White Coat's dark and twisted legacy. His voice was low but unwavering, every word slicing through the room like a blade. What had begun as a covert Cold War experiment—an attempt to create enhanced soldiers—had mutated into something more insidious. It had transcended borders and infiltrated governments, corporations, and research institutions. It was no longer just an operation—a sprawling, self-sustaining, and constantly evolving machine. Its methods had grown more sophisticated, and its reach was more pervasive, but its goal remained chillingly unchanged: absolute control.

"The Cold War ended," Volkov said, his gaze distant as if reliving memories he'd rather forget. "But White Coat didn't. It adapted and became quieter, more subtle. But don't mistake subtlety for weakness. Its roots are everywhere now—financing wars, engineering crises, shaping nations. And its ultimate purpose hasn't wavered."

Rhett's fists clenched as Volkov's words painted a picture more horrifying than anything he'd imagined. Operation White Coat wasn't just a relic of the past; it was alive, thriving, and moving toward its ultimate goal—a world where freedom was a carefully controlled illusion and humanity was rewritten.

Elena sat frozen, her knuckles white as she gripped the table's edge. "Why now?" she asked, her voice barely above a whisper. "Why escalate now?"

Volkov's lips twisted into a bitter smile. "Because they're close," he said. "Closer than ever. If they succeed, it won't just be soldiers or operatives they control but entire populations—a new humanity engineered to serve. And no one will be safe—not your families or friends. Not even you."

The room fell into a suffocating silence as what they faced settled over them like a crushing weight. Rhett's thoughts raced, his mind churning with images of what the future could hold if they failed. This wasn't just about justice or revenge—it was a fight for the very survival of humanity as they knew it.

Finally, Volkov stopped speaking, his eyes haunted. "You have one chance," he said quietly. "One chance to stop this before it's too late."

Rhett rose slowly, his expression stern as stone. He deliberately holstered his weapon and met Elena's gaze. Her dark eyes mirrored his resolve, her fear tempered by fierce determination.

"We end this," Rhett said, his voice a low growl.

Elena nodded firmly. "Together."

Without another word, they stepped into the biting cold of the Copenhagen night, the echoes of Volkov's revelations lingering like ghosts in the frosty air. The streetlights cast long shadows as they moved with purpose, every breath misting in the icy wind.

The fight wasn't over—it had only just begun. And the stakes had never been higher.

CHAPTER 15

Dangerous Affection

The air in the Copenhagen safe house hung heavy and oppressive with the gravity of what Rhett Kardon and Elena Morales had uncovered. The dimly lit room seemed to hold its breath, bearing witness to their silence as they sat surrounded by scattered maps, encrypted files, and hastily scrawled notes. Outside, the muffled hum of the city streets barely penetrated the thick walls, a distant reminder of the world moving on obliviously.

They hadn't spoken much since their encounter with Viktor Volkov—the man whose revelations had shattered any illusion of containment. Operation White Coat wasn't a Cold War ghost, not a relic buried in the past. It was a living, breathing monstrosity—an evolving web of global influence controlled by governments, corporations, and shadow networks. Its goal wasn't mere military supremacy but the subjugation of humanity on a terrifying scale.

Rhett sat heavily in his chair, exhaustion carving deep lines into his face. He rubbed his hands over his eyes, dragging them down his cheeks as if trying to erase the weight of what they now knew. The stale air smelled faintly of coffee and dust, the only illumination from a single desk lamp that flickered weakly, casting warped shadows over peeling wallpaper. The light accentuated the strain etched into Rhett's rugged features—the set jaw, the faint tremor in his fingers as he clenched and unclenched them.

At the window, Elena stood silhouetted against the city's amber glow. Her arms were crossed, her posture rigid, though the slump of her shoulders betrayed her fatigue. Strands of her dark hair framed her face, catching the faint light as her gaze swept the quiet street below. The fire in her green eyes hadn't dimmed; if anything, it burned brighter now, fueled by Volkov's words. Whatever exhaustion her body endured, her spirit refused to falter.

"You should get some sleep," Rhett said, breaking the silence. His voice was rough, gravelly from hours of tension. It carried an edge of concern, though he tried to mask it.

Elena turned slightly, arching an eyebrow in disbelief. "Do I look like someone who can sleep right now?" she asked, her tone sharp but not unkind.

Rhett allowed himself a faint smirk, the shadow of humor cutting through his otherwise somber demeanor. "Fair point," he muttered, leaning forward and resting his elbows on his knees. Sleep was a luxury for people who didn't have enemies tracking their every move. For people who weren't trying to dismantle a decades-old conspiracy capable of reshaping humanity.

After a beat, Elena spoke, her voice quiet but resolute. "Volkov knew too much," she said without turning from the window. "The facilities, the names, the experiments... If he's dead, that knowledge dies with him."

"And if he's not?" Rhett asked, his eyes narrowing. "If he's playing us, leading us straight into a trap?"

Elena exhaled slowly, finally stepping away from the window. She moved to the desk, bracing her hands on its surface as she stared at the maps and files spread out on it. Her eyes were colder now, sharp with purpose. "Then we deal with him like the rest of them."

Rhett studied her in the dim light, noticing her jaw set and the hard edge in her tone. There was pain there—an anger that burned alongside her relentless determination. He recognized it because it mirrored his own. They were both fueled by a need to stop something larger than themselves, born of betrayal and loss.

"Volkov's not our only lead," Rhett said after a pause, his voice measured. "The data we pulled from Montenegro's lab—those coordinates, the names—are still our best shot. We'll find the next piece, one way or another."

Elena nodded, though her gaze stayed fixed on the table. "Finding the next piece isn't enough, Rhett," she said in a low voice. "We have to end this. All of it. If we don't, there's no stopping them."

He stood, the chair scraping softly against the floor as he moved beside her. His hand rested lightly on the desk's edge, the other near the holster at his side. "We will," he said firmly. "One step at a time. Piece by piece."

Elena's eyes flicked up to meet his, and for a moment, the weight between them seemed to ease, their shared resolve anchoring them. "One step at a time," she echoed, her voice steadier now.

Outside, the faint sound of a car engine hummed in the night—a distant, steady reminder that the world kept turning even as theirs teetered on the brink. Together, they turned back to the maps and files. Their mission wasn't just personal anymore; it was about a future no one else could see was under threat.

Trust, Distrust, and Everything in Between

The partnership between Rhett and Elena had been born in fire—necessity and danger forging a bond neither could fully define. But the closer they worked, the more complex that bond became. The cracks in their defenses and the unspoken understanding moments all pointed to something more profound than shared survival.

Rhett wasn't used to letting people in, and his years in the CIA taught him to build walls so thick that not even guilt or grief could slip through. Trust was a weakness; his father's betrayal had burned into him with cruel finality. Yet Elena's unyielding drive, her refusal to be anything less than relentless, chipped away at those walls in ways that unsettled him. She wasn't just a mission partner or a resource; she was a challenge—a fire that matched his own, both in intensity and purpose.

And Elena wasn't oblivious to the pull between them. She felt it, too, an ember glowing quietly beneath their constant vigilance. But she couldn't afford to give it life. Not when her focus was razor-sharp, her mind consumed by her brother's disappearance and the monstrous conspiracy that had ensnared him. Rhett might understand her pain—he might even share it—but acknowledging their connection felt dangerous, like taking a step too close to the edge of a cliff.

"What's next?" Elena asked, dropping into a chair across from Rhett. She rubbed her sore feet, leaning back with a sigh. Her exhaustion was evident, but her voice carried the same fierce resolve it always did. "Where do we go from here?"

Rhett's gaze flicked to the maps and documents on the table. "We follow the money," he said after a moment. "Volkov was just the brain behind this. Someone else is funding it—someone with global reach. They're the ones we need to find."

Elena scoffed lightly, a dry smile tugging at her lips. "You mean besides half the Russian government and probably your CIA?"

Rhett shot her a look, his expression unamused but tinged with grudging agreement. "Trust me, I'm not exactly loyal to either."

Her smile softened, though her eyes remained sharp, studying him like she was trying to solve a puzzle. "Good," she said. "Because loyalty to them gets you killed."

The corners of Rhett's mouth twitched upward in a faint smirk. "You're not wrong," he admitted. "But that's why we're here—to burn this thing to the ground before they can build it into something unstoppable."

Elena nodded, her expression hardening again. Despite their banter, a seriousness in her gaze mirrored his own. She respected his pragmatism, even if it sometimes felt like he was holding something back. But in moments like this—when the world felt impossibly heavy, and the silence between them carried more than words ever could—it felt like those walls between them cracked just enough to let the other in.

The Vulnerability Beneath

For a long moment, neither spoke. The room settled into a heavy quiet, filled only with the soft hum of the desk lamp and the distant sounds of the city outside. Rhett found his eyes drawn to Elena as she leaned forward, her attention fixed on the scattered maps and files. She had a way of carrying herself that fascinated him—her movements deliberate, her focus unrelenting. Even in her quiet moments, there was an energy about her, a fire that refused to die.

"What about you?" he asked suddenly, his voice low but cutting through the silence. "What happens when this is over? When you find out what happened to your brother?"

Elena hesitated, her green eyes flicking up to meet his. He thought she might deflect, but then her expression softened. "I survive," she said. "That's what we do, right? Survive and keep moving."

Her words were quiet but heavy, laced with a truth Rhett knew all too well. He nodded slowly, his jaw tightening. He had spent his entire life surviving, chasing answers that only ever seemed to lead to more questions. But he saw something different with Elena—a determination beyond mere survival. She wanted justice and closure. And maybe, just maybe, she wanted peace.

A Line Crossed

Without thinking, Rhett reached out, brushing a stray strand of hair from Elena's face. The gesture was small, almost instinctive, but it carried a weight neither could ignore. For a moment, she froze, her eyes locking onto his. The air between them felt electric, charged with an intensity they couldn't name.

And then she kissed him.

The kiss was fierce, almost desperate—a collision of pent-up frustration, anger, and something far more complicated. For a few seconds, everything else fell away. The weight of their mission, the dangers closing in around them, the unspoken barriers between them—it all dissolved in the heat of that moment.

When they finally pulled apart, Elena looked at him, her breathing uneven. "That shouldn't have happened," she whispered, though her words had no conviction.

Rhett smirked faintly, his voice low and rough. "Probably not. But I'm not sorry."

Elena rolled her eyes, a reluctant smile tugging at her lips. "Of course you're not."

For a moment, they allowed themselves to linger in the fragile quiet that followed. But they both knew the kiss hadn't solved anything—it had only complicated what was already fragile. They couldn't afford this, not now.

A Final Gamble

They packed their gear quickly, the tension between them still palpable but unspoken. The enemy was closing in, and the only option was to vanish completely, following Volkov's revealed money trail. Their path would take them deep into the conspiracy's heart, to the forces that funded and sustained Operation White Coat.

Rhett and Elena sat in a dimly lit compartment as the train pulled away from Copenhagen. Outside, the city lights blurred into darkness, the rhythmic clatter of the wheels filling the silence.

"You ready for this?" Rhett asked, his voice steady but noting something more profound.

Elena met his gaze, her expression hard but resolute. "Always."

They were hurtling toward the unknown, danger, answers, and an endgame neither could fully predict. But they would face it together.

For now, that was enough.

CHAPTER 16

The Dead Scientist

The tension was palpable as Rhett Kardon and Elena Morales stepped off the midnight train into the outskirts of Berlin. Their enemies were closing in, and time was running out. Every clue, every trace, and every step forward seemed to bring them closer to uncovering the full scope of the conspiracy—and closer to the inevitable confrontation that Rhett knew was coming.

Their next lead wasn't just a financial trail—it was a name that repeatedly resurfaced in old Operation White Coat documents and Montenegro's notes: Dr. Artyom Sokolov. An expert geneticist and one of the operation's architects, Sokolov had vanished years ago, presumed dead or living in obscurity under an alias. But Rhett and Elena's investigation suggested otherwise—he was alive and held more answers than anyone else.

The catch? They had found his body, or at least what was left of it. And the circumstances surrounding his death pointed to something far more sinister than a random murder.

Berlin's Underworld: A Dangerous Encounter

Berlin's underworld was an intricate, shadowy web of ex-CIA operatives, rogue mercenaries, arms dealers, and informants who traded secrets like currency. It was a dangerous ecosystem where trust was a liability and deception a survival skill. Rhett and Elena moved through the city like ghosts, blending into the shadows and remaining vigilant. They had learned through bitter experience that no ally could be fully trusted, and every enemy lurked just out of sight, waiting for the perfect moment to strike.

Their mission began with a dangerous lead pointing to Sokolov, a name tied to a web of covert operations gone awry. Their first stop was Richter, an ex-CIA handler who had gone rogue years ago, reinventing himself as an information broker. Rhett had once helped Richter vanish from the Agency's radar, a debt that ensured cooperation—at least on the surface. But in this world, every favor came at a price, and Rhett knew better than to expect altruism.

The meeting was held in Kreuzberg, a smoky, dimly lit dive bar where anonymity was the unspoken rule. The air was thick with the smell of stale beer and cigarettes, a haven for those operating in the grey zones of legality. The patrons kept to themselves, their conversations low and furtive. Rhett and Elena entered with practiced ease, their eyes scanning every corner for potential threats before settling into a booth near the back.

Richter was already there, nursing a glass of whiskey. His grizzled face split into a sly grin as Rhett slid into the seat across from him, Elena close by, her presence as much a deterrent as an asset.

"Kardon, you bastard," Richter greeted his voice with amusement and wariness. "I knew you'd come knocking eventually."

Rhett's expression remained cold, businesslike. "Sokolov," he said, skipping the pleasantries. "You heard what happened to him?"

Richter's grin faded. He leaned forward, his elbows resting on the table. "Yeah, I heard. Poor bastard turned up dead in some grimy hostel last week. The official story says heart attack, but we both know that's bullshit."

Rhett nodded, his jaw tightening. "I need everything you've got on him."

Richter hesitated, his fingers drumming a slow rhythm against his glass. "You sure you want to go digging? I hear people are getting taken out just for whispering his name."

Elena, who had been silently observing, leaned in now, her voice sharp and unwavering. "We're not whispering, Richter. We're telling you to talk."

Richter's chuckle was low and begrudging. "I like her," he muttered, reaching under the table to retrieve a worn file. He slid it across the table, the folder thick with notes, photos, and documents. "Everything I've got is in there. But listen, Kardon—this is big. Bigger than you think. Sokolov wasn't just some unlucky operative; he was part of something... messy. And people way above our pay grade are watching."

Rhett took the file; his expression was unreadable. "Who's watching?" he pressed.

Richter shook his head. "You don't want to know. Just watch your backs. There's interest in this from people you don't cross—unless you've got a death wish."

Elena exchanged a glance with Rhett, her hand subtly moving to her concealed weapon. The tension in the air was palpable. They both understood the stakes now, and the weight of the file in Rhett's hands felt heavier than it should. Without another word, they slipped out of the bar, disappearing into the Berlin night, their mission growing darker with every step.

The Hostel Room

The following day, Rhett and Elena pulled up to the hostel where Dr. Artyom Sokolov's body had been discovered. The building was a shabby relic of neglect, its paint peeling and windows clouded with grime. Located on the city's edge, it was the place where people disappeared into obscurity—a haven for drifters and those avoiding questions.

Inside, the smell of damp carpet and cheap cleaning supplies filled the air. The night clerk, a gaunt man with bloodshot eyes, barely looked up from his crossword puzzle as Rhett slipped him a bribe. The man pocketed the cash and handed over the key without hesitation. "Third floor. End of the hall," he muttered before returning to his newspaper as if nothing unusual had occurred.

The room was dim and oppressive, with a single overhead light casting a sickly yellow glow. A narrow bed with a sagging mattress was pushed against the wall, and a rickety desk was cluttered with scraps of paper and a dented lamp. The air was heavy with the staleness of neglect, but a faint, sharp scent lingered beneath it that Rhett's senses immediately picked up. It was the unmistakable metallic tang of blood.

"Doesn't look like a heart attack, does it?" Elena whispered, her tone laced with skepticism as she glanced around the cramped space.

Rhett shook his head, his expression grim. "No. This was staged."

He moved to the desk, his eyes narrowing as he sifted through the mess. Among the clutter were handwritten notes scrawled in Russian, some pages covered in intricate diagrams of DNA sequences and cryptic formulas. A few of the sheets had been hastily torn, their edges were jagged, while others showed signs of scorching as if someone had tried to destroy them in a hurry.

"They were looking for something," Rhett muttered, piecing through the papers. "And they didn't find it."

Elena stood near the window, pulling back the frayed curtain to peek into the street below. "Then whatever they wanted is either gone... or hidden."

Rhett nodded, his jaw tightening. Sokolov's death wasn't a random tragedy. This was a cleanup operation—and they were running out of time to find out what he had died protecting.

Clues in the Darkness

As they sifted through the papers, Rhett found something that made his blood boil. One of the diagrams was a match—the same genetic structure used in Operation White Coat's experiments.

"He was still working on it," Rhett muttered, holding the papers for Elena to see. "Even after all these years."

Elena's eyes widened. "Which means someone killed him to keep this buried—or to take it for themselves."

Rhett nodded, his mind racing. "And whoever it was, they missed something. Sokolov wouldn't have kept all his research here—he was too smart for that."

They searched the room more thoroughly, tearing through drawers, flipping the mattress, and checking every nook and cranny. Finally, Rhett found a small flash drive taped to the underside of the bed frame.

"Got it," Rhett whispered, holding up the drive.

Elena grinned. "Now let's find out what was worth killing for."

A Race Against Time

They didn't have time to linger. Rhett's instincts screamed that they were being watched. The hostel's shadows seemed to stretch and shift, carrying a palpable tension that set his nerves on edge. Whoever had staged Sokolov's death wouldn't take kindly to their presence.

"We need to move," Rhett muttered, his voice low but urgent. Elena nodded, and without another word, they slipped out of the room and down the creaking stairs.

The cold Berlin streets greeted them with biting wind and the muffled sounds of a city waking up. They blended into the crowd, their movements deliberate yet unremarkable, disappearing into the flow of pedestrians like smoke. Rhett constantly scanned their surroundings, catching fleeting glances of unfamiliar faces that lingered a moment too long. He couldn't shake the feeling they were being tracked, but they had one advantage: speed.

Back at the safe house, a dimly lit apartment tucked away in a rundown block, they wasted no time. Rhett slid the flash drive into the laptop, his fingers moving swiftly across the keyboard. The screen illuminated their tense expressions as he bypassed layers of encryption with a precision born from years of practice.

When the files finally opened, the weight of their contents hit them like a freight train. It wasn't just Sokolov's scattered notes—it was a full-scale blueprint for something more sinister.

"They were planning to start over," Elena said, trembling with horror and disbelief. "Not just soldiers—entire populations."

Rhett's hands clenched into fists, his jaw tight with anger. "This is what my father wanted all along," he said bitterly, the words like venom on his tongue. "This is what he built me for."

The truth was out, but it left them with even more questions—and a growing sense of dread.

The Betrayal Unfolds

The laptop's screen suddenly went black as they scrolled through the files. Momentarily, an encrypted message appeared: "You are already too late."

Rhett's stomach dropped. They'd been compromised. Someone knew they had the files—and their enemies were already closing in.

Before he could warn Elena, the door to the safe house burst inward with a deafening explosion. The force blew debris across the room, and a team of armed operatives swarmed in, their weapons trained on Rhett and Elena.

"Move!" Rhett barked, instinct taking over. He grabbed his gun, diving for cover behind the overturned couch as bullets tore through the air. Elena rolled to the side, landing behind a table and returning fire with sharp, precise shots.

"They've boxed us in!" Elena shouted, her voice barely audible over the cacophony of gunfire.

Rhett's mind raced. They were outnumbered and cornered but not beaten. His eyes darted to the flash drive still clutched in his hand—they couldn't let it fall into enemy hands.

"Window!" he shouted, pointing to the far wall. He unleashed a volley of shots, forcing the operatives to duck for cover, giving Elena a second to move.

She nodded, sprinting toward the window as Rhett laid down suppressing fire. Together, they launched themselves through the glass, shattering it into a thousand shards as they plummeted into the cold alley below.

They hit the ground hard but kept moving, disappearing into the maze of Berlin's backstreets with their enemies on their heels.

The Chase

The streets of Berlin erupted into chaos as Rhett and Elena sprinted through narrow alleys, the sound of gunfire ricocheting off the walls. Shadows danced in the flickering glow of streetlights, and the relentless pounding of boots on pavement closed in behind them.

"Faster!" Rhett urged, his voice sharp as he pulled Elena around a corner just as a spray of bullets shattered a brick wall where they'd been seconds before.

Elena's breathing was ragged, but she kept pace, her weapon clutched tightly. "How many are there?" she hissed, glancing back to glimpse their pursuers.

"Too many," Rhett replied, his tone grim. "But we're not sticking around to count."

Relying on instinct and his intimate knowledge of the city's labyrinthine backstreets, Rhett led Elena through a maze of sharp turns and hidden passages. He darted through abandoned courtyards and vaulted over rusted fences, always staying one step ahead. The operatives' shouts grew more frustrated, their gunfire sporadic as they struggled to keep up.

Finally, they burst onto the banks of the Spree River just as the first light of dawn brushed the sky with hues of pale gold and gray. Rhett's chest heaved with exertion, and his breath was visible in the cold morning air.

"We can't stop here," he said, scanning their surroundings as the distant shouts grew fainter. "We need to disappear—fast. They'll turn this city upside down to find us."

Elena nodded, her jaw set with determination. "Then let's make sure they never do."

Without hesitation, they slipped into the shadows again, the fight far from over.

Chapter 17

Chased by Shadows

The streets of Berlin turned into a blur as Rhett Kardon and Elena Morales sprinted through the maze of narrow alleyways. The distant wail of sirens and the pounding of their boots on slick cobblestones filled the air, but the shouts and heavy footfalls behind them were getting closer. Their escape from the ambush at the safe house had been razor-thin, and now their pursuers were closing in fast.

A sharp crack of gunfire split the air, followed by the panicked screams of civilians scattering for cover. Rhett didn't hesitate—he grabbed Elena's arm and yanked her sharply into a side alley, their sudden turn narrowly avoiding a barrage of bullets that peppered the wall behind them. The acrid scent of gunpowder mingled with gasoline and damp concrete, the city's grit seeping into their every breath.

"Move!" Rhett barked, shoving a stack of crates behind them to slow their pursuers. They ducked low, sliding behind a row of overflowing dumpsters as another spray of gunfire echoed down the alley. His heart thundered in his chest, adrenaline pushing his senses into overdrive.

Elena leaned against the wall, her chest heaving as she tried to catch her breath. Dirt and sweat streaked her face, but her green eyes burned with determination.

"We can't keep this up," she hissed, keeping her voice low. "They're tracking us—every step we take."

"We'll lose them," Rhett growled, peeking around the corner. His hand tightened on his weapon, his mind racing through options. "We've done it before."

"Not like this," she countered, her tone sharp but steady.

"We don't have a choice," he shot back. "We just need to get to the extraction point."

The sound of boots pounding on pavement grew louder, echoing like a drumbeat in the confined space. Rhett's eyes darted toward a fire escape above them, its rusted ladder hanging just out of reach. He motioned to Elena. "Up. Now."

Without hesitation, she scrambled onto a dumpster and launched herself up, pulling the ladder down with a sharp metallic screech. Rhett followed, scaling the fire escape as their pursuers rounded the corner below. Bullets ricocheted off the metal railings as they climbed, and the operatives' shouted orders.

Reaching the rooftop, Rhett and Elena sprinted toward the far edge. "We're not out of this yet," he muttered, glancing over his shoulder.

"Then let's make it count," Elena said, her voice hard with resolve. They disappeared into the Berlin night with a running leap, leaving their pursuers scrambling below.

The Extraction Plan

The extraction point was a few blocks away, on the other side of a canal that cut through the heart of Berlin. Rhett had arranged a rendezvous with a contact—a former agent who owed him a favor. They just needed to get there in one piece.

"How much further?" Elena asked, keeping her voice low.

Rhett checked his watch. "Two blocks. But we need to stay off the main roads."

They moved cautiously, sticking to the shadows and weaving through back alleys. Rhett's heart pounded in his chest, not from exertion but from the knowledge that they were being hunted.

"They'll have every exit covered," Elena whispered, glancing over her shoulder.

"Then we'll make our exit," Rhett replied. His mind raced, calculating their options.

The Chase Escalates

The canal was just within reach when the screech of tires tore through the night. A black SUV careened around the corner, its headlights cutting through the darkness, blocking their path. Doors flew open, and armed operatives spilled out, their rifles raised and ready.

"Move! Move! Move!" Rhett shouted, grabbing Elena's arm and yanking her toward a narrow sidewalk.

Gunfire erupted, the deafening roar of automatic weapons echoing off the buildings. Bullets ricocheted off brick walls, spraying sparks and debris. Rhett's enhanced reflexes kicked in and every movement was calculated and precise. He fired a quick burst over his shoulder, forcing the operatives to scatter and take cover.

They sprinted down the alley, but the sound of boots pounding pavement signaled reinforcements closing in. Turning a corner, they skidded to a halt—another squad of operatives was advancing from the opposite direction.

"They've boxed us in!" Elena hissed, her voice taut with frustration.

Rhett's eyes darted around, taking in their surroundings. Every nerve in his body was electrified, his mind racing. They were outnumbered and outgunned, but surrender wasn't an option. His gaze locked onto a rusted fire escape bolted to the side of a nearby building.

"There!" he barked. "Up the ladder—Go! Go! Go!"

Elena didn't hesitate. She scrambled onto a stack of crates, reaching for the fire escape's bottom rung. Rhett fired off another volley, suppressing the operatives as Elena climbed. The sharp reports of his shots punctuated the chaos, each landing with deadly accuracy.

"Come on!" she shouted as she reached the top. Rhett followed his movements swiftly and fluidly. He fired even as he ascended. Below, the operatives regrouped, shouting orders as more gunfire erupted, peppering the metal escape with sparks.

Reaching the rooftop, Rhett didn't stop. "Keep moving!" he yelled, grabbing Elena's hand and pulling her forward.

The rooftops of Berlin stretched out before them, a jagged maze of chimneys and antennas. They sprinted across the uneven terrain, their boots thudding against the concrete. The operatives weren't far behind, their shadows flickering in the moonlight.

"We can't keep this up!" Elena gasped, her breath ragged.

"We don't have to," Rhett replied, eyes locking onto the canal ahead. "We just need to make it to the water."

At the edge of the roof, they stopped. The canal shimmered far below, the water dark and forbidding under the moonlight. Rhett pulled off his

jacket, tossing it aside.

"We jump," he said firmly.

Elena turned to him, her eyes wide with disbelief. "You're out of your mind!"

"You've said that before," he shot back with a half-grin. "Now jump!"

Without waiting, Rhett launched himself off the roof, the wind rushing past him in a deafening roar. A second later, Elena followed, the world blurring into a rush of cold air and adrenaline.

They hit the water hard, the icy chill biting their skin like knives. The shock stole Rhett's breath, but he forced his body into motion, kicking against the numbing cold. He surfaced, gasping for air and struggling beside him.

He grabbed her arm, pulling her toward the canal's shadowy bank. Behind them, the operatives reached the rooftop edge, their shouts drowned out by the splash of water and the pounding of Rhett's heartbeat.

They didn't look back. The fight wasn't over, but they had slipped away into the night, for now.

The Rooftop Escape

The rooftops of Berlin stretched out like a jagged labyrinth under the moon's pale glow. Chimneys, antennas, and satellite dishes jutted into the night sky, casting long shadows over the uneven terrain. Rhett and Elena sprinted across the rooftops, their breaths ragged, their movements driven by sheer adrenaline. Behind them, the pounding of boots and the sporadic crack of gunfire echoed in the still air, a relentless reminder that their pursuers were closing in.

"We can't outrun them forever!" Elena gasped, stealing a glance over her shoulder. The silhouettes of armed operatives were only a few rooftops away, their weapons glinting in the moonlight.

"We don't need to," Rhett replied, his voice tight but resolute. His eyes locked onto the canal ahead, its dark waters shimmering faintly. "We just need to make it to the water."

Bullets whizzed past them, striking chimneys and tearing through air ducts. One round ricocheted off a metal pipe inches from Elena, making her flinch. Rhett grabbed her arm, steadying her. "Keep moving!" he shouted.

They reached the edge of the roof, skidding to a halt. Below, the canal stretched like an inky ribbon, its surface deceptively calm but foreboding. The drop was steep, and the water looked icy enough to freeze them on impact.

"We jump," Rhett said, already shrugging off his Jacket and tossing it aside.

Elena stared at him, her chest heaving. "Are you insane?" she demanded, her voice edged with both fear and frustration.

"You've said that before," Rhett replied wryly. The sound of their pursuers' boots grew louder and closer. And stepped to the edge. "Jump!"

Without waiting, Rhett launched himself into the void, the wind tearing past him as gravity dragged him toward the freezing water below. A heartbeat later, Elena followed, her scream swallowed by the rush of air.

They hit the canal with a force that knocked the breath from Rhett's lungs. The icy water stabbed at his skin, stealing his strength and slowing his movements. Disorientation threatened to take over for a moment. But he forced himself to surface, gasping for air.

"Elena!" he shouted, his voice ragged. He spotted her struggling against the current, her limbs sluggish from the cold. Kicking hard, Rhett powered through the numbing water, grabbing her arm and pulling her toward him. "I've got you," he muttered, his teeth chattering.

Above them, shouts echoed from the rooftop. Their pursuers had reached the edge, shining flashlights down into the canal. A burst of gunfire sent ripples through the water, bullets splashing dangerously close.

"Dive!" Rhett barked, pulling Elena under the surface. The cold burned their lungs as they swam blindly, desperate to put distance between themselves and the operatives above.

Underwater Evasion

The canal provided temporary cover, but Rhett knew it wouldn't be long before their enemies figured out where they went. They swam to the far side, keeping low in the water, and slipped beneath an old dock.

"Stay still," Rhett whispered, pulling Elena close. "They'll search the water but won't find us if we stay quiet."

They waited in tense silence as searchlights swept across the canal—the distant hum of a helicopter added to the growing tension.

Rhett's hand rested on his gun, ready to act if necessary. But for now, they were hidden, out of sight.

"How are you so calm?" Elena whispered, her breath warm against his ear.

Rhett gave a slight shrug. "I've been in worse situations."

Elena let out a soft, incredulous laugh. "Of course you have."

After what felt like an eternity, the searchlights moved on, and the helicopter drifted away.

"Now," Rhett whispered. "We move."

They swam quietly to the shore and climbed out of the water, shivering from the cold. Rhett's clothes clung to his skin, but he ignored the discomfort. They were almost at the extraction point.

The rendezvous location was beneath an old railway bridge, hidden from prying eyes. As they approached, a dark figure emerged from the shadows—their contact, an ex-MI6 agent named Carter.

"Cutting it close, aren't we?" Carter said with a grin, his British accent thick and amused.

"You have no idea," Rhett muttered, glancing around to ensure they hadn't been followed.

"Got what you need?" Carter asked, eyeing the flash drive in Rhett's hand.

Rhett gave a curt nod. "Now get us out of here."

The Road Ahead

With Carter's help, they slipped out of Berlin and headed toward their next destination. But Rhett knew that this was only the beginning. The conspiracy ran more profound than he had imagined, and every answer led to more questions.

As they sped through the dark countryside, Elena leaned against Rhett, her exhaustion finally catching her.

"What now?" she whispered, her voice barely audible.

Rhett stared out at the road ahead, his jaw tight. "We stop them, Elena. No matter what it takes."

And in that moment, Rhett knew that he wasn't just running from his past anymore—he was running toward the fight of his life.

CHAPTER 18

A Narrow Escape

The hum of the tires on the highway was the only sound in the van as Rhett Kardon and Elena Morales sped through the night. Their extraction from Berlin was behind them, but tension lingered in the air. They had survived another brush with death, but their enemies were still out there—relentless, waiting for their next move.

The flash drive, safely tucked into Rhett's Jacket pocket, was the key to everything. Inside it were the remnants of Montenegro's and Sokolov's research—a blueprint for genetic control on a scale that defied imagination. It wasn't just soldiers they wanted to engineer—it was the next phase of humanity. And someone, somewhere, was willing to kill to ensure the operation's success.

The Road to Safety

Their ex-MI6 contact, Carter, drove with the detached calm that only came from years of navigating dangerous situations. His sharp eyes scanned the highway, checking for tails. Rhett sat beside him, quietly plotting their next move.

"We need to get off the grid for a while," Rhett muttered, adjusting the map on his lap. "They're going to hunt us down like dogs if we stay visible."

Elena, seated in the back, pulled a blanket around her shoulders. The chill from the canal water still clung to her.

"You think we bought ourselves any time with that escape?" she asked, her voice tinged with exhaustion. The adrenaline from the chase had faded, leaving behind only the bone-deep fatigue of survival.

Rhett shook his head. "Not enough. They'll regroup. We need to figure out exactly what's on this drive—what they're after—and fast. Once we do, we take the fight to them."

Carter chuckled softly. "Always the optimist, Kardon. But you know as well as I do that this kind of thing doesn't end cleanly. Whatever's on that drive, you're up against people who don't just disappear when you punch them."

"Then we make them disappear," Rhett said coldly, his gaze hardening.

Decoding the Files

They found an abandoned farmhouse deep in the German countryside, far from prying eyes. It was a relic of the past—empty and crumbling but secure enough for their purposes.

Elena set up the laptop on the rickety kitchen table, her fingers rushing across the keyboard. She had learned enough from her time chasing her brother's case to know how to decrypt files and find hidden data—skills that had saved her life more than once. Now, those skills were their only hope.

"How long is this going to take?" Rhett asked, standing by the window and peering out into the night.

Elena gave him a quick smile. "Depends. If they encrypt this with basic security protocols, we'll be inside in an hour. If they layered it with Cold War-level paranoia, maybe three days."

Rhett grunted, shifting his weight. "We don't have three days."

Elena's smile faded. "Then let's hope whoever encrypted it wasn't a genius."

Enemies Close Behind

By the time the first file loaded, the pale light of dawn began creeping over the distant hills, shrouding the landscape in a cold, gray haze. The farmhouse was silent except for the faint hum of the laptop and the creak of floorboards beneath Rhett's restless pacing. He moved like a predator in a cage, his instincts screaming that danger was closer than they could see.

"Got something," Elena whispered, her voice cutting through the heavy stillness. She leaned closer to the screen, her fingers flying over the keyboard. "This isn't just research—it's a ledger. Names account... a full list of everyone involved in keeping Operation White Coat alive."

Rhett froze mid-step and moved to her side, his broad frame looming over her shoulder. His eyes scanned the screen, and his jaw tightened as he processed the information. The list was staggering in its length and damning in its content. Familiar names leaped out at him—politicians with untouchable reputations, corporate magnates who controlled the global economy, military generals who commanded armies, and intelligence officers from both sides of the Cold War divide. These were the architects, the beneficiaries of a shadowy empire hidden in plain sight that had thrived for decades.

"This isn't just an operation," Rhett said, his voice low and taut with anger. "This is an empire—a network. They've been laying the groundwork for this for generations."

Elena's fingers hovered over the keyboard as her eyes narrowed, her mind racing. "And now they're ready to bring it all back," she said darkly. "With or without Volkov."

Rhett's hands curled into fists, his knuckles white. "Then we burn it down—every piece of it. Every name on that list."

The rising sun did little to warm the cold resolve in his voice. This wasn't just about stopping Operation White Coat anymore. This was about exposing a legacy of betrayal and ensuring that no one—no matter how powerful—would be safe from the reckoning to come.

The First Betrayal

The farmhouse's front door exploded inward with a deafening crash, the force of the blast sending splinters flying across the room. Armed operatives poured in, their movements precise and practiced, weapons sweeping the space like hunting predators.

"Down! Down! Down!" Rhett roared, grabbing Elena and dragging her behind the overturned table just as a hail of gunfire erupted. Bullets tore through the wooden walls, shredding furniture and smashing through windows. Glass rained down as the air filled with the acrid smell of gunpowder.

Elena clutched the laptop to her chest, her breaths coming in short, panicked gasps. Rhett's pistol was already in his hand, and he fired a quick burst over the table's edge, forcing the operatives to scatter momentarily.

"We're pinned!" Elena shouted, her voice barely audible over the chaos.

Rhett's mind worked at lightning speed, assessing the situation. The operatives moved brutally, flanking the farmhouse, their intention clear: there would be no prisoners.

"Back door!" Rhett barked, his tone sharp and commanding. "Go—now!"

Elena didn't hesitate. She grabbed the laptop and darted toward the rear exit, crouching low as bullets tore through the air above her. Rhett covered her, his shots precise, buying her precious seconds. Stationed near the kitchen, Carter returned fire with deadly precision, dropping one operative but quickly realizing how outnumbered they were.

"They're circling!" Carter shouted, his voice strained as he emptied his clip.

"Then we make it quick," Rhett growled. He fired again, hitting a charging operative, then motioned for Carter to follow. "Move!"

Elena reached the back door and threw it open, the dense forest beyond offering their only hope of escape. Rhett and Carter followed Rhett's shots, keeping their enemies at bay as they sprinted into the underbrush.

The forest swallowed them whole, its shadows providing a momentary reprieve. But the operatives weren't far behind. Shouts echoed through the trees, and the telltale crack of branches underfoot warned Rhett that their pursuers were closing in.

"This way!" Rhett hissed, grabbing Elena's arm and steering her toward a narrow game trail. "We stick to the shadows and keep moving!"

As the sound of their pursuers grew louder, Rhett's resolve hardened. They had survived ambushes before, but this wasn't just about survival. The laptop held the keys to unraveling the conspiracy, and they couldn't let it fall into enemy hands.

He glanced at Elena, her face set with determination despite the fear in her eyes. "We're not done yet," he said, his voice firm.

"No," she replied, gripping the laptop tighter. "Not even close."

And together, they disappeared into the forest, their escape only just beginning.

Hunted in the Woods

The forest swallowed them whole, the thick undergrowth and towering trees providing some cover as they ran deeper into the wilderness. But Rhett knew their enemies wouldn't stop—they were trained killers, and they would keep coming until Rhett and Elena were dead.

"We split up," Rhett said breathlessly as they reached a small clearing. "It'll buy us time."

Elena hesitated for a moment, then nodded. "See you on the other side, Kardon."

They exchanged a glance—an unspoken promise to survive—before Elena veered off to the left, disappearing into the trees.

Rhett took the opposite direction, moving with the kind of stealth and precision only years of training could provide. He was a ghost in the forest, blending into the shadows as he doubled back toward their pursuers.

A Fight for Survival

The next few hours unraveled in a relentless storm of violence and survival. The forest, once silent and serene, transformed into a warzone. Rhett moved like a predator in the shadows; his every step was calculated, and his every breath was sharp and measured. The scent of damp earth and blood hung heavy as he stalked his prey.

Near the ravine's edge, he spotted two operatives advancing cautiously, their weapons sweeping the dense underbrush. Rhett crouched low, blending into the shadows, his heart pounding like a war drum. When they came too close, he struck with brutal precision. He lunged from his cover in a flash, his knife glinting in the dim light. The first operative didn't even have time to shout before Rhett silenced him, his movements swift and lethal. The second turned, panic flashing in his eyes, but Rhett's pistol was already raised. The gunshot cracked through the forest, and the man crumpled to the ground.

The echoes of the shot hadn't faded before Rhett was on the move again, his senses razor-sharp despite the exhaustion clawing at him. The forest seemed alive with danger—the crack of a twig, the distant shouts of pursuers, the bark of orders over radios. They were hunting him, closing in, but Rhett refused to be cornered.

Gunfire erupted somewhere behind him, and Rhett veered sharply to the left, plunging deeper into the wilderness. His boots slipped on the damp ground as he navigated treacherous terrain, his breath coming in ragged bursts. His body screamed for rest, his muscles burning with fatigue, but he forced himself onward. Stopping wasn't an option—not with the stakes this high.

Through the haze of exhaustion, the image of Elena clutching the laptop burned in his mind. The files she carried were more than just information—they were the key to bringing down a network of lies and control that had thrived for decades. If they were caught, if the laptop fell into enemy hands, it would all be over. Every sacrifice they'd made, every life lost, would mean nothing.

The forest grew darker as the sun dipped lower, the dense canopy swallowing the last traces of daylight. Rhett paused briefly, his back pressed against the rough bark of a tree, his chest heaving as he listened to the sounds of the hunt. A distant voice called out, closer than before. They were tightening the noose, and he had to keep moving.

With renewed determination, Rhett gritted his teeth and pushed forward, his exhaustion forgotten in the face of his resolve. This wasn't just survival—it was war. And he wasn't about to lose.

Reunited

As the sun dipped below the horizon, casting the forest in shades of amber and shadow, Rhett emerged from the dense underbrush, his steps heavy but determined. At the edge of a narrow river, Elena stood waiting, her silhouette framed by the fading light. Her face was streaked with dirt, her hair damp from sweat, but her eyes were sharp and unwavering, scanning the treeline until they locked onto him.

"You made it," she whispered, her voice steady but betraying a flicker of relief. She exhaled slowly as if she'd been holding her breath since they'd separated.

Rhett allowed himself a weary smile. "Told you I would." His tone was light, but the exhaustion in his voice spoke volumes. His clothes were torn and bloodied, the grime of the day's battle clinging to him like a second skin.

They didn't waste time with questions or reassurances. The sound of the river rushing past was a reprieve, but danger still loomed just beyond the shadows. Rhett knelt by the water, splashing his face and taking a quick drink, while Elena kept watch, her fingers tightening around the grip of her weapon.

"We're not out of this yet," Rhett said, rising to his feet.

Elena nodded, her jaw set with determination. "Then let's finish it."

Without another word, they moved, their silhouettes fading into the encroaching night.

The Final Stretch

With the flash drive secure and their pursuers momentarily shaken off their trail, Rhett and Elena didn't allow themselves even a moment of rest. The stakes were too high. The files they had uncovered pointed to something far worse than they had imagined—a hidden lab deep within Eastern Europe, shrouded in secrecy and fortified against anyone who might try to uncover its horrors. It was there that the final phase of Operation White Coat was already in motion.

Rhett studied the map on the laptop's cracked screen; his jaw clenched in grim resolve. "If we can reach the lab," he said, his voice low but steady, "we can stop them. For good." His words hung heavy in the air, the enormity of their mission pressing down on both.

Elena leaned over his shoulder, her eyes scanning the intricate network of coordinates and encrypted documents. "This isn't just a lab," she murmured, her voice tight with anger. "It's their heart—where it all comes together. If we take it out, the whole operation collapses."

Rhett looked up at her, his eyes burning with the same fierce determination that lit hers. "We're not just stopping an operation, Elena. We're dismantling an empire."

She nodded, gripping the table's edge so tightly her knuckles turned white. "Then let's finish this," she said, her voice sharp and resolute.

Rhett powered down the laptop and slipped the flash drive back into its hidden compartment in his pack. "We'll need to move fast," he said, mentally mapping their route. "If they catch wind of this, we won't get another chance."

Elena adjusted her gear, and her movements were efficient and precise. "They'll be expecting us, but that's their mistake," she said, her lips curling into a determined smirk. "They don't know what's coming."

Rhett couldn't help but grin, a flicker of dark humor breaking through the tension. "Let's make sure they never forget."

Together, they stepped out into the cold night, the weight of the flash drive heavier than it seemed, carrying the potential to expose the deepest secrets of a global conspiracy. Their path led into the heart of the unknown, where the fight wasn't just for survival—it was for justice, freedom, and redemption.

CHAPTER 19

Revelations

The narrow road through the Carpathian Mountains wound like a serpent, cutting through dense forests and jagged cliffs as Rhett Kardon and Elena Morales made their way toward their final destination: the hidden lab at the heart of Operation White Coat's operations. Their escape from Berlin had bought them precious time, but the enemy was still out there—watching, waiting, and ready to strike.

In the back of their stolen SUV, the flash drive lay tucked inside Rhett's Jacket pocket, a ticking time bomb of secrets. What they had uncovered so far painted a chilling picture of a conspiracy that had never ended. But the whole truth was still buried in the encrypted files they hadn't yet accessed—files that might hold the key to stopping the resurrection of the operation once and for all.

Elena sat in the passenger seat, her sharp green eyes fixed on the winding road ahead. She was quiet—too quiet. Rhett could feel the weight of unspoken thoughts hanging between them, like a storm waiting to break.

"What's on your mind?" Rhett asked, his voice low as he navigated a sharp curve.

Elena glanced at him, her expression unreadable. "What if... what if we don't stop it? What if it's already too late?"

Rhett tightened his grip on the wheel. "It's not too late." His tone left no room for doubt, though the gnawing uncertainty in his gut told a different story. "We end this. No matter what."

The Approach

T he final leg of the journey took them off the main road onto a narrow path overgrown with weeds and flanked by towering evergreens. They parked the SUV a mile from the lab, and the road ended abruptly at the edge of a steep incline. The forest stretched before them, thick and impenetrable. Rhett and Elena shouldered their gear and set out on foot, their movements cautious and deliberate.

Every rustle of leaves, every snap of a twig underfoot, felt amplified in the forest's stillness. The air was crisp, carrying the faint scent of pine and damp earth, but beneath its natural beauty lay an unmistakable tension. Rhett's instincts prickled with unease.

As they moved closer to the lab, Rhett stopped abruptly, raising a hand to signal Elena. Ahead, partially obscured by moss and brush, was a ventilation shaft—one of the lab's few vulnerabilities. It was their entry point.

"We'll go in through there," Rhett whispered, crouching low as he pointed to the grate. "Once inside, stick to the plan: get to the server room, download everything, and destroy the lab."

Elena nodded, her expression resolute as she checked her pistol. "And we make it out alive, right?" she asked, her tone light but laced with tension.

"Always," Rhett replied, managing a faint, reassuring smile. But the gravity of their mission loomed large between them, unspoken but undeniable.

They crept forward, weaving through the undergrowth with practiced stealth. Each step brought them closer to the hidden entrance, closer to the heart of a conspiracy that had already claimed so many lives. Rhett's senses were on high alert, his muscles taut with anticipation.

And then the stillness shattered.

A cold, mechanical voice echoed through the trees: "Drop your weapons. Now."

Ambushed

Rhett froze, his pulse spiking as his eyes darted toward the source of the voice. Figures emerged from the shadows—silent, faceless operatives clad in tactical gear. Their weapons were raised, laser sights cutting through the gloom.

Elena's hand hovered near her pistol, her sharp eyes flicking to Rhett for direction. He gave a subtle shake of his head, signaling her to stand down.

"Do it," the voice demanded, sharper this time. "Or we will open fire."

Rhett slowly raised his hands, his heart pounding as he met Elena's gaze. "Stay calm," he murmured, his voice barely audible.

Reluctantly, Elena complied, lowering her weapon to the forest floor. Her expression was a mix of fury and frustration, but her movements were controlled, her resolve unbroken.

The operatives moved in, and their precision was a testament to their training. One of them stepped forward, his rifle trained on Rhett's chest. "You've led us on quite the chase, Kardon," the man said, his voice cold and impersonal. "But it ends here."

Rhett's jaw tightened, his mind racing as he calculated their next move. He didn't believe in fate, but they weren't going down quietly if this was the end.

A Fight for Survival

With a single motion, Rhett seized the moment, his enhanced reflexes propelling him forward with blistering speed. He lunged at the nearest operative, his fist connecting with the man's jaw in a brutal arc. The impact sent the operative sprawling, his rifle clattering to the forest floor. Chaos ignited instantly. Elena pivoted, her pistol snapping off precise, deafening shots that cut through the night.

The forest transformed into a battlefield, the cacophony of shouts and gunfire reverberating against the dense trees. Leaves and dirt exploded into the air as bullets struck the ground, and the rustling of branches gave way to the sharp crack of breaking twigs underfoot. Rhett moved with the ferocity of a cornered animal, each strike calculated, his enhanced strength and speed giving him the edge—at least for the moment. Beside him, Elena was a blur of motion, ducking and weaving with lethal precision, every shot she fired finding its mark.

But the tide turned quickly. The operatives were fast—too fast. Rhett's heart sank as he caught the fluid synchronization in their movements, the unnaturally sharp reflexes that mirrored his own. Realization hit him like a blow: these weren't ordinary soldiers. They were products of Operation White Coat.

An operative slammed into Rhett, driving his shoulder into his ribs with enough force to knock the wind from him. Pain shot through his side, but Rhett spun with the momentum, using it to slam his attacker into a tree with bone-crunching force. He turned just in time to see Elena struggle. Outnumbered, she was driven to the ground, her pistol kicked from her hand and lost in the underbrush.

"Elena!" Rhett roared, his voice cutting through the chaos like a blade. His heart raced as he fought toward her, his movements desperate and unrelenting. Another operative closed in, his knife flashing in the moonlight. Rhett sidestepped the attack and disarmed him with a vicious twist, sending the weapon flying.

"Elena! Fall back!" Rhett bellowed, his tone commanding but laced with urgency.

Scrambling to her feet, Elena lunged for an opening, but the operatives were relentless. Their weapons were raised, their formation tightening like a noose around the pair. Rhett gritted his teeth, his mind racing for a solution, but the sheer number of their attackers left no doubt—the fight was lost for now.

As the operatives began to close in, Rhett locked eyes with Elena. "This isn't over," he growled under his breath, his gaze burning with defiance.

The war was far from finished, and they both knew it. Even as they were forced into retreat, the fire in their hearts burned brighter than ever. This was just the beginning.

Face-to-Face with the Enemy

Bound and disarmed, Rhett and Elena were yanked through the dense underbrush, their boots dragging against the muddy ground as their captors shoved them forward. The hidden entrance to the lab loomed ahead—an unassuming steel door embedded into the hillside, camouflaged by vines and dirt. With a sharp hiss, the door slid open, and the chilling hum of machinery spilled out, echoing through the forest like a warning.

Inside, the air was sharp and sterile, the atmosphere suffocating. Rows of monitors lined the walls, streaming endless rivers of data, live surveillance feeds, and cryptic diagrams that hinted at the horrors unfolding deeper within the lab. Overhead lights buzzed softly, their cold glare reflecting off gleaming floors and metallic surfaces.

At the center of the sterile chaos stood Elliot Granger—Congressman and the political architect of Operation White Coat, the man who had turned human lives into experiments. His suit was flawless, as crisp as if he'd just stepped out of a boardroom, but his posture carried the weight of a puppeteer who held all the strings. His sharp and unnervingly calm gaze locked onto Rhett with a gleam that spoke of victory.

"Welcome home, Kardon," The Congressman said smoothly, his voice laced with smug satisfaction. The words oozed through the air like poison. "You've come a long way to witness the end of your story."

Rhett straightened, his fists clenching against the zip ties biting into his wrists. His jaw tightened, his glare a mix of hatred and defiance. "You're not writing the ending, Granger."

Granger's smirk widened, a predator savoring the moment before the kill. He stepped closer, his polished shoes clicking against the floor, his gaze drifting to

Elena. "Ah, but I already have," he murmured, his voice a dangerous whisper. "You just don't know it yet."

Elena's breathing hitched, but her expression stayed fierce; her eyes locked on Granger like a dagger. Rhett shifted instinctively closer to her, his muscles coiled despite his bindings, his mind racing. Granger thought he'd won, but Rhett knew better. This wasn't the end—it was the beginning of a reckoning.

"You'll regret this," Rhett said, his voice low and unrelenting, each word a promise.

Granger chuckled softly, echoing through the sterile room like a death knell. "We'll see, Kardon. We'll see."

As the steel doors slammed shut behind them, the hum of the lab seemed to grow louder, as though the walls themselves were alive with anticipation. The trap had been sprung, but Rhett wasn't done fighting.

The Horrifying Revelation

As they were marched deeper into the heart of the facility, Rhett and Elena were surrounded by a world that should never have existed. The walls were alive with the hum of machines, cables snaking across the floor like veins feeding some monstrous entity. The air was cold, sterile, and laced with a faint chemical odor that burned their nostrils. Overhead, lights pulsed eerily, casting an unsettling glow on the horrors they began to pass.

Rows of chambers stretched endlessly on either side of the corridor—massive glass tubes filled with figures suspended in a luminous, viscous liquid. Bodies. Human replicas, their features flawless but lifeless. Each one was meticulously engineered—too perfect, too identical, as though a machine had stamped them out. Their eyes were closed, their expressions peaceful, but something about their stillness felt unnatural. Male. Female. Young. Old. Rows upon rows of them, waiting like tools in a shed for the day they would be unleashed.

Rhett's gut twisted with revulsion as its sheer scale hit him. This wasn't just a lab but a factory built to manufacture a new humanity.

"This," Granger's voice broke through the hum of machines, calm and dripping with pride, "is the future." He swept his arm toward the rows of chambers as if unveiling a masterpiece. "Perfect obedience. Perfect control. No dissent. No chaos." His eyes gleamed with a fanatical light. "Imagine a world where no one questions authority, wars cease, and everyone serves their purpose without complaint. No hunger. No rebellion. A world engineered for peace."

Rhett's fists clenched, the zip ties cutting into his skin, but he barely noticed the pain. His chest heaved with rage and disgust as he tore his gaze from the chambers to Granger's smug expression. "That's not peace," Rhett growled, his voice trembling with barely restrained fury. "That's a prison."

Granger's smirk deepened, the gleam in his eyes as cold and calculating as the room they stood in. "You can't see it now, but you will. Soon enough," he said, his voice dripping with smug certainty.

Rhett's fists clenched, every muscle in his body coiled and ready to strike, but Granger's words hit harder than any blow. "We've made some breakthroughs," Granger said, his voice cold and cutting. "All thanks to the work your father started with you. You should feel honored, Kardon. His legacy lives on—refined, enhanced, and nearly perfected."

Rhett's jaw tightened, his breath coming in sharp bursts, but Granger wasn't finished. He stepped closer, his smug smile deepening. "Oh, we're still working out a few bugs. But the ability to read minds? That's no longer a theory. It's reality. And you?" Granger leaned in, his eyes glinting with cruel amusement. "You're going to make the perfect test subject."

Rhett barely had time to register the meaning before Granger moved. In a flash, Rhett was forced to the ground, Granger's grip like iron as he grabbed a fistful of his hair and yanked his head to the side. The syringe appeared, gleaming under the harsh light—a cruel harbinger of what was to come.

"This is Operation White Coat's update," Granger grinned. "Let's see how you handle it."

The needle pierced Rhett's neck, the fluid burning like liquid fire as it surged into his veins. There was only darkness for a moment—a suffocating void stretching forever. Then it came: a tidal wave of euphoria so potent it felt like drowning in light, followed by an excruciating, skull-splitting pain that drove Rhett to his knees. He clutched his head, his vision spinning, his mind fraying at the edges.

Through the chaos, he caught sight of Elena. She was frozen. Her face was pale as if she'd seen a ghost. But her dark eyes blazed, her fury an anchor pulling him back from the abyss. She didn't flinch, didn't look away. Their eyes locked. At that moment, no words were needed.

They understood each other perfectly. They would not bow, not break. Whatever Granger had unleashed, whatever hell awaited, they would face it together. And they would end it.

This place had to burn.

They wouldn't leave until they had destroyed every trace of Granger's twisted vision, every monstrosity he had created. And if that meant tearing the entire facility apart with their bare hands, so be it.

Rhett's resolve hardened, his voice low but fierce. "You think you've won, Granger, but you're wrong."

Granger tilted his head, amused. "Oh, and why is that?"

"Because you underestimated us," Elena said coldly, her voice steady as steel.

Rhett leaned closer, his eyes locked on Granger's. "And we're going to bring this place down around you."

Granger's smile faltered ever so slightly, but the guards shoved them forward, deeper into the facility. The air felt heavier, charged with an unspoken tension. They were outnumbered, disarmed, and surrounded by the nightmare they had been trying to stop.

But Rhett and Elena weren't beaten. Not yet. Somewhere, deep inside this labyrinth of horrors, was a weakness—a crack in the machine Granger had built. And when they found it, they would strike with everything they had.

No matter the cost.

Breaking Free

Granger turned away, his steps slow and deliberate, every inch of him radiating smug confidence. "You've already lost, Kardon," he said over his shoulder, echoing through the sterile hall. "You just don't know it yet."

And that was his mistake.

Rhett's eyes flicked to the nearest guard, assessing his position and movements with deadly precision. In one explosive motion, Rhett surged forward, twisting his wrists to loop the bindings around the guard's neck. The man's startled cry was cut short as Rhett yanked him backward, using the momentum to choke him out. The guard's body hit the floor with a dull thud, his weapon clattering from his grip.

"Move!" Rhett barked at Elena, already twisting to confront the next threat.

The room erupted into chaos. Alarms blared, red warning lights bathing the walls in a pulsing glow. The other guards spun to react, but Rhett was already on them, his enhanced reflexes turning him into a blur of motion. He sidestepped a swinging baton, disarming the guard with a bone-snapping twist of his arm before driving an elbow into his throat. The man crumpled.

Elena moved like a shadow at Rhett's side, her agility and speed honed to deadly efficiency. She ducked a blow, grabbed a fallen weapon, and fired a sharp burst of rounds that dropped two more guards before they could react.

"Behind you!" Elena shouted.

Rhett spun, his instincts firing before his mind could process. A guard lunged with a knife, but Rhett caught his wrist mid-swing, twisting the blade back into the man's side. The guard gasped, his eyes wide with shock before slumping to the floor. Rhett snatched the fallen rifle, the familiar weight settling into his hands like an extension of his body.

"They'll keep coming!" Elena called; her voice edged with urgency as she shot another operative charging from the corridor.

"Then we keep moving," Rhett growled.

He grabbed a few spare magazines from the nearest fallen guard, tossing one to Elena before they bolted for the door. The air was thick with smoke and the acrid smell of gunpowder as alarms wailed louder, the facility now fully aware of their escape.

"Central server room," Rhett muttered, scanning the hallway ahead as they sprinted forward. "If we take it out, we cripple this entire operation."

"Let's make it count," Elena shot back, reloading her weapon with a sharp click.

They moved like predators through the facility's sterile corridors, every corner a new risk, every sound a potential ambush. Footsteps pounded in pursuit behind them, but Rhett and Elena were faster. The training, the desperation, the sheer will to survive propelled them forward. Rhett's enhanced reflexes guided him with surgical precision—ducking, firing, and moving as if the chaos around him were in slow motion.

A squad of operatives emerged ahead, their rifles raised. Rhett didn't hesitate. "Cover me!" he shouted to Elena.

Elena slid into cover, unleashing a barrage of suppressive fire that sent the operatives diving for cover. Rhett charged straight through the smoke, his rifle barking in rapid bursts. He dropped the first two men before they could react, closing the distance to disarm the third with a brutal strike to the jaw.

"Clear!" Rhett yelled as the last guard hit the floor. Elena joined him, breathing hard but steady, her eyes blazing with adrenaline.

Ahead, the door to the central server room loomed, reinforced steel glowing ominously in the red emergency lights.

"They'll reinforce this position any second," Elena said, her voice tense.

Rhett raised his weapon, sweat streaking down his face. "Then we finish this—now."

Together, they stormed the door, a final blaze of gunfire and fury their only path forward.

The Final Stand

T he facility was chaos. Alarms screamed through the corridors, red warning lights pulsing like a heartbeat as Rhett and Elena tore through wave after wave of guards. Gunfire rattled the walls, bullets slicing the air around them, but neither faltered. Rhett moved like a force of nature; his strikes were brutal and efficient—bone-crunching impacts and sharp bursts of gunfire that dropped enemies with deadly precision. Elena flowed like a shadow at his side, weaving through the chaos, her shots snapping off with pinpoint accuracy.

They burst through the final door to the server room, slamming it shut behind them just as another barrage of rounds peppered the steel. Inside, the servers hummed ominously, rows of blinking lights casting a faint glow across the sterile space. But something far worse filled the air.

A voice crackled over the intercom—Granger's voice, smug and victorious. "You think you've won, but you're too late. Initiating self-destruct. In five minutes, this facility and all its secrets will be ash."

The countdown began, a robotic voice filling the room. "Five minutes. Self-destruct sequence activated."

Elena ran to the nearest terminal, her fingers flying over the keyboard. "We don't have time!" she shouted, her voice edged with panic. "The data transfer will take longer than that."

"Do what you can!" Rhett barked, planting himself between her and the door. He reloaded his weapon, his movements sharp and controlled despite the rising tension. A loud clang echoed as the guards outside began pounding on the door, their shouts growing louder.

Rhett's knuckles whitened around the grip of his rifle. The seconds ticked away—each one louder, sharper, like a hammer in his ears. The door creaked, hinges straining under the pressure of the assault.

"They're coming!" Elena called, sweat dripping down her face as she fought to extract the files. "Rhett, I need another minute!"

"You've got it," he growled.

The door burst inward with a deafening crash. Guards flooded into the room, their weapons blazing. Rhett met them head-on, his rifle barking in short, controlled bursts. A guard lunged at him, but Rhett pivoted, using the butt of his weapon to drive the man into a server, sparks erupting on impact. Another enemy appeared, and Rhett tackled him, slamming him into the floor with bone-shattering force.

"Thirty seconds!" Elena screamed, her hands a blur as she willed the transfer to finish faster.

Rhett grabbed a fallen guard's pistol, dual-wielding now as he fired into the oncoming operatives. Blood and smoke filled the air, the walls trembling as the countdown blared louder. "Fifteen seconds."

"Time's up!" Elena shouted, yanking the flash drive from the terminal.

"Move!" Rhett roared, grabbing her arm and pulling her toward the exit.

The server room erupted behind them, sparks shooting from overloaded circuits as flames spread. Rhett led Elena through the smoke-choked corridor, ducking gunfire and leaping over debris as the countdown reached its final stretch.

"Three... two... one..."

They dove through the facility's outer door just as the explosion ripped through the structure, a shockwave of fire and debris blasting out behind them. Rhett tackled Elena to the ground, shielding her as fragments of steel and concrete rained down like deadly hail.

The silence followed was deafening, broken only by the crackle of flames and Rhett's ragged breathing. Slowly, he looked back to see the lab consumed by fire, Granger's empire reduced to smoldering ruins.

"You get it?" Rhett panted, his voice hoarse.

Elena held up the flash drive, her hands trembling but steady. "I got it."

Rhett pushed himself to his feet, offering Elena a hand. "Then we finish this—for good."

Together, they turned toward the horizon, the glow of the burning facility at their backs, their resolve burning even brighter. The fight wasn't over, but they'd struck a blow that would never be forgotten.

Victory at a Cost

They burst through the last door, the fiery glow of destruction chasing them like predators. The earth trembled beneath their feet as the lab erupted behind them in a violent roar, the shockwave slamming into them like a freight train. Rhett barely had time to grab Elena before the force threw them forward, their bodies hitting the ground hard. The sound was deafening—a chorus of collapsing steel, shattering glass, and the hungry roar of flames consuming everything in their path.

There was only chaos for a moment—smoke and fire twisting into the night sky, debris raining down like burning meteors. Rhett coughed, choking on the acrid smoke as he pushed himself up, his muscles aching with every movement. He blinked through the haze, his ears ringing, and turned to look back.

The lab was gone. What had been a fortress of horrors was now a blazing inferno, reduced to rubble and ash. Flames licked at the twisted remains of metal beams, and thick black smoke billowed into the sky. Everything inside—the experiments, the servers, Granger's vision—was gone.

Rhett staggered to his feet, chest heaving. His mind raced, his pulse still pounding in his ears. It was over—for now.

Beside him, Elena struggled up, brushing soot from her face, her hair wild and streaked with ash. Her breaths came fast, but her eyes blazed with an unshakable fire as she held up the flash drive, still clutched tightly in her hand. "We did it," she said, her voice hoarse but filled with raw triumph. "We got what we came for."

Rhett met her gaze, his jaw tight as he looked at the drive. The data they'd risked everything for was enough to rip apart the entire operation and expose the twisted empire Granger had spent decades building. But Rhett's gut told him the fight wasn't over. Not yet.

He turned his eyes to the raging inferno, its flames lighting the dark sky like a warning. "This was just the beginning," he said, his voice low but steady, the promise of vengeance burning behind his words.

Elena nodded, her fingers curling tighter around the drive. "Then we finish it."

The two stood together, silhouetted against the destruction they had wrought—battered, bruised, but unbroken. The flames roared on behind them, but ahead lay the next battle, the final reckoning.

And this time, Rhett swore, there would be no escape for the people who started this.

CHAPTER 20

The Next Lead

The charred ruins of the underground lab hissed and smoldered beneath the incredible night sky expanse, ghostly smoke tendrils rising to mingle with the stars. The destruction Rhett Kardon and Elena Morales had unleashed was absolute, a fiery punctuation mark in their relentless pursuit of justice. But even as the lab lay in ruins, the shadow of the conspiracy loomed large, pressing heavily on them. The puzzle was far from solved, its edges jagged and incomplete. Too many players remained in the game, their motives hidden behind deceit.

Elena perched on a jagged boulder just outside the blast radius, her body sagging with exhaustion but her spirit unbroken. She dragged the sleeve of her Jacket across her face, smearing ash and sweat into dark streaks on her skin. Her green eyes glimmered faintly in the pale moonlight as she watched Rhett. He stood a short distance away, his broad shoulders silhouetted against the flickering embers, his gaze fixed on the horizon. The quiet intensity in his posture told her his mind was already churning, mapping out their next steps.

"So, what now, Kardon?" Elena asked, breaking the heavy silence. Her voice carried a weariness that spoke to the battles they'd fought, but beneath it was the unmistakable edge of determination. "The lab's gone, but we both know this isn't over."

Rhett didn't answer immediately. His jaw tightened, his thoughts racing through the tangled web of enemies and leads they had uncovered. Destroying the lab was a blow, but it was a glancing one. Granger, Volkov, and the shadowy network backing Operation White Coat wouldn't falter—they would regroup, adapt, and strike back. Time wasn't on their side. If they hesitated, they'd lose the fleeting advantage the destruction of the lab had given them.

"We move on, Copenhagen," Rhett said finally, his voice low and steeled with resolve. He turned to meet Elena's gaze, the firelight behind him casting sharp shadows on his face. "There's one last piece of the puzzle there—something Granger's been guarding. And I'd bet my life Volkov's people are already waiting for us."

Elena exhaled sharply, the name of their subsequent battleground settling between them like a live wire. She rose to her feet, her movements deliberate as she adjusted the straps of her gear. "Copenhagen," she repeated, nodding slowly. Her expression was stern, but a flicker of anticipation lit her eyes. "Then we finish this."

Rhett's lips pressed into a thin line. "We don't stop until it's done," he said, his tone leaving no room for doubt.

The two of them stood there for a moment longer, the weight of the mission ahead palpable. Then, without another word, they turned away from the ruins, their silhouettes blending into the darkness as they set their sights on the next phase of the fight. Copenhagen was waiting. And so were the answers.

A Race to Copenhagen

Rhett and Elena moved with urgency, and their every action was calculated and precise. They didn't have the luxury of hesitation—the window of opportunity was closing fast. Their enemies would soon recover from the blow they'd dealt, and when they did, the hunters would inevitably become the hunted.

Carter, their ever-resourceful MI6 contact, had come through once again. In less than 24 hours, he secured fake passports, fresh identities, and seats on an untraceable flight from Eastern Europe to Denmark. The plan was high-risk, but they didn't have time for a safer option. Every second they delayed gave Granger and Volkov more time to lock down their operations and erase the traces of Operation White Coat.

The flight to Copenhagen was fraught with tension, the air between them thick with unspoken thoughts. Rhett sat rigidly in his seat, his gaze fixed on the window, but his mind was a storm of strategies and contingencies. Elena, seated beside him, flipped through her passport for the hundredth time, her fingers tracing the alias stamped inside. They both knew the stakes. The data they carried—the culmination of their work and the destruction of the lab—was a weapon powerful enough to expose Operation White Coat. But it was a double-edged sword that would do them no good if they didn't survive long enough to wield it.

As the plane descended over the Danish coast, the distant glow of Copenhagen's city lights reflected faintly in the glass. Elena broke the silence, her voice soft but laced with a quiet exhaustion. "You ever get tired of running?" she asked, her eyes on the horizon rather than Rhett.

Rhett turned to her, the corner of his mouth lifting in a crooked grin. Despite everything—the danger, the pressure, the weight of what lay ahead—there was a glimmer of humor in his expression. "Running's the easy part," he replied, his tone light but edged with a truth they both understood.

Elena huffed a quiet laugh, shaking her head. "Guess we'll see about that," she murmured, her focus returning to the city below. The plane dipped lower, and the soft hum of its engines filled the silence between them.

As they approached Copenhagen, the weight of their mission pressed down once more. There was no turning back. Every move from here on out would bring them closer to their goal—or their end.

The Arrival

They landed just before dawn, the icy air stinging their skin as they stepped out into Copenhagen's still, muted streets. The city was a labyrinth of narrow alleys, serene canals, and cobblestone roads, its early morning quiet broken only by the faint hum of distant activity. It was the perfect place to disappear—but also an ideal setting for an ambush.

Their destination was a safe house Carter had arranged, tucked discreetly within a narrow, unassuming building in the heart of Nyhavn. The harbor outside was beginning to stir with life—locals preparing their cafes for the day, fishermen tending to their boats bobbing rhythmically on the water. The scene was deceptively peaceful, starkly contrasting the storm of danger and secrets that followed Rhett and Elena.

Inside, the safe house was sparsely furnished but functional, with a heavy wooden table at its center. The dim lighting added to the sense of urgency as Elena began unpacking their salvaged files, spreading the documents across the table like puzzle pieces. She leaned over them, her expression tense but focused, her fingers deftly sorting through bank statements, schematics, and pages of encrypted communications.

"This is what we have," Elena murmured, her voice steady as she sifted through the information. Her green eyes flickered across the documents, pausing when her hand fell on a worn photograph. She picked it up slowly, holding it to the light.

It was an old, grainy image: Viktor Volkov and Dr. James Kardon—Rhett's father—standing side by side in front of a sterile-looking research facility. The faint smiles on their faces, coupled with the stark backdrop, sent a chill down her spine.

Rhett stood beside her, his jaw tightening as he studied the photo. His broad shoulders seemed to tense even further, his hands curling into fists at his sides. "They were working together," he said, his voice low and cold. "Longer than we thought."

Elena glanced at him, her gaze searching his face for any sign of the storm brewing beneath his calm exterior. "And Copenhagen," she said quietly, setting the photograph down deliberately, "is where it all connects."

Rhett's eyes didn't leave the table. His focus locked on the pieces in front of him. "Then we pull the thread," he said, his tone resolute. "And see how far it unravels."

The morning light began creeping through the shutters, but neither moved. The files on the table were more than evidence—they were a map to the truth, and every step forward would bring them closer to the needed answers. Or to the dangers waiting for them in the shadows.

Into the Depths of the Conspiracy

T he documents painted a clear yet unsettling picture: their destination was an abandoned research facility on the outskirts of Copenhagen. Officially, it was listed as a decommissioned Soviet outpost, a relic of the Cold War left to decay amidst overgrown weeds and crumbling walls. On paper, it was forgotten—irrelevant. But to Rhett, it was the kind of place that screamed hidden agendas and covert meetings. Its isolation and obscurity made it ideal for the clandestine dealings Volkov thrived on.

Rhett leaned over the table, his eyes scanning the highlighted coordinates scribbled in faded ink. The location was marked with cryptic notes in the files, its significance buried beneath layers of coded language. But it all pointed to one undeniable conclusion.

"If Volkov's in Copenhagen, that's where he'll be," Rhett said, his voice hard and steady. His fingers grazed the edge of the old photograph before tucking it securely into his Jacket pocket. The image of his father standing beside Volkov felt heavier now, like a phantom weight pressing against his chest. There was more to their connection than he'd imagined, and he wasn't leaving Copenhagen without answers.

Elena crossed her arms, her sharp gaze on the map spread before them. "It makes sense," she said, her tone laced with grim understanding. "The location is remote enough to avoid scrutiny but not so far that it's inaccessible. If they're meeting to regroup or finalize plans, it's the perfect spot."

Rhett straightened, rolling his shoulders to shake off the tension building in them. "Then we need to get there first," he said firmly. "If Volkov's involved, he won't be coming alone. And if Granger sent anyone to clean up after the lab..." He trailed off, the implication clear. Time wasn't just a luxury they didn't have—it was a weapon their enemies would use against them.

Elena grabbed her bag, anticipating Rhett's voice's unspoken urgency. "We'll need to stay off the grid," she said. "No public transportation, no obvious routes. If they've got eyes on us, we can't give them a trail to follow."

"Agreed," Rhett replied, his mind already piecing together a plan. He glanced at the files one last time before folding the map and slipping it into his gear. The research facility was more than just a meeting point—it was the next step in unmasking Operation White Coat. And it might hold the key to the truth about his father's involvement.

Rhett turned to Elena, his expression set with resolve. "We move now," he said, his voice leaving no room for argument. "If we're going to intercept them, we can't afford to be late."

Elena nodded, her lips pressing into a thin line. "Let's go," she said, slinging her bag over her shoulder. Together, they stepped out of the safe house, disappearing into the waking streets of Copenhagen. The path ahead was uncertain, but one thing was clear: whatever waited for them at the facility, they would face it head-on.

The Facility

The drive to the abandoned outpost was tense, the winding country roads carrying them far from the bustling city into the quiet desolation of the countryside. The further they traveled, the more the landscape seemed to close in around them. Dense woods bordered the narrow roads, their skeletal branches arching overhead like ominous sentinels. The air grew colder, the silence oppressive, broken only by the occasional rustle of leaves in the wind. Rhett gripped the wheel tightly, his senses on high alert. Every curve in the road felt like an invitation to an ambush.

"This place looks like a ghost town," Elena murmured, her voice cutting through the stillness as they approached their destination. The facility loomed ahead, its rusted gates barely visible through the creeping fog. Twisted metal and peeling paint hinted at decades of neglect, and the structure stood like a monument to forgotten secrets. "Are we sure this is it?"

"Only one way to find out," Rhett replied, his tone grim. He eased the car to a stop and reached for his weapon, the cold metal a familiar comfort in his hand. "Stay sharp. They'll be expecting us."

They slipped through a gate gap, moving like shadows across the cracked asphalt. The compound was a wasteland of decay—crumbling buildings, shattered windows, and walls streaked with grime. The air was damp and heavy with the mingling scents of mildew and rust. Every sound seemed amplified in the stillness: the crunch of gravel beneath their boots, the faint creak of a distant hinge swinging in the wind.

Elena scanned the area, her weapon raised and her eyes sharp. "Hard to believe anyone would set up shop in a place like this," she murmured, her voice barely above a whisper.

"That's the point," Rhett replied, his voice low and focused. "Nobody comes out here unless they've got something to hide."

The darkened corridors of the main building stretched before them, a labyrinth of shadows and decay. Rhett took the lead, his eyes constantly scanning for movement and his grip on his weapon steady. The hairs on the back of his neck stood on end, and every instinct screamed that they weren't alone.

"If Volkov's here, we find him," he whispered, a measured calm that belied the tension in his body. His gaze darted to Elena, her focus just as unyielding. "And we get answers."

Elena nodded, her jaw set with determination. Together, they pressed deeper into the compound, each step bringing them closer to the truth and whatever dangers lay waiting in the shadows.

An Unexpected Ally

As they moved deeper into the facility, the faint echo of footsteps broke the oppressive silence. Rhett raised his hand in a swift, silent signal for Elena to stop. They froze, straining to pinpoint the sound as it grew louder—measured, deliberate, and unhurried. Whoever it was, they weren't trying to hide.

Out of the shadows, a figure stepped into view. A woman, her presence commanding despite her unassuming attire. She looked to be in her late fifties, her dark clothing practical yet well-fitted, her demeanor calm and composed. Her sharp eyes swept over Rhett and Elena with a quiet calculation, the corners of her mouth curving into a faint, knowing smile.

"I was wondering when you'd show up," she said, her voice smooth and controlled, carrying an air of authority. "My name is Katya Volkov."

Rhett's jaw tightened, his weapon steady but his grip firming at her words. "Volkov's daughter?" he asked, the suspicion in his tone cutting through the tension.

Katya inclined her head ever so slightly, her expression unreadable. "Daughter, yes. But don't make the mistake of assuming I share his goals," she said evenly. "He's not who you think he is. None of this is."

Elena's eyes narrowed, her weapon remaining trained on Katya. "And why should we trust you?" she asked sharply, her voice low but steady.

Katya held their gaze, her smile fading as her tone turned serious. "Because I know how to stop him. And if you want any chance of shutting this down, you'll need my help."

The words hung like a challenge, and the dim corridor suddenly felt more minor. Rhett and Elena glanced at each other, a silent question passing between them: Could they risk trusting her, or would this alliance prove just as dangerous as the enemies they were hunting?

The Truth Unfolds

In a concealed room buried deep within the facility, Katya unveiled the chilling truth about the conspiracy. The sterile space was cluttered with monitors, files, and old blueprints, their contents painting a picture more horrifying than Rhett or Elena had anticipated. This wasn't just about creating enhanced soldiers for battlefield superiority. It was a sweeping, insidious agenda aimed at redefining power on a global scale.

Volkov and his backers weren't satisfied with controlling armies—they wanted dominion over governments, economies, and even entire populations. They aimed to engineer loyalty, obedience, and superiority through advanced genetic manipulation, creating a world where power was not just wielded but biologically ensured.

"This isn't just your father's legacy, Kardon," Katya said, her tone heavy with the weight of the revelation. She turned to face Rhett, her expression both grim and resolute. "It's your future. They've been shaping you—and others like you—for decades. You're not the only prototype."

Her words hit like a hammer. Rhett felt a cold knot tighten in his stomach, his mind racing to process what she said. The room seemed to close in around him, the horrifying implications settling over him like a suffocating shroud. "What do you mean, others?" he asked, his voice low and edged with disbelief.

Katya held his gaze, her eyes sharp and unyielding, as if daring him to confront the truth. "There are more like you," she said quietly. "Enhanced, conditioned, and placed where they can do the most damage—or the most good, depending on who's pulling the strings. And they're already in play."

Elena's breath caught, her expression darkening. "You're saying they're active? Operative?"

Katya nodded slowly, her lips pressing into a thin line. "Not just active—integrated. Politicians, agents, business leaders. Some don't even know what they are or have been made into. Volkov's vision goes beyond soldiers. This is about reshaping the world, one piece at a time."

Rhett's fists clenched at his sides, his pulse hammering in his ears. His father's involvement in the operation had always been a shadow hanging over him, but this—this was more than he could have imagined. And now, it wasn't just his father's actions he was questioning. It was his existence.

"We need to stop this," he said, his voice firm despite the turmoil surrounding him. "All of it."

Katya's gaze softened, though her determination didn't waver. "Then you'll need to face the truth about yourself first," she said. "Because they've planned for this moment. And if you're not ready, they'll win."

The Final Plan

Katya extended a small flash drive toward Rhett, her expression grim and resolute. "Everything you need to stop them is on this," she said, her voice steady but urgently heavy. "But you don't have much time. The summit in Zurich is two days from now. That's where they'll initiate the final phase."

Elena's brow furrowed, her green eyes narrowing with concern as she stepped closer. "And if we can't stop them?" she asked, her tone edging with defiance and dread.

Katya's gaze flickered between them, her shoulders sagging slightly as the weight of her words pressed down. "Then you won't recognize the world when they're done with it," she said quietly, the gravity in her voice cutting through the tension. "This isn't just power they're playing with—it's control on a scale no one has ever seen."

Rhett gripped the flash drive tightly, his jaw clenching as the reality of what lay ahead settled over him. "Then we don't fail," he said, his voice firm, his resolve unshakable.

A Lasting Bond

As they gathered their gear and prepared to leave, Rhett glanced at Elena. The mission had stripped away their old identities, reshaping them into something more substantial, unspoken but undeniable. They weren't just partners anymore—they were bound by a trust forged in the crucible of survival, the kind that only came from staring death in the face and refusing to blink.

"This ends in Zurich," Rhett said softly, his voice carrying both resolve and the weight of everything they'd been through.

Elena met his gaze, her lips curving into a small but determined smile. "Let's finish it," she replied, her tone fierce, her eyes alight with the fire of someone who wasn't just ready for the fight—she was prepared to win.

CHAPTER 21

Viktor Volkov

The train ride from Copenhagen to Zurich was steeped in an almost unbearable tension. Rhett Kardon, Elena Morales, and Katya Volkov sat in a dimly lit compartment, the rhythmic clatter of the train wheels the only sound filling the silence. Each of them was locked in their thoughts, their expressions shadowed by the weight of what lay ahead. Zurich wasn't just another city—it was the epicenter of everything Operation White Coat had built since the Cold War. If they failed to act, the final phase of the operation—a global rollout of genetic manipulation—would plunge the world into a new kind of tyranny, one controlled by an invisible elite.

The atmosphere in the compartment was stifling, heavy with unspoken doubts and the enormity of their mission. Rhett leaned against the window, his sharp gaze fixed on Katya Volkov. She was an enigma—a potential ally whose every word and action was tainted by her connection to her father, Viktor Volkov. For Rhett, that name was a specter haunting the mission and his own life. Katya's involvement blurred the lines between friend and foe, making trust fragile and conditional.

Rhett broke the silence. His voice cut through the tension like a blade. "So, where does your loyalty lie, Katya?" His tone was calm, but there was no mistaking the weight behind the question.

Katya didn't flinch. Her sharp blue eyes met his without hesitation, and for a moment, the two of them seemed to measure one another in the stillness. "My loyalty?" she repeated, her voice steady and deliberate. "It's to ensure my father's legacy doesn't destroy everything. I can't erase what he's done, but I can make damn sure it stops here."

Elena leaned forward, her elbows resting on her knees as she scrutinized Katya. Her expression was guarded, but her voice carried an edge of urgency. "You're sure he'll be at the summit? That Zurich is where this ends?"

Katya nodded, her jaw tightening as her expression turned grim. "Zurich is the final meeting point," she said, her words deliberate and heavy with certainty. "They've called in everyone they need—corporate CEOs, high-ranking government officials, intelligence operatives. It's the last piece of the puzzle. The full-scale launch will be unstoppable if they get the green light at that summit. If we don't stop them now, we'll lose everything."

Rhett leaned back, his eyes narrowing as he processed her words. Zurich wasn't just another mission. It was their last chance. For a brief moment, the train rocked gently beneath them, and the clatter of wheels felt like a countdown. The stakes couldn't have been higher, and failure wasn't an option.

The Arrival in Zurich

Zurich welcomed them with a biting chill and a steel-gray sky heavy with the promise of snow. With its immaculate streets and towering financial institutions, the city bustled with the quiet efficiency of a global power center. It was the perfect place to hide something monumental in plain sight. Amid the banks, multinational headquarters, and streams of hurried professionals, the clandestine summit would blend seamlessly, unnoticed by the untrained eye.

Rhett, Elena, and Katya checked into a modest hotel under carefully crafted aliases, their every move calculated to avoid drawing attention. But Rhett wasn't naive. He knew better than to believe they were invisible. Eyes could be anywhere, and their enemies were far too skilled to overlook the arrival of two rogue agents and Volkov's daughter.

Tension hung as heavy as the cold outside inside their tiny, nondescript room. The ticking clock was a constant reminder: less than twenty-four hours remained before the summit would commence, setting into motion a plan decade in the making. Time was slipping away faster than they could prepare.

Rhett stood by the window, gazing at the city's cold, efficient beauty. Elena joined him, her reflection in the glass mirroring his grim determination. The two had faced impossible odds before, but this felt different—final.

"This is it," Rhett murmured, his voice barely above a whisper as his breath fogged the glass. "One way or another, it all ends here."

Elena didn't look away from the view, her jaw tightening as her eyes tracked the distant movement of people below. "Then we make sure we're the ones who end it," she replied, her voice steady, her resolve unshaken.

Rhett nodded, the weight of their mission pressing against him like the icy wind outside. Zurich wasn't just the next step in their journey—it was the endgame.

Reconnaissance and Preparation

The atmosphere in the cramped hotel room crackled with urgency as Rhett, Elena, and Katya pieced together their plan. The summit location was as daunting as it was opulent: an ultra-luxurious private estate in the Swiss Alps, a short drive from Zurich. It was a fortress in every sense of the word, guarded by elite private military contractors, advanced surveillance drones, and state-of-the-art biometric scanners. The estate wasn't just designed to keep intruders out—it was a vault for secrets meant never to see the light of day.

Rhett's mind churned through the details, piecing together an infiltration plan like assembling a fragile, high-stakes puzzle. Every move needed to be flawless. One misstep and the entire mission would collapse. There was no room for error.

Elena crouched over a map spread across the hotel bed, her sharp eyes scanning its details as she traced potential entry points with her finger. "We'll need a distraction to get past the main gate," she said, her tone clinical and focused. "Once we're inside, it's a straight race against time. We hit the main hall, grab the intel, and get out before they know we're there."

Katya leaned back in her chair, her expression amused despite the tension. "Speed and chaos," she said with a smirk. "Good thing that runs in the family, right?" Her words carried an edge of dark humor, though her eyes betrayed a flicker of unease.

Rhett glanced up from his notes, meeting her gaze with a tight smile. "You'd better hope they do," he replied, his tone sharp but not unkind. His focus shifted back to the map, his mind already running through contingencies for when—because it was never if—things went wrong.

The minutes ticked by as they refined the plan, the weight of what lay ahead pressing down on all of them. The estate was an impenetrable fortress, but it wasn't their first impossible challenge. And this time, failure wasn't an option.

The Infiltration Begins

Nightfall came swiftly, wrapping the Swiss Alps in an icy, impenetrable darkness. The moonlight barely pierced the dense canopy of the forest surrounding the estate, its glow casting faint silver streaks on the snow-dappled ground. The air was sharp with the mingled scents of pine and frost; their lungs had a cold sting with every breath. Rhett, Elena, and Katya moved with the precision of predators, their steps muffled by the forest floor as they closed in on the compound.

The estate loomed ahead, its silhouette barely discernible through the trees. High walls crowned with razor wire marked the perimeter, and faint red lights blinked from hidden security cameras that dotted the property like watchful eyes. The faint hum of drones patrolling overhead added to the tension, their mechanical precision a constant reminder of the estate's impenetrable defenses.

They crouched behind a cluster of rocks just beyond the outer fence, their breaths fogging in the frigid air. Rhett scanned the area with binoculars, tracking guards' movements as they patrolled in pairs. Their paths were methodical and practiced. This wasn't just a show of force—it was a carefully designed defense meant to repel even the most determined intruders.

"We only get one shot at this," Rhett whispered, his voice barely audible over the faint rustle of the wind. His eyes flicked to Elena and Katya, their faces illuminated by the dim light of a tactical map spread between them. "We take out the guards, get inside, and find Volkov before anyone realizes we're here."

Elena nodded, her face grimly determined as she studied the layout. "Two guards at the west gate," she murmured, pointing to the map. "If we time it right, we can neutralize them without raising an alarm. After that, it's a straight shot to the control room."

Katya gave a slight nod, her expression calm and unreadable, though her fingers flexed nervously around the grip of her weapon. "I'll handle the security systems," she said, her voice steady. "The cameras, alarms, drones—all of it. But once we're in, you'll need to move fast. I can't keep the systems offline forever."

Rhett allowed himself a faint smirk, the faintest glimmer of humor breaking through the tension. "Just make sure we don't die in the process," Katya added, glancing at him with a raised brow.

"Fair enough," Rhett replied, his tone dry but confident.

The plan was simple on paper but fraught with risk in execution. Every move had to be precise. One mistake—a missed patrol, a delayed takedown, or a camera out of sync—and the entire compound would erupt into chaos. For a brief moment, they remained huddled in silence, listening to the forest and the faint murmur of activity from the estate. Then, Rhett motioned forward, the signal to move.

They slipped through the underbrush like shadows, the icy air clinging to them as they approached the first checkpoint. The guards at the west gate stood vigilant, their weapons slung but their postures alert. Elena darted forward with practiced grace, her silenced weapon dropping the first guard with a whisper of sound. Rhett followed, taking out the second before the man could react.

The gate was open. The path ahead was clear—for now. And the clock was already ticking.

CHAPTER 22

Inside the Belly of the Beast

They breached the defenses with precision born of necessity, slipping into the main building undetected. Every movement was calculated, and every takedown was swift and silent. The guards fell without a sound, their unconscious bodies hidden in the shadows. Rhett, Elena, and Katya moved like well-oiled machines, their steps synchronized as they navigated the estate's labyrinthine corridors.

But as they descended deeper into the compound, the air grew heavier, the walls seeming to close around them. The cold, clinical opulence of the upper levels gave way to something darker—hallways lined with steel and concrete, faintly lit by recessed, flickering lights. It wasn't just the architecture; it was the weight of the place, a palpable sense of something sinister buried at its core. Rhett could feel it pressing down on him, a foreboding that set his instincts on edge. This wasn't just a fortress but a tomb for secrets too dangerous to see the light of day.

Finally, they reached the heart of the estate. A set of heavy double doors loomed ahead, flanked by biometric scanners and a pair of unconscious guards they had dispatched moments earlier. Rhett glanced at Elena and Katya, nodding once before pushing the doors open.

The room inside was vast, its grandeur a stark contrast to the cold, utilitarian corridors they'd passed through. A long, obsidian table dominated the center, polished to a mirror finish reflecting overhead lights' dim glow. Around the table sat figures that exuded power—corporate magnates, high-ranking officials, intelligence operatives. Their faces were calm, their postures relaxed, as if they weren't conspiring to reshape the world. The weight of their collective influence was suffocating, the kind of authority that could topple nations with a signature or a whispered command.

At the head of the table stood Viktor Volkov. His presence was commanding, his posture exuding a calm authority that spoke of absolute control. His silver hair was immaculate, his tailored suit flawless, but his eyes—cold, sharp, and piercing—sent a chill through the room. He didn't flinch as Rhett burst in, weapon raised, his sharp gaze locking onto Rhett as though he had been expecting this moment all along.

"Ah, Kardon," Volkov said smoothly, his deep voice echoing through the room with a practiced ease. A faint, amused smile played on his lips. "I wondered when you'd finally catch up."

The calm voice and the subtle disdain in his words were maddening. Rhett's grip on his weapon tightened as the enormity of the confrontation crystallized. This wasn't just a man—it was the architect of everything they had been fighting against, the living embodiment of the monstrous agenda they had uncovered. And he wasn't afraid.

The silence that followed was deafening, the air crackling with the tension of what was coming.

The Confrontation with Volkov

The room seemed to hold its breath as Rhett, Elena, and Katya stood at the threshold, their weapons drawn and their resolve unshakable. Across from them, Viktor Volkov remained unperturbed, flanked by an elite security team clad in tactical gear, their guns trained and ready. The figures seated at the obsidian table watched in silence, their composed faces betraying no hint of alarm, as if they, too, understood that the balance of power lay firmly on their side.

The tension in the air was suffocating, the kind that precedes a storm no one can outrun.

"It's over, Volkov," Rhett growled, his voice cutting through the charged silence like a blade. His eyes locked onto the man orchestrating the horrors they'd uncovered. "You're not launching anything tonight."

Volkov's smile widened to a cold, razor-sharp expression of superiority and absolute confidence. "Over?" he said, his voice smooth and mocking. "You think you've won? You don't even know what game you're playing."

With a deliberate flick of his wrist, Volkov activated a control panel embedded in the table. A shimmering holographic display materialized above them, casting a ghostly blue light across the room. It showed a vast, intricate network: operatives strategically embedded in governments, corporations, and intelligence agencies, their influence radiating outward like the threads of a spider's web. Names, faces, and locations flickered across the display—proof of the machinery driving Operation White Coat's agenda.

Elena's breath hitched, her eyes scanning the hologram with growing horror. This wasn't just a conspiracy but an empire already rooted too profoundly to unravel quickly.

Volkov's voice dropped to a chilling whisper, his tone dripping triumphantly. "We've already won, Kardon. The pieces are in place. The summit is just a formality. It's too late to stop us."

Rhett's grip on his weapon tightened, his knuckles whitening as rage and frustration churned inside him. "You're wrong," he snarled. "There's always a way."

Volkov leaned forward slightly, his expression one of amusement, as if Rhett's defiance were nothing more than a futile gesture. "Ah, the indomitable spirit," he said with mock admiration. "You're more like your father than you know. He thought he could stop it, too." His words hung like taunts, a deliberate provocation designed to twist the knife.

Katya stepped forward then, her voice sharp and cutting. "Enough," she snapped, drawing Volkov's attention. "You've overplayed your hand. Do you think this display of power makes you untouchable? It makes you vulnerable."

Volkov's smile faltered for the briefest of moments, a flicker of doubt crossing his face. It was enough.

"This isn't over," Rhett said, his voice low and filled with resolve. "Not while we're still standing."

The moment stretched taut, and the room was poised on the edge of chaos. Rhett could feel the weight of the fight to come, the battle that would decide the mission and the fate of everything they had fought to protect.

A Battle of Wits and Strength

The tension snapped like a taut wire, and chaos erupted instantly. Volkov's guards sprang into action, raising their weapons, but Rhett and Elena were faster, moving as if the storm had been theirs to unleash. Gunfire rang out, ricocheting off the obsidian table and shattering the air. Rhett charged forward, his movements a blur of brutal precision, taking down the nearest guard with a strike so swift the man didn't have time to react. Elena followed close behind, her silenced weapon dispatching enemies with cold efficiency, her focus unshaken.

Positioned behind cover, near the control panel, Katya worked furiously to hack into the estate's security system. Her fingers flew across the keyboard, bypassing layers of encryption. "Automated defenses offline," she muttered, sweat beading her forehead as alarms blared. "And the exits—locked. No one's leaving until we're done."

The guards fought fiercely, but the room was a whirlwind of destruction. Rhett's enhanced reflexes turned the chaos into a deadly ballet. Each punch and strike was precise, and his body moved faster than his enemies could track. Elena darted between covers, her sharp eyes calculating every shot, ensuring none of the guards reached Katya. Blood slicked the polished floor, and the once-pristine conference room was reduced to a battleground.

Amid the pandemonium, Volkov moved with a predator's calm. He didn't flee or hide—instead, he stepped into the fray with calculated ease. Rhett turned, his senses homing in on the man who had haunted him for so long. Volkov met his gaze, and for a moment, the world seemed to narrow to just the two.

"You think you can stop this, Kardon?" Volkov said, his voice carrying over the noise like a cold wind. "You're nothing more than a failed experiment."

Rhett clenched his jaw and surged forward. Their clash was immediate and violent, a collision of raw power and skill. Volkov wasn't just a strategist or a figurehead—he was a product of the same experiments that had created Rhett, his strength and reflexes honed to deadly perfection.

They moved with lightning speed, and their strikes blurred. Rhett blocked a brutal kick aimed at his ribs, countering with a devastating elbow strike that Volkov barely avoided. Volkov retaliated, his fist crashing into Rhett's jaw with enough force to send him staggering. But Rhett recovered instantly, using the momentum to launch a spinning kick that connected with Volkov's side, sending him skidding across the room.

Each move felt deliberate as if this fight had been inevitable, written in their shared DNA. Every punch, even, was a calculated strike, their movements a deadly mirror of each other. The guards around them fell away, either unconscious or retreating, leaving the two men locked in a primal struggle at the center of the chaos.

Elena shouted something from the corner, but Rhett barely registered her voice. His world had narrowed to Volkov, representing everything he had fought against and feared about himself.

Volkov smirked, blood dripping from the corner of his mouth. "You're strong, Kardon," he said, his voice strained but still taunting. "But strength alone won't save you."

Rhett didn't reply. Instead, he lunged again, his fists a blur as he drove Volkov back. Every strike carried the weight of his determination, anger, and refusal to let Volkov's vision come to fruition.

The fight raged on, fast and brutal, as if it were more than a battle—it was a reckoning.

The Final Revelation

As the brutal fight tore through the once-pristine conference room, Volkov's true intentions began to surface, each revelation more chilling than the last. This wasn't just about creating enhanced operatives for warfare or espionage—it was far more insidious. Volkov's ambition reached beyond armies and governments. He sought to control humanity, manipulating genetic code globally to engineer a new version of mankind, reshaped to fit his vision of perfection.

"You were the first, Kardon," Volkov spat, his voice venomous and charged with conviction. Blood trickled from the corner of his mouth. His expression twisted into a grimace of pain and triumph. "But you won't be the last. This is evolution, and you can't stop it."

His words hit Rhett like a physical blow, even as their fight raged on. Rhett blocked a vicious swing from Volkov and countered it with a brutal punch connected to his opponent's ribs. But his mind churned with the implications of what Volkov had said. Evolution? Global control? It wasn't just about creating a select few enhanced operatives—it was about reshaping the very fabric of society. And Volkov was determined to be the architect of this new humanity.

Rhett's thoughts snapped to the flash drive they'd recovered. It wasn't just the blueprint for Operation White Coat but also the key to shutting it all down. During their briefing, he'd seen the encrypted files, pieces of code designed to disrupt the operation's infrastructure. The answers were within their grasp, but only if they acted fast.

Volkov lunged again, a wild fury in his movements, but Rhett anticipated it. He dodged the attack with a surge of strength and tackled Volkov to the ground. The impact sent a shockwave through Rhett's body, but he ignored the pain, using his weight to pin Volkov beneath him.

"Elena! Now!" Rhett shouted, his voice cutting through the chaos. His eyes flicked to where she stood, hunched over a terminal Volkov's guards had been using to monitor the compound.

Elena's hands moved with blistering speed, plugging the flash drive into the console and typing commands to initiate the shutdown. The holographic display in the room flickered and changed, lines of code racing across the screen as the system began to respond.

"We're in!" Elena yelled back, her voice filled with urgency. "It's working—but I need time!"

Volkov thrashed beneath Rhett, a feral growl escaping his lips. "You think you've won?" he snarled, his voice filled with venom. "You're too late! The summit was only the beginning!"

Rhett's grip tightened, his jaw clenching. "The beginning ends here," he hissed, holding Volkov down as Elena worked to dismantle the empire he had built. Time was running out, but Rhett wasn't about to let Volkov's vision of evolution become humanity's nightmare.

The Shutdown and Escape

Elena's fingers danced across the control terminal, her face illuminated by the flashing red glow of warning lights as alarms screamed through the compound. Lines of code cascaded across the screen in an almost hypnotic rhythm, each command dismantling a piece of Volkov's carefully constructed network. Communications were severed, data stores began to self-erase, and decades of covert research—the horrifying fruits of Operation White Coat—started disappearing into digital oblivion.

The sound of boots pounding against metal echoed faintly behind her. Elena knew the guards were regrouping, but she couldn't afford to look away, not even for a second. Her voice was tense but resolute as she shouted over the chaos, "I just need a few more seconds—hold them off!"

Rhett and Katya moved like a shield around her, keeping the remaining guards at bay. Rhett fought with a ferocity born of purpose, every punch and strike deliberate, his movements fluid despite the weariness seeping into his muscles. With a sidearm she'd taken from a downed guard, Katya fired with precision, her sharp eyes scanning the room for any threats that could reach Elena.

The terminal beeped as Elena typed the final sequence. A countdown appeared on the screen—ten seconds to complete the shutdown. The alarms grew louder, the red lights brighter, as the system reached critical collapse.

"We've got it!" Elena yelled triumphantly as the countdown hit zero. The terminal screen flashed one last time before going black. The alarms stopped abruptly, replaced by an eerie silence over the compound. Every server, every database, and every backup in Volkov's empire had been obliterated. The nightmare was over.

Behind her, Rhett exchanged a glance with Elena before turning his attention to Volkov. The man had regained his footing, staggering slightly but still radiating a dangerous aura. Volkov lunged at Rhett in a last-ditch effort, but Rhett sidestepped with precision, using the momentum to drive his elbow into Volkov's temple. The force of the blow sent Volkov crumpling to the ground, unconscious.

Rhett stood over him, breathing heavily, his chest heaving with the effort of the fight. The room seemed frozen in time, the weight of their victory sinking in.

But the reprieve was short-lived.

"We're not done yet," Katya said, her voice sharp as she reloaded her weapon. The sound of approaching reinforcements echoed in the corridors outside. "Volkov's guards will be on us in minutes, and this place isn't going to stay quiet for long."

Elena grabbed her gear, pulling the flash drive from the terminal and stuffing it into her pocket. "We have what we came for," she said, her voice urgent. "Now, we need to get out before they trap us here."

Rhett nodded, his gaze sweeping over the room one last time before locking on the exit. "Move!" he barked, taking point as the three exited the compound.

The fight was over, but the walls were closing in fast. Their escape had only just begun.

The Aftermath

They barely escaped, their bodies moving on pure adrenaline as the final alarm blared through the compound. The roaring flames drowned the sound of the countdown as a m. A fireball erupted behind them, engulfing the estate in an explosion that tore through the night. The shockwave sent them sprawling onto the forest floor, a wave of heat rolling over them even at a distance. The once-impenetrable fortress was reduced to rubble, a flaming monument to the destruction of Operation White Coat.

Rhett, Elena, and Katya lay on the cold ground, their chests heaving as they gulped in the icy night air. The acrid smell of smoke mixed with the earthy scent of the forest, and for a moment, the world was silent save for the crackle of distant flames and the rustle of leaves in the wind.

Elena rolled onto her back, her face streaked with soot and exhaustion, her breath visible in the freezing air. "We did it," she whispered, her voice barely audible but laced with disbelief and relief. She stared up at the stars barely visible through the dense canopy of trees as if seeing them for the first time.

Rhett pushed himself onto one elbow, his gaze fixed on the inferno in the distance. The mission was over—or at least this part of it. He gave a slight nod, his expression unreadable but his body betraying the toll of the night's events. "Yeah," he said softly, though the weight in his voice told a different story.

Katya sat up slowly, cradling her arm where a bruise was forming. Her sharp blue eyes scanned the forest for any sign of pursuit, her instincts still on high alert. "We bought the world some time," she said, her tone pragmatic but edged with weariness. "But this isn't the end."

Rhett's jaw tightened as he followed her gaze into the darkness, his mind already turning over the possibilities. There would always be more shadows, more enemies waiting in the dark. Volkov's network was vast, and while they had dismantled its core, the ripple effects would take time to unfold. Someone else could pick up where he had left off—someone just as ambitious and dangerous.

"But we stopped this," Elena said, sitting up and meeting Rhett's gaze. "We destroyed Operation White Coat. We gave people a chance."

"For now," Rhett replied, his voice low. His eyes remained on the horizon, where the glow of the fire was beginning to fade into the night. He allowed himself a moment of silence, a fleeting acknowledgment of their victory. They had torn down a monster that had been decades in the making, threatening to reshape humanity.

Katya stood, brushing the dirt from her clothes and wincing at the stiffness in her shoulder. "We need to move," she said. "Someone will come looking for what's left of this place. We can't be here when they do."

Rhett nodded, rose to his feet, and extended a hand to Elena. She took it, her grip firm despite her exhaustion. Together, the three of them began to make their way deeper into the forest, the faint light of dawn beginning to pierce through the trees.

As they walked, Rhett allowed himself a rare moment of reflection. The fight wasn't truly over—it never was. But for now, they had won. Operation White Coat was destroyed, and the nightmare it promised was averted. The world was safe, at least for a bit longer. That would have to be enough.

CHAPTER 23

A Web of Lies

The betrayal cut Rhett Kardon more deeply than any bullet or blade ever could. For years, his instincts had been his lifeline, a razor-sharp sixth sense that had guided him through firefights, ambushes, and the murky waters of international espionage. Those instincts had never failed him—until now. Seated in a dimly lit safe house, Rhett sifted through the encrypted files and documents he and Elena Morales had retrieved from their ambushed mission in Zurich. Each keystroke on the laptop revealed a vast conspiracy so insidious that even Rhett, with all his years of experience, felt a creeping sense of doubt.

The files painted a chilling portrait of Operation White Coat's resurgence. Names, coded communications, and financial transactions unraveled a global web of power and influence. CEOs, high-ranking officials, and intelligence operatives from rival nations were implicated, their cooperation revealing not just a conspiracy but a machine—one that had been engineered to outlast empires. What Rhett had assumed was an isolated threat now revealed itself as a blueprint for global domination, its roots buried deep within the world's most trusted institutions.

Rhett leaned back in his chair, rubbing his temples as exhaustion tugged at him. The safe house was quiet save for the soft hum of the laptop. The names in the files weren't abstract figures. Many were people he had crossed paths with during his career—trusted allies, mentors, even friends. And now, he was forced to confront the bitter truth: the enemy wasn't just out there. It was everywhere.

A sharp pang of guilt cut through him as he stared at a name that brought his worst fears to life. It wasn't just strangers implicated in this scheme. A trusted contact who had been a lifeline during past missions was deeply entangled in Operation White Coat's revival. Rhett clenched his fists. The ambush in Zurich wasn't just an attack—it had been a calculated move designed to eliminate him before he could peel back the layers of deception. They had planned for him and accounted for his every move. And they had almost succeeded.

But they hadn't.

As rage replaced doubt, Rhett's jaw tightened. Betrayal stung, but it also kindled a fire within him. He would turn their arrogance into their undoing. If they thought this would break him, they were wrong. This wasn't just a fight for survival anymore—it was a war to dismantle the system that had corrupted the very fabric of humanity.

Unraveling the Threads

Hours passed, the flickering light of the safe house growing dimmer as Rhett and Elena worked side by side. Places of decrypted files across the battered wooden table revealed the sprawling scope of the conspiracy. Offshore accounts funneled billions to clandestine research labs. Corporate executives disguised as philanthropists orchestrated funding drives under the guise of humanitarian aid. Politicians delivered legislation that conveniently aligned with White Coat's goals.

"This isn't just an operation," Rhett muttered, tracing his finger over a complex chart of connections. "It's an ecosystem."

Elena's eyes burned with the intensity of sleepless determination as she skimmed another decrypted report. "They're not hiding anymore," she said, her voice tight with disgust. "They've built this thing into a shadow government that spans nations and industries."

Rhett studied a particularly damning file: a joint venture between rival intelligence agencies, one he had believed dissolved decades ago. The Cold War rivalry between the U.S. and Russia, he realized, had been nothing more than a smokescreen. Operation White Coat had been a secret collaboration designed to outlast political ideologies and shift seamlessly into a new era.

"They played us," Rhett said bitterly. "Everyone—every government, every agency—we were pawns in their game."

Elena's gaze hardened as she pulled another file forward. This one detailed an experiment conducted under the guise of medical research. It outlined the development of genetic manipulation tools that could influence behavior, suppress dissent, and instill programmed loyalty.

"This isn't just control," Elena said, her voice barely above a whisper. "It's erasure. They're rewriting what it means to be human."

Rhett's hands curled into fists. The implications of what they uncovered weren't just horrifying but personal. The enemy had not only created him but had used his entire life as a stepping stone in their climb toward ultimate power.

A Shadow Cast by Granger

A mid the flood of data, one name stood out like a beacon in the dark: Elliot Granger. Seeing his name tied to the operation wasn't surprising—Rhett had suspected as much for months. But the sheer volume of evidence implicating him confirmed what Rhett had feared. Granger wasn't just involved. He was the linchpin.

Granger's connections reached into every aspect of the operation. His financial backing ensured the operation's continuity, while his charm and influence shielded it from scrutiny. Rhett couldn't shake the image of Granger standing at the helm, orchestrating everything with calculated precision.

"He's the architect," Rhett said, shoving a printout across the table toward Elena. "If we take him down, we can unravel this whole thing."

Elena studied the document, her expression grim. "He's not just the architect, Rhett. He's untouchable. If we go after him without concrete evidence, he'll bury us before we can take a step."

Rhett nodded, his jaw tight. "Then we get the evidence. All of it."

A Lead in Prague

T heir next move became clear: Granger's financial network was the key to exposing the operation. According to the files, one of his primary staging points was a secure safe house in Prague. It was a fortress, protected by layers of security and staffed with some of White Coat's most loyal operatives. But it was also a trove of information—if Rhett and Elena could infiltrate it, they could deliver the evidence to bring Granger's empire crashing down.

Elena frowned as she studied the plan. "It's a hell of a risk," she said. "If they catch us, we're done."

"We don't have a choice," Rhett replied, his voice steely. "If we wait, they'll tighten the noose. We hit them before they see us coming."

A Sudden Attack

B efore they could finalize their strategy, the distant crunch of tires on snow shattered the fragile quiet of the safe house. Rhett's instincts kicked in immediately. He motioned for Elena to stay low, his hand moving to the sidearm holstered at his hip.

The sound of approaching vehicles grew louder. Through the cracked blinds, Rhett saw black SUVs pulling into the clearing. His stomach churned. Their position had been compromised.

"We need to move," Rhett hissed, pulling Elena toward the back exit. But before they could escape, the front window exploded inward in a hail of gunfire. Glass rained down on them as bullets tore through the walls, filling the room with splinters and smoke.

"Go!" Rhett shouted, covering Elena as she darted toward the rear door. His shots fired back, forcing the attackers to take cover, but the odds were grim. These weren't just foot soldiers—they were enhanced operatives, faster and deadlier than any enemy Rhett had faced before.

Into the Forest

The two plunged into the forest, the cold night air biting at their skin as they navigated the uneven terrain. The sound of pursuit was relentless—crunching snow, sharp commands, and the occasional burst of gunfire. Rhett's mind raced as he scanned the darkness for an escape route.

"We need to split them up," Rhett said, his voice low and urgent. "They're too coordinated." Elena nodded, her breathing heavy but controlled. "How?"

"Follow me," Rhett replied, veering toward a rocky ridge. The incline was steep, the ground slick with snow and ice, but it provided the needed cover. Rhett used the terrain to his advantage, leading their pursuers into narrow chokepoints where their numbers became a liability.

As they reached the top of the ridge, Rhett turned, his weapon raised. The operatives emerged from the shadows, their movements precise and unyielding. But Rhett was ready. Using the high ground, he picked them off individually, his enhanced reflexes giving him the edge he needed.

Elena held her ground, her shots steady and controlled. Together, they fought with the desperation of people with nothing left to lose—and everything to fight for.

The Path Ahead

When the final operative fell, the forest was silent once more. Rhett and Elena stood amidst the carnage, their breaths visible in the frigid air. The snow was stained with blood, the echoes of the battle fading into the night.

"This isn't over," Elena said, her voice steady despite the exhaustion etched into her features.

Rhett nodded, his jaw set. "Not by a long shot."

Together, they turned toward the darkness, their resolve unbroken. Prague awaited, and with it, the chance to bring Operation White Coat to its knees.

CHAPTER 24

The Facility

The night was cold and still, as Rhett Kardon and Elena Morales approached the BioGenesis facility, hidden deep in the dense forests of southern Denmark. Their breaths came in quiet puffs, the chill biting at their exposed skin, but neither slowed. They moved like shadows, the crunch of their boots muffled by the snow. The facility loomed ahead, a stark, angular structure barely visible beneath the canopy of trees. This was the beating heart of Operation White Coat's twisted ambitions.

Rhett's mind raced as he scanned the perimeter. The compound wasn't just a laboratory; it was a fortress. Razor-wire fences stretched high, their coils glittering faintly in the moonlight. Automated turrets pivoted with machine-like precision, scanning the grounds for any movement. Above, drones buzzed softly, their infrared sensors sweeping the area. On the ground, guards patrolled in synchronized patterns, their movements unnervingly efficient. These weren't ordinary soldiers. Like Rhett, they were enhanced.

Elena crouched beside him, her night vision goggles casting an eerie green glow across her determined face. "This isn't just a research lab," she whispered. "It's a military-grade stronghold."

Rhett nodded grimly, his sharp eyes tracking the movement of a drone overhead. "We've faced worse," he muttered, though even he knew the odds were daunting. He pointed toward the western edge of the facility where the patrols overlapped, leaving a narrow, thirty-second gap in coverage. "That's our entry point. We take out the cameras and move fast."

Elena studied the area, her sharp mind calculating their chances. "And if we miss the window?" she asked, her tone light but her expression serious.

"We won't," Rhett replied, his voice steady. "We don't have a choice."

With that, they moved. Low to the ground and silent, they darted from tree to tree, the forest around them dark and oppressive. The faint hum of the drones overhead mingled with the rhythmic crunch of snow under their boots. Ahead, the west gate appeared—a heavy, reinforced structure flanked by two enhanced guards. A camera rotated lazily above it, its red light a menacing beacon.

Rhett raised a hand, signaling Elena to halt. From his gear, he pulled out a compact EMP device. "Disable the cameras," he murmured. "Be ready to move."

Elena nodded, her weapon poised as she took position. Her breathing slowed, and her focus narrowed to the task at hand. Rhett activated the EMP with a faint click, sending a precise pulse that darkened the camera above the gate. At that exact moment, Elena fired two silenced shots. The guards crumpled silently, their enhanced bodies hitting the snow in near-perfect unison.

"Clear," she whispered.

Rhett was already moving, dragging one of the guards into the shadows while Elena dealt with the other. They quickly disabled the guards' communications and slipped through the gate. Beyond, the compound loomed even more, its towering walls and featureless design built for secrecy.

The air inside was cold and sterile. The faint hum of machinery filled the silence, broken only by the occasional murmur of voices or the distant clatter of boots on metal floors. Rhett's enhanced vision picked up heat signatures deeper within the facility, and his senses were on high alert.

"We're in," Elena said quietly. "Now what?"

Rhett glanced at her, his jaw tight with determination. "We find Granger. And we end this."

A Maze of Secrets

The labyrinthine facility was a study in calculated precision. The corridors stretched endlessly, with reinforced doors bearing cryptic labels and warnings. The sterile walls reflected the harsh fluorescent lighting, creating an unsettling clinical atmosphere. Rhett and Elena moved efficiently, sticking to the shadows and avoiding the patrols that swept the halls.

As they ventured more deeply, the facility revealed its true purpose. The air grew colder, tinged with the metallic scent of blood and chemicals. Behind thick observation windows, they glimpsed sterile labs filled with ominous machinery. Rhett's stomach churned as he recognized some of the equipment—machines he had seen during his time in the program. Machines that had been used on him.

"This place..." Elena began, her voice barely a whisper. "It's worse than I imagined."

Rhett didn't respond. He couldn't. Every step deeper into the facility unearthed memories he had fought to bury in cold, sterile rooms, needles piercing his skin, and the detached eyes of scientists as they measured his every reaction. This wasn't just a lab. It was a factory churning out something monstrous.

They rounded a corner and entered a large chamber, and Rhett froze. Before them stood rows of cylindrical tanks filled with a greenish liquid. Suspended inside were human figures—men, women, children—all motionless, their faces eerily serene. Electrodes were attached to their temples, and scars crisscrossed their bodies.

"They're still running the experiments," Rhett muttered, his voice thick with anger.

Elena approached one of the tanks, her face pale. "This isn't just about soldiers," she whispered. "They're conditioning them. From birth."

Rhett clenched his fists, rage boiling inside him. He had known Operation White Coat was about control, but this—this was something else. These weren't test subjects. They were victims, robbed of their humanity before they even had a chance to live.

"They're creating obedience," he said, his voice cold. "This isn't just control—it's enslavement."

Elena turned to him, her eyes wide with horror. "We have to stop this."

Rhett nodded, his resolve hardening. "We will. But first, we get the proof."

The Betrayal

As they neared the central server room, Rhett's enhanced hearing picked up the sound of voices. He motioned for Elena to stop, his heart sinking as he recognized one of them.

Garrett.

Garrett stepped into view, flanked by two heavily armed guards. The sight hit Rhett like a punch to the gut, anger igniting in his chest. Garrett. A man Rhett had once trusted with his life—a brother forged in battle—now walking freely through the heart of the enemy's stronghold.

Elena froze beside him, her jaw tight, her eyes burning with betrayal. "He sold us out," she hissed, venom in every word.

Rhett's blood boiled. Without hesitation, he stepped into the open, his weapon snapping up, aimed squarely at Garrett's chest. The guards immediately lifted their rifles, ready to fire, but Garrett raised his hand, a calm command to stand down. His face was infuriatingly composed, like a man who believed he was still in control.

"You don't have to do this, Rhett," Garrett said, his voice steady, but there was something else beneath it—something Rhett couldn't place. Regret? Fear? "You don't know what you're up against."

Rhett's finger hovered on the trigger. His voice was low, sharp, and deadly. "I know enough. Enough to see you standing on the wrong side."

Garrett's expression hardened the facade cracking. "It's not that simple. You think you can fight them? You think you can win? They're bigger than you, bigger than anything you can imagine. This isn't a war you can survive."

"You made your choice," Rhett snapped, his weapon unwavering. "Now face the consequences."

The room erupted in chaos.

The guards fired first, bullets shredding through the narrow corridor, ricocheting off steel walls, and sending sparks cascading through the air. Rhett and Elena moved in perfect unison, their enhanced reflexes taking over. Rhett dropped to one knee, firing three quick rounds that punched through the first guard's armor, dropping him like a stone. Elena rolled to the side, her silenced pistol barking twice, each shot finding its mark. The second guard crumpled his rifle, clattering to the floor.

In the split second of stillness that followed, Garrett lunged.

He collided with Rhett, the force driving them both into the wall with a sickening crack. Garrett's fists flew the brutal precision of his Navy SEAL training clear in every strike. Rhett grunted as a punch connected with his ribs, pain flaring, but he pushed through it, adrenaline pumping through his veins. This was no ordinary fight—it was personal.

"You betrayed everything we fought for!" Rhett snarled, driving his elbow into Garrett's face.

Garrett staggered back, blood streaming from his nose, but he recovered quickly, his eyes wild with determination. "I'm trying to save you, damn it!" he shouted, swinging a knife that appeared in his hand. Rhett barely dodged the blade, twisting to grab Garrett's wrist and wrench it back with bone-snapping force. The knife clattered to the floor.

"You sold your soul," Rhett growled through gritted teeth.

With a roar, Rhett drove his knee into Garrett's ribs, the impact sending him crashing to the ground. Garrett coughed, blood flecking his lips, his breaths ragged as he clutched his side. The fight was over.

"You should have stayed out of this," Garrett rasped weakly, his voice barely audible.

Rhett loomed over him, his expression cold, his words like ice. "You made your choice." He turned his back, not sparing another glance at the man who had once been his brother.

"Elena," Rhett said sharply, signaling her to move. She stepped over the fallen guards, her pistol still ready, her expression unreadable.

Together, they pressed forward toward the server room, leaving Garrett's lifeless body behind, broken and defeated. The air was thick with the stench of gunpowder and betrayal, but Rhett pushed it aside. There was still a war to win, which was far from over. Granger's empire would fall.

The Data Heist

The server room was a stark contrast to the chaos outside. Rows of humming machines filled the space, their screens displaying encrypted data streams. Elena plugged a drive into the central terminal, her fingers flying across the keyboard as she initiated the download.

"This is everything," she said, her voice urgently tight. "The experiments, the funding, the network—it's all here."

Rhett stood guard, his weapon ready as his enhanced senses tracked the vibrations of approaching boots. "How long?" he asked.

"Two minutes," Elena replied, her focus unwavering.

As the download progressed, the seconds stretched into eternity. Rhett's pulse quickened as the first wave of reinforcements arrived. The ensuing firefight was brutal, but Rhett and Elena held their ground, their combined skill and determination keeping the enemy at bay.

The download was completed with a sharp beep, and Elena pulled the drive free. "Got it," she said.

"Time to go," Rhett said, already moving.

The Escape

The facility descended into chaos as Rhett and Elena triggered the charges they had planted. Explosions rocked the compound, sending plumes of fire and smoke into the night sky. The two sprinted through the collapsing structure, dodging falling debris and evading the remaining guards.

They emerged into the forest just as the final explosion tore through the facility. As they ran, the fiery glow lit up the sky, and their breaths were visible in the freezing air. Behind them, the BioGenesis lab crumbled into ash.

"We did it," Elena panted, her voice a mix of exhaustion and triumph.

Rhett didn't respond. His mind was already on the next step. The drive in his possession held the truth about Operation White Coat, but the fight wasn't over.

"We're not done yet," he said, his voice steady. "Next stop: Zurich."

Without another word, they disappeared into the shadows, leaving the burning facility behind.

CHAPTER 25

The Nightmare Continues

The BioGenesis facility's destruction was a fleeting victory, like a match struck in a storm. As Rhett Kardon and Elena Morales drove through the snow-covered countryside toward their next safe house, the magnitude of their mission hung heavily between them. The icy wind howled outside, but the silence was thick and oppressive inside the vehicle. The glowing dashboard cast a faint light on Rhett's tight grip on the steering wheel and Elena's furrowed brow as she stared out the window, lost in thought.

They carried with them the stolen data—a trove of damning evidence exposing Operation White Coat's evolution into something far more sinister: Operation Genesis. What had started as an initiative to create enhanced soldiers had become a blueprint for reshaping humanity, engineering entire societies from birth. The implications were terrifying, but the path forward was equally daunting. Zurich awaited the next battleground in a war neither of them had chosen but were now compelled to fight.

The Fallout from Betrayal

Garrett's betrayal lingered like a phantom in the car, unspoken but unavoidable. For Rhett, the wound cut deeper than he let on. Garrett had been more than a comrade; he had been a brother, someone Rhett had trusted with his life. Seeing him standing alongside their enemies, a cog in the machine they were fighting, was a betrayal Rhett hadn't been prepared for.

Elena broke the silence, her voice steady but gentle. "You know this wasn't on you, right?"

Rhett's eyes didn't leave the road. "Doesn't matter," he muttered. "I should've seen it."

"None of us did," she replied firmly, facing him. "You gave him the benefit of the doubt because that's who you are. That doesn't make you wrong—it makes him wrong."

Rhett's grip on the wheel tightened. "He made his choice," he said after a long pause. "And now we have to live with it."

Elena nodded, though her gaze softened. "We make our own choices, too, Rhett. Garrett's actions don't define ours."

Her words struck a chord, though Rhett didn't respond. The betrayal stung, but it also fueled him. If Garrett had shown him anything, it was how far their enemies would go to protect their plans. And Rhett was determined to show them how far he would go to stop them.

Uncovering Operation Genesis

The safe house on the outskirts of Hamburg was as nondescript as they came: a two-story brick building set back from the main road, its windows shuttered and its interior cold. They arrived just before dawn, exhaustion heavy on their shoulders but urgency driving them forward. Inside, the air smelled faintly of damp wood and dust, the sparse furnishings offering no comfort.

Elena wasted no time, setting up the laptop on the rickety dining table and plugging in the stolen data drive. Rhett stood behind her, arms crossed, as streams of encrypted files filled the screen. Line by line, the truth of Operation Genesis unraveled before them.

"This is worse than we thought," Elena murmured, her fingers flying across the keyboard as she decrypted file after file. Charts, diagrams, and protocols filled the screen, each more chilling than the last.

Rhett leaned closer, his jaw tightening as the full scope of Genesis became clear. "They're not just enhancing people," he said, his voice low and sharp. "They're rewriting them. Programming entire populations from birth."

Elena nodded grimly. "Obedience, aggression, suppression of critical thinking—these are traits they're engineering into the genome. If Genesis goes live, humanity's future won't just be controlled—it'll be manufactured."

Rhett began to pace, his mind racing. The data revealed that Genesis wasn't a distant threat; it was imminent. The files detailed plans for deployment at an international summit in Zurich, which is just days away. Disguised as a conference on genetic advancements, the summit would bring together the world's most powerful players, all complicit in the operation's launch.

"This summit is their launchpad," Elena said, pulling up the schematics of the venue. "Once Genesis goes live, it's over. They'll release the genetic modifications through air, water, even vaccines."

Rhett stopped pacing, his expression grim. "Then we take it down. Zurich becomes ground zero for their failure."

A Struggle with Power

As Rhett stared at the glowing screen, memories he had fought to bury clawed their way back. He saw the sterile labs of his youth, the cold gaze of scientists who had viewed him not as a child but as an experiment. He felt the pricks of needles, the cold touch of electrodes on his skin. His enhanced reflexes and strength—gifts born of those experiments—had kept him alive, but they had also marked him as a product of the very system he now sought to destroy.

The temptation whispered in his mind: What if you used what they made you to stop them? What if you became something greater?

The thought was intoxicating, but it also terrified him. He clenched his fists, trying to banish the dark allure of embracing his enhancements fully. When Elena touched his arm, her steady presence pulled him back.

"Don't let it consume you," she said quietly. "That's how they win."

Her words anchored him, grounding him in the person he had fought to remain, not a weapon but a man.

Planning the Infiltration

The hours passed in a blur as Rhett and Elena prepared for Zurich. The summit was more than a gathering—it was a fortress. Security surrounded the venue, including private military contractors, biometric locks, and cutting-edge surveillance. Every operation detail required precision; there would be no room for error.

"We'll use these credentials to get past the first checkpoint," Elena said, sliding two forged IDs across the table. "After that, it's all about staying ahead of their security."

Rhett studied the blueprints of the venue. "The control room is in the lower levels," he said, tracing a path with his finger. "Once we're in, we'll have about 40 minutes to extract the data and shut down Genesis."

"And Granger?" Elena asked, her voice tight. Rhett's gaze hardened. "He'll be there. But our priority is the data. Granger's time will come."

A Voice from the Shadows

As dawn broke, a secure line buzzed on the laptop. Katya Volkov's voice came through, sharp and commanding. "You're running out of time," she said. "The summit is your last chance to stop this."

Katya, the daughter of one of Operation Genesis's architects, had become an unlikely ally. Although her motives were her own, her knowledge of Genesis and its inner workings had proven invaluable.

"Tell us what we're walking into," Rhett demanded.

"The summit is a fortress," Katya replied. "Private military contractors, automated defenses, and the world's most powerful people protecting their investment. You'll have less than an hour to get in, secure the protocols, and shut down the activation sequence."

"And if we fail?" Elena asked.

Katya's tone darkened. "Then Genesis becomes reality, and humanity becomes their experiment."

The Calm Before the Storm

The summit day arrived quickly, and the hours leading up to it filled with quiet determination. Rhett and Elena reviewed their plan one final time, and their forged credentials were secured alongside their gear. They knew the risks: Zurich would be their most dangerous mission yet. If they succeeded, they could dismantle Genesis before it took root. If they failed, there would be no second chances.

As they prepared to leave the safe house, Rhett paused, looking at Elena. "No matter what happens," he said, "we finish this."

Elena nodded, her green eyes fierce. "We finish this."

With their resolve unshaken, they stepped into the cold dawn, the road to Zurich stretching before them.

Moving Toward Zurich

Zurich loomed like a monolith of power, its sleek architecture a façade for the darkness beneath. The summit venue, an expansive estate surrounded by high-tech security, was more fortress than a conference hall. As Rhett and Elena approached, their hearts pounded with anticipation.

The forged credentials worked as planned, granting them access past the first perimeter checkpoint. But the true challenge lay beyond: penetrating the inner sanctum, reaching the control room, and shutting down Genesis before the activation sequence could begin.

Every step felt like a gamble, every glance a potential threat. But as Rhett and Elena moved deeper into the lion's den, one thought sustained them: This was the moment that would decide everything.

The Reckoning Ahead

Zurich wasn't just another mission—it was the final battleground. The summit wasn't just a meeting but the culmination of years of planning, the launchpad for a new world order. Rhett and Elena knew the odds were against them, but they also knew the stakes. Billions of lives hung in the balance, and the future of humanity rested on their shoulders.

As they prepared to infiltrate the summit, Rhett's mind flashed with images of the people who had brought him here: his father, Garrett, and Granger. They had all played a role in shaping the war he now fought. But Rhett knew one thing with absolute certainty—he wasn't fighting for them. He was fighting for the world they had tried to destroy.

"This is it," Elena said, her voice steady as they stood at the final checkpoint.

Rhett nodded, his resolve unshakable. "Let's finish this."

And with that, they stepped into the heart of the storm, ready to face whatever awaited them.

CHAPTER 26

Mind Reading

The wind howled across the tarmac, a cold, biting force that whipped around Rhett Kardon and Elena Morales as they climbed the steps of the private jet. The engines roared, thunder echoing through the darkness, a promise of turbulence ahead. Above them, the evening sky churned with storm clouds, bruised and restless, mirroring the dread weighing heavy in Rhett's chest. Zurich awaited. Their mission—already a precarious gamble—was teetering on the brink of disaster.

Inside Rhett's mind, the stolen data seared like a brand, impossible to forget. Operation Genesis wasn't just an experiment but a blueprint for domination. Granger didn't merely want enhanced operatives. He wanted control of humanity itself. Genesis reached beyond physical perfection into the sinister realm of engineered thoughts, manufactured emotions, and the complete eradication of free will. Rhett's fists clenched, the revelation echoing like a curse: Granger didn't want an army. He wanted a species.

Elena collapsed into a seat inside the jet, her face drawn with exhaustion but her eyes still alight with determination. Rhett remained standing, his gaze fixed on the rain-streaked window as the jet rumbled down the runway. The blurred world outside reflected his inner chaos, but everything was agonizingly sharp inside his head. The abilities Granger had unlocked in him—enhanced reflexes, inhuman strength—were evolving. And the new gift, his telepathy, was tearing him apart.

At first, the whispers had been manageable—stray thoughts slipping into his mind like faint echoes. But now, they were crashing waves. He could feel them. Every fear, every agony, every buried trauma from those around him struck like a hammer, fracturing his sense of self. Thoughts that weren't his mingled with his memories, distorting them into a nightmarish blur. Sweat beaded on his temple as he pressed his fists against the armrests, his jaw tight against the rising tide of chaos.

"Rhett," Elena's voice broke through the storm in his mind. He turned toward her, her sharp green eyes filled with concern. "Are you okay?"

The words caught in his throat. He didn't need telepathy to feel her worry, her exhaustion, her silent fear that he was unraveling before her eyes. But he could feel them as though her emotions were his own.

"I'm fine," he muttered, the lie brittle on his tongue.

Elena didn't push, but her gaze lingered. They both knew fractures couldn't afford to show now. The weight of their discovery sat heavy between them: if they didn't stop Genesis in Zurich, Granger's vision would reshape the world.

The jet lifted into the sky, the engines screaming against the storm. Rhett sank into his seat, his fingers gripping the armrests as lightning split the darkness outside. Granger's plan, the countless lives sacrificed, and the unbearable noise in Rhett's head swirled together like a vortex, threatening to consume him.

"We'll stop him," Elena said, her voice soft but resolute. "Whatever it takes."

Rhett forced himself to nod, drawing strength from her unyielding resolve. But deep inside, he knew the truth: he wasn't just fighting Granger anymore. He was fighting himself—and the battle was growing harder to win.

The Flight to Zurich: A Battle Within

As the plane climbed into the inky night sky, Rhett sat rigid, his hands gripping the armrests like they were the only things tethering him to reality.

His mind was a storm of noise, every thought, every emotion from those around him crashing into him like relentless waves. Across from him, Elena watched him closely, her sharp green eyes narrowing. She could see it—something inside him was fracturing.

"Rhett," she said, her voice gentle but insistent. "You need to talk to me. This thing—your abilities—it's tearing you apart."

He clenched his fists, his knuckles white as he tried to block out the cacophony in his head. The pilot's unease about turbulence ahead. The flight attendant's fear of losing her job. Elena's growing concern for him. It was all there, layered over his thoughts, suffocating him.

"It's getting worse," Rhett admitted, his voice tight and low. "I can't control it. It's like everyone's thoughts are all in my head at once. Constant. Loud. I can't shut it off."

Elena leaned forward, her voice steady and grounding. "Listen to me. We'll figure this out, but you need to stay with me right now. If we don't stop Genesis, this won't just be your burden—it'll be the whole world's."

Her words cut through the chaos, grounding him for a moment. Rhett nodded slowly, though the pressure inside him didn't ease. He could feel the weight of his abilities crushing him, but he forced himself to meet Elena's gaze.

"I'll hold it together," he said, his voice rough but resolute. "For now."

"For the world," Elena added, her eyes fierce.

As the jet soared into the stormy night, Rhett steeled himself, the fight within him as daunting as the battle ahead.

An Unraveling Mind

Rhett closed his eyes, trying desperately to focus, to silence the cacophony inside his mind. He had hoped for even a moment of calm, but the noise only grew louder, a relentless storm he couldn't escape. Memories surged through him—fragments that didn't belong to him, shards of lives he'd unintentionally touched during their journey.

He saw Garrett's regret in those final moments, bleeding out in the Danish facility, his thoughts tangled with guilt and betrayal. He felt Elena's childhood fears, a visceral pang of abandonment that still lingered in the recesses of her mind. And then there was his father—cold, calculating, and detached, always studying Rhett like an experiment rather than seeing him as a son. His father's voice echoed, sharp and clinical: You were never meant to feel, only to function.

The memories came in waves, slamming into him with unrelenting force. Rhett's breathing grew shallow as he clutched his head, pressing his palms hard against his temples in a futile attempt to keep his mind from splintering further. What was real? What was illusion? The line between himself and others was vanishing, dissolving into chaos.

A hand on his shoulder brought him back, grounding him. He opened his eyes to find Elena crouched beside him, her gaze steady, her presence like a lifeline. "Stay with me, Rhett," she said softly, but her tone carried weight. "We need you."

He exhaled slowly, forcing himself to focus to find some fragile semblance of control. For now, he could hold it together. But he knew it wouldn't last. The walls in his mind crumbled, the boundary between his identity and the flood of others' memories thinning. And when they collapsed utterly, he didn't know what would be left of himself.

A Contact in Zurich

They touched down in Zurich just before dawn, the city cloaked in a dense mist that hung over the river like a veil. The streets were still and cold, the quiet before the storm. Rhett and Elena moved swiftly through the deserted alleys, their breaths visible in the frigid air as they approached a discreet café near the water's edge.

Inside, their contact was already waiting. Katya Volkov sat at a corner table, her sharp eyes scanning the room like a hawk. Every movement she made was deliberate, her presence a study in control. Shadows had shaped her—raised under the weight of her father's clandestine work in Russia, a mirror of Rhett's grim history. But where Rhett had resisted the darkness, Katya had wielded it like a weapon, dismantling the network from within.

"You're late," Katya said, not bothering to look up as she sipped her coffee.

"We ran into complications," Elena replied evenly, sliding into the seat across from her.

Katya's gaze flicked to Rhett, her expression unreadable. "You look like shit."

Rhett forced a faint smile. "I've had better weeks."

Katya leaned forward, her voice dropping to a conspiratorial whisper. "The summit begins in twelve hours. Granger's here, along with the biotech execs, Russian operatives, and half the shadow brokers in Europe. If you're going to stop them, it has to be now."

Rhett's jaw tightened, his mind racing through scenarios. "What's the plan?"

Katya smirked faintly, her eyes gleaming with danger. "Infiltrate the summit, identify the Genesis operatives, and neutralize them. Clean. Quiet. Simple."

"Nothing about this is simple," Rhett said, his voice low and tense.

Katya's smile sharpened. "Welcome to the game, Kardon. Play it well, or you lose everything."

The clock was ticking, and failure wasn't an option.

A Descent into Chaos

With Katya's forged credentials, Rhett and Elena infiltrated the summit, posing as security consultants for a biotech firm. The venue was a sprawling conference center, its opulence a facade for the sinister dealings within. Diplomats, scientists, and corporate executives milled about, sipping champagne and exchanging pleasantries, all under the pretense of humanitarian progress. But Rhett knew better—Genesis was the real agenda, its shadow looming over every whispered conversation.

When Rhett stepped through the doors, his telepathic abilities surged, hitting him like a tidal wave. Thoughts and emotions poured in, chaotic and unfiltered: ambition, betrayal, greed, fear. Each pressed against him, a storm of unspoken desires and hidden agendas. His grip on himself wavered as the sheer weight of the collective tension bore down on him.

Elena glanced at him, her sharp eyes narrowing as she caught the strain in his expression. "Rhett, are you okay? Can you handle this?"

He rubbed his temples, forcing himself to focus, to filter the noise. "I don't have a choice," he muttered through gritted teeth. "We need to find Granger."

Her gaze lingered on him briefly, worry flickering across her face before she nodded. They moved deeper into the maze of power players and double-dealing, Rhett's every step guided by the undercurrent of thoughts swirling around him. Granger was here, and Rhett was determined to confront him before Genesis became unstoppable.

Granger's Revelation

They moved through the crowd, their eyes scanning the sea of faces, the tension building with every step. Rhett's senses were heightened by the thoughts and emotions of the gathered elite pressing against his mind like a rising tide. Finally, near the back of the room, they spotted him: Granger. He stood in quiet conversation with a Russian operative, his demeanor calm, his expression coolly confident.

Rhett's heart pounded as he closed the distance. This was it—the confrontation he'd been waiting for. Granger wasn't just the architect of Genesis; he was the key to unraveling it.

Granger turned as Rhett approached, a slow, deliberate motion that sent a chill down Rhett's spine. He smiled—a cold, knowing smile that carried no warmth. "Rhett Kardon," he said, his tone mocking. "I wondered when you'd show up."

"This ends now, Granger," Rhett said, his voice low and edged with fury.

Granger chuckled softly, his confidence unnerving. "Oh, Rhett. Still clinging to your illusions of control? Genesis is already in motion. You're too late."

"We'll see about that," Rhett growled, stepping closer, his fists clenched.

Granger's smile widened, his voice dropping to a sinister whisper. "You don't get it, do you? Genesis isn't just about control—it's about evolution. You, of all people, should understand that."

Rhett's vision blurred as the words struck deep, stirring memories long buried. His telepathic abilities surged, pulling him into the storm of Granger's mind—into the dark, twisted core of the Genesis conspiracy.

A Battle of Wills

What followed was a battle unlike any Rhett had ever fought—a war waged not with fists but with minds.

Granger's thoughts lashed like a fortress of steel and fire, a labyrinth of lies, ambition, and cold calculation. But Rhett pushed deeper, his telepathy piercing through the carefully constructed defenses, pulling him into the darkest corners of Granger's psyche. The truth lay there, stark and chilling: Granger believed humanity was broken, a flawed species in desperate need of salvation. And Genesis was his answer.

Through Granger's eyes, Rhett saw a world remade by genetic engineering. Obedient citizens are devoid of rebellion. Soldiers bred for perfection. Leaders are stripped of free will and programmed only for loyalty. It was a world stripped of chaos—but also of humanity.

Yet beneath the arrogance, Rhett uncovered something unexpected: fear. Granger was terrified of failure, losing control, and becoming obsolete in the perfect world he sought to create. That fear was a crack in the fortress, and Rhett drove into it with all his strength.

"You're just a man, Granger," Rhett said, his voice sharp and unyielding, cutting through the mental storm. "And men like you always fall."

Granger's confidence faltered, his defenses crumbling under his insecurities.

The Final Confrontation

Rhett locked eyes with Granger, ready to rip the truth from his mind, when the alarms blared, their piercing wail cutting through the tense silence. A voice over the intercom crackled with urgency: "Security breach. All units to alert." The summit had been compromised.

Gunfire erupted, sharp and sudden, as chaos consumed the conference center. Operatives from multiple factions stormed the building, each vying for control of Genesis. Granger vanished into the fray, his inner circle shielding him as chaos unfolded.

Rhett spun toward Elena. "We move now!" he barked, his voice cutting through the cacophony. The two dove into the chaos, their movements sharp and deadly, cutting through the melee precisely. Rhett's heightened reflexes gave him the edge as he disarmed and neutralized attackers in seconds, his every strike efficient and brutal. Elena was a force of her own, her silenced pistol snapping off clean, calculated shots that dropped their enemies one by one. The conference center became a warzone, the air thick with smoke and screams. Through the storm of violence, Rhett's focus remained razor-sharp. They had come too far, risked too much, to fail now. Genesis had to be stopped—no matter the cost.

Rhett and Elena burst into the heart of the summit—a sleek, sterile control room bathed in the cold glow of monitors. A console displayed a countdown at its center: Genesis Protocol—Initiation Imminent. The room was eerily silent compared to the chaos outside, but the tension was suffocating. Rhett stepped forward, his fists clenched, knowing the weight of the decision before him.

The console held the key to everything. With a single command, he could use Genesis to enhance himself beyond anything human—becoming a force no one could challenge. He could ensure no enemy, no threat, could ever rise again. But the cost would be steep. To wield that power would mean becoming what he despised: another architect of control, a tyrant cloaked in good intentions.

Rhett's mind raced as the countdown ticked on, the temptation clawing at him. Behind him, Elena's voice broke through his storm of doubt. "Rhett," she said, her voice steady but filled with urgency, "you know what's right. Don't become what you hate."

Her words cut deep, grounding him. He turned to her, seeing the unwavering trust in her eyes. Rhett exhaled slowly, his jaw tightening as he made his choice. He wouldn't fix the world by destroying its soul.

Without hesitation, he moved to destroy Genesis—for good.

Rhett's Decision

Rhett stood before the glowing console, the countdown ticking in bold red numbers. The chaos of the summit faded into the background, replaced by a heavy, almost suffocating silence. His mind felt clear for the first time in days—no noise, no voices, no invasive thoughts—just clarity.

The choice had been made.

Taking a deep breath, Rhett placed his hands on the console, his fingers hovering over the keys. Every memory, every sacrifice, and every life lost flashed in his mind, fueling his resolve. This had to end. Genesis wasn't salvation; it was control—a tool that would strip humanity of its soul. Granger's twisted dream would die here.

Rhett's movements were deliberate, his hands steady as he input the final commands. The console beeped in protest as safeguards were bypassed. A final prompt appeared on the screen: "Confirm Erasure of Genesis Protocol." Without hesitation, Rhett pressed the key.

The monitors flickered, and the countdown froze before disappearing altogether. A soft hum filled the room as the program erased itself, its power extinguished.

"It's over," Rhett whispered, his voice barely audible, but the weight of the words hung in the air.

Behind him, Elena stepped closer, her expression a mixture of relief and exhaustion. "You did it," she said quietly, brushing his shoulder.

Rhett turned to her, a faint smile tugging at his lips. "We did it."

The world outside wasn't fixed, but it was free—and that was a fight worth winning.

CHAPTER 27

Moral Dilemma

R hett Kardon stood motionless in the control room, his hand still resting on the console where he had dismantled the Genesis protocol moments earlier. The cold hum of machinery faded into silence, and a heavy stillness filled the room. It was the kind of silence that came with the weight of irreversible decisions, the kind that pressed down like an unseen force.

The screen before him was dark now, its countdown extinguished, and the potential for unimaginable power erased. Genesis—the tool that could have made him invincible and capable of reshaping the world—was gone. Rhett had chosen destruction over control, freedom over dominion. But the enormity of his actions settled over him like a storm cloud.

He exhaled slowly, his chest tightening as doubt began to creep in. Had he done the right thing? Genesis had been a weapon, but it had also been a solution—a chance to end chaos, to create order. He had seen the future it promised, both its perfection and cost.

Rhett clenched his fists, forcing himself to stand tall. Power built on the sacrifice of humanity's soul wasn't salvation—it was oppression. And as the silence deepened, Rhett resolved to live with his choice, no matter the doubts.

Aftermath: Facing Elena

The control room had grown eerily quiet, its sterile walls bearing the weight of everything they had endured. Rhett lingered, his body tense as his mind replayed his decision. He knew destroying Genesis was the right choice, but its gravity still pressed heavily on his chest.

Elena approached him, her movements slow, cautious. She had seen the storm in his eyes during the final moments before he struck the killing blow to the program. She studied him carefully, gauging whether he had come through the other side intact.

"You, okay?" she asked, her voice soft but steady.

Rhett turned toward her, his expression unreadable. "I'm not sure," he admitted, running a hand through his dark hair. "It's gone, but... I can't shake the feeling that it's not over. That they'll find another way."

Elena's lips pressed into a thin line, her green eyes thoughtful. "Maybe they will," she said after a pause. "But we stopped them here. We stopped this. That matters, Rhett."

He exhaled deeply, the tension in his shoulders easing slightly. "It doesn't feel like enough."

"It never does," she replied, stepping closer. "But you made the right call. You didn't let the power consume you. That's more than most could say."

Her words struck a chord, resonating with the battle he'd fought within himself. The temptation to wield Genesis had been overwhelming—a seductive promise of order and control. But he had chosen differently. Not because it was easy but because it was necessary.

"Thanks," Rhett said, his voice quieter now, the gratitude in his tone evident.

Elena nodded, her expression softening. "Always."

The Temptation of Power

For a fleeting moment, as Rhett's fingers hovered over the keyboard, the allure of Genesis threatened to consume him. The power it offered wasn't just the ability to control others but the promise of control over himself. With Genesis, he could silence the chaos in his mind and refine his fractured telepathy into something precise and manageable. He could finally be free of the burden that had haunted him since his father's experiments.

The thought was intoxicating. Genesis could make him perfect. It could make him the weapon Granger had always dreamed of, but with one crucial difference—he could wield that power for good—end wars. Dismantle corruption. Build a better world.

But then Elena's voice cut through the fog of his thoughts, her earlier words echoing in his mind: "Don't become what you hate."

Rhett clenched his jaw, his hand balling into a fist. Genesis wasn't a tool for salvation but a weapon of control. No one—especially him—could be trusted to wield it without consequences. The cost would always be too high.

With a sharp breath, he made his choice. His fingers danced across the keyboard, inputting the sequence that would dismantle Genesis forever. The glow of temptation faded, replaced by the steady hum of resolve.

A Fractured Mind

The fight to destroy Genesis wasn't just external—it also raged within Rhett. His telepathic abilities, heightened by adrenaline and stress, flared uncontrollably in the moments following the protocol's destruction. Thoughts and emotions from the remaining operatives and scientists in the building flooded his mind, their whispers a cacophony that threatened to pull him under.

He stumbled, gripping the edge of the console as his knees buckled. The noise was deafening—fear, anger, betrayal, hope—all bleeding together into an unrelenting tide.

Elena was at his side instantly, her hands steadying him. "Stay with me, Rhett," she urged, her voice cutting through the chaos like a lifeline. "Focus on me. Block the rest out."

He nodded weakly, his breaths shallow as he struggled to regain control. Slowly, painfully, he pushed the noise into the background, isolating it until it was a dull roar rather than an overwhelming flood.

"I'm here," he rasped, his voice strained but steady. "I'm still here."

Elena's grip on his arm tightened briefly, her relief palpable. "Good," she said. "Because we're not done yet."

The Escape

The alarms blared as Rhett and Elena fled the control room, their footsteps echoing through the sterile halls of the summit facility. Operatives swarmed from all directions, their clipped commands and heavy boots signaling the beginning of a relentless pursuit.

"This way!" Rhett barked, leading Elena down a side corridor as bullets ricocheted off the walls behind them. The chase was on, and their window for escape was narrowing by the second.

The battle that ensued was brutal and unrelenting—a deadly dance of bullets, fists, and raw determination. Rhett's enhanced reflexes and strength gave them an edge, but their enemies were numerous and relentless. Together, he and Elena fought through the labyrinthine corridors, their partnership forged in fire.

When they finally burst into the cold Zurich night, the city stretched before them, silent and unaware of the chaos that had unfolded. They didn't stop running until the summit was a distant shadow behind them.

A New Beginning

Hours later, Rhett and Elena stood on the edge of a quiet overlook, the city lights twinkling faintly in the distance. The air was crisp, carrying the scent of rain and renewal. They were battered and bruised but alive.

Rhett glanced at Elena, her silhouette framed against the soft glow of the horizon. "Do you think it's over?" he asked, his voice low.

She didn't answer immediately, her gaze thoughtful. "No," she said finally. "But we stopped this. And we'll stop whatever comes next."

Rhett nodded, a faint smile tugging at his lips. "Together?"

Elena looked at him, her green eyes steady. "Always."

And with that, they turned toward the unknown, their steps steady as they disappeared into the night. The fight wasn't over, but Rhett felt ready to face whatever came next for the first time in a long time. Together, they would protect the fragile freedom they had fought to preserve. And for now, that was enough.

CHAPTER 28

Elena's Betrayal?

Zurich's narrow streets lay cloaked in an eerie quiet, the echoes of the earlier cataclysm hidden beneath the city's tranquil façade. Rhett Kardon and Elena Morales moved swiftly through the maze of cobblestone alleys, their senses sharp, their presence almost spectral as they slipped through the city's historic charm. The air was heavy, damp from the mist that curled along the ancient stones, and every sound—the faint rustle of leaves, the distant hum of an engine—felt amplified in the stillness.

The summit was behind them now, reduced to literal and figurative ruin. They had dismantled Operation Genesis and neutralized Elliot Granger, but the victory rang hollow in Rhett's chest. Instead of triumph, an unease gnawed at him—a lingering shadow that even the destruction of their enemies couldn't dispel. His instincts, honed by years of danger and sharpened by his telepathic abilities, buzzed with tension. The ground beneath their feet felt on the verge of giving way.

Rhett paused abruptly at the faint hum of a surveillance drone. He raised a hand, signaling Elena to stop. They pressed against the cold stone of a nearby building, its surface slick with condensation. The drone's lights swept the street ahead, casting long, shifting shadows before disappearing into the mist.

"We're clear," Elena murmured, her voice steady but low.

Rhett nodded, but the unease within him didn't waver. They moved again, sticking to the darkened alleys. Patrols would be tightening the noose around Zurich soon enough. News of the summit's destruction would ripple through the city and beyond, drawing more than just the attention of local authorities. Their window for escape was narrowing, yet Rhett's focus was elsewhere—on Elena.

Doubts Beneath the Surface

Rhett's telepathic abilities, still raw and unpredictable from the chaos of the summit, betrayed him. Fragments of Elena's emotions brushed against his consciousness as they walked. Her resolve burned like a steady flame beside him, but something else flickered at the edges—an echo of hesitation, a guarded undercurrent that didn't quite fit the situation.

He tried to suppress the whispers in his mind, to push away the doubts. She had repeatedly stood by him through impossible odds, proving her loyalty. But the seed of suspicion had been planted, and his fractured telepathy nurtured it, twisting every fleeting thought into something sinister.

"Elena," Rhett said quietly, his voice cutting through the night like a blade.

She glanced at him, her green eyes narrowing slightly. "What?"

Rhett hesitated, the tension in his chest tightening further. "Do you feel it?" he asked finally. "Something's... off."

Elena's brow furrowed, her expression sharpening into focus. "Off? You mean besides the fact that we just brought down the most dangerous conspiracy in history, and now half the city's on high alert?"

He forced a smile, but it was brittle. "Yeah, besides that."

Elena stopped and turned to face him fully, her silhouette outlined by the soft glow of a distant streetlamp. Shadows danced across her face, making her look both fierce and weary. "What's going on, Rhett?" she asked, her tone steady but edged with concern. "Talk to me."

Rhett looked into her eyes, searching for answers even as his telepathy tugged at the edges of her thoughts. He felt the frustration she kept hidden, the weight of exhaustion pulling at her—but there was something deeper, something he couldn't name. It wasn't fear, not exactly, but it felt adjacent. It was enough to keep his unease simmering.

"It's probably nothing," he said finally, his voice flat.

Her gaze didn't waver. "You don't believe that."

Rhett hesitated again. His frustration wasn't just with her—with himself, with the chaos in his mind that turned even moments of respite into battlegrounds. "The telepathy," he admitted at last. "It's making me doubt things, even when I know I shouldn't."

Elena's expression softened, and she stepped closer, lowering her voice. "I get it," she said. "I can't imagine what it's like to carry that. But you're still you, Rhett. And I'm still on your side."

Her simple but firm words cut through the haze clouding his mind. For a moment, the whispers quieted. Rhett nodded, his tension easing slightly as they resumed their path through the shadowed alleys. Zurich stretched out ahead of them, cloaked in uncertainty. The fight against Genesis was over, but the road forward felt no less perilous.

The Safe House

The safe house was barely more than a forgotten room tucked into a derelict building on the city's outskirts. Its walls were bare except for cracks that spidered through the plaster, and the dim glow of a single bulb cast the room in stark shadows. Rhett sat near the small, chipped table, his gaze fixed on Elena as she secured the door.

The silence between them was heavy, the weight of unspoken doubts pressing down like the air before a storm. Rhett watched her movements—the way her hands moved over the locks, the faint tremor in her fingers as she finished the task. Elena Morales was usually unshakable, and her every action was precise and deliberate. But tonight, something was different.

"You've been quiet," Rhett said, his voice cutting through the silence like a razor.

Elena turned slowly, her green eyes locking onto his briefly before darting away. "Just tired," she said, her tone too controlled to be convincing. "It's been a long night."

Rhett leaned back in his chair, his gaze unflinching. "What's really going on?"

Her posture stiffened, her jaw tightening. She crossed her arms, her fingers brushing instinctively against the holster at her hip. "What are you trying to say?"

Rhett didn't flinch, his focus unwavering. "I'm saying you're not acting like yourself."

The room felt suddenly smaller, the tension between them filling the air like an electric charge. Elena's expression hardened, her eyes narrowing. "I don't know what you think is going on, but I've been here with you through all of this. You know that."

"I do," Rhett said. "But I also know when something's changed."

Elena's lips pressed into a thin line, and for a moment, Rhett thought she might lash out. Instead, she turned away, pacing to the room's far corner. Her shoulders rose and fell with each breath, but her silence spoke louder than any words.

"Talk to me, Elena," Rhett said, his voice softer now but no less firm. "If there's something you need to tell me, now's the time."

When she turned to face him, her expression was conflicted. The fierce determination he had always admired was still there, but it was joined by something raw—regret, guilt, and a flicker of vulnerability she rarely allowed to show.

"I've made mistakes, Rhett," she said quietly, her voice thick with emotion. "And I don't know if they're the kind you can forgive."

A Confession

The words hit Rhett like a physical blow, his chest tightening as the air between them grew heavier. He stood slowly, his movements deliberate as he took a step closer. "What kind of mistakes?" he asked, his tone low but edged with a warning.

Elena hesitated, her gaze dropping for a moment before meeting his again. "Before we met, I was involved with people connected to Genesis," she admitted, each word spoken as though it cost her something. "They had leverage on me—things I couldn't ignore."

"What kind of leverage?" Rhett pressed, his mind racing.

"My family," she said. "They threatened my sister and her daughter. Told me if I didn't cooperate, they'd…" She trailed off, her voice cracking slightly.

Rhett's anger flared, his fists clenching. "So, you worked with them? Fed them information?"

"Not on you," Elena said quickly, her tone urgent. "Never on you. I did what I had to do to keep my family safe, but I never betrayed you, Rhett. That's why I stayed. That's why I fought."

Her words hung in the air, heavy with emotion. Rhett's instincts screamed at him to be cautious, but his telepathy picked up no hint of deception—only guilt, pain, and a desperate hope for understanding.

He exhaled slowly, running a hand through his hair. "You should've told me."

"I know," Elena said, her voice barely above a whisper. "But I didn't know if I could."

Rhett studied her, the silence between them thick with unspoken emotions. Trust was fragile, a delicate thread frayed by her confession. But it wasn't broken—not yet.

"We have a lot to figure out," Rhett said finally. "But right now, we don't have time for anything else. We have to keep moving."

Elena nodded; her green eyes steady despite the turmoil within them. "Together?"

"Together," Rhett said, though the word carried more weight than he expected.

As they turned toward the window, the first hints of dawn began to break across the Zurich skyline. The fight against Genesis was over, but the battle for trust—for a path forward—had just started. Together, they stepped into the uncertain light, ready to face whatever came next.

CHAPTER 29

Return to Washington

The flight back to Washington, D.C., was supposed to mark the end of one chapter and the beginning of a well-deserved reprieve. Rhett Kardon had imagined a moment to breathe, to assess the battle scars left behind by the dismantling of Operation Genesis. Instead, the high-altitude solitude of the jet only amplified the unease gnawing at him. The launch had been stopped, but the conspirators behind Genesis were still out there, lurking in the shadows, refining their plans, and waiting for the perfect moment to strike back.

Rhett's thoughts were a tangled web of questions as the jet sliced through the quiet night sky. The CIA—his former sanctuary—was now a potential battlefield. His father's haunting legacy, Granger's political ambitions, and a network of betrayals hung like storm clouds over his return. He had burned bridges and toppled schemes, but the consequences of those actions remained unresolved, dangling like a blade above his head.

The most troubling truth was simple: he no longer knew whom to trust.

A Fraught Homecoming

The private jet touched down on the icy tarmac of a secluded airfield just outside Washington, D.C. Frost coated the runway like a thin veil, and the early morning sun struggled to pierce the heavy blanket of gray clouds. Rhett Kardon descended the jet's steps first, his sharp blue eyes scanning the landscape. His coat did little to ward off the bite of the frigid air, but it wasn't the cold that unsettled him.

The city loomed on the horizon, a sprawling collection of monuments and powerhouses symbolizing resilience and treachery. To outsiders, Washington, D.C., represented authority and democracy; to Rhett, it was a chessboard where every piece was shrouded in shadow, and each move threatened catastrophe.

He paused for a moment, taking in the distant skyline. Memories of the past months surged unbidden: the experiments that had given him abilities he never wanted, the betrayal by Granger that had nearly broken him, and the fallout of Genesis—an experiment in human control that he had destroyed, but not before it had irrevocably changed him.

Behind him, Elena Morales stepped off the plane. Her movements were as measured and purposeful as always. She adjusted her scarf against the wind, her green eyes scanning the surroundings with unspoken precision. The tension between them was palpable, a thread stretched taut but not yet severed. They had survived the fires of Genesis together, but the scars ran deep, and their trust was fragile at best.

Their breath curled visibly in the morning air as they walked toward a waiting black sedan. The vehicle idled near the edge of the runway, its exhaust trailing faintly into the frozen air. Every step felt heavier than it should have, as though the ground beneath them carried the weight of their subsequent decisions.

As they reached the car, Rhett hesitated, turning to Elena. "If we go back," he said, his voice low and steady, "there's no guarantee we'll come out clean."

Elena tilted her head slightly, a faint smirk playing on her lips. "I wasn't expecting clean," she replied, her tone carrying its usual sharpness. "Just survival."

Rhett allowed himself the faintest smile. "Fair enough."

Without further comment, they climbed into the car. The interior was warm, and the steady hum of the engine offered a deceptive sense of calm. Rhett settled into his seat and gazed out the window as the car pulled away from the airfield. Each mile brought them closer to the city, where power played out in whispers, and the consequences of failure were written in invisible ink.

The Washington Monument jutted into the pale sky like an austere sentinel, while the Capitol dome gleamed faintly through the weak sunlight. Yet for all its grandeur, the city seemed eerily silent, as though it were holding its breath in anticipation of their arrival.

Elena remained quiet beside him, her hands resting loosely in her lap. She glanced at him once, her expression unreadable, then returned to the road ahead. Rhett's mind churned with possibilities, each more dire than the last. Washington was a place of secrets and shifting alliances, where victories were never clean, and defeats always left scars.

"This feels too easy," Rhett muttered, breaking the silence.

"It won't stay that way," Elena replied, her tone calm but firm. "It never does."

Rhett nodded, her words grounding him. She was correct; the quiet was a prelude. In Washington, the storms came not in thunderclaps but in whispers, and survival meant being ready to strike before the storm hit. Rhett's resolve hardened as the car sped more profoundly into the city. Whatever lay ahead, they would face it head-on. The fight wasn't over—not yet.

The CIA's Warning

Langley was their first destination. The sprawling CIA headquarters loomed ahead, a fortress of glass and steel that stood as a monument to power and secrecy. The sedan rolled to a stop at the secure gates, and Rhett felt the knot in his stomach tighten. Langley had been his professional home for years, where purpose and duty had aligned. Now, it felt like enemy territory.

Elena remained silent as they were escorted inside, her sharp gaze taking in every detail of the sterile corridors. The polished floors reflected the cold fluorescence of overhead lights, and the muted hum of activity reverberated faintly through the walls. Rhett's instincts prickled as he observed the glances exchanged by passing agents, the subtle tension in their movements. Something was off.

They were led into a windowless briefing room, where Deputy Director Andrews waited. A sharp-eyed bureaucrat with an air of calculated authority, Andrews epitomized the kind of man who thrived in the murky waters of intelligence work. His tailored suit and steely demeanor spoke of precision, control, and the confidence of someone who always had a contingency plan.

"Kardon," Andrews said, his voice clipped. "You've put us in quite a predicament."

Rhett leaned back in his chair, his posture relaxed but his body coiled, ready for whatever came next. "I'm not here to talk politics, Andrews. I'm here for answers."

Andrews gave him a thin smile devoid of warmth. "Answers," he echoed, his tone laced with sarcasm. "You've caused quite the mess with this Genesis business. There are powerful people who aren't pleased, Kardon. They wanted you to stop asking questions. Instead, you burned the whole thing to the ground."

Rhett's jaw tightened. "If you know something, say it," he demanded, his tone sharp.

Andrews' smile faded, replaced by a calculating look. "You're playing a dangerous game, Kardon. The people behind Genesis aren't just operatives—they're power brokers. They don't forgive, and they don't forget."

The warning landed heavily. Rhett exchanged a glance with Elena, whose posture remained steady but tense. Andrews' words weren't just an observation but a veiled threat. Langley wasn't just a repository of secrets; it was a battlefield, and Rhett was deep in enemy territory.

"Then it's a good thing I'm not looking for their forgiveness," Rhett replied, his voice low but resolute.

Andrews studied him for a long moment before leaning back in his chair. "You have allies in this building," he said, his tone softer but no less pointed. "But you also have enemies. Watch your back."

As they left Langley, Rhett's mind churned with possibilities. The conversation with Andrews had confirmed his worst fears: the conspiracy behind Genesis ran more profound than he'd imagined, and the people involved were still pulling strings.

Elena broke the silence as they walked toward the car. "That went about as well as expected."

Rhett smirked bitterly. "We're on our own. Just the way they like it."

The Surveillance Trap

Back in Georgetown, Rhett's unease intensified. The safe house was secure, tucked into a quiet neighborhood corner, but Rhett's instincts told him they were being watched. As he bolted the door behind them, his telepathic abilities flickered at the edges of his consciousness. Thoughts—scattered, faint—whispered like static in his mind.

"They've got us under surveillance," Rhett muttered, moving to the window and carefully peering out. The street was quiet, but he could feel unseen eyes tracking their every move. He stepped back and turned to Elena. "The question is, who's watching—and why?"

Elena shrugged out of her coat and hung it on a chair. "Welcome back to Washington," she said with dry humor. "It's like old times."

Rhett chuckled darkly, though the sound lacked humor. He moved to the table and opened his laptop, pulling up surveillance detection programs. Red blips appeared on the screen, marking the presence of drones and operatives around the building.

"They're waiting for something," Rhett said, his tone grim.

"Or trying to make us sweat," Elena replied.

"They picked the wrong targets." Rhett's voice was steel as he leaned back, his resolve hardening. If their enemies wanted a fight, they'd get one.

Mackenzie's Intel

Desperate for information, Rhett contacted Mackenzie Price, a rogue analyst with a reputation for slipping through the cracks. When her reply came—a single line instructing him to meet her at midnight—Rhett felt a flicker of hope.

Mackenzie delivered devastating intel at the abandoned C&O Canal: Granger wasn't just regrouping but building something worse. Dubbed Apex, the new Operation promised total domination, a successor to Genesis that aimed not to control humanity but to reshape it entirely.

"Granger's not done with you yet," Mackenzie warned. "If anything, you're his top priority now."

Rhett pocketed the drive, his resolve hardening. The fight wasn't over—not by a long shot.

Into the Lion's Den

Back at the safe house, Rhett and Elena pored over Mackenzie's intel. Granger's network was vast, his ambitions unchecked. If they didn't act now, Apex would become unstoppable.

"We take it down piece by piece," Rhett said, his voice steady. "Every ally, every resource. We dismantle it until there's nothing left."

Elena nodded, her green eyes sharp with determination. "Then let's get to work."

The fight against Granger wasn't just about stopping an operation—it was a battle for humanity's future. As dawn broke over Washington, Rhett and Elena prepared for the war ahead, their resolve unshakable. Together, they would face the shadows—and this time, they wouldn't stop until the game was over.

Chapter 30

Elliot Granger's Vision

The sun hovered low over the Washington skyline as Rhett Kardon stood at the edge of an empty park. The political power games of Washington, D.C., felt distant, like a silent machine humming beneath the city's surface, ever-present but unseen. However, the enemy he was about to face was far from invisible. Elliot Granger, a powerful California congressman, was the puppet master pulling the strings—working behind the scenes to rebuild Genesis and reshape the world in his image.

Rhett knew this would be the most brutal fight of his life. Granger wasn't just another corrupt politician; he had a vision—one dangerous enough to change the course of history.

A Meeting in the Shadows

Rhett adjusted his coat as the crisp autumn air wrapped around him, carrying the scent of fallen leaves and the promise of an approaching storm. The park was eerily quiet, its empty benches and dim streetlights casting long, haunting shadows. He wasn't alone. Somewhere among the trees, his contact waited—Katya Volkov, a former Russian intelligence operative turned informant. Their alliance was uneasy, but their goals aligned for now: dismantling Granger's empire.

Katya emerged from the shadows like a phantom, her footsteps silent, her movements deliberate. Her piercing gaze swept the park, cold and calculating. She stopped a few paces from Rhett, her presence as sharp as the chill in the air.

"Granger isn't just a politician," she began, her voice low and edged with warning. "He's built an empire inside your government. He's untouchable. If you want to take him down, you must be ready for war."

Rhett's fists clenched, his jaw tightening. "I've fought worse," he said evenly. "I just need to know where to hit him."

Katya reached into her coat and handed him a flash drive, her eyes never leaving his. "Everything you need is on here. But if you move too soon, you'll tip your hand. Granger has eyes everywhere—your agency, your government. The moment he senses you coming, he'll bury you."

Rhett took the flash drive, his grip firm. He met her gaze with unwavering determination. "Then we make sure he doesn't see us coming."

Katya smirked faintly, nodding once before slipping back into the shadows. Rhett pocketed the drive, his resolve hardening. The fight was coming, and he'd be ready.

Granger's Secret Agenda

That night, Rhett and Elena sat hunched over the files Katya had provided, their faces lit by the cold glow of the laptop screen. The documents laid bare a vision more chilling than I had anticipated. Granger's ambitions weren't confined to enhanced soldiers or corporate domination—Genesis was a plan for societal control on a global scale.

Granger extended to intelligence agencies, multinational corporations, and even foreign governments. His network was vast, his influence insidious. Genesis wasn't just about creating operatives with enhanced abilities—it was about engineering obedience. In Granger's future, rebellion would be extinguished before it even sparked, and free will would become an illusion for all but a select few who held the reins of power.

Rhett stared at the screen, his jaw tight, his stomach twisting in anger. This wasn't just a political coup—it was a meticulously crafted blueprint for tyranny. And the most insidious part? The people Granger had manipulated believed they were building a better, safer world.

Elena placed a steady hand on his shoulder, her voice breaking the heavy silence. "We can stop this, Rhett. We know his plan. Now it's up to us to act."

Rhett nodded slowly, his resolve hardening despite the crushing weight of what lay ahead. This wasn't just about taking down Granger or dismantling Genesis—it was about defending freedom. He exhaled, his voice low but firm. "Then we don't waste any time."

Inside the Belly of the Beast

R hett knew brute force wouldn't be enough to take Granger down. They had to expose him to dismantle his empire and tear apart his network from within. The first step was infiltrating one of Washington's most exclusive political events: a private fundraiser hosted by Granger himself.

With forged invitations, Rhett and Elena slipped into the grand ballroom disguised as security consultants. The opulence was suffocating—crystal chandeliers hung overhead, while tables adorned with fine linens surrounded a gleaming dance floor. The room buzzed with quiet tension, filled with politicians, lobbyists, and intelligence operatives—all cogs in Granger's vast, carefully constructed machine.

Rhett could feel the charged atmosphere, the air thick with ambition and quiet fear. His telepathy hummed beneath the surface, offering him fragmented glimpses of whispered conversations: deals being struck, alliances cemented, betrayals unfolding in real-time.

"He's here," Elena whispered, her tone clipped but calm. She nodded toward the far side of the room.

Rhett followed her gaze. Elliot Granger stood at the center of a cluster of admirers, exuding quiet confidence. His suit was immaculate, his movements deliberate, and his smile practiced and easy—an untouchable man who held the room in his grip.

Rhett's jaw tightened. The sight of Granger's smug composure fueled his determination. "Let's make sure that changes," he muttered, calculating his next move. This was their moment to strike—and Rhett wouldn't waste it.

Granger's Vision Revealed

They moved through the glittering crowd like shadows, focusing on one man. Granger. Rhett and Elena trailed him carefully, always close enough to listen but never drawing attention. The opulent ballroom buzzed with muted conversations and the clink of champagne glasses, a theater of power and deception. To everyone else, Granger was the star of the evening—a charismatic visionary speaking of national security and prosperity.

But Rhett's telepathy told a far darker story.

As Granger shook hands and delivered polished remarks, his thoughts bled unfiltered and raw into Rhett's mind. "The world is broken," the inner voice seethed, resonating with cold certainty. And I'll be the one to fix it. Order must be absolute. People must be controlled."

Rhett's jaw tightened, his fists clenching at his sides. Granger's words were calculated, his demeanor magnetic, but his mind was a storm of ambition and tyranny. He didn't see himself as a dictator—he saw himself as a savior—a zealot in a tailored suit.

Elena, ever observant, touched Rhett's arm lightly, pulling him back from the edge of his rising anger. "We have to act now," she whispered, her voice barely audible over the hum of the crowd. "Before he slips away again."

Rhett nodded, his eyes never leaving Granger. "This ends tonight," he murmured, his voice low and resolute.

Granger moved to another cluster of admirers, his easy smile masking the monstrous ambition that only Rhett could hear. The moment to strike was coming, and Rhett would make sure Granger's reign of shadows would fall.

The Confrontation

As the glittering event wound down, the echoes of polite laughter and clinking glasses faded into the distance. Rhett and Elena moved with purpose, slipping through the maze of opulence until they found him. Granger stood in a secluded hallway, his back turned, reviewing something on his phone. The glow cast long shadows on the walls.

"You've gone too far, Granger," Rhett said, his voice cutting through the silence like a blade. It was cold, steady, and filled with the weight of everything he had uncovered. "This ends now."

Granger turned slowly, his expression calm, his eyes calculating. A faint, practiced smile tugged at his lips, designed to unnerve. "Ah, Kardon," he said smoothly. "Still clinging to the idea that you can stop this? You don't see it, do you? This isn't something you can dismantle. It's already in motion."

Rhett took a deliberate step forward, his gaze locked on Granger like a predator sizing up its prey. "Then I'll tear it apart piece by piece," he growled. "Starting with you."

Granger didn't flinch. Instead, his smile widened, radiating a quiet arrogance that made Rhett's fists clench. "You can try, Kardon," he said, his tone soft but venomous. "But the world I'm building doesn't need people like you. It needs those who understand that control is the only path to peace."

Rhett's chest tightened, his fury burning beneath the surface. Granger's words weren't just an ambition but a declaration of war. "Peace without freedom isn't peace," Rhett said, his voice low, deadly. "It's slavery."

The hallway felt like a battlefield for a moment, and the tension between them was thick enough to cut. Both men knew this was only the beginning.

The Fight for Control

Before Rhett could respond, the air shifted. Shadows peeled away from the corners of the hallway as Granger's guards emerged, weapons raised and eyes cold.

"Kill them," Granger ordered, his voice calm, his smile untouched by the chaos he had just unleashed.

The hallway erupted into a storm of violence. Rhett and Elena moved instantly, their instincts and training taking over. Rhett lunged forward, his enhanced reflexes giving him a split-second advantage. A guard swung a baton, but Rhett ducked low, driving his fist into the man's ribs with a force that sent him crashing into the wall.

Elena moved like a shadow beside him, her silenced pistol snapping off deadly shots. Each movement was precise and calculated. Together, they fought as one—two halves of a seamless, lethal whole. Rhett disarmed another guard, spinning his rifle around and using it to block a strike before driving the butt into the man's jaw. Elena dropped an operative with a single headshot, her focus unyielding.

But Granger's guards weren't ordinary operatives. They were elite—highly trained and ruthless. One guard swept low, catching Rhett off guard, but his telepathic abilities flared to life. He felt the intent behind the move a second before it happened, shifting his weight to counter the attack. He spun, using the momentum to drive his elbow into the man's temple.

The strain of the fight mounted the flood of thoughts from his enemies pressing against Rhett's mind like a crashing wave. Every flicker of intent, every strategy formed in their heads, surged into his consciousness, allowing him to anticipate their moves—but at a cost. His vision blurred, and his breaths grew ragged.

"Elena!" Rhett called out, his voice sharp as he spun to cover her flank. She nodded, her expression fierce, and they pressed forward.

The fight was brutal, the hallway littered with the fallen, but Granger had slipped away into the chaos. Rhett's fists clenched as he realized the battle wasn't over.

Granger's Escape

In the chaos of the fight, Granger disappeared into the shadows. Rhett's jaw tightened, a growl of frustration escaping his lips. The faint sound of retreating footsteps echoed through the hallway, a taunting reminder of how close they were to losing him.

"He's headed for the garage," Elena said, her voice steady but urgent as she reloaded her pistol quickly. "We can't let him leave."

Rhett nodded sharply, wiping blood from the corner of his mouth. "Then we don't stop moving."

They sprinted through the building, weaving through the labyrinth of corridors. Alarms blared, the red glow of emergency lights casting distorted shadows on the walls. More guards poured into their path, guns blazing. Rhett dove into cover, firing back with deadly accuracy. His telepathy flared, giving him split-second insights into their movements. He rolled out, taking two guards down with clean shots.

"Move!" he barked, pushing forward.

Elena was at his side, her silenced pistol barking as she picked off enemies with cold precision. A guard lunged at her from a side door, but she spun, striking him in the throat with the butt of her weapon before finishing him with a shot to the chest. "Rhett, keep going! We're almost there!"

The corridors blurred together in a whirlwind of gunfire, shouts, and the sharp tang of smoke. Rhett's muscles burned, but his focus was unrelenting. He couldn't let Granger escape. Not now.

Bursting into the parking garage, they spotted Granger slipping into a sleek black SUV. "There!" Elena shouted. Rhett didn't hesitate. With adrenaline surging through his veins, he charged forward, raising his weapon. Granger's men scrambled to cover him, but Rhett and Elena were faster, their combined fury a force of nature. This wasn't just a chase anymore—it was the final stand.

The Final Confrontation

They burst into the underground parking garage, their footsteps echoing off the cold concrete. The space was dimly lit, with shadows stretching across rows of expensive vehicles. Granger stood beside a sleek black car flanked by two remaining guards at the far end. Despite the chaos above, his expression was calm and composed, as if he had already won.

Granger turned slowly, his hands clasped behind his back, his voice steady and filled with quiet certainty. "You're wasting your time, Kardon. Even if you kill me, the vision will live on. Genesis isn't a man—it's an inevitability."

Rhett's grip on his weapon tightened, his breathing heavy but controlled. "Not if I burn it all down," he growled, his voice low and lethal.

The guards moved to draw their weapons, but Rhett was faster. A single shot echoed through the garage, dropping one of them instantly. The second guard lunged, but Elena's pistol barked twice in quick succession, and he crumpled to the ground.

Granger remained unmoved, his composure unshaken. "You're fighting evolution, Kardon. A better world—one without chaos, without rebellion—is within reach. You could be part of it."

"I've seen your better world," Rhett said, taking a step forward, his gun trained on Granger's chest. "It's a prison."

Granger smirked, raising his chin defiantly. "Then take your shot. But you'll only delay the inevitable."

The tension hung heavy in the air, the hum of the idling car the only sound. Rhett's finger hovered over the trigger, his mind racing. Killing Granger wouldn't stop Genesis, but letting him escape would seal their fate.

"Rhett, now!" Elena shouted, her voice cutting through his hesitation.

With a sharp exhale, Rhett fired, shattering the windshield of Granger's escape vehicle. The congressman dove for cover, and the fight reignited in a storm of bullets and fury.

A Decision that Defines Everything

For a moment, the world seemed to hold its breath. Rhett stood there, his weapon raised, his finger hovering over the trigger. The cold air of the underground parking garage pressed against him, heavy with the weight of his decision. This was it—the moment he could end it all. One pull of the trigger and Granger would be gone. No more schemes, no more Genesis.

But as Rhett stared into the calm, composed eyes of Elliot Granger, he knew the truth. Killing him wouldn't stop the network he had built. It wouldn't erase the vision Granger had etched into the minds of his allies. It would only make him a martyr, his twisted dream gaining strength from his death.

The tension in Rhett's chest burned as he lowered his weapon, his gaze never wavering. "You'll answer for what you've done, Granger," he said, his voice steady, low. "But not like this."

Granger's calm facade flickered, his lips curling into a faint smirk. "You've changed, Kardon. Maybe you're more like me than you realize."

Rhett shook his head, his jaw tightening as his eyes locked onto Granger's. "I'm nothing like you," he said, his voice resolute. "You take freedom and call it control. I'll destroy everything you've built—and I won't need to become a monster to do it."

Granger's smirk faded, replaced by cold calculation as the sound of approaching footsteps echoed through the garage. Rhett stepped back, his focus unbroken. This wasn't over. It was just beginning.

The Arrest

The sharp wail of approaching sirens shattered the stillness of the night, echoing through the underground garage as red and blue lights reflected off concrete walls. Rhett and Elena stood in the shadows, their breaths visible in the cool air as law enforcement vehicles swarmed the scene. Officers moved with precision, their tactical formations a testament to Katya's intel reaching the right hands.

Granger's sleek black car, once a symbol of his untouchable power, was intercepted by an armored police vehicle, its path abruptly blocked. Doors slammed open, and armed agents surrounded the car, weapons drawn.

"Step out of the car with your hands up!" an officer barked, his voice amplified and commanding.

Rhett and Elena watched intently as the car door opened slowly. Granger emerged, his hands raised in surrender, but his face betrayed no fear. Even now, his expression was composed, his gaze sharp and calculating. He allowed himself to be cuffed, his cold demeanor unshaken.

"It's over, Granger," one of the lead agents said, securing him. "You're done."

Granger's lips curled into the faintest smile—a quiet defiance that sent a chill through Rhett. The man had lost the battle, but his expression carried the ominous weight of someone who believed the war was far from over.

Elena's voice broke the silence. "Do you think this will stick?"

Rhett didn't answer immediately, his eyes following as Granger was led toward a waiting vehicle. His once-pristine suit was now rumpled, stained by the residue of his failed escape. It should have been a triumph, but Rhett felt no relief.

"It's a start," he said, his tone measured. "But men like Granger don't fall easily. He's built too much, buried too deep. This is just the beginning."

As the flashing lights receded into the night, the weight of their victory settled over them, tempered by the knowledge of what lay ahead. Granger's arrest was a crack in his empire, but Rhett knew it wouldn't be enough to shatter it completely.

"There's always another Granger," Rhett said, his voice edged with weary resolve. "Another threat. Another battle."

Elena nodded, her gaze distant, reflecting on his words. "So, what now?"

"For now, we breathe," Rhett replied, turning to her with a faint smile. "We've taken the first step."

Elena's lips curved into a small smile, the tension in her shoulders easing. "It's more than a step. We showed them they're not untouchable. That they can fall."

Rhett looked toward the emptying garage, his mind already racing ahead. She was right—they had struck a blow, but the war would only escalate. Granger's arrest would send shockwaves through his network, forcing its remnants to scatter, regroup, or retaliate. It was a victory, but the most brutal fights were still to come.

As the night settled into a quiet calm, Rhett allowed himself a rare moment of solace. The weight on his shoulders remained, but it felt lighter for the first time in a long while. Turning to Elena, he said, "You did good tonight."

She smirked, her confidence returning. "So did you, Kardon. Looks like we make a decent team."

Rhett's smile widened, though his thoughts lingered on the battles ahead. "Yeah," he said softly. "We do."

Together, they walked toward the exit, leaving the chaos behind. Shadows still loomed ahead, but for the first time, Rhett felt hope. They had pushed back against the darkness and were ready to do it again.

CHAPTER 31

Granger's Vision

The tension in the air was suffocating. Rhett Kardon stood by the window of a safe house in the heart of Washington, D.C., watching the early morning light creep over the skyline. Granger was finally behind bars, but Rhett knew better than to believe it was over. Men like Granger didn't fall without leaving behind contingencies.

The government, intelligence community, and shadow power networks were still intact. And Rhett sensed that Granger's downfall was only the first crack in an intricate machine designed to outlast any individual.

The question was: How deep did Granger's influence run?

The Aftermath of the Arrest

Rhett leaned against the cold window frame, staring at the quiet city below. The distant hum of traffic and the faint glow of streetlights offered a stark contrast to the chaos of the night before. The weight of recent events pressed down on him, heavier than ever. They had taken Granger into custody, but the battle was far from over.

A specialized intelligence task force had been mobilized within hours, storming offices, seizing records, and detaining personnel tied to Operation Genesis. It was a calculated strike aimed at crippling the network Granger had built. But Rhett knew the real danger wasn't in the documents or the people they arrested—it was in the ideas Granger had seeded. Genesis wasn't just an organization but a belief system, a blueprint for control. And unless they uprooted it entirely, the seeds would grow back, more potent and more insidious.

Behind him, Elena sat at a cluttered table, her fingers flying over the keyboard as she sifted through encrypted files they'd recovered. The screen glowed with an endless maze of data—names, locations, covert operations—all evidence of how deeply Genesis had infiltrated the world.

"It's like pulling at a spider's web," Elena muttered, pausing to rub her tired eyes. "Every time we find one strand, five more show up. Corporations, government agencies—they're all tangled in this."

Rhett's fists tightened at his sides, his jaw clenching. "We're not just dismantling an organization," he said quietly, his voice heavy with resolve. "We're cutting out a cancer that's been spreading for years."

Elena glanced up, her eyes meeting his. "And if we don't?" she asked softly.

Rhett didn't hesitate. "Then we fight harder." His gaze hardened as he turned back to the window, the battle ahead looming larger than ever. This wasn't the end—it was only the beginning.

Granger's Leverage

The sharp knock on the door reverberated through the tense air of the safe house. Rhett's instincts took over immediately, his hand gripping his sidearm as he nodded for Elena to check it. She moved cautiously, her steps silent and precise. With her pistol at her side, she cracked the door open just enough to see who was there.

"It's Mackenzie," Elena said, relaxing slightly but not completely lowering her guard.

Mackenzie Price, the rogue hacker who had been their lifeline for critical intel, slipped into the room, her laptop tucked under one arm and her posture tensioned. This immediately set Rhett on edge. Her dark hoodie was damp from the night air, and her expression was grim—grimmer than usual, which said something.

"We've got a problem," she announced, bypassing pleasantries as she strode to the table and flipped open her laptop. The screen flared to life, casting an eerie glow across her face.

Rhett joined her at the table, his jaw tightening. "What kind of problem?"

Mackenzie tapped a few keys with practiced precision, pulling up an encrypted message that scrolled with lines of code and fragmented instructions. "Granger's people were ready for this. He didn't just build an empire—he built a failsafe. If he were ever arrested, contingencies would activate automatically."

Elena leaned over Mackenzie's shoulder, her green eyes scanning the screen. "What kind of contingencies?" she asked, her voice sharp.

Mackenzie sat back slightly, rubbing her temple as if the weight of the revelation had followed her into the room. "Data fail safes. Hidden across multiple servers, spread around the globe. They contain everything—his research, the experiments, the infrastructure for Genesis's next phase. If we don't disable them, it'll all be unleashed."

Rhett's stomach knotted as he processed the implications. Granger hadn't just accounted for the possibility of failure; he had weaponized it. "How bad are we talking?" he asked, though he already knew the answer wouldn't be good.

"Bad enough," Mackenzie replied, her tone as flat as the look she gave him. "The files I've decrypted suggest the data isn't just a backup—it's a blueprint for escalation. New locations, new targets, new recruits. And some of it looks like it's already live."

Elena let out a sharp curse under her breath, stepping back and running a hand through her hair. "Of course, he planned this. He's always two steps ahead. He knew we'd come after him."

Mackenzie nodded grimly. "It's worse than that. He didn't just know—it was part of his strategy. Even in custody, he's still pulling strings. If these servers activate fully, everything we've fought to stop will come back tenfold."

Rhett's eyes narrowed, his mind racing. "Where are these servers?" he demanded.

Mackenzie tilted her head, her fingers flying across the keyboard as she brought up a map. Dots appeared on the screen, each marking a different global location. "That's the fun part," she said grimly. "They're scattered across four continents. Hidden in places you'd never expect—private research labs, abandoned facilities, offshore data centers. Granger was paranoid about redundancy. Even if we destroy one, the others can still operate."

"And some of them are still active?" Rhett asked, his voice cold and steady.

"Very active," Mackenzie confirmed, zooming in on one of the marked locations. "This one, for instance—outside Singapore. It's an old pharmaceutical facility, repurposed for data storage. That's where the most sensitive Genesis files are being routed. But it's not alone. There's another in the Arctic Circle, buried in a bunker under the ice. And another in a private compound in Brazil."

Elena shook her head, incredulous. "He's turned the whole world into his playground. How the hell are we supposed to shut all this down?"

"We don't," Rhett said, calm but resolute. "Not all at once. We prioritize the most dangerous sites and take them out systematically."

Mackenzie's fingers hovered over the keyboard. "It won't be easy," she warned. "Granger's network didn't just hide these servers—layers of encryption, physical security, and, in some cases, private armies protect them. This isn't just a clean-up job. This is war."

Rhett folded his arms, his mind already working through the logistics. "Then we treat it like a war. We hit them hard, one by one, and we don't stop until there's nothing left."

Elena met his gaze, her green eyes fierce. "If we're going to do this, we need resources. We can't take on this kind of operation alone."

"I'll get you what you need," Mackenzie interjected, her tone firm. "But it won't be quick. I can pinpoint the vulnerabilities in their systems, but you'll need to handle the boots-on-the-ground part. And you're going to need allies."

Rhett nodded, his determination unwavering. "Then we find them. Whatever it takes."

The room fell into a tense silence, the enormity of the task before them settling over the trio like a weight. But beneath the tension was a flicker of hope—a shared understanding that they had come too far to turn back now.

"This is what Granger didn't plan for," Rhett said, his voice steady. "He thinks he's untouchable, that his web is too big to unravel. But he didn't count on us."

Mackenzie smirked, her expression revealing the faintest hint of approval. "Then let's prove him wrong."

The Race Against Time

The ticking clock loomed over them like a countdown to disaster. Each second carried the weight of lives, choices, and the fragile hope of undoing Granger's empire. Rhett paced the room, his sharp gaze fixed on the satellite maps glowing on Mackenzie's laptop. The stakes were clear: if they didn't act fast, Granger's failsafe would activate, releasing sensitive data, experimental research, and tactical plans to loyal operatives. It would undo everything they had fought to dismantle.

"We have three primary targets," Rhett said, pointing to the glowing markers on the map. His tone was steady, but the tension in his voice was unmistakable. "Shut these down, and we sever the network before it regroups. But Granger's people won't hesitate to defend them."

He gestured to the first marker. "Zurich. A covert research lab disguised as a biotech firm. It's housing critical Genesis data—if it falls into the wrong hands, they could launch the next phase."

Elena leaned over the table, her green eyes scanning the map. "I'll handle Zurich," she said firmly. "I know the city. I can get in and out without drawing attention."

Rhett nodded, moving to the second marker. "The South Pacific. An offshore server is hidden on a heavily guarded island. It holds the operational blueprints for Genesis."

"You're taking that one alone?" Elena asked, her brow arching.

Rhett smirked grimly. "It's what I do best. Smaller footprint, less chance of detection."

Mackenzie, her fingers flying across the keyboard, chimed in. "That leaves Hong Kong," she said, zooming in on the third marker. "A luxury estate doubling as a communications hub. Encrypted messages are coordinating Granger's allies. If we don't cut those lines, they'll regroup faster than we can move."

"I need you to dismantle it remotely," Rhett said, turning to Mackenzie. "Take out their comms and give us a chance."

Mackenzie snorted, confidence lacing her tone. "Hack a billion-dollar network protected by elite security? No problem. But I'll need time—and if they trace me, things will get messy."

"We'll buy you that time," Rhett said resolutely. "This is our chance. If we pull it off, Granger's failsafe goes dark. If we fail..."

Elena's voice cut in, sharp and unwavering. "We won't."

For the next hour, they finalized plans, reviewed schematics, and prepared gear. The room buzzed with tension and determination. As they geared up, Elena glanced at Rhett. "You sure about the South Pacific alone?"

Rhett met her gaze, calm and resolute. "I've got it. Focus on Zurich. Mackenzie, keep the comms open."

Mackenzie grinned. "Don't worry about me. Just make sure you come back."

Rhett smirked faintly. "That's the idea."

The gravity of what lay ahead settled over them as they prepared to part ways. Each mission carried enormous risk; the odds stacked high. But they had already defied the impossible once—and they weren't stopping now.

"See you on the other side," Elena said, her voice steady with quiet resolve.

Rhett nodded. "On the other side."

Zurich: Elena's Mission

The cobblestone streets of Zurich shimmered under a drizzle, and the chill of the night bit through Elena Morales' coat as she approached the imposing research facility. Disguised in a lab coat and armed with forged credentials, she blended seamlessly into the crowd of employees entering the building. Her heart raced beneath her composed exterior, and every step was a calculated risk in a mission fraught with danger.

Inside, the facility was a maze of gleaming corridors, sterile workstations, and the faint hum of state-of-the-art equipment. Security was formidable—guards patrolled in pairs, surveillance cameras monitored every corner, and biometric scanners restricted access to the deeper levels. But Elena's training kicked in. She adopted the air of a distracted lab assistant, moving with purpose and confidence as she navigated past checkpoints.

Reaching the lower levels, the atmosphere shifted. The air was colder, and the faint antiseptic scent mingled with the mechanical hum of high-tech equipment. She passed glass-enclosed labs where scientists worked in intense concentration, oblivious to her presence. Finally, she arrived at her target: a secure server room containing the genetic data and blueprints at the heart of Genesis.

Two guards stood outside, their stances rigid. Elena calculated her options, knowing her cover wouldn't hold if they questioned her. Spotting a cart of lab equipment nearby, she shoved it hard. The crash of metal echoed through the hallway, and the guards immediately moved to investigate.

Elena slipped past them, using her stolen credentials to enter the server room. Rows of servers blinked with cold efficiency. She plugged a portable drive into the nearest terminal, her fingers moving swiftly to bypass the encryption. The progress bar crawled forward, every second stretching unbearably.

Mackenzie's voice crackled in her earpiece. "Chatter on their comms. They know something's up. You need to hurry."

"I'm almost there," Elena whispered, her voice tight.

When the transfer was completed, she yanked the drive free and slipped it into her pocket. But before she could leave, the door burst open, and the guards stormed in, weapons raised.

"Freeze!" one barked.

Elena didn't hesitate. She toppled a server rack into their path, diving for cover as bullets ripped through the room. Her silenced pistol barked twice, dropping one guard, but the other managed to sound the alarm before she neutralized him.

Alarms blared, red lights flashing as reinforcements converged. Elena sprinted through the corridors, dodging security. A guard blocked her path, lunging at her with a baton. She ducked, slamming an elbow into his ribs and finishing with a sharp kick that sent him sprawling. Swiping his keycard, she unlocked a side exit and slipped into the freezing Zurich night.

Behind her, shouts and footsteps closed in. She scaled a fence, her muscles straining, and dropped into an adjacent alley just as guards spilled out of the building. She didn't stop running until she was several blocks away, her breath ragged and adrenaline pumping.

When she reached the safe house, Mackenzie glanced up from her laptop. "You look like hell," she quipped.

Elena smirked, brushing damp hair from her face. "You should see the other guys."

Rhett's voice came through the secure comms, relief evident. After her briefing, he said, "Good work. But this confirms it—Granger's network is bigger than we thought."

Elena's resolve hardened. "Then we'll keep hitting them. This was just the start."

The Zurich mission succeeded, but the fight against Genesis was far from over.

South Pacific: Rhett's Fight in the Shadows

The ocean's roar was a constant backdrop as Rhett Kardon stepped off the small boat, his boots sinking into the damp sand of the secluded island. The night was pitch-black, and the dense jungle ahead was illuminated only by the faint glow of floodlights surrounding a distant facility. This was the heart of Granger's failsafe—a remote server hub hidden from prying eyes, protected by layers of terrain and elite operatives. Rhett was here to dismantle it alone.

As he moved into the jungle, the air grew thick with humidity, the earthy scent mingling with the tang of salt. Each step was deliberate, his enhanced senses scanning for threats. He spotted the first trap—an IED woven into the undergrowth—and disarmed it with practiced precision. The jungle felt alive, every rustle of leaves or snap of a branch sending his instincts into overdrive.

He caught the faint sound of boots crunching against the forest floor and distant voices. Granger's operatives patrolled in tight, coordinated units, their flashlights slicing through the darkness. Rhett melted into the shadows, his movements soundless. A patrol passed mere feet from his position, their rifles sweeping the area. He waited until they were gone before pressing forward, inching closer to the facility.

The jungle thinned, revealing a fortified compound surrounded by flood-lights and patrolling guards. Rhett crouched at the edge of the clearing, studying the cameras' patterns and the guards' movements. Finding a blind spot, he efficiently scaled the fence, landing softly on the other side. Darting between shadows, he moved closer to the server room.

The first skirmish came quickly. Two guards spotted him near the entrance, opening fire with suppressed weapons. Rhett moved like lightning, his enhanced reflexes allowing him to evade the bullets. He closed the distance, disarming one guard with a brutal twist and slamming him into the ground. The second guard lunged, but Rhett countered with a sharp elbow strike, dropping him instantly.

The reinforced doors of the server room loomed ahead. A shadow moved in his peripheral vision as Rhett examined the electronic lock. He turned to see a man emerge from the darkness—tall, broad-shouldered, and clad in tactical gear. The man's gaze locked onto Rhett, radiating menace and recognition.

"You must be Kardon," the man said, his voice gravelly. "I've been waiting for this."

Rhett's muscles coiled, recognizing the calm confidence of someone like himself—an enhanced operative. The man attacked without warning, and his first punch narrowly missed Rhett's head. Rhett countered with an uppercut that landed solidly, but his opponent barely flinched, his body absorbing the impact.

What followed was a brutal, unrelenting clash. Every move was precise, every strike designed to kill. Rhett's training and reflexes were pushed to their limits as he fought an opponent who matched him blow for blow. They tore through the clearing and into the compound, slamming each other into walls and counters. Pain lanced through Rhett's ribs as he was thrown across the room, but he forced himself to rise, blood streaking his face.

"You're good," the man said, circling him like a predator. "But you'll never be good enough. Granger made sure of that."

Rhett wiped the blood from his lip, his eyes narrowing. "Granger made a mistake," he said coldly. "He didn't account for this."

Using his telepathic abilities, Rhett anticipated his opponent's next move, the disorienting flashes of thought giving him a critical edge. Feinting left, he drove his knee into the man's solar plexus, knocking the wind out of him. As the man staggered, Rhett grabbed a length of metal piping and struck with all his strength, hitting him in the head and sending his opponent crashing.

Chest heaving, Rhett stood over the fallen operative before turning to the server controls. Planting an EMP device, he set the timer. Sparks erupted from the servers as the device activated, their data erased in a cascade of failure.

Staggering out of the compound, Rhett inhaled the cool night air as the facility behind him erupted in a controlled explosion. The operation had been a success but at a cost. His body screamed in protest as he limped back into the jungle, every step a reminder of how close he'd come to losing.

As he disappeared into the shadows, Rhett allowed himself a fleeting moment of satisfaction. The South Pacific server was destroyed, but the war against Genesis was far from over. This was just one victory in a fight that demanded everything he had—and more.

Mackenzie's Digital War in Hong Kong

In the dim glow of the safe house's makeshift command center, Mackenzie Price sat hunched over her laptop, her fingers dancing across the keyboard in a blur. The room was silent except for the rhythmic tapping of keys and the occasional beep from her monitors. On-screen, lines of code scrolled rapidly, interspersed with flashing warnings and countermeasures—evidence of the digital war she was waging.

The Hong Kong servers were an impenetrable fortress with firewalls and encryption protocols designed to repel even the most skilled hackers. Mackenzie wasn't just professional—she was relentless, exploiting vulnerabilities faster than enemy teams could patch them. But these weren't amateurs. The sharp enemy hackers launched counterattacks like precision strikes, forcing her to adapt quickly.

"Come on," she muttered, her focus razor-sharp. Each keystroke was a calculated blow, cutting through their defenses while dodging their countermeasures. Every second inside their system was risky, but she thrived on the pressure.

Her earpiece crackled, Elena's voice cutting in from Zurich. "Mackenzie, we're not hearing much. What's your status?"

"I'm a little busy keeping us alive, thanks," Mackenzie snapped, her voice dry but tinged with tension. "These guys are good—damn good. I've got two teams trying to boot me out, and they're not holding back."

Elena's tone stayed calm. "Can you hold them?"

"Hold them? Sure. Outrace them? That's the real game." Her confidence broke through her stress, though her fingers never slowed.

Rhett's voice cut in next, steady and reassuring. "Keep going. We're counting on you."

"No pressure," Mackenzie muttered, a faint smirk on her lips. Her screen flashed red as a surge attack threatened to overload her system. She countered instantly, redirecting the assault back to its origin. "Nice try," she murmured under her breath.

The tug-of-war was relentless, her heart pounding as seconds stretched into minutes. When doubt began to creep in, one of her algorithms hit its mark. The final layer of encryption crumbled, revealing a treasure trove of data: names, transactions, and locations of Granger's remaining allies.

"We've got them," she whispered, scanning the data. Relief flooded her—but only for a moment. A new warning blared on her secondary monitor. The enemy team deployed measures to erase the data and shut her out.

"Not so fast," Mackenzie growled, launching a rapid-fire sequence of commands. Her laptop hummed with effort as she implanted malware into their core operating systems, crippling the communications hub from within.

"Elena?" she called into her earpiece, her voice tight.

"Status?" Elena pressed.

"Almost there. They're trying to wipe everything, but they're too slow." A final surge rattled her system, her screen flickering ominously. She steadied herself, muttering under her breath, "Not today."

With one decisive keystroke, her malware detonated. The servers collapsed in a cascade of digital failure. The screen went dark, leaving only one message: System offline. Data erased.

Mackenzie exhaled sharply, leaning back in her chair as the tension drained from her body. "It's done," she said, her voice a mix of triumph and exhaustion. "Hong Kong is dark. The communications hub is gone."

Elena's voice carried relief. "You did it. We're clear."

Rhett followed, calm but firm. "Good work. Now pack up—they'll trace you."

The Final Failsafe

T he safe house buzzed with tension as Mackenzie Price hunched over her laptop. The glow of the screen highlighted the determination etched on her face. Her fingers flew across the keyboard, navigating the labyrinthine remnants of Granger's network. When she thought the battle was over, a hidden failsafe appeared, its countdown ominously ticking.

The screen flashed red: "Global Dissemination Protocol: ACTIVE." Below it, a timer ticked mercilessly: 9:57... 9:56... 9:55.

Her stomach dropped. "We've got a problem," she muttered, her voice tight.

"What kind of problem?" Rhett's voice crackled through the comms, already braced for bad news.

"Granger set up a dead man's switch," Mackenzie explained, eyes locked on the screen. "If this hits zero, every Genesis file goes global—operatives, research, everything. We'll lose it all."

"How long do we have?" Elena's voice was sharp, cutting through the tension.

"Ten minutes. Maybe less," Mackenzie replied, already digging into the code.

"Can you stop it?" Rhett asked, calm but urgent.

"I can try," she said, her fingers flying faster. "But this thing is locked down tighter than anything I've seen. Granger wasn't playing games."

"Do your best," Rhett urged. "We'll guide you."

Mackenzie blocked out the world, her focus absolute. Each line of code revealed another trap, another layer of defense. She peeled back the encryption like the layers of an onion, every breakthrough countered by new defenses. The timer marched forward, mocking her efforts: 6:12... 6:11... 6:10.

"Talk to me, Mackenzie," Elena pressed. "What do you need?"

"Time," she snapped, sweat trickling down her temple. "And maybe a miracle."

Rhett's voice cut through, steady and resolute. "You've got this. Trust yourself."

Mackenzie's heart raced as she reached the final layer. Her screen glowed with a tangle of deceptive commands, the trigger mechanism buried beneath layers of false code. One wrong move could prematurely activate the protocol.

1:00... 0:59... 0:58.

"I'm in the last stage," she said, her voice taut. "But this thing is booby-trapped. If I mess up, it's game over."

"Don't mess up," Rhett said, his tone steady.

Mackenzie's hands trembled as she analyzed the final sequence, her mind racing through possibilities. Her instincts locked onto the trigger. It was brilliantly hidden but not impenetrable. She took a deep breath, her fingers poised. 0:20... 0:19... 0:18.

"Come on," she whispered, her heart pounding. With a final keystroke, she executed the command. The screen froze, the room holding its breath. Then, the timer disappeared, replaced by the words: "Protocol Terminated."

Mackenzie exhaled sharply, slumping back in her chair. "It's done," she said, her voice shaking with relief. "Failsafe disabled. The files are secure."

Elena's voice broke through, filled with gratitude. "You did it. You stopped it."

Rhett's tone carried quiet admiration. "You just saved us all." Mackenzie let out a nervous laugh. "Yeah, well, let's not do that again."

As the weight of their victory settled in, Mackenzie knew the fight wasn't over. Granger's shadow loomed large, and the subsequent battle would be even more complex. But for now, they'd won—and that was enough

Victory at a Price

The safe house was steeped in heavy silence, broken only by the faint hum of Mackenzie's laptop as she finished securing the last Genesis files. The air felt thick with exhaustion, the adrenaline that had fueled them through near-impossible odds now replaced by bone-deep weariness. Outside, the world continued oblivious to how close it had come to disaster, the dawn just beginning to creep over the horizon.

Rhett leaned back in a battered chair, his body aching with the aftermath of battle. He stared at the worn floorboards, his mind a storm of conflicting emotions. They had won, but the cost of that victory hung over him like a shadow. Granger's empire lay in ruins, the Genesis network dismantled—but the scars of the fight ran deep in the world and within himself.

Across the room, Mackenzie sat cross-legged on the floor, her laptop perched on her knees. Her fingers hovered over the keyboard, hesitating for the first time that night. The rush of the digital war she'd waged had faded, leaving only a quiet fatigue. Sighing, she closed the laptop and leaned back against the wall.

"Well," she said, her voice cutting through the silence, "that was a thing."

Elena, slouched beside Rhett on the worn couch, let out a dry laugh. "A thing? That's the word you're going with?"

Mackenzie shrugged, a faint smirk tugging at her lips. "What do you want me to say? We saved the world. You're welcome."

Rhett chuckled softly, though his gaze remained distant, fixed somewhere in the past or the future. Elena noticed and shifted closer, her hand resting lightly on his. He met her green eyes, finding concern and quiet relief mirrored there.

"It's over, Rhett," she said softly. "We did it."

His lips twitched into a tired smile. "For now," he replied, the weight of their journey evident in his tone.

Elena frowned slightly but didn't press. She understood better than anyone how deep his wounds ran—not just the physical ones but the invisible scars left by Genesis. The betrayal, the loss, and the constant battle to hold on to his humanity in the face of Granger's twisted vision of control had taken their toll.

"Hey," Mackenzie said, cutting through the tension. "I get that we're all in our feelings, but can we take a moment to acknowledge we pulled off the impossible? Granger's empire is toast, Genesis is gone, and none of us died. That's a win."

Rhett glanced up, his expression softening. "You're right, Mack. It's a win."

"But?" Mackenzie prompted, raising an eyebrow.

Rhett sighed, his thoughts drifting. "But it doesn't feel like the end. Granger might be finished, but what about the ambition behind Genesis? That hunger for control? It's still out there. Someone will pick up where he left off."

Elena squeezed his hand gently. "Then we'll be ready. Whatever comes next, we'll face it together."

The room settled into a comfortable silence, each lost in their thoughts. The toll of the mission weighed on all of them, but for the first time, they allowed themselves a moment of peace.

Rhett stood, his movements deliberate as he stretched stiff muscles. He glanced at Elena and Mackenzie, his expression softening as he took in the people beside him. "Get some rest," he said, his voice firm but kind. "We've earned it."

Mackenzie snorted, packing up her gear. "Rest? Sure. Right after, I make sure no one's tracking us."

Elena smiled, leaning back. "She'll crash eventually."

Rhett nodded, his gaze already drifting toward the window. The faint light of dawn illuminated the city, stirring to life, blissfully unaware of the battles fought in its shadows. A rare flicker of hope stirred in his chest as he stood there, watching the new day begin.

"For now," he murmured to himself. And for now, that was enough.

CHAPTER 32

The Temptation

The safe house was quiet, the tension inside thick enough to suffocate. Rhett Kardon sat alone, elbows on his knees, staring at the decrypted files before him. Operation Genesis had been dismantled, Granger's network severed, but something gnawed at Rhett's mind—a temptation he hadn't anticipated.

These files were not just a record of past atrocities but a blueprint for the future. He could feel the weight of the knowledge pressing down on him. This technology could change the world—ending wars, eradicating threats, and even making individuals like him the new standard of humanity. The question that haunted him was: If you have the power to shape the future, what's stopping you from using it?

The First Whisper of Power

The air in the room was heavy, laden with unspoken tension as Elena entered quietly, her footsteps soft against the worn hardwood floor. The pale morning light seeped through the blinds, casting shadows across the scattered files and documents covering the table. Rhett sat hunched over them, his elbows on his knees, his fingers steepled against his lips. Though his eyes were fixed on the papers, his gaze was distant, as if staring into the abyss of what they had uncovered.

"What's going on?" Elena asked, her voice calm but edged with concern. She crossed the room and slid into the chair beside him, her movements deliberate and steady.

Rhett gestured toward the table, his voice low but burdened. "It's all here," he said. "Every experiment. Every enhancement. Every life they ruined for Genesis. Everything they dreamed of building."

Elena leaned forward, scanning the pages. Her sharp green eyes took in the dense diagrams, genetic blueprints, and lists of test subjects—some marked "successful," others "deceased." The scope of it was staggering, a roadmap of human experimentation and manipulation.

"It's dangerous, Rhett," Elena said, her voice firm. "We need to destroy it. All of it."

Rhett hesitated, his hands tightening into fists. "What if we don't?" he countered, his tone tinged with conflict. "What if we use it for good? To cure diseases, to stop suffering, to fix the world?"

Elena's expression hardened. "That's what Granger thought," she said, her voice cutting through the air like steel. "That kind of power always corrupts. You've seen it. I've seen it. No one can wield this without becoming the monster they swore to destroy."

Rhett turned to her, desperation flickering in his eyes. "What if it's different this time? What if we're different?"

Elena placed a firm hand on his arm, her gaze steady but compassionate. "You know it doesn't work that way. Genesis didn't just change bodies—it broke people. Minds, souls. It isn't just dangerous; it's a weapon that no one can control."

The words hit Rhett like a blow. He leaned back, running a hand through his hair as the weight of her argument settled in. He had lived as proof of what she said. Every enhancement, every decision tied to Genesis had left scars—on him and countless others.

"What if someone else finds it later?" he asked quietly. "What if we destroy it, and they rebuild something worse?"

"Then we make sure no one gets the chance," Elena replied, her voice resolute. "We destroy it, but we also expose it. Let the world see what Genesis really was and what it did. That truth is the only way to stop it from happening again."

Rhett stared at her hand on his arm, the strength of her conviction grounding him. Finally, he let out a long breath, his shoulders sagging. "You're right," he said. "It's not ours to use. It's ours to end."

Elena nodded, relief softening her features. "Together," she said.

As sunlight crept further into the room, Rhett gathered the files, stacking them neatly as if preparing for a ritual. Each page felt heavier than the last, a lifetime of horror they would finally erase.

"Let's burn it," Rhett said, his voice steady now.

Elena stood with a faint smile on her lips. "Let's make sure it never rises again."

Side by side, they began dismantling the legacy of Genesis, ensuring it would never return. Together, they chose hope over power—and a future untainted by the past.

A Conversation with Mackenzie

The safe house was quiet, the hum of Mackenzie's laptop the only sound in the dimly lit room. Rhett found her sitting cross-legged on a worn armchair in the corner, her face illuminated by the pale glow of the screen. She barely glanced up as he entered, her fingers flying over the keyboard.

"I figured you'd show up," she said without preamble, her tone dry but not unfriendly. "Can't sleep, huh?"

Rhett pulled up a chair, sitting across from her with a tired sigh. "Something like that," he replied, his gaze shifting to the screen. "How much of this data have you processed?"

Mackenzie smirked, leaning back slightly. "More than I probably should have," she said, closing one file and opening another. "The stuff in here, Rhett—it's the kind of thing that keeps you up at night. Genetic manipulation, behavioral conditioning, enhancement protocols... Granger didn't just want to control the world. He wanted to rebuild it from the ground up."

Rhett rested his elbows on his knees, his hands clasped together. "And you've gone through all of it?"

"Not all," Mackenzie admitted, her tone turning serious. "But enough to know this isn't just dangerous—it's apocalyptic if it falls into the wrong hands. Or any hands, really."

Rhett hesitated, running a hand through his hair as conflicting thoughts swirled in his mind. "What if we could control it?" he asked, his voice measured but tinged with curiosity. "What if we could ensure it only got used for the right reasons?"

Mackenzie froze, her fingers hovering over the keyboard. Slowly, she turned to face him, her expression a mix of disbelief and exasperation. "Control it?" she echoed, her voice dripping with skepticism. "You've got to be kidding me."

"I'm serious," Rhett said, leaning forward. "What if this is a chance to do something good? To fix things instead of just breaking them?"

Mackenzie snorted, shaking her head as she closed the laptop with a decisive snap. "Control is an illusion, Rhett. Trust me, I've seen people try to harness things like this before. It always ends the same way—disaster."

Rhett frowned. "So, you think we just destroy it? Pretend it never existed?"

"Exactly," Mackenzie said, her tone sharp. "You don't harness a hurricane, Rhett. You don't try to guide an avalanche. You run. You warn everyone else to run. And if you're lucky, you survive."

Rhett's jaw tightened, his mind racing with possibilities and consequences. "What if it's different this time? What if we—"

"'We'? Rhett, come on," Mackenzie interrupted, her voice rising slightly. "You've seen what this kind of power does to people. It turns them into Granger. Or worse. You want to play God with something like Genesis? Fine. But don't expect me to stand by and watch it happen."

Rhett fell silent, her words hitting harder than he expected. He looked at Mackenzie, the unflinching resolve in her gaze, and felt a pang of doubt creeping in. She was right—he had seen the destruction Genesis had wrought, not just on the world but on the people who thought they could control it.

"You're smarter than this," Mackenzie continued, her voice softening slightly. "You've spent your whole life fighting to stop people like Granger. Don't let his dream pull you in just because it's dressed up as something noble."

Rhett sighed, leaning back in his chair and rubbing his temples. "It's just... hard to let go," he admitted. "Knowing what's possible, knowing how much good we could do."

Mackenzie leaned forward, her tone severe but not unkind. "I get it, Rhett. I really do. But some things aren't meant to be controlled. Sometimes, the best thing you can do is let them burn."

The room fell into a heavy silence, their conversation settling over them like a cloud. Rhett looked at Mackenzie, her sharp eyes steady and unwavering, and realized that she wasn't just trying to convince him—she was trying to protect him from himself.

Finally, he nodded, the tension in his shoulders easing slightly. "Alright," he said quietly. "We destroy it."

Mackenzie gave him a small, approving smile. "Smart choice. Now, let's make sure it stays that way."

As she reopened her laptop and began preparing the files for erasure, Rhett leaned back in his chair, his gaze fixed on the faint glow of the screen. The temptation was still there, lingering like a shadow in the back of his mind. But he felt the weight lifting for the first time, replaced by a sense of clarity.

He wasn't Granger. And he wasn't going to be.

The Ghosts of the Past

The room in Rhett's dream glowed with an eerie, golden light, its shadows stretching ominously across the worn mahogany chessboard between him and his father. Dr. James Kardon sat opposite, unchanged by the years. His sharp eyes, tailored suit, and air of superiority exuded the same cold authority Rhett had grown to loathe. Time hadn't softened the man; it had sharpened him, making his presence even more oppressive.

The chess game was mid-play. Rhett's king was cornered and surrounded by hostile pieces. His father reached out, moving a knight with precision. The soft click of the piece, like a gavel, struck judgment.

"The world is strategy," his father intoned, his voice smooth, clinical. "Every decision, every move—it all depends on how well you play."

Rhett's hands trembled over the board, the weight of his father's words suffocating. This wasn't just chess; their unending battle for control and freedom from expectations had crushed him since childhood.

"I don't want to play your game," Rhett said, his voice shaking but resolute.

Dr. Kardon leaned back, a calculating smile tugging at his lips. "You're already playing," he said, the menace in his voice undeniable. "The moment you stepped into that lab, the first move was made. There's no walking away now."

The words struck like a physical blow. Memories surged—needles piercing his skin, the sterile lab's fluorescent lights, the relentless drills. Rhett had spent years fighting to escape his father's shadow, but it loomed more significant here than ever.

"You think you're different," Kardon continued, his bishop sliding into position. "But you're like me. You see the board, the moves, and you can't resist. That's who we are."

Rhett moved a pawn forward, defiance in his shaking hands. "I'm not playing to win. I'm playing to end this."

His father's smile widened, devoid of warmth. "An admirable sentiment. But naïve. The game never ends, Rhett. Destroy the board, and another will appear. Another player. Another move."

The golden light dimmed, the board fracturing into fragments as Kardon delivered checkmate. Rhett woke with a gasp, the dream's weight pressing down on him like a vice.

He sat in the dark, the city's glow faint against the walls. His father's words echoed, but Rhett clenched his fists, resolved to harden. He wasn't playing to win. He was playing to destroy the game—for good.

A Dangerous Offer

The morning sunlight filtered through the blinds of the safe house, casting faint patterns across the cluttered table. Rhett sat in the stillness, a mug of coffee cooling in his hands. The dream of his father still lingered, a shadow at the edge of his thoughts. The battle with Granger might have ended, but the war—against the network, the ideology, and the scars of Genesis—was far from over.

The chime of the secure laptop broke the silence, pulling him from his reverie. Frowning, Rhett leaned forward, sliding the device closer. The notification wasn't from the usual channels. It was from a private, encrypted network—one reserved for the highest operatives. Few even knew it existed.

A simple message blinked on the screen:

"The work doesn't have to end. We can continue where Granger left off. Together."

Below the text, a set of coordinates appeared—an abandoned government property outside the city. There was no name or signature—just the chilling invitation.

Rhett's stomach tightened. He recognized this for what it was: not just a trap but a test. Granger's empire had fallen, but its architects, the shadowy figures who had funded and directed Genesis, were still alive. And now, they were reaching out—not as enemies but as potential allies.

"You've already made your first move. There's no walking away now," his father's voice echoed in his mind, a specter from his dream.

The door creaked softly behind him. Elena stepped into the room, her hair tousled from sleep. She froze when she saw his expression, her green eyes narrowing. "What's wrong?" she asked.

Wordlessly, Rhett turned the laptop toward her. Elena's face darkened as she read the message. "They're trying to recruit you," she said flatly.

"Or test me," Rhett replied, his jaw tightening. "Either way, they're not finished."

"You're not seriously considering this," Elena said, crossing her arms.

"I don't know," Rhett admitted. "If I go, I might learn more. But if I don't…"

"They'll find another way," Elena interrupted. "You've seen what these people do. You can't fight them by becoming part of their game."

Rhett met her gaze, her unwavering conviction grounding him. Slowly, he closed the laptop. "They're not getting what they want," he said firmly.

Elena let out a breath. "Good. Once you go down that road, there's no coming back."

Rhett stood, his resolve solidifying. "This fight isn't over. But it's going to end on my terms."

The Internal Struggle

The hours before the meeting dragged like an eternity, each second weighed down by the enormity of the choice before Rhett. The safe house was cloaked in silence, broken only by the distant hum of the city and the occasional creak of the floorboards. Rhett sat hunched in a chair, his elbows on his knees, his hands clasped tightly as he wrestled with the invitation.

The words repeated in his mind, relentless and haunting: "We can continue where Granger left off. Together. "Promise and threat intertwined, offering not just power, but the illusion of purpose—a chance to transform destruction into an opportunity—a chance to create a world without fear, chaos, or war.

Across the room, Elena watched him carefully. She recognized the storm brewing in his eyes, the same silent battle she'd seen before. When the lines between right and wrong blurred, Rhett always struggled. Quietly, she stepped closer, breaking the stillness.

"You're thinking about it," she said evenly, though concern tinged her voice.

Rhett didn't answer. His jaw tightened, his gaze fixed on the floor. The weight of the decision felt suffocating, like a noose tightening with every passing second.

Elena's tone sharpened. "They're offering you control, Rhett. But it's a lie. They don't want you to lead—they want to use you, just like they used Granger. Just like your father."

Her words cut deep, igniting anger and doubt. Rhett shot to his feet, pacing like a caged animal. "What if I could use them?" he snapped. "Turn their power into something good? Stop this cycle from repeating?"

Elena stepped into his path, her voice firm but filled with quiet urgency. "You've seen what that kind of power does. It consumes people—twists them. If you go, you're giving them exactly what they want. They'll make you into another Granger."

Her words stilled him. The room fell silent, the weight of her conviction sinking in. He turned away, his shoulders heavy with the burden of choice.

"Elena," he said softly, almost pleading, "what if they're right? What if this is the only way to fix a broken world?"

She reached out, her hand steady on his arm. "The world is broken, Rhett. But power like theirs doesn't fix it—it shatters it. You fix it by choosing to be better. By refusing to compromise everything you stand for."

Her words settled over him like a lifeline, pulling him back from the edge. Slowly, Rhett nodded, the anger fading into clarity. "You're right," he said, his voice steadier now. "If I go, I'm playing their game. And I'm done playing."

Relief softened Elena's face as she offered a faint smile. "Good. Because the world doesn't need another Granger. It needs you."

Rhett exhaled deeply, the storm within him quieting. The fight wasn't over, but his path was clear now. "Let's make sure they never get the chance to try again," he said firmly.

Elena nodded, her resolve matching his. "Together."

The Meeting

The drive to the meeting was suffocatingly silent, tension filling the air like a storm about to break. Rhett gripped the steering wheel, his thoughts churning. Elena had made it clear she didn't trust the invitation, warning him it was a trap. But Rhett couldn't ignore it. He needed answers. If the people behind Genesis were regrouping, he had to confront them, even if it meant stepping into the lion's den.

The abandoned government building loomed ahead, a decaying relic shrouded in shadows and overgrown vines. Parking a safe distance away, Rhett approached on foot, his senses on high alert. The faint glow of lights from within told him the place wasn't empty. Someone was waiting.

The air inside was stale and damp. Rhett's footsteps echoed down a long corridor, every step heightening his awareness of the eyes he knew were watching.

At the end of the hall, he entered a cavernous room illuminated by a single, harsh overhead light. A long table stood at its center, flanked by shadowy figures who rose as he entered.

They were power incarnate—high-ranking officials, corporate titans, and faceless operatives. An undeniable intensity undercut their calm composure. At the head of the table stood a silver-haired man in a sharp suit, his presence commanding and calculated. "Mr. Kardon," he said with a thin smile, his tone rich with condescension. Welcome. We've been watching you."

Rhett crossed his arms, refusing to sit. "Say what you came to say."

The man gestured smoothly. "You've dismantled Genesis. Impressive. But you've also proven its potential. Imagine what we could accomplish together. No more chaos, no more unpredictability—just order and progress. And you, Mr. Kardon, could lead it."

Rhett's eyes narrowed. "Your 'progress' is just another word for control."

The woman beside him, a diplomat with ice in her gaze, spoke. "Control brings peace. Evolution requires sacrifice. You understand this better than anyone."

Rhett's fists clenched. He saw through their polished words the oppression they indeed promised. "You're wrong," he said coldly. "The world doesn't need you. It needs freedom."

The Temptation Deepens

The voices around the table were calm, calculated, and insidious. Their polished words woven a vision that shimmered with false promises. Rhett listened as the men and women spoke of a world without chaos, without pain—one where suffering was a relic of the past. Their offer was as seductive as it was chilling: the power to bring order to a fractured world, prevent conflict before it began, and create a future guided by precision and control.

The room felt like a trap, every word they spoke tightening the invisible net around him. Rhett's silence was taken as contemplation, but his mind churned, grappling with the magnitude of their proposal. For a fleeting moment, he imagined a world where no child went hungry, no wars ravaged cities, and humanity's flaws were smoothed away by design.

But that moment shattered as he looked at the faces around the table. Their expressions were serene, their suits impeccable, but their eyes betrayed them. These weren't people driven by compassion—they were driven by calculation. They didn't seek peace; they sought power. They weren't architects of progress; they were engineers of oppression.

"This isn't about peace," Rhett said at last, his voice slicing through their carefully constructed narrative. The room stilled, their polished smiles faltering. "It's about control. And I won't be part of it."

The silver-haired man at the head of the table leaned forward, his calm demeanor cracking just enough to reveal the steel beneath. "Control is necessary to secure humanity's survival," he said smoothly. "Left to its own devices, humanity destroys itself. You know this."

Rhett's jaw tightened. "What you're offering isn't survival—it's servitude. You want to take away choice, to shape the world in your image, no matter the cost."

The diplomat spoke to the man's left, her voice measured but cold. "Guidance isn't tyranny, Mr. Kardon. Someone has to lead humanity forward. Why shouldn't it be us?"

"Because you don't see humanity as people," Rhett shot back, his voice rising. "You see them as pieces on a board, pawns in your game. And people like you don't lead—they conquer."

The room's tension became tangible, and the air was heavy with unspoken threats. Rhett knew what his refusal meant. He wasn't just rejecting their offer; he was declaring war.

"You're making a mistake," the silver-haired man warned, his voice sharp. "The future is inevitable. You can stand with us or be swept aside."

A Choice Made

The room was heavy with silence, the offer's weight crushing in intensity. Rhett stood before the polished table where the architects of power sat, their expressions composed but their eyes gleaming with ambition. Their proposal hung in the air like a siren's call, promising a future reshaped by order and precision—a world without chaos, without suffering. It was a temptation that clawed at the edges of Rhett's resolve.

His fists clenched at his sides as the enormity of the decision bore down on him. They offered him the tools to rewrite the rules, prevent wars before they began, and save lives by eliminating unpredictability. But the cost of that vision loomed large. The world they described wasn't built on freedom—it was built on control. Their promises of peace were masks for domination.

The silver-haired man at the head of the table leaned forward, his voice smooth and measured. "This isn't about control, Mr. Kardon. It's about creating a better future. A future you could lead."

Rhett's jaw tightened. "And what happens to those who don't fit into your perfect vision? The ones who refuse to conform?"

The man's smile didn't waver. "Progress demands sacrifice. The greater good requires hard choices. You understand that, don't you?"

Rhett's gaze swept the room, lingering on the faces of the people who believed so fervently in their cause. There was no empathy in their eyes, only calculation. These weren't visionaries—they were conquerors dressed in the language of salvation. He thought of the countless lives destroyed by Granger's ambitions, of the experiments, the manipulation, the suffering. He thought of Elena's warning: power like this would consume anyone who touched it.

The answer came to him with startling clarity.

"I'm not interested in your future," Rhett said, his voice steady but resolute.

The man's smile faltered. "You're making a mistake. This is inevitable."

Rhett stepped toward the door, his movements deliberate. "Your inevitability isn't mine."

He paused as he reached the exit, glancing back at the stunned figures around the table. "I'll fight for a world where people can choose their own future. And I'll make sure you never control it."

With that, Rhett walked into the night, the weight of their offer lifting from his shoulders. The battle ahead would be fierce, but his resolve was unshakable. He wasn't fighting for power—he was fighting for freedom. And he would risk everything to win.

Breaking the Cycle

As Rhett stepped out of the shadowy building and into the cool night air, the weight that had settled on his chest began to lift. The crisp breeze brushed against his face, carrying the faint scent of rain and earth—an anchor to the world he had chosen to protect. The voices from the meeting still echoed in his mind, their promises slick with manipulation, their temptations carefully wrapped in logic. But the decision had been made, and with it, Rhett felt a rare sense of clarity. He had walked away from their vision and claimed something they could never offer: freedom.

For too long, others had dictated his life—his father's experiments, the CIA's missions, Granger's schemes. Each had shaped him into a tool, a pawn in their games. But tonight, Rhett had taken control of his fate, rejecting the siren call of power and choosing a path not defined by control but by resistance.

Elena waited for him near the car, leaning casually against the door. The faint streetlamp glow illuminated her face, her sharp green eyes watching him intently as he approached. Her expression was calm, but her posture betrayed tension.

"Did you get what you needed?" she asked, her voice even but edged with concern.

Rhett stopped a few feet away, meeting her gaze. In her eyes, he saw trust and the unwavering resolve that had kept him grounded. "Yeah," he said, his voice steady. "I did."

"And?" she pressed, her tone softening slightly. "Was it worth it?"

He glanced back at the building, its dark silhouette looming behind him. "I needed to see them," he said deliberately. "To hear it from their own mouths.

They're not building a better world—they're building a prison. And they think I'd help them lock the doors."

"You told them no," Elena said, her lips curving into the faintest of smiles.

Rhett nodded, a quiet determination settling over him. "I told them no."

Relief flickered across her face before resolve reclaimed it. "Good. Because if you'd said yes, I'd have dragged you out myself."

Rhett chuckled, the sound low and rough. "I don't doubt it."

They stood silently for a moment, the enormity of what had just transpired settling between them. For Rhett, rejecting their offer wasn't just about resistance but about reclaiming himself. He wasn't his father's creation, the CIA's operative, or Granger's pawn. He was his own man, and he had chosen his fight.

"What now?" Elena asked, her voice calm but carrying a flicker of hope.

"Now we finish this," Rhett said, his voice firm. "We take them apart, piece by piece. No more talking. No more offers. Just action."

Elena's eyes hardened with purpose. "Good. Because I'm not done fighting, either."

As they climbed into the car and drove into the night, the shadows of the past receded. The road ahead was uncertain, the enemies relentless, but Rhett felt something he hadn't in years: hope.

He had chosen freedom and would fight for it—no matter the cost.

A New Beginning

The days after Genesis's fall were eerily still, as though the world was holding its breath. Rhett and Elena had lived in chaos for years, each moment a battle against the ticking clock. Now, the urgency was gone, replaced by a quiet that felt almost foreign. The mission was complete—Granger's network was dismantled, and the Genesis files were destroyed. The immediate fight was over, but the scars it left behind would linger.

Rhett stood on the balcony of a secluded safe house overlooking the ocean. The rhythmic crash of waves against the shore filled the air, steady and grounding. He gripped the cold metal railing, his eyes fixed on the endless horizon. The Genesis Operation was behind them, but the weight of what they'd done and its cost remained.

The door creaked open, and Elena joined him, a steaming mug of coffee in her hands. She leaned against the railing, her green eyes scanning the water. "You've been quiet," she said softly.

Rhett offered a faint smile. "Just thinking."

"About what?" she asked, taking a sip.

He hesitated, his voice low, when he finally spoke. "What happens when the next Granger comes along? Or the next Genesis?"

Elena set her mug down, turning to him. "There will always be another threat, Rhett. But we stopped this one. That has to matter."

"It does," Rhett admitted. "But I've spent so long fighting. I'm not sure I know how to stop."

Her hand rested lightly on his arm, her touch steady. "You don't have to stop. You have to remember why you're fighting—for the people who don't even know what was at stake."

Rhett looked at her, the weight in his chest easing slightly. "What about you? What's next for you?"

Elena smiled, a rare softness in her expression. "You think I'd let you do this alone? Someone's got to keep you in line."

Rhett chuckled; the sound was unfamiliar but welcome. "I guess I owe you that."

The sun dipped lower, painting the sky with streaks of orange and pink. For the first time in years, Rhett felt the stirrings of something he thought he'd lost: hope.

"You know," he said quietly, "I don't think I ever really understood what freedom felt like. Not until now."

Elena tilted her head, her smile widening. "And how does it feel?"

Rhett exhaled, the tension in his shoulders easing. "It feels like I can finally breathe."

"Then let's figure out what to do with it," she said. "Together."

"Always," he replied.

Rhett felt a profound sense of peace as the stars began to scatter across the sky. The battles ahead would come, but for now, he had this moment, this freedom, and he wasn't alone.

CHAPTER 33

An Internal Struggle

The wind howled through the D.C. streets as Rhett Kardon stood on the rooftop of an old government building, the cold night air biting into his skin. He had walked away from Granger's vision, from the temptation of power, but the internal battle was far from over. The knowledge that had come with dismantling Genesis—the files, the enhancements, the technology—still haunted him. What if he had made the wrong choice?

Inside him, a war raged. Every instinct, every lesson from years in the field, told him that power corrupts. But another voice, quieter but insistent, whispered that he could have saved the world with that power. He could have protected the people he cared about.

He clenched his fists. "Did I just walk away from the only way to end this?"

The Fallout Begins

Rhett stepped into the safe house, the muted scent of coffee and the faint hum of Mackenzie's laptop pulling him momentarily from the storm in his mind. The dim light reflected off the walls, casting long shadows that mirrored the weight hanging over him. He had walked away from power—from the seductive promise of reshaping the world—but the choice hadn't come without a cost.

Elena stood by the window, her silhouette framed by the faint streetlights outside. She turned at the sound of the door, her sharp green eyes narrowing as they searched Rhett's face. "Are they still in your head?" she asked, calm but taut.

"They let me go," Rhett said, shrugging off his coat, his tone carrying a weariness he couldn't quite shake. "But not without a message."

Perched on the couch's armrest, Mackenzie glanced up from her laptop. The screen's glow animated her face, and her brow furrowed with concern. "A message like, 'We'll destroy you,' or something more creative?"

Rhett let out a dry chuckle, sitting heavily on the couch. "Something like that. They're regrouping already. People like them don't quit."

Mackenzie leaned forward, setting her laptop aside. "They'll come at you from angles you don't expect. They'll want you gone."

Elena crossed the room, sitting across from Rhett. "Do you regret it?" she asked, her voice soft yet firm.

Rhett shook his head. "No," he said, his voice resolute. "I made the right choice. But that doesn't mean I'm not ready for what's coming."

Elena nodded, her expression steady. "Good. Because we're not done, they'll try to rebuild, but we'll stop them. Together."

Mackenzie smirked, already reopening her laptop. "This time, we'll make sure they can't pick up the pieces."

Rhett looked at both women, their unwavering determination cutting through his lingering doubt. He leaned forward, resting his elbows on his knees. "Alright," he said, a faint smile breaking through. "Let's finish this."

Nightmares and Memories

That night, sleep brought Rhett no solace. The nightmares came swiftly, vivid, and unyielding, dragging him back into the cold corridors of his past. The hum of fluorescent lights buzzed in his ears, sterile and oppressive, while the sharp, metallic scent of antiseptic filled his lungs. In the dream, he was a boy again—small, frightened, and powerless—strapped into the familiar chair where his father's experiments had always begun.

Dr. James Kardon towered above him, an imposing figure wrapped in clinical detachment. His father's voice was calm, measured, and utterly devoid of warmth. "You're special, Rhett," he said, each word dripping with certainty. "Sacrifice is the price of greatness."

Young Rhett looked at his trembling hands, his fingers clutching the armrests as though they might anchor him. He didn't feel special. He felt trapped, like a cog in a vast, unknowable machine. James turned to a tray of gleaming instruments, lifting a syringe filled with a faintly glowing liquid. The substance pulsed, alive with potential and laden with menace.

"It's for the greater good," James murmured, his tone clinical but chilling. "You have to become what the world needs."

Rhett wanted to scream, to tear away from the straps holding him down, but his body betrayed him. He could only watch as the syringe moved closer, his father's expression carved from stone, resolute in his belief.

The dream shifted, becoming a kaleidoscope of fear and memory. He saw the faces of Genesis operatives, Granger's smug smile, and the promises of control and perfection. Their words mirrored his father's, and the line between past and present blurred. The question that haunted him surfaced again: By rejecting their offer, was he abandoning the chance to fix the world? Or was he preserving what humanity they still had left?

Rhett jolted awake, his chest heaving, sweat drenching his skin. The room was dark, the moonlight casting faint silver lines across the walls. He pressed a shaking hand to his face, his mind still trapped in the echoes of the dream.

Beside him, Elena stirred. Her hand found his arm, grounding him with a gentle squeeze. "You're not him, Rhett," she whispered, her voice soft but firm. "You're not your father."

Her words cut through the lingering shadows, anchoring him. Rhett turned to her, meeting her steady green eyes. He found a quiet strength in her gaze, a reminder that he wasn't alone.

"I don't know if I can escape it," he admitted, his voice rough. "It's always there, waiting to pull me back."

Elena's grip tightened, her voice unwavering. "You're not running from it. You're fighting it. And you're not doing it alone."

Her words eased the tension in his chest. He nodded her reassurance, a balm to his fractured thoughts. The nightmare's grip loosened, and Rhett felt the weight of his father's shadow begin to lift for the first time that night.

He wasn't alone. And that made all the difference.

A Visit from the CIA

The knock on the door wasn't unexpected, but the visitor was. When Rhett opened it, Deputy Director Andrews stood on the threshold, immaculate as ever in his tailored suit. His rigid posture and calculating eyes spoke volumes. Behind him, two plainclothes agents lingered in the shadows, silent but undeniably present—a reminder of the authority Andrews carried.

"Director Andrews," Rhett said, his tone neutral but sharp. "What brings you here this early?"

Andrews stepped inside without waiting for an invitation, his gaze sweeping the room before settling on Rhett. His expression betrayed nothing but cold precision. "Kardon," he said, his clipped voice carrying a weight that immediately thickened the air. "You've stirred up quite the mess."

Rhett shut the door behind him, leaning against it. "If dismantling a global conspiracy is a 'mess,' then you're welcome."

Andrews didn't smile. Instead, his lips pressed into a thin line. "You've made some powerful enemies. People are unhappy with how you handled things. They want answers. Control."

Rhett met Andrews' icy gaze without flinching. "Then they'll be disappointed."

Andrews stepped closer, his tone low but sharp. "Do you even understand the fire you've started? Granger's network is in ruins, but the people behind him. They're still here. They don't like loose ends, and right now, you're one hell of a loose end."

Rhett's jaw tightened, his voice steady. "If they want control, they'll have to take it. I won't hand it over."

Andrews studied him for a long moment, his eyes narrowing. "Some people think you made the wrong call. That you should've worked with them instead of against them."

Rhett's lips curled into a faint smirk. "Let me guess. You're one of them."

Andrews didn't answer directly. Instead, his voice dropped to a near-whisper. "You had the chance to reshape the world, Kardon. And you walked away. Do you think they'll just let that go?"

Rhett stepped forward, his tone ice-cold. "Granger's vision was about ownership, not progress. If anyone thinks I'll help rebuild it, they're mistaken."

Andrews' expression softened into something almost pitying. "Watch your back. This city eats people like you alive."

"Let it try," Rhett shot back.

Andrews lingered momentarily, then turned, his agents falling in line. At the door, he glanced back. "Neutral ground doesn't exist in this game. Choose a side."

When the door clicked shut, the room felt heavier. Elena emerged, crossing her arms. "That didn't sound like a friendly chat."

"It wasn't," Rhett replied.

Mackenzie, still at her laptop, called from the corner. "They're testing you. Don't let them win."

Rhett straightened, resolved to solidify. "They won't."

Elena's gaze softened, though her voice was firm. "Good. Because this fight is just beginning."

Rhett smirked. "Then let's make sure we finish it."

A Meeting with Carter

The dimly lit bar smelled faintly of whiskey and regret, the kind of place where questions were left at the door. Rhett spotted Carter in the corner, nursing a beer. The reclusive former MI-6 officer didn't look up as Rhett approached, but there was no mistaking the flicker of recognition in his posture. Rhett slid into the chair across from him without a word.

Carter finally glanced up, his sharp eyes taking in Rhett's expression. "Figured you'd show up," he said, setting the bottle down with a soft clink. "You've got that look again."

Rhett smirked faintly, though there was no humor in it. "Guess I'm predictable."

Silence hung between them, heavy with shared history. The low murmur of the bar's patrons faded into the background as Rhett turned a bottle in his hands, his thoughts churning. Finally, Carter broke the quiet.

"So, what's the plan now?" he asked, his tone casual but his gaze sharp. "You walked away from Granger's people. But you think they'll just let you go?"

Rhett shook his head. "No. They'll come. Not today, maybe not tomorrow, but they'll come."

Carter leaned back, studying him with the unflinching look of someone who'd seen too much. "And you? You ready for that?"

Rhett stared at the amber liquid in his bottle, the dim light catching its surface. "I thought I was," he admitted. "But now... I don't know. What if I threw away the only chance to fix things?"

Carter's lips pressed into a thin line. "Fix things? Rhett, power like that doesn't fix—it corrupts. The people offering it don't want to save the world. They want to own it."

Rhett frowned, gripping the bottle tighter. "But what if I could've used it? Turned it against them?"

"You'd lose yourself before you even started," Carter said firmly. "And that's exactly why they hate you. Because you won't cross that line."

Rhett exhaled, leaning back. "They're not just after me. They'll come for everyone who helped."

Carter nodded grimly. "Then you've got a bigger fight ahead than you realize."

Rhett's jaw tightened. "Let them come. I'm not backing down."

Carter smirked faintly, lifting his beer. "Here's hoping you've got the stamina for it."

Rhett met his gaze, resolve to harden. "I'll keep going, Carter. For them. For the people who don't have a choice."

Carter nodded, his tone quiet but firm. "Then don't lose sight of that. It's all that'll keep you from becoming one of them."

The Enemy Strikes Back

Just as Rhett was beginning to feel like the dust was finally settling, the first blow landed with surgical precision, shattering any illusion of peace. It started with an innocuous alert—a flagged breach in a government system. Within minutes, it escalated into a coordinated cyberattack targeting multiple classified networks. Among the breached systems were the highly sensitive Genesis research files—data that had been painstakingly locked away after the operation's collapse.

Mackenzie yelled across the room, cutting through the silence of the safe house like a blade. "Rhett, we've got a problem. A big one. Someone's making a play for the Genesis files. They're trying to recover the data."

Rhett froze for a fraction of a second, his heart slamming against his ribs as her words registered. "What kind of play?" he asked, reaching for his gear. The tension in his voice mirrored the knot tightening in his chest.

"It's not just a probe—it's a full-scale breach," Mackenzie replied, her tone sharp and focused. The faint clatter of her typing filled the background. "Whoever's behind this isn't messing around. They've already hit three systems, and the data's bleeding. If they break through the final layers of encryption, they'll have everything."

Rhett clenched his jaw, slinging his tactical bag over his shoulder. Granger's allies weren't regrouping quietly in the shadows. They were moving aggressively, wasting no time in piecing together the shattered remnants of Genesis. The thought sent a chill down his spine. The files contained more than just blueprints and research—they were the foundation of a global operation that could reshape humanity. Everything Rhett had fought for would unravel if those files fell into the wrong hands.

"Do we know where the attack's coming from?" Rhett asked, his voice steady despite the storm building inside him.

Mackenzie hesitated for a beat. "Not yet. They're using sophisticated proxies—layered, like Russian dolls. But I've traced one of the servers to an offshore data hub in the Baltic. That might be their anchor point."

Elena entered the room, already geared up. She had overheard the conversation and didn't need an explanation. Her green eyes were sharp, her expression set. "We don't have time to wait for a full trace. If they get their hands on that data, it's game over."

Rhett nodded, his resolve hardening. "Then we stop them."

Mackenzie's voice chimed in, a mixture of urgency and determination. "I'll keep digging on my end, try to slow them down. But if you're planning to hit the source, you'll need to move fast."

Rhett glanced at Elena; their unspoken understanding was clear. "We'll move," he said, his tone resolute. "Send me everything you've got on that data hub. Coordinates, access points, weaknesses—whatever we can use."

"Already on it," Mackenzie replied. "Be careful, Rhett. This isn't just a grab for data—it's a declaration. They're rebuilding, and they're not waiting for permission."

"Wait!" Mackenzie's voice rang out, sharp and urgent. "There's something here—labeled 'James Kardon Final Contact.'" Her fingers flew over the keyboard, the glow of the monitor reflecting off her wide eyes. As the file opened, her breath hitched.

"It's...a resignation letter," she said, her voice laced with disbelief. "From Dr. James Kardon."

Rhett froze mid-step, the words hitting him like a thunderclap. "What did you say?" he asked, turning back toward her.

Mackenzie leaned closer to the screen, reading aloud. "He wanted to retire from the program and stay on as a consultant. He...he suggested that his death be faked so he could disappear. 'Ride off into the sunset,' his words."

The room went silent, the hum of the monitors the only sound. Rhett's heart pounded as he stepped closer, staring at the screen. There it was—his father's signature, the unmistakable scrawl he had seen so many times growing up. His stomach twisted as his gaze moved to the address at the bottom: the family's lake house.

"That doesn't make sense," Rhett said, his voice low but edged with fury. "Why would they let him leave? He knew too much. He was too valuable."

Mackenzie hesitated, glancing up at him. "What if they didn't let him leave? What if he...found a way?"

Rhett clenched his fists, his mind a storm of memories and questions. He stared at the address, the words burning into his mind. The lake house. It was a ghost from his past, a place he hadn't thought of in years—a place he thought he had left behind.

Elena stepped into the tense silence, her voice calm but firm. "We have bigger problems right now, Rhett. If this is true, it can wait."

Rhett tore his gaze from the screen, his jaw tight. "You're right," he said, though the words tasted bitter. "We deal with this later. But if he's alive..." His voice trailed off, the unspoken promise heavy in the air.

Mackenzie and Elena exchanged a look, but neither said a word. They knew Rhett well enough to recognize the storm brewing inside him. The mission wasn't over—not yet.

Rhett felt the weight of the moment settles on his shoulders. This was the fight he had been preparing for, the next chapter of a war he thought he had ended. There was no turning back now. Granger's allies had made their move, and Rhett intended to finish what he had started—once and for all.

An Infiltration Gone Wrong

T he team moved like shadows, blending into the darkness that cloaked the desolate industrial zone. The unmarked warehouse stood ahead, its cold steel walls hiding the stolen Genesis files that could reignite the nightmare they had fought so hard to end. Mackenzie's intel had been clear: this was the enemy's new stronghold, the hub where Granger's allies were regrouping. Rhett, Elena, and Carter were here to dismantle it—once and for all.

Elena moved to the security panel near the perimeter, her fingers dancing across the keys as she bypassed the alarms with surgical precision. Carter dispatched the guards with the silent efficiency of a predator, his Special Boat Service training evident in every calculated movement. Rhett led them forward, his enhanced senses tuning in to every creak, every distant hum of machinery. Each step deeper into the facility tightened the tension in his chest.

Inside, the air was sterile and almost unnervingly quiet. The team navigated the labyrinth of corridors with practiced precision, their breaths barely audible. The server room was ahead, its glow visible through the reinforced glass. The mission had gone too smoothly, but Rhett's instincts screamed a warning he couldn't shake.

"Elena, how much longer?" he whispered, scanning the dim corridor.

"Almost there," she replied, her voice a mix of calm and urgency. The lock beeped, the door hissed open, and they entered. The room was a gleaming hive of activity, monitors displaying streams of data being consolidated. Elena plugged in Mackenzie's custom decryptor, her fingers flying across the keyboard.

Then Rhett heard a faint shuffle, a breath other than their own. His enhanced senses picked up vibrations and the faint scrape of boots in the air. It was too late.

"It's a trap!" he barked.

The room exploded in chaos. Gunfire tore through the silence, and the operatives burst in with unnerving precision. These weren't ordinary soldiers; they moved like predators, their strength and reflexes unnatural. Enhanced operatives are the products of the same experiments that created Rhett.

The fight was a brutal symphony of violence. Rhett moved like lightning, his body a weapon honed by years of survival. His strikes were deadly and calculated, but his opponents were his equals, their enhanced abilities matching his blow for blow. Elena fired in short bursts, every shot finding its mark. Carter fought with raw, unrelenting force, his knife flashing in the dim light.

The air was a cacophony of gunfire, shouted orders, and the visceral clash of combat. Blood splattered against the sterile walls as Rhett took down one operative after another, his mind a storm of focus and fury. But for every enemy they felled, another seemed to emerge from the shadows, their numbers relentless.

Rhett could feel Granger's shadow in every blow. These operatives were living reminders of the Genesis Operation's dark promise, a twisted vision of control and power. The files were tantalizingly close, but every passing second threatened to push them out of reach.

"We can't hold this position!" Elena shouted, reloading with practiced speed.

Rhett's eyes flicked to the decryptor, its progress bar inching forward agonizingly slowly. "We don't leave without those files!" he growled, his fists connecting with the nearest operative's jaw in a bone-crunching strike.

Carter, blood dripping from a gash on his temple, planted his back against Rhett's. "We've got maybe two minutes before we're overrun!" he shouted.

The stakes were crushing. The files represented everything they had fought to destroy, but they wouldn't live to see them erased if they didn't move fast. Rhett's mind raced, calculating every possible move.

Then, with a sharp beep, Elena's decryptor chimed. "Got it!" she yelled.

"Fall back!" Rhett ordered, his voice cutting through the chaos. The team moved as one, fighting their way out of the room, the operatives in relentless pursuit. The corridors became a battlefield, every step a desperate push for survival.

The fight wasn't just about escaping but defying the power that had haunted them for so long. Bloodied but unbroken, the team fought their way into the night, the flames of the facility's self-destruct sequence roaring behind them. The files were theirs, but the battle was far from over. Granger's vision lived on in the operatives they had faced, and Rhett knew the war against it had only begun.

A Costly Victory

The aftermath of the battle was a grim scene of destruction and loss. Flames danced across the smoldering ruins of the facility, their light casting jagged shadows against the night sky. The acrid stench of burning metal and chemicals hung heavy in the air, a bitter reminder of the mission's cost. Rhett stood at the edge of the devastation, his shoulders weighted with exhaustion and the harsh reality of their fight.

Behind him, the team gathered, battered and bloodied but alive—most of them, at least. Carter leaned against a chunk of crumbled concrete, his face pale and slick with sweat. A makeshift bandage clung to his side, barely stemming the flow of blood from a gunshot wound. His jaw was set in defiance, but the pain in his eyes betrayed him. Fighters like Carter never gave in, but Rhett knew even he had limits.

"I'm fine," Carter muttered, though his voice was tight. Elena crouched beside him, her hands steady as she checked the wound. She didn't believe him, but time wasn't on their side.

Nearby, Mackenzie hunched over her laptop, her trembling fingers racing across the keys. "I stopped most of it," she said, her voice hoarse with frustration. "But fragments got out. I don't know where they're going, but whoever's on the other end is good. Really good."

Rhett's jaw clenched. The Genesis files—the foundation of Granger's twisted vision—had been their target, their prize to destroy. The facility was gone, obliterated in the flames, but the leaked fragments proved their fight wasn't over.

Elena rose, her soot-smudged face drawn with exhaustion. She placed a hand on Rhett's arm, her touch grounding. "We did what we could," she said softly. "We stopped them from taking everything."

Rhett's eyes stayed locked on the ruins. "It's not enough," he said, his voice low and resolute. "This isn't over."

Carter coughed, wincing as he shifted. "He's right," he rasped. "This war doesn't end with one battle. It never was going to."

Mackenzie slammed her laptop shut, her voice sharp with determination. "Then we track the leaks. We find out who's got the data. And we stop them. Again."

Rhett turned to face his team. Bruised and broken, they still stood, defiant in the face of defeat. "We will," he said, his voice firm. "Piece by piece, if that's what it takes."

The flames burned behind them, a testament to the cost of the fight. The night was far from over, but they weren't done. Not yet.

The Final Choice

Back at the safe house, the weight of the night's events pressed down on Rhett like a leaden shroud. The team had returned battered and weary, each of them carrying scars—both physical and emotional—from their harrowing escape and the pyrrhic victory at the facility. Rhett stood by the window, staring at the darkened city skyline, the faint glow of streetlights barely illuminating the shadowy expanse before him. The battle was over, but the war raged on in his mind.

The Genesis Operation should have been reduced to ash and memory, erased in the flames of the destroyed facility. But it wasn't. Fragments of its twisted vision remained scattered across networks, hidden in corners of the digital world where they could be rebuilt and repurposed. That knowledge was still out there, waiting for someone bold—or reckless—enough to wield it. Rhett felt the pull of it, the temptation like a whisper in the back of his mind, urging him to consider the possibilities.

He clenched his fists, the tension coiling in his chest. The temptation gnawed at him relentlessly. With the remnants of Genesis, he could do what Granger had promised but failed to achieve: control chaos, prevent wars, and end suffering. He could reshape the world into something better, something just. All it would take was stepping over the line he had fought to draw.

Behind him, Elena watched in silence. She had seen this battle in him before, the push and pull between his ideals and the darker instincts he tried to suppress. She understood the struggle better than anyone but knew she couldn't choose him.

Finally, she stepped forward, her voice breaking the heavy silence. "What are you going to do, Rhett?" she asked, her tone steady but tinged with quiet urgency.

Rhett didn't answer right away. He let the question hang in the air as he stared into the night, his thoughts churning. He had spent so much of his life fighting to stop people like Granger, who believed the ends justified the means and thought control was the answer to the world's chaos. And now he was, standing at the same crossroads, faced with the same temptation.

He turned to look at Elena, her unwavering green eyes locking onto his. She didn't need to say anything else; her presence was enough to remind him of who he was fighting for—not just the world, but the people in it—people like her, who believed in something greater than power or control.

Rhett took a deep breath, his shoulders squaring as he chose. "I'm going to burn it all down," he said, his voice low but resolute. "Every last piece of it."

Elena nodded, her expression softening with a mixture of relief and pride. "Then we'll do it together."

Rhett felt the tension in his chest ease, replaced by a quiet determination. The road ahead would be long and dangerous, but he knew now where he stood. Genesis, its remnants, and everything it represented would not be salvaged. They would be destroyed—entirely and irrevocably.

There was no room for compromise. Not this time. Not ever.

A New Beginning

I n the following days, Rhett set to work, methodically dismantling the last remnants of Genesis. Every file was erased, every connection severed, and every operation trace was obliterated. It wasn't just an operation—a reckoning, a promise fulfilled. He tore through the network relentlessly, leaving no room for anyone, not himself, to piece it back together.

The weight of his decision bore down on him with every step. The Genesis files represented everything Granger promised: control, stability, and hope. But Rhett knew that power like that was poison, seductive, and destructive. To wield it, even for good, was to risk becoming what he had fought to destroy.

Elena stood by him through it all, her quiet resolve steady in the chaos. "You're doing the right thing," she said one night, her voice soft but firm.

Rhett nodded, though the ache of what could have been lingered. "Power isn't the answer," he replied. "It never was."

As the last server burned, Rhett felt something shift within him. Genesis was gone. And with its destruction, he had reclaimed something more significant—his humanity.

CHAPTER 34

The Tortured Father

The old, crumbling house stood at the edge of a forgotten town deep in the Virginia woods—a ghost from Rhett Kardon's past. The structure was a shadow of the home he remembered, long abandoned, overrun by ivy and decay. Yet, this was where Rhett had tracked his father. Dr. James Kardon, the architect of Operation White Coat and the man behind Rhett's very existence, was finally within reach.

Rhett hesitated outside the door, a heavy weight pressing on his chest. For years, his father had haunted his thoughts—first as a distant, unloving parent and later as the mastermind behind the nightmare Rhett had uncovered. Now, the moment to confront him was here.

With a deep breath, Rhett pushed the creaking door open and stepped inside.

The Face of the Past

In the living room, he found Dr. James Kardon. The man who had once been a towering presence now sat slumped in an old armchair, his hair gray and his eyes hollow. Time and regret had worn him down, leaving only a shadow of the brilliant scientist who had once believed he could change the world.

James glanced up as Rhett entered, recognition flickering in his tired eyes. "Rhett." His voice was hoarse, barely more than a whisper. "I knew you'd find me eventually."

Rhett stood frozen, anger and sorrow warring within him. After all these years, he had imagined this moment countless times—confronting the man who had used him, demanding answers. But now, faced with the reality of his broken father, all those rehearsed confrontations dissolved.

"You have a lot to answer for," Rhett said, his voice hard. "What you did to me... What you did to all of us."

James exhaled slowly, a weary sound as if he had been carrying the weight of the world for too long. "You're right," he murmured. "I do."

The Confession Begins

The room was dimly lit, the air thick with unspoken words. Rhett sat across from his father, the old wooden chair creaking under his weight. James Kardon, once a towering figure in Rhett's life, now seemed smaller—weathered and haunted by years of betrayal and regret. For a long moment, they sat in silence, the distance between them filled with the ghosts of the past.

Finally, James spoke, his voice quiet, almost fragile. "I didn't want this for you, Rhett. I never did."

Rhett's jaw clenched, his hands tightening into fists. The flood of memories—cold labs, needles, the weight of his father's dispassionate gaze—rushed to the surface. His voice, when it came, was sharp and edged with years of pain.

"You experimented on me. On your own son. How could that not be what you wanted?"

James shook his head slowly, his eyes distant, lost in thoughts only he could see. "It was supposed to be different," he murmured. "White Coat wasn't about power—it was about peace. About making sure humanity survived what was coming."

"What was coming?" Rhett snapped, his voice rising. "War? Chaos? You thought building soldiers like me would save the world?"

James leaned forward, his expression heavy with something resembling shame. His hands rubbed together absently, a nervous tic Rhett had never seen before. "We didn't build soldiers, Rhett," James said, his voice a raw whisper. "We built solutions. Or at least, that's what we told ourselves."

He paused, the weight of his own words sinking in. "The world was spiraling into madness—nuclear threats, political instability. Everywhere we looked, there was a new crisis, a new disaster waiting to happen. We thought we could create a new kind of human, one that wouldn't make the same mistakes. One that could lead."

Rhett's stomach churned. The justifications, the rationalizations—it all sounded so clinical, so detached from the reality of what had been done. His voice was cold when he responded. "And you thought you had the right to play God."

James flinched at the accusation, but he didn't deny it. Instead, he looked Rhett in the eye, his expression a mixture of resolve and sorrow. "We were arrogant. I see that now. We thought we could engineer a better future and control the chaos. But we didn't understand what we were unleashing. Not fully."

Rhett leaned back in his chair, crossing his arms. "You didn't care. You didn't stop to think about what it would do to me—or the others. You treated us like test subjects, not people."

James's voice cracked as he replied. "I cared, Rhett—more than you'll ever know. But I believed the ends justified the means. I thought... I thought I was saving you from the future I saw coming."

Rhett stared at him, his chest tightening. "You weren't saving me," he said, his voice low. "You were turning me into something I never wanted to be."

The silence that followed was heavy and oppressive. For the first time, James looked genuinely broken. "I can't change what I did," he said softly. "But maybe... maybe you can stop it from happening again."

Rhett stood, the chair scraping against the floor. His voice was steady, but his words were final. "That's the only reason I'm still here. To make sure no one else becomes your 'solution.'"

James nodded slowly, the flicker of a resigned smile crossing his lips. "Then I guess there's hope for you yet."

A Father's Regret

James's eyes glistened with unshed tears, his once-steady demeanor crumbling before Rhett's eyes. "I thought I was doing the right thing," he whispered, his voice tinged with desperation, making Rhett's stomach tighten. "At the time, it felt like the only choice. The world was unraveling, and we thought—no, I thought—I could stop it."

He leaned back in his chair, running a trembling hand through his thinning hair. The weight of his past, of the choices he'd made, seemed to press down on him, making him appear smaller, older, and infinitely more fragile. "I was wrong, Rhett. I see that now. But by the time I realized what I had done, it was too late. Too much damage had been done. Too many lives..." His voice cracked, trailing into a silence that felt heavier than words.

Rhett stood there, arms crossed, his jaw clenched. His heart twisted with conflicting emotions—anger that burned hot and bright, sadness that seeped into the cracks, and a strange, reluctant empathy that made him feel like a traitor to himself. He had spent so much of his life chasing answers, searching for someone to blame, and now, here was his father—a broken man weighed down by his own mistakes—offering a truth that Rhett wasn't sure he wanted to hear.

"You didn't just ruin my life," Rhett said quietly, his voice barely more than a whisper. "You ruined countless others. People died because of you. Families were destroyed. And for what? A dream of a perfect world?"

James flinched at his words, his guilt manifesting in the deep lines of his face. "I know," he said, his voice barely audible. "I know what I did. And I'll carry that with me until the day I die."

The raw honesty in his father's tone struck something deep within Rhett, cutting through his carefully built defenses. It wasn't absolution and wasn't enough to erase the scars of the past, but it was real. For the first time, he saw James not as the cold, clinical scientist who had experimented on his son but as a man who had been consumed by his hubris and was now left to pick up the shattered pieces of his soul.

Rhett exhaled sharply, turning away to stare out the window. The world outside seemed too quiet and normal for the turmoil within him. "Do you even understand what you did to me?" he asked, his voice trembling despite his efforts to keep it steady. "You took away my choices, my future. You turned me into something I never asked to be."

"I know," James said again, his voice steadier this time. "And I wish I could undo it. Every day, I wish I could go back and make a different choice. But I can't, Rhett. All I can do is tell you the truth and hope that somehow, you can make something better out of the wreckage I left behind."

Rhett turned back to face him, his expression hard but no longer filled with the fire of pure anger. "I'm not you," he said firmly. "And I'm not going to make the same mistakes you did."

James nodded slowly, a faint, bittersweet smile tugging at his lips. "No, you're not," he said softly. "And that's why you're the one who can fix this."

The Revelation of Control

As Rhett stared at his father, the weight of their conversation settled over him like a suffocating blanket. Dr. James Kardon sat before him, a man broken by regret yet still clinging to the remnants of the ideals that had driven his life's work. It was in how he spoke and avoided Rhett's gaze—it all pointed to a truth that made Rhett's stomach churn.

"You still believe it, don't you?" Rhett asked softly, his voice carrying both accusation and disbelief. "You still think you were right."

James hesitated, the silence between them stretching painfully. He looked away, shame flickering across his features. "I believe in what I tried to do, Rhett," he admitted, his voice low and tentative. "I believe the world needs order. It needs someone to step in when chaos takes over. But I also know..." He paused, struggling with the weight of his following words. "I know I was wrong in how I went about it."

His gaze lifted to meet Rhett's. Sorrow was etched deep into his face. "And I know I failed you."

Rhett's chest tightened, his breathing shallow as emotions surged within him. Anger, sadness, and frustration collided in a cacophony that threatened to overwhelm him. He clenched his fists, his knuckles white. "You didn't just fail me, Dad," he said, his voice trembling. "You betrayed me."

James flinched as though Rhett's words had physically struck him. "I know," he whispered, the words barely audible. "I thought... I thought I was doing what was necessary. That I could make a better world for you, for everyone. But I see now that I only made things worse."

Rhett shook his head, his jaw tightening. "You didn't just make things worse—you destroyed lives. You destroyed mine." He felt his voice crack, and he hated the vulnerability that came with it. "You turned me into something I never wanted to be, and for what? Some ideal that only existed in your head?"

James's shoulders slumped, his hands wringing together in a gesture of helplessness. "I can't take it back," he said. "If I could undo it all, I would. But I can't. All I can do now is try to make sure no one else suffers for my mistakes."

Rhett stared at him, searching his face for remorse, hope, or maybe redemption. But all he saw was a man who had built a house of cards and was now watching it collapse.

"You can't fix this, Dad," Rhett said quietly. "But I can. And I will."

A Choice Forged in Pain

The silence stretched between them, thick and heavy, as if the years of unspoken words and unresolved pain had taken physical form. Rhett and his father sat in the small, dimly lit room, the air charged with the weight of everything lost. The distant hum of a fan was the only sound, a faint, mechanical reminder of the world outside, a world neither of them felt entirely part of anymore.

James's gaze flickered to the table, his fingers tracing the edge as if searching for something to hold onto. On the other hand, Rhett sat stiffly, his fists resting on his knees, his eyes fixed on the man who had shaped so much of his life—both in ways that had built and broken him. The shared silence wasn't peaceful; it was a battlefield of memories, regrets, and choices neither could undo.

Finally, Rhett stood, the chair scraping against the floor. His movements were deliberate, every motion carrying a gravity that filled the room. He looked down at his father, his expression a mixture of quiet pain and unwavering resolve. "I didn't come here for an apology," he said, his voice steady but strained, as though each word was a struggle. "I came here to make sure this ends."

James looked up at him, his face drawn and weary. There was no defiance in his expression, no attempt to defend or excuse himself. Instead, there was a kind of resignation, an acceptance that he had always known this moment would come. He nodded slowly, the motion almost imperceptible, as if the weight of his acknowledgment was too much to bear. "I know," he said softly, his voice carrying the exhaustion of a man who had long since stopped fighting against his failures.

Their eyes met, and for a moment, something unspoken passed between them—not forgiveness, not reconciliation, but an understanding that this was the only path left.

A Moment of Reckoning

Rhett stared down at his father, whose actions had cast a long shadow over his life. This man had carefully orchestrated every major event in Rhett's journey—not out of love or guidance but through manipulation and deceit. His father's words, commands, and even moments of apparent kindness had been calculated as tools to control Rhett like a puppet on a string. Every choice Rhett thought he'd made for himself had been subtly engineered by the man lying before him now.

But as Rhett stood there, staring into the weary, defiant eyes of the man who had molded him into a reflection of his ambitions, something inside him shifted. The fire that had driven Rhett this far—fueled by anger, resentment, and a desire for vengeance—dimmed. He saw his father not as a larger-than-life figure but as a broken, desperate man clinging to the illusion of power.

And in that moment, Rhett realized something profound. This wasn't about revenge. Revenge would only perpetuate the same cycle of control and destruction that had plagued their relationship for years. Nor was it about justice. Justice, while noble, wouldn't erase the years of pain or give Rhett back the life he might have lived.

No, this was about freedom—freedom from the chains of bitterness that bound him, freedom from the invisible hand that had steered his every move, and freedom to become his own man finally. For the first time, Rhett understood that true liberation wouldn't come from defeating his father but from stepping beyond him. He knelt, not in submission, but in release, whispering words he never thought he'd say: "I forgive you."

The End of the Line

Dr. James Kardon gave his son a sad, knowing smile. The lines on his face, carved by years of ambition, control, and regret, deepened as he met Rhett's unwavering gaze. There was no malice in his expression now, no hint of the domineering presence that had shaped so much of Rhett's life. Instead, there was something softer—something almost broken. "I know, Rhett," he said quietly, his voice tinged with a bittersweet acceptance. "That's what I always hoped for."

The words hung in the air between them, heavy with meaning. Rhett stood silent, trying to decipher their intent. Was this his father's final manipulation, a way to claim the moral high ground even in surrender? Or was it the closest James Kardon could come to admitting his faults and acknowledging the damage he had done? Rhett didn't know, and perhaps it didn't matter. The weight of this moment was not about understanding his father's intentions; it was about finally stepping out of his shadow.

James closed his eyes slowly as if surrendering to the inevitability of time and the consequences of a lifetime of choices. He had spent years choosing power, controlling those around him, and justifying it all as love. Yet now, in the quiet of this moment, he seemed to accept the truth: his empire, influence, and even his son's accomplishments—all came at a cost. And that cost was trust, connection, and the kind of legacy that mattered most. James appeared at peace for the first time, the weight of his regrets finally lifting from his shoulders.

"Rhett," James called out. Handing Rhett a flash drive. "This should be the last bit of information you need to end this once and for all."

Rhett took the flash drive and took one last look at the man who had been both his greatest adversary and his greatest teacher. There was no anger in his heart, no lingering desire to exact revenge. That part of him had been set free. He turned and walked away, each step feeling lighter than the last. He didn't look back—not because he hated his father, but because he no longer needed to. Whatever forgiveness he could give, he had given. Whatever understanding he might someday find, he would see on his terms.

The past stayed behind with James, left to haunt its keeper. Rhett walked forward into a future that was finally his own.

The Road Ahead

The crisp air hit him like a cleansing wave as Rhett stepped out into the cold night. For a moment, he stood still, his breath forming faint clouds in the moonlight. Around him, the world seemed impossibly quiet, as if it, too, was holding its breath. He tilted his head back to look at the stars scattered across the dark expanse above. They had always been there, distant and indifferent to the chaos of his life. And now, standing in their silent witness, a sense of clarity settled over him.

He couldn't change what had happened. He couldn't rewrite the years spent under his father's control nor undo the mistakes that had shaped him. The pain, resentment, and struggle were part of his story, etched into his bones. But they didn't define him. He realized that now. The past was unchangeable, but the future? The future was his. For the first time in years, he felt the weight of that possibility and its freedom.

Elena was waiting by the car, her figure illuminated by the soft glow of a street lamp. She leaned against the door, arms crossed, her expression unreadable. She didn't move as Rhett approached, her eyes searching his face for answers he hadn't yet spoken.

"How did it go?" she asked softly, her voice steady but laced with curiosity and concern.

Rhett exhaled slowly, the tension in his chest finally easing. He felt lighter, like the years of carrying his father's shadow had dissolved into the night. He met Elena's gaze, and his voice held no trace of bitterness or anger for the first time in a long while. It was just quiet finality.

"It's over," he said.

Elena studied him for a moment, her brow furrowing slightly as if trying to gauge the depth of his words. Then she nodded, understanding without pressing for details. She opened the car door, and Rhett slid into the passenger seat, closing the door on the cold and everything that had come before this moment.

As the car pulled away, Rhett turned his gaze toward the horizon. The night stretched ahead, vast and unknown, but for once, it didn't feel daunting. It felt like freedom. And Rhett was ready for whatever came next.

A New Beginning

They drove through the quiet streets, the soft hum of the engine filling the silence between them. Outside, the city lights blurred past, streaks of gold and white against the dark canvas of the night. It was a familiar route, but it felt different tonight, as though the world had shifted. Rhett leaned back in his seat, watching the glow of the passing streetlamps reflect off the windshield. For the first time in years, he felt a calm he couldn't quite explain—a weight lifted, a chapter finally closed.

The shadow of his father, which had loomed over him for so long, was gone. The burden of living up to impossible expectations and constantly striving for a sense of approval that was always out of reach had dissolved into the night. He had spent years chasing after something he could never truly attain, only to realize that the freedom he craved had always been within his grasp. All it required was the courage to let go.

The future stretched out before him now, vast and unknown. It was uncharted territory, and the uncertainty didn't scare him for once. It thrilled him. He didn't have a plan, didn't have answers to every question, but for the first time, he didn't need them. Rhett had spent too long defining himself by what others expected, by what his father demanded. Now, stripped of those constraints, he saw himself.

He was no longer just James Kardon's son or the product of someone else's ambition. He was simply Rhett. And that was enough.

As the car turned onto a quieter road, he glanced at Elena beside him, her calm presence grounding him. He smiled faintly, feeling a sense of peace he hadn't known in years. Whatever came next, he was ready.

CHAPTER 35

Father's Confession

The drive back to Washington was quiet, but Rhett Kardon's mind was anything but. His father's words haunted him, unraveling everything he thought he knew about himself, his past, and the purpose of Operation White Coat.

Dr. James Kardon's confession had been a cold truth: Rhett was not born in the traditional sense. His father hadn't just wanted to build the perfect soldier—he had wanted to create the future, starting with Rhett.

Now Rhett knew the full scope of the experiments, the lies, and the manipulation—but there were still questions that James had deliberately left unanswered.

The pieces didn't quite fit. Why was Rhett designed the way he was? What had his father indeed intended? And more importantly, who else knew the full extent of the operation's objectives?

A Lasting Legacy

Back at the safe house, Rhett sat at the edge of the bed, his hands clasped tightly together as his mind raced through the implications of what he had discovered. The files, the experiments, and the tests all connected in a horrifying pattern. His father's work wasn't just a scientific endeavor or a twisted vanity Operation. James Kardon had a vision so grandiose and terrifying that it sent a chill down Rhett's spine. Rhett wasn't merely an experiment; he was meant to be the first—a prototype for something far more profound and dangerous.

The dim light from the desk lamp cast long shadows across the room, but Rhett barely noticed. His thoughts were consumed by the implications of what his father had planned. He wasn't just shaping the future; he was trying to redefine what it meant to be human. Rhett was supposed to be the bridge, the proof of concept for a new kind of leader—genetically engineered, enhanced, superior. And once perfected, his father had intended to create more—an entire generation, perhaps even a whole species, modeled after Rhett.

Elena sat across from him, her expression a mixture of concern and determination. She had been patient, but the silence was unbearable. "What's going on, Rhett?" she asked, her voice steady but tinged with worry. "What aren't you telling me?"

Rhett exhaled deeply, running a hand through his hair as the truth settled over him. "It wasn't just about me," he said finally, his voice low and heavy. "My father wanted to create more—more like me. A future where everyone would be... engineered."

Elena's eyes widened, the weight of his words sinking in. "He wanted to replace humanity?"

Rhett nodded slowly, his jaw tightening. "He thought he was building a better world. But this wasn't about making people stronger or smarter. It wasn't even about creating soldiers. He wanted something permanent—an entire species designed according to his vision, engineered to be superior and obedient. He thought he could control evolution itself."

Elena leaned back, her face pale. "And you? What does that make you?"

Rhett's voice dropped to a whisper, filled with fear and resolve. "The first step. But I'm not going to let it go any further."

A Disturbing Discovery

Determined to unravel the full extent of his father's plans, Rhett worked tirelessly into the early hours, his eyes fixed on the laptop screen. The files on the flash drive James Kardon had given him were a labyrinth of encrypted data, but Rhett methodically sifted through them, peeling back layer after layer of secrets. What he found was more horrifying than he could have imagined.

Operation White Coat hadn't ended with him. The experiments that had shaped his existence were only the beginning of a far-reaching, insidious plan. The files detailed candidates from across the globe—individuals handpicked for their genetic potential, subjected to the same enhancements they had undergone. What he had once believed to be a singular, horrific aberration was revealed to be the blueprint for a new era. He wasn't unique; he was a prototype.

As Rhett delved deeper into the files, one name caught his attention: Subject Omega. Unlike the others, whose enhancements mirrored his own to varying degrees, Omega was something else entirely. It wasn't just another experiment. Omega was the culmination of everything his father had envisioned—a being designed to surpass even Rhett in every way. The data suggested that Omega was more potent and faster and equipped with advanced neural modifications, capable of strategic thought and control on an unparalleled scale. It wasn't just an operation—it was the final phase.

"What is this?" Rhett muttered, scrolling through the details, his voice barely above a whisper. A cold realization washed over him: Omega wasn't dormant. Preparations had been underway to activate the operative and use it as the leader of the next generation of engineered beings.

Mackenzie, who had been silently scanning the files over Rhett's shoulder, straightened, her face pale. "They were getting ready to launch this phase," she said. "If Granger hadn't been stopped, Omega would've been activated by now."

Rhett's jaw tightened, his fists clenching in anger. "We didn't stop them soon enough," he said through gritted teeth. "This isn't over. Omega is still out there. And someone—someone alive—is waiting to finish what my father started."

The room fell silent, the weight of the discovery settling heavily over them. Rhett took a deep breath, his resolve hardening. If Omega were out there, he would stop it. Whatever it took.

A Race Against Time

Rhett felt the urgency in his chest like a drumbeat, steady and relentless. Time was slipping away, and the stakes couldn't be higher if Subject Omega were operational. This wasn't just about stopping another experiment but preventing a catastrophe. Omega wasn't an ordinary target—it was the culmination of his father's twisted vision, a weapon designed to shape the future of humanity. The thought sent a shiver down his spine, but Rhett pushed it aside. There was no room for hesitation now.

Elena moved swiftly, grabbing her gear with practiced efficiency. Her expression was calm but steely, her resolve evident in every movement. "Where do we start?" she asked, slinging a tactical bag over her shoulder.

Mackenzie's fingers flew across her laptop keyboard, her face illuminated by the screen's glow. "There's a facility in Greenland," she said, her voice clipped with focus. "It's an old Cold War base, decommissioned for decades—until now. Satellite images show unusual activity, and intercepted chatter mentions a high-value subject being transferred there in the last 48 hours."

Rhett paced the room, the weight of the mission settling over him. "If Omega is there, it's not just a transfer point. It's a staging ground," he said, checking his weapons. His movements were precise, fueled by the adrenaline coursing through him. "We go in, confirm Omega's location, and shut this down. No hesitation, no half-measures. This ends tonight."

Mackenzie turned her screen toward them, pointing to the coordinates on the map. "The facility is buried under ice, with only one primary access point. It's heavily secured, but we'll be landing far enough away to avoid detection. From there, it's a hike to the entrance."

Elena nodded, tightening the straps on her gear. "And once we're in?"

"We improvise," Rhett said firmly, his gaze sweeping over the team. "We've faced worse odds. If Omega is as advanced as the data suggests, we won't have the luxury of planning for every scenario. But we will stop this."

The room fell silent for a moment, the gravity of their mission hanging heavy in the air. Then Rhett slung his weapon over his shoulder, his jaw set with determination. "Let's move out. We're not letting this happen—not on our watch."

Greenland's Frozen Fortress

The flight to Greenland was cloaked in a heavy silence, the kind that spoke louder than words ever could. Rhett sat by the small window, staring into the endless darkness, his thoughts a maelstrom of anticipation and dread. This mission wasn't just the culmination of his father's twisted legacy; it was the end of a journey that had begun before he existed. The stakes weren't just personal—they were monumental. Failure wasn't an option.

Elena sat across from him, methodically checking her gear. Her usual sharp remarks were absent, replaced by a focused determination. Engrossed in her laptop, Mackenzie occasionally muttered updates about their target, but she kept her voice low as if afraid to disturb the charged atmosphere. The hum of the plane's engines was the only sound, a steady reminder that every moment brought them closer to the confrontation they had dreaded.

When the plane descended over Greenland, the landscape came into view—an endless, desolate expanse of snow and ice. The terrain was brutal, a stark reminder of the isolation they were walking into. Snow-covered hills stretched as far as the eye could see, and the howling wind whipped across the tundra, carrying an eerie sense of foreboding. The abandoned Cold War base came into view only briefly, a shadowy outline buried beneath layers of ice and secrecy. This was a place forgotten by time, and for good reason.

The team landed several miles from the base, their pilot giving a quick nod before taking off again. They were on their own now. Under the cover of darkness, they began trekking through the snow, each step crunching loudly in the otherwise deafening silence. The cold bit at Rhett's exposed skin, but he barely noticed. His senses were on high alert, his pulse steady but deliberate. Every crunch of snow beneath their boots felt amplified, a grim reminder of their exposure.

"This place gives me the creeps," Mackenzie whispered, her breath visible in the icy air.

"It should," Rhett said, his eyes scanning the horizon. "We're walking straight into a lion's den. Stay sharp."

The base loomed closer, its dark silhouette barely visible against the white expanse. Whatever awaited them inside, Rhett knew one thing: this was the moment everything would be decided.

Breaking Into the Facility

The entrance to the facility loomed ahead, a stark, steel structure half-buried in the icy terrain. Armed guards patrolled the perimeter, their movements precise and mechanical. Their sharp eyes scanned the darkness, and their synchronized steps spoke of training far beyond standard military protocols.

"These aren't ordinary guards," Rhett whispered, crouching behind a snowdrift. His voice was calm but laced with tension. "They're enhanced. Just like me."

Elena nodded, her grip tightening on her weapon. Mackenzie scanned the area with binoculars, noting the patterns in their patrols. "They're not leaving much room for error," she murmured.

"We don't need much," Rhett replied. His jaw tightened, and his eyes hardened. This was the moment he had trained for, though the irony wasn't lost on him—he was using the very skills and enhancements his father had forced upon him to dismantle the legacy those experiments had built.

The team moved like shadows, swift and silent. Rhett led the way, his heightened senses picking up every sound, every flicker of movement. When they struck, it was with brutal efficiency. The guards were highly skilled, their reflexes sharp, but Rhett's enhancements made him faster, stronger, and more precise. One by one, they fell, leaving only the echo of their muffled struggles in the frigid night air.

Every takedown was a grim reminder of what Rhett had become. These men and women were like him—engineered, improved, and ultimately used. They weren't just guards but products of the same ruthless vision he was fighting to destroy.

Once inside, the facility's cold, sterile interior greeted them. The air was heavy with an unshakable sense of unease. Fluorescent lights cast harsh shadows across the metallic walls, and the faint hum of machinery filled the silence. The halls were lined with rooms, their glass walls revealing rows of medical equipment and strange, unidentifiable devices. It was a haunting reminder of his father's work, a vision of science untethered by morality.

Rhett paused, his gaze lingering on one of the rooms. He could almost hear the echoes of past experiments—the cries, the sterile voices of scientists, the hum of machines reshaping lives without consent. This was where his father's vision had reached its apex, where ambition had eclipsed humanity.

"We keep moving," Rhett said, his voice firm. The ghosts could wait. Right now, they had a mission to finish.

The Confrontation with Omega

They found it at the heart of the facility—the culmination of all the horrors they had uncovered. Subject Omega stood in the center of a sterile, brightly lit laboratory encased in a reinforced glass chamber. The figure was massive, towering over the team as they entered. Its body was a masterpiece of genetic and technological engineering—muscles rippled beneath an almost inhumanly perfect physique, and its eyes glowed faintly with an eerie, calculated intelligence. Omega was everything Operation White Coat had aspired to create: a living weapon designed to surpass humanity.

Around the chamber, scientists worked feverishly, their fingers flying across consoles in a desperate attempt to complete the activation sequence. Alarms blared, bathing the room in flashing red lights as the intruders were detected. Rhett's presence seemed to unnerve them, but their determination to finish their work overrode their fear.

One of the scientists stepped forward, his voice trembling but resolute. "You were supposed to lead, Rhett," he said, his tone almost mournful. "You were the prototype. The beginning. But Omega... Omega will replace you. He's perfect."

As if on cue, the chamber hissed open, and Omega stepped out, its movements fluid and precise. Its glowing eyes locked onto Rhett, and momentarily, the room seemed to hold its breath.

Then the chaos erupted.

Omega moved like a blur, closing the distance between them with terrifying speed. The fight was instantaneous and brutal. Rhett met the first strike head-on, his enhanced reflexes barely enough to deflect the crushing blow. But Omega was relentless—stronger, faster, and impossibly resilient. Every punch, every block sent shockwaves through Rhett's body, testing his limits in ways he had never experienced.

"Elena, cover me!" Rhett shouted, his voice strained as he ducked a devastating kick. Elena responded instantly, her gunfire forcing Omega to recalibrate momentarily. It wasn't enough to slow him for long, but it bought precious seconds.

Meanwhile, Mackenzie worked frantically at a nearby terminal. "The systems controlling his enhancements are linked to the mainframe," she yelled over the noise. "If I can disable them, he'll lose his edge—but I need time!"

Rhett gritted his teeth, every fiber focused on surviving the onslaught. This wasn't just a fight for his life—it was a fight for humanity's future. With each blow he landed, with every second he held Omega at bay, he knew one thing: they couldn't afford to fail.

Rhett's Breaking Point

The fight with Omega was unlike anything Rhett had ever faced. Each punch, each block, and shock waves through his body, testing the limits of his endurance and resolve. Omega's strength was overwhelming, and its precision was deadly. Every move seemed designed to exploit weaknesses Rhett hadn't even realized he had. This wasn't just a battle of strength—a fight against the embodiment of everything his father had envisioned, a perfect creation of power without restraint.

As Omega landed a brutal blow that sent Rhett staggering back, he felt a flicker of doubt creep into his mind. Could he even win this? He had spent his entire life fighting against the very essence of what he had become, resisting the temptation to let his enhancements define him. He had fought for his humanity, for control over the abilities his father had forced upon him. But now, standing toe-to-toe with Omega, he realized that holding back wasn't an option anymore. To end this, he had to embrace the power he had always feared.

"I'm not like you," Rhett growled through clenched teeth, grappling with Omega as they collided in a furious struggle. Their movements were a blur, fists meeting flesh echoing through the lab. "But I'll do whatever it takes to stop you."

Something shifted inside Rhett then—a surge of strength, of purpose, fueled not by rage or pride but by a deep, unshakable resolve. He drew on every ounce of training, every lesson he had learned through pain and sacrifice, channeling it into one final effort. With a guttural roar, Rhett surged forward, breaking Omega's hold and using its momentum against it. He twisted, throwing Omega to the ground with a force that cracked the reinforced floor.

Omega staggered, its movements faltering for the first time. Rhett didn't hesitate. He delivered a final blow with a strength he hadn't known he possessed, rendering Omega motionless. The lab fell silent, the only sound the ragged rhythm of Rhett's breath echoing in the sterile space.

He stood over Omega's lifeless form, his chest heaving, blood trickling from a cut above his brow. He stared momentarily, the weight of what he had done settling over him. The fight was over. The nightmare his father had created had been stopped. But at what cost?

Destroying the Legacy

Rhett stood over the lifeless body of Omega, his breaths coming in ragged gasps. His body ached from the fight, bruised and battered, but the pain was drowned out by the weight of the moment. This was the culmination of everything his father had built and everything Rhett had fought to dismantle. Omega, the embodiment of Operation White Coat's ambitions, lay motionless at his feet, a stark reminder of what unchecked ambition could create.

The room was eerily silent, save for the faint hum of the computers lining the lab's walls. On those screens flickered the last remnants of his father's research: data, blueprints, genetic sequences—all the knowledge that had led to Rhett's creation and, ultimately, to Omega. It was all there, glowing ominously in the sterile light of the monitors.

Rhett's eyes fixed on the terminal in front of him. One keystroke and it would all be gone. Years of experiments, sacrifices, and horrors would be wiped from existence. But as his fingers hovered over the keyboard, hesitation gripped him. This wasn't just about destroying data. It was about erasing his father's legacy—a legacy that, for better or worse, was intertwined with his existence.

Elena stepped beside him, her presence steadying. She placed a hand on his arm, her voice soft but firm. "It's time, Rhett. End this."

He turned to her, seeing the trust and determination in her eyes. She had been with him and was now here to see it through. Nodding, Rhett took a deep breath. His hand steadied as he entered the final command, his fingers striking the keys with resolute purpose.

The screens began to flicker, lines of code disappearing into oblivion. The machines' hum dulled and then ceased entirely. The primary monitor displayed one last confirmation: System Wipe Complete. Then the screen went black, and with it, Operation White Coat was gone—erased from existence as if it had never existed.

Rhett stepped back, exhaling deeply as the enormity of what he had done settled over him. Once a hub of his father's twisted dreams, the lab was now lifeless and still. The legacy of James Kardon had been destroyed—not with a grand proclamation, but with a single keystroke.

"It's over," Rhett said quietly, his voice heavy with relief and sorrow. And for the first time in years, he felt free.

A Hard-Fought Victory

They left the facility in silence, their footsteps crunching through the snow as they returned to the extraction point. The cold wind bit at their faces, but none of them spoke. The weight of what had transpired inside that lab hung heavy, settling over them like the Arctic chill. Rhett walked before the group, his shoulders squared but his mind far away. They had won, but it didn't feel like a triumph. It felt like survival.

The helicopter waited for them, its rotors cutting through the frigid air in a rhythmic hum. As they climbed aboard, Rhett paused at the open door, his eyes lingering on the facility in the distance. It was silent now, its once-bright lights extinguished. Inside, Omega lay defeated, and the remnants of Operation White Coat had been reduced to ash and memory. He had accomplished what he set out to do—he had ended his father's twisted vision. But the cost was something he hadn't fully anticipated.

Once aboard, the team buckled in, still silent as the helicopter lifted off. Elena sat across from Rhett, her eyes flicking to him with concern, but she didn't say anything. She knew better than to try. Mackenzie busied herself with the equipment, but her usual sharp quips were absent. Everyone needed time to process.

Rhett stared out the window as the frozen wasteland below grew smaller and smaller. The battle was over, but the scars it left behind felt permanent. He had fought against everything he feared becoming—a weapon, a tool for someone else's ambition—and in doing so, he had come face-to-face with the parts of himself he had always tried to ignore. The strength, power, and potential for destruction were all part of him. But so, too, was the resolve to use that power for something better. That was what set him apart. That was who he indeed was.

The facility disappeared into the horizon, swallowed by the endless expanse of ice. Rhett leaned back in his seat, his breath fogging in the cold cabin air. The mission was over, but the scars and lessons would remain. He wasn't sure where the future would take him, but he felt ready to face it for the first time.

Moving Forward

Back in Washington, the weight of the mission lingered on Rhett's shoulders. The sterile corridors of the briefing facility felt worlds apart from the icy desolation of Greenland. Still, the echoes of Operation White Coat remained with him, a burden he knew he'd carry forever. The images of the lab, the data he'd erased, and Omega's relentless gaze flashed through his mind. His father's legacy was gone, but the scars it left would haunt him for the rest of his life.

But now, for the first time, Rhett felt something he hadn't experienced in years: control. The horrors of Operation White Coat no longer dictated his path. His past no longer defined him. Standing in the dimly lit conference room, the faint hum of city life filtering through the windows, Rhett realized he had something his father never did—a choice.

Elena stood nearby, her arms crossed as she leaned against the table. She was exhausted, with dark circles under her eyes and disheveled hair from days without rest, but her expression was resolute. She had stood by him through everything, and her presence now reminded him that even in his darkest moments, he hadn't been alone.

Rhett turned to her, a tired but genuine smile on his face. "Let's make sure no one ever tries this again," he said, his voice steady but filled with determination.

Elena straightened, meeting his gaze with a slight nod. "Together," she said, her words carrying the weight of a promise.

At that moment, something shifted. The shadow of his past—the long, dark reach of his father's ambitions—began to recede. Rhett Kardon had spent his life trying to escape what he had been made into, trying to outrun the legacy of James Kardon. But now, he wasn't running anymore. He had faced it, fought it, and dismantled it piece by piece. And for the first time, he felt ready to move forward.

With Elena by his side, Rhett turned and left the room, leaving behind the ghosts of what once was. The future stretched ahead of him, uncertain but full of possibility. And for the first time, he wasn't afraid. He was ready to face whatever came next.

EPILOGUE

Finding Family

T he sun dipped low over the horizon, its fiery hues reflecting off the tide rolling in from the ocean exhale. Rhett Kardon stood at the edge of a dock, his eyes fixed on the rippling surface as if the answers to his past and future lay just beneath. The journey that had brought him here had been long, brutal, and filled with choices that would haunt him for the rest of his life. But as the cool evening breeze brushed against his face, he felt something he hadn't allowed himself to feel in years—peace.

Rhett had been born an experiment, a product of his father's unrelenting ambition. For so long, he had defined himself by what had been done to him, the power forced into his veins and the shadow of Operation White Coat looming over his life. But his journey had proven something more significant: the man he had become wasn't the result of experiments or manipulation. His flawed, painful, and deeply human choices had shaped him.

He thought of the battles fought, the lives saved, and those lost. He thought of Elena's unwavering support, Mackenzie's sharp brilliance, and Carter's unyielding resolve. They were more than allies; they were his family. Together, they had torn down a vision of oppression and control, replacing it with something fragile but infinitely more powerful—hope.

Rhett inhaled deeply, the crisp scent of the salty air grounding him. His fight wasn't over; it might never be. But for the first time, he wasn't running from who he was. He was embracing it.

Because freedom wasn't about escaping the past; it was about facing it, owning it, and choosing to rise above it. Rhett Kardon was no longer the sum of someone else's experiment. He was a man who had decided to fight for a world worth living in. And as the stars began to scatter across the darkening sky, he made a silent promise: whatever came next, he would be ready.